The Heritage

$25P$.

ff

faber and faber

First published in 2008
by Faber and Faber Limited
3 Queen Square London WC1N 3AU

Typeset by Faber and Faber
Printed in England by Mackays of Chatham

The right of Will Ashon to be identified as author of this work has
been asserted in accordance with Section 77 of the Copyright,
Designs and Patents Act 1988

A CIP record for this book
is available from the British Library

ISBN 978–0571–23104–1

2 4 6 8 10 9 7 5 3 1

For Leila

In the spiral form, the circle, uncoiled, unwound, has ceased to be vicious; it has been set free.

Vladimir Nabokov

We'd like to say shit politely to you, in your false language. Because we bumpkins, we yokels, have absolutely no manners, you realise.

Louis Scutenaire

We the undersigned state both collectively and individually that we are tired of running from you and tired of fighting you. As from the release of this statement, we secede from CTRL and all the norms, strictures and relations of power it places upon us. We are the Vanished and we go to join the Vanished and with this act of violence we and those who will follow us declare War on you and your so-called civilisation.

First Communiqué of the Vanished

Preface

The first time I saw the Vanished was on television. Although, of course, they weren't the Vanished then.

I was recovering from an operation at the time and would have struggled to move from the bed even if I were not chained to it. In such circumstances, it had quickly become my habit to lie on my side with the TV opposite me, my eyes unfocused, the colours forming and dissolving in abstract patches on my retina, the babble of voices and music and sound effects a stream flowing down the well of my left ear. It offered me relief from myself – a step out of time – and I was grateful for any relief I could get.

I don't know what caused me to snap from my reverie on this particular day and at this particular moment. I suppose something was said in the preamble to the news report which registered inside me and returned me to consciousness. Whether it was a single word that woke me, a phrase, or even the tone of voice, I'll never know. Whatever the trigger, the colours became recognisable shapes and I found myself concentrating. I was looking for escape. Why else would anyone watch television?

On the screen in front of me was a ragged column of perhaps two hundred people moving through a street in what was bound to be London, shot from above, probably the top of a tall building. About half of the crowd were holding up large white placards, though from this angle it was impossible to make out what was printed on them. A political demonstration of some sort, I presumed. Nothing in itself to catch my interest there.

The shot changed to street level, right down on the tarmac and

3

looking up as the protesters filed by. The camera focused in on the placards the demonstrators were holding. Each of them, a metre wide and twice as tall, was held in front of its carrier's head. Each showed a face printed in black, the texture a smudged pointillism, as if it had been enlarged from a newspaper.

There was something compelling about those giant faces, though it was hard to say what. They smiled or frowned, looked into the lens or stared past, were young or old or in between, unkempt or neat, their expressions intimate or formal. A proportion of the pictures appeared to have been taken on holiday, others at school, others in police custody, a very few at Christmas parties, the paper crowns adding a touch of festivity to proceedings. They all bumped and bounced along, the shrieks of the whistles in the mouths of their bodies keeping rough time with the rhythms set by the drummers studded between them.

The next take was filmed from the centre of the road in the path of the demonstration. The front line of marchers had a long banner unfurled across their chests, the words warping and bunching but clear: WHO TOOK THE VANISHED?

As I read the question I flinched.

The camera cut to another huge ribbon of cloth, this one held high above the protesters' heads: WHERE DO THE VANISHED GO?

Behind, before the shot changed, I caught sight of my only friend's huge face printed across one of those boards, not even a picture I knew, no metal in her skin, her hair short and fringe flicked, a shy smile, her lips held carefully over her embarrassing teeth. But definitely her, the obstruction in my throat doubling its size.

I hadn't known what I was waiting for until then. I found myself kneeling on the floor – one arm extending to the side of the screen, the other stretched out behind me, handcuffs linking me to the bed – searching for and finding glimpses of Valerie, Seb and Marcus on those boards, but never again the one I hoped for, no matter how hard I looked.

4

The crowd had started to chant some sort of slogan, patchily and almost self-consciously at first and then with increasing vigour and certainty. I tried to get closer to the screen, struggling to make out what they were shouting, stitches dragging like teeth across my belly. Three syllables, the first two short, the last long, the beat of it simple but driven on by the drums. 'TAYMEETOOOO, TAYMEETOOOO, TAYMEETOOOO.' Try as I might I could make no sense of it.

The placards had risen up on straightened arms now to reveal the faces of their carriers. The whistles had fallen to their chests, and their heads were bent back beyond the boards' upper reaches, their faces tearing open with what looked like rapture. It was at that moment, watching their mouths, that their words fell into place in my head. 'TAKE ME TOO, TAKE ME TOO, TAKE ME TOO.'

This so completely articulated my own sentiments at the time that I thought I must be imagining it. No. It was perfectly clear. There was no mistake. These people, it seemed, had ransacked my mind and stolen not only my closest friend but my thoughts as well.

I began to listen to the voice-over, the reporter's tone calm and well-modulated as he explained the unlicensed nature of the demonstration and its proximity to Downing Street. Policemen with plastic shields were shown closing in round the marchers and pushing them back. The director cut to a graphic detailing the positions of important government ministries in relation to the protesters' location, then switched to an airborne shot, the rough square of bodies slowly rotating.

'But seemingly nothing could dampen the demonstrators' fervour and their chanting continued unabated for the best part of an hour. Until at one p.m. this happened.'

The camera was behind the police lines this time, row after row of helmets before the dancing portraits, the incantation thundering out, its intensity increased, if anything, with repetition. Then, from amongst it all came the sound of a gunshot, a thin snap, utterly unlike its fictional avatar, enough, however, to come through clear against the shouting, enough to send helmets flinching back, enough to tip the camera on a downward swirl, only returning to its position in time to catch the placards toppling. Enough to make me start back from the screen.

There was a cut to an overhead still, a red circle overlaid to pick out the middle of the square of bodies, a pixel-splash of yellow at its centre.

'And here is freeze-framed footage of the gunshot, the discharge from the barrel clearly visible. Police now believe the shot was fired from a starting pistol found at the scene and hence was harmless, but they weren't to know this at the time. They immediately fired tear gas into the crowd . . .'

I heard shouting and screaming, the muffled thump of canisters breaking open, saw smoke, a policeman in a gas mask ushering the camera away, and then, through it all, picked out the chant gathering new strength, reasserting itself.

' . . . which was when chaos descended. Police sources tell us that they believe some of the protesters let off smoke bombs and tear gas themselves, the resultant cloud completely obscuring all the participants in this developing drama . . .'

I would imagine you know the rest. You may even know it as well as I do. You probably have the footage stored somewhere. Perhaps you watch it, as I have, for inspiration, for resolve.

I'm going to presume, you see, that if you have these words in front of you then you're familiar with the Vanished, or at least believe you are. It seems unlikely to me that you could have found this text by chance. It's not as if it's readily available and downloadable from any of the usual outlets. And while it's not exactly illegal to be in possession of any of my work, I know that it's frowned upon – officially, unofficially, *commercially*. The only way you could have it is if you've specifically searched it out, if you already knew where to look.

What follows is a departure for me. That sums it up perfectly. The best way for you to read it is as a story, a personal work, a *memoir*, I suppose, though that word repels me. Much of it alludes to the atmosphere and events in which so many of us were radicalised so it may even be of some historical interest to you.

It is also a signed confession, a confession of betrayal and, as is the case with many confessions, a justification, too. Though I hope that through these words and the single action which will follow I make right what I've made wrong. In some small way, anyway, in some sense. The truth is that this book wasn't written for you, but for one person and one person only. And that one person will probably never read it, will they, Olivia?

To the rest of you I apologise now, before I begin. I apologise if you've risked anything for this, if you feel cheated by this. I don't think what follows is going to give you the strength you need, the encouragement, the rigour necessary to see through what you're contemplating. Quite the contrary, in fact. Although it's also possible I could be wrong.

All I can offer you in compensation is the final moments of my first glimpse of the Vanished, so that you know it means as much to me as it does to you, so that my betrayals can be seen by you in context, so you can be sure, despite everything, that we remain on the same side.

Eventually, in silence, the smoke and gas clears, the clouds blow off in upward sweeps, their remnants hanging close to the ground. These curtains pull back to reveal confused policemen, alien in their breathing apparatus, their batons and guns hanging useless, taking careful steps between abandoned placards, all lying face up on the ground, giant playing cards in a game no one yet understands. And, yes, of course, all the so-called protesters, the *demonstrators*, these misinterpreted activists, all gone, not a sign of a single one of them. As if they've dissipated into the air as easily as the smoke.

– misstitch014

7

Our secession, it should be immediately apparent, is a secession like no other. Not only do we have no territory, we deny our very physicality. And we secede not from a State but from a whole set of social relations. Still, we claim it as a secession, a rejection of all authorities. The ghosts of your conscience, you fight us, we haunt you.

Extract from *Second Communiqué of the Vanished*

Let's call her Allason. That wasn't her name, but I never called her by her name and I was to find out her name wasn't her name, anyway. So I don't suppose it would matter to her.

I met her at Yarleigh Falls Young Offenders Unit, a privately run secure facility that had won Flagship Status for its pioneering Rehabunishment work and where I had found myself incarcerated after my brother's definitive victory in what I took to be our long-running battle for parental affection. A central tenet of Rehabunishment was the enrolment of Customers (as we were known) into a workplace situation in which essential New Economy skills could be acquired. Allason and I were both signed up to the Anti-Social Behaviour Programme and working in the Unit's onsite call centre.

Despite the tedium of the work and the difficulty of mimicking the vowel sounds of the Indian subcontinent, it was a popular option, particularly amongst claustrophobes, the huge, high-ceilinged former church in which we operated providing rare comfort after a night struggling for breath in a locked cell. While the work itself was tedious, repetitive and soul-befuddling, to pull your headset's microphone down until it touched your neck, lean back in your chair and see twenty or thirty foot of clear air between you and the ceiling was compensation enough. I had never fully appreciated space before, deadened to it by the surfeit around me. Now, beyond the threat of a group audit, it was the only thing which tipped me from my bunk in the morning.

I had never smoked before my incarceration but, upon finding that the whole prisoner economy ran on the cigarette trade and that to hoard was to invite violence and, furthermore, upon the realisation that I had no future worth investing health in, I had thrown myself into the practice with considerable gusto.

It was one of those cold, damp English mornings which probably don't exist anymore, the air heavy with water, breath great gushes of vapour. Each of us stood marooned in our personal cloud, a judder of tempers, break's end already looming, the orange of our boiler suits brighter than any flame. I engrossed myself, as usual, in the study of technique: the girls who arched their hand back, the white tube pointing floorward, clasped lightly at the very tips of their fingers; the girls with hand folded over itself, wrist bent right back so that each tiny ember was angled up to an invisible sky; those holding between thumb and index finger, their remaining digits shielding their precious diminishment; the amateurs, quickly abandoned by me, who pushed it right down into the skin where index meets middle; the solitary smoker who never took it from her mouth, her hands almost bursting through her pockets as she chugged away, her teeth – probably less than a decade old – tarred to a mottled brown, her smile pure defiance after spitting the spent butt.

From amongst all this, looming from the fog of our living and dying, came Allason Benylind, with such suddenness, from such silence, that I dropped my cigarette when she spoke, the ember somersaulting down through the gloom to sizzle out in a puddle at my feet.

'You the hacker, innit?'

She was so tall and I so short that she stooped over me, her neck plunging down from the hunch of her right shoulder. Her face was unfeasibly symmetrical, almost feline in shape. The holes where her piercings should have been gave her a forlorn aspect, as if someone had been puncturing polystyrene with a red-hot biro. Her bleach job was weeks or months out of date, pulled back tight from her face in a badgerish helmet. Her teeth, when she finally opened her mouth wide enough for me to see them, huddled in a petrified clump. She seemed impossibly glamorous.

By the time I had finished the cigarette she lit and passed me I was able to speak again. I explained the commonly held misapprehension concerning my computer skills, that I'd been set up, that I was not merely innocent of the crime for which I'd been convicted but actually incapable of committing it. She laughed. Everyone in the Unit was innocent, nobody had even been there and we all had a watertight alibi.

'You got a computer, yeah?'

'Not exactly.'

'In ya yard.'

'My brother –'

'There y'are den. Most of em in ere never touch one. You got one in ya yard. Got a job for ya. Come.'

And with that I was summoned into her world.

Everything I'd told her was true. My brother David was the worm-maker. He tricked me into unleashing Scaramanga#4 (his imagination failing him only in its naming) one bright summer morning by pretending to let slip that a friend had emailed him a picture of Leonardo Bloom in the nude. A pretty, boyish film actor of the day, his image played tricks on my hormones, as David well knew, and it was while frantically searching the Inbox that I animated Scaramanga. It crashed two thirds of the computers in the City of London, wiped 20 per cent from stock prices and led to my arrest shortly after my darling brother called the police. This was entrapment, I thought. David, an adult, would go to prison, I, a minor, would go home. He turned out to be considerably more thorough than that. I should have realised at the time this was more than standard sibling rivalry, that something deeper lurked behind his actions.

With money which I can only assume he stole using his considerable digital talents, this brother of mine hired the top computer lawyer in the country, a celebrated media star fond of grand statements about 'hacking the law' and 'cyber rights' who nevertheless had a remarkable acquittal rate. I, on the other hand, was assigned Barbara Manx, an overworked and often tearful legal aid solicitor lost deep in the midst of divorce. It was only when I was allocated her philandering husband as my barrister that I began to grow fearful for my future. And for my sexual well-being, as he wasted little time in making an entry-level pass at me.

It was only much later that I found out the lengths David had gone to in order to bring together this dream team. As it happened, he was wasting his time and money. The fact that I had refused to speak when the police had first arrested and interviewed me was held, in the judge's final summary, to be ample evidence of my guilt.

Which is a long-winded way of emphasising that my fear was genuine when Allason led me away. There was no chance that I would be able to help her, but I knew from my time at the Unit that 'refusal' was disallowed. I'm sure you find it odd that I was so fearful of auditing, but you must remember that it was new then, only just introduced into the criminal justice system, unknown outside, a source of considerable emotional pain and humiliation. The only precursor was something called a 'focus group' and this had been voluntary. When motor cars were first driven on the roads of England people used to faint and scream. You've all grown up with it. To you it's as comforting as a beaker of warm milk.

And yet I wasn't afraid. Not really. I was too busy watching the independent ruminations of her two buttocks as she walked, falling into step behind her, trying to move my hips in the same way, a child in the rear of such sophistication. My world suddenly expanded, possibility working on my respiratory system like spring air, my vicious circle turned dirty-virtuous. Which is when, high on it all, I collided with her instantly stationary self.

'You lookin at muh batty?'

'No. No.' Panic running through me like the first fag of the day. 'No. Not like that. No.'

'Not like dat . . . ?' She let the question flop over me, the fog clearing to reveal geometries of red brick towering above us, everything sharp and still. Looked at me so hard I felt as if I was vanishing beneath her scrutiny, so hard her eyes began to glaze, so hard their sightlines began to mesh, pupils pushing in towards her nose – 'Like what den . . .? *Funny?*'

Finally realising the joke, I managed to wheeze a strangled laugh, aspire toward complicity.

'Ow old are ya?'

'Fourteen.'

'Look about twelve. When ya fifteen?'

'Next month.'

'Me an all. What date?'

'The twelfth.'

'No shit! We're twins innit? Thass my birthday an all. That's like a fousand to one or sutt'n yeah?'

My failure to answer, to think of a funny or interesting response, making me shrink further. That blank look saturating me again, then sudden movement, her back receding.

'Come then, Titch. Off to work, innit?'

Allason proved to be correct. I was a computer expert of sorts, at least by the lowly standards Yarleigh Falls encouraged and enforced, mediocrity being its guiding principle, the virtue to which it asked us to aspire. More than a passing acquaintance with a mouse qualified you here.

The chief perk of working in the call centre was supposed to be internet access. Each operative toiled at a computer screen on which the next customer's details and the script we read from appeared as our phone automatically dialled their number. During breaks we were allowed to use these monitors to check for emails from friends and relatives and to 'surf the net' within the circumscribed confines of PrisonWeb. I soon found that the few emails I received were made unreadable by the hearty enthusiasm of the censorship and that PrisonWeb was a small database of Morally Improving articles on drugs, crime and sexually transmitted diseases. In my naivety I assumed that this censorship was the self-evident reason for the low (in fact, zero) uptake of the service. In this, as in almost everything else, I was wrong.

'Go'n then.'

'What?'

'Start it up.'

'Start up what?'

'The fing. The fing it does.'

'What thing?'

'The emmale. The emmale innit?'

'The what?'

'The emmale. The rasclart emmale.'

'The . . .' – hesitating, scared of offence – 'e mail?'

'What I said.'

'. . .'

'Do you know your address?'

'Fairview Block, Cell 12.'

'Your, er. Your email address.'

'Know that, man. I was jokin.'

'So?'

'Nah. Dun know.'

'You know your Customer Number?'

'Takin the piss? 2321XYL.'

'Then it's 232 . . . ?'

'1XYL.'

'At yarleighfalls dot pris dot gov.'

'. . .'

'Are you expecting anything?'

'Yeah man.'

'. . .'

'. . .'

'. . . Nothing, I'm afraid.'

'Nutt'n?'

'Nothing. Have you given the address to anyone?'

'Wha? All that 232 at yarleigh dot shiz?'

'Yeah, all that.'

'Nah man.'

'Well that might explain it.'

'. . . ?'

'Why you haven't got any messages. If no one knows your address.'

'. . .'

'Why don't we send it to a few people? Your address? So they can write back.'

'Seen, seen. Gwan den.'

' . . . well, do you have any addresses?'

'. . .'

' . . . nah.'

'Oh.'

She had examined the ceiling carefully, the lines round her eyes like arrows leading to treasure. Then, with a creamy smile, returned to me facelift smooth.

'Ya know your address?'

'Yeah.'

'Then I'll send you one innit?'

'Erm, okay, let me just . . . There you go. Do you want to sit here to type . . . ?'

'Nah man. I'll dictake. I failed typin innit?'

'Okay. What do you wanna say?'

'Lemme see.' A breath. '"Dear Titch. This is my address. Then put the address in. Write back soon. Oh, and tell me sutt'n I dun know. Big ups. Lady Sadie." Alrigh?'

'Erm, yeah. Yeah, great. Erm. *Sadie?*'

I felt her pity pouring over me. 'Well, Lady Allason don't rhyme, innit? An Sadie's well sexy. Yagetme?'

Which is how our correspondence started.

For the first couple of weeks I was typing both sides, Allason waiting outside while I wrote my response then rushing in to check it and relate her next instalment. I didn't mind. It used up twice the time. It also broke up the monotony of the day, giving me something to think about while I ran through sales scripts with eighty-year-olds who didn't even have a computer let alone know what kind of processor was supposed to be inside. It gave me something to focus on during other people's audits. But more than any distraction it was intimate, a first small conspiracy of friendship.

Then, one bright morning when, despite the cigarette smoke, the air smelt of cut grass and clean boys, as I walked out to fetch her she signalled to me to stay where I was. I ignored her, of course, a mixture of arrogance and devotion propelling me forward, unable to stop myself, to admit to any change.

'Ya deaf, bitch? Stay.'

Stopping me was that easy, the ensuing silence leaching strength from me, left standing on the steps, minuscule in an architecture of raised brows and sharp-edged, faux-sympathetic smiles.

She re-emerged fifteen minutes later with such a self-satisfied look on her face that I presumed she had spent the time with her right hand in her knickers instead of on a mouse. But she signalled me inside with the angle of her head and when I checked my mail her reply plopped into my Inbox like a pebble into a still pool.

yo mizz tich! check it! ladie sadie in ya arear! yes man! rollin! some fink u dint no – me mam aint even me mam! 4 real! more nex time! peace out! 1 luv! ladie 2 da sadie

It was inevitable, I suppose, that our relationship would change at this point. The Unit's Customers enforced a rigid social system, a hierarchy of such complexity and subtlety that newcomers inevitably stumbled into trouble. This appeared to be its main purpose. Any breach of etiquette was met with outrage, disgust and then unpleasant auditing, with the result that such apparent breaks with tradition actually had the effect of

18

reinforcing what they were supposed to have damaged. So, fed on a diet of newbie error, every week would see a further hardening and refinement of each Customer's place within the hierarchy. The auditors, keen to aid our Rehabunishment and well versed in the power of social shame, encouraged this situation, our auditing a constant reiteration of the idea that our problem was with 'finding our place'.

Allason and I were quite clearly in breach of the code. In the normal running of things it was acceptable for her to demand my help and unthinkable that I would refuse to give it. But to continue to spend time alone when we could and should have been smoking cigarettes was clearly abnormal, and causing a growing unease amongst the other call-centre girls. It quickly became apparent from the looks I got off the strangers serving my fish oil in the dining hall that this unease was being transmitted to the main body of Customers. I think only Allason's standing within the wider community (shoplifters being accorded an exalted status) prevented repercussions much earlier in the process. So we stopped talking to one another. Or rather, Allason stopped talking to me. And thankfully, I took the hint.

But this wasn't the sacrifice that might have been expected because we now communicated daily (sometimes twice daily) by email. And, freed from the embarrassment of each other's presence, unconcerned now about how our friendship might be viewed or what reprisals might be visited upon us, these communications bloomed, growing in length and detail and honesty. Sadie, as I now thought of her, told me how she was given up by her mum when she was just hours old, about the homes she'd lived in, her various foster families, skiving off school, nicking stuff from Woolies, eating her tea on her lap in front of the telly. I treasured it, this soap opera full of excitement and alien detail. Tea in front of the telly! We had always been made to eat together, the children crouched over our plates as a barrage of questions and interest and enthusiasm poured down on us from the mouths of our deluded, involved parents. We didn't even have a microwave, whereas Sadie picked what she wanted from the freezer and heated it herself, before carrying her steaming food on a tray over to the warm, welcoming glow of the TV on which she could watch *whatever she wanted!* And secretly, rather than truly empathising with the pain and hurt and sense of loss she obviously felt over her disappeared mother, I experienced instead a first tug of romance and delicious freedom in her lack of attachments. Everything about her captivated me, her misspellings a stream of creativity washing over me rather than the drip-drop of ignorance.

All I could offer in return were tales of my mother not letting me stop playing the clarinet even though I hated it, of my grandmother leaving me a music box in her will, of my father damaging the neighbour's roses whilst cutting the hedge. Of being forced to go to the recycling centre every weekend. Of my mother's over-enthusiastic response to my third place in the Area Under-11s swimming heats. Of my family's oppressive need to be involved in everything I did, to inhabit the inside of my head. Yet strangely, Sadie loved my emails as much as I loved hers, my boring, circumscribed life seeming as exotic to her as hers did to me, like something from those old books they'd had at junior school, she said. Like a fairytale world.

The sense of release that Sadie's messages gave me was enhanced by a strange anomaly. While the emails I occasionally still received from various family members were littered with the black blocks of censorship, Sadie's mails reached me untouched. I have never been able to find out definitively why this should have been. At first I allowed myself to believe that the censor had taken pity on us and allowed us our little game, a benevolent dictator overseeing each word of our developing friendship. But then, as I examined the mails I'd received from Mum, replete with exclamation marks and exhortations to keep my chin up and make a go of it (unanswered, all unanswered), I became convinced that a machine was responsible for the excisions. There seemed to be no sense in what was taken out, merely a very long list of keywords cut without any reference to context. Sadie and I appeared to have found a loophole in the system, an oversight which meant the technology hadn't been set up to take internal emails into account. After all, why would two Customers be emailing each other? What could they possibly have to say to one another?

We answered the question over and over. I would tell Sadie about how my father used to make me and my brother go door-to-door with him on Sundays delivering leaflets for the Labour Party. Sadie would respond with a detailed explanation of the best way to remove security tags from garments while in a dressing-room cubicle. To scare her, I would fire back with the ingredients of my mother's nut loaf. In turn, she would wax lyrical on the lushness of her favourite alcopop. Elated, I would complain that my school had no uniforms with which to disguise the combination of dowdiness and worthiness which constituted what my parents had instead of taste. Outraged that such a school was possible, she would regale me with tips on the modifications needed to her uniform so that, when people saw her, they didn't puke. And in this way, we became more than friends. And I survived all the degradations and humiliations designed for girls of stronger stock than mine.

I only talked to her once more at the Unit. We had reached our first break of the day and I leant back in my chair as the girls around me rolled away from their desks and, in a confusion of wire, disentangled themselves from their headsets before limping and huffing toward the exit, the giant room slowly reaching the quiet equilibrium of computer hum, the non-silent silence enhanced by church acoustics so it seemed, with your eyes closed, as if the banks of machines went on for ever, an infinity of processors. Waiting for complete peace, for the most absolute of privacy, I occupied myself as I did every day with examining the stained glass window which had been installed in place of a too blatantly single-faith image when Yarleigh Falls had been converted.

I'm still not sure whether the picture showed one body splitting into two or two bodies merging. The profiled faces looked away from each other, one to the left, the other to the right, each the back of the other's head, their skin the colour of a department-store latte, their single torso draped in angel-white robes, each fold detailed in black, the wire from their headsets two spirals reaching up and then circling down to meet beneath them like a snubbed heart. The hand to the left, shaped into a child's pistol, pointed up into the sky, the hand to the right pointed forward. The smiles on the profiled faces suggested hidden pleasure, the same shape I imagined my mouth taking when an email arrived. It wasn't the image that held my attention, though, so much as the colours, particularly on a day like today, at this point in the morning, when sunlight came straight through from behind and the red panes in particular took on an intensity even greater than the pixels on the screen in front of me.

Rebooting myself, I checked my mail, opened it leisurely and, with the usual warmth of anticipation, began to read.

The realisation seemed slow, as if I was being hit in the stomach again and again, frame by frame, the impact of each blow stretched, my mind smearing with betrayal, a whole lifetime of hopes dropping through my bowels, my mouth filling with sand, the cold touch of sweat rippling out across me. In truth, it must have taken less than a minute for me to read, re-read and re-re-read the short message, for me to rise, my chair careering off on its casters, for me to march/run from the room, tears already cool on the hot skin of my face, for me to push through the ossified gaggles of smokers to where Allason (Allason again, a stranger) stood geezering with her own set, for me to scream, louder than I had ever screamed before, my rage surprising me, 'WHY DIDN'T YOU FUCKING TELL ME?'

The silence. The whole yard made of silence. I could hear the sky, the clouds moving. I could hear children in a playground somewhere. Mothers chatting in coffee shops. The sea.

Asteroids colliding with planets a thousand years ago. I could hear the incessant skitter of my heart as it pumped more blood to my face, flooding the tributaries of my cheeks.

She didn't even look up at me, jerkily faked a smile, a shrug, a half eyeroll, not to me, despite the glance I tried to hold on to. To the others, all the others still around us. Which is when I felt them, the witnesses, no alibi possible this time. I turned and ran between them, a cleared path greeting me instead of the jeers I expected, a bank of orange fluoro to each side. Finally made it to the toilet block and there abandoned myself to the sobs which ran through my body in great spasms, as if a rat was trying to escape from my intestines.

Sadie was getting out. Having failed every attempt to parole her, she had served her sentence in its entirety and the authorities could no longer hold her. In one week's time she would be gone. My brain looped the information and my stomach kept on dropping.

I refused to check my email for the next six days. I refused to eat, my food swept round my plate, code for the cameras above. I refused to talk in my emergency auditing, jaw clenched, arms crossed, a perpetual shrug. The world smudged into an endless mid-afternoon, even my distraction distracted. But on that sixth day I woke hungry, breakfasted well, made my way to the call centre, energetically sold financial products to people who couldn't afford them and waited impatiently for my break. Checked. Saw the packets of data drop one after the other, a tumble of apologies and promises. Im a keep riting. Im a keep riting 2 u. My resolve suddenly shining, polished, those six days a wilderness I had left behind, I typed my reply. You'd better.

I don't know whether I really believed her. I can't remember with any sense of clarity. I think I thought she meant it but that once she was out what she meant might change. It's easy to make promises when you're locked in a cell every night. There's nothing else to do. But once Sadie exploded back into the world, why would she remember me? I wasn't being self-pitying about it, just honest. So I recall myself as unsurprised, stonily unfazed, as another six days passed after she'd gone, my Inbox refusing to fill however many times I checked. Until, with all the inevitability of a supervisor's prompt, on that sixth day the message finally came, the longest she had ever sent me, a barrage of blacked out expletives and misspelled explanations.

She didn't have a computer of her own, of course, and no money for internet cafés. Finally, she had discovered that the local library had a machine and that she could book time on it. After two separate hours caught up in the thickets of her own ignorance and growing frustration, **sum fit brer** had shown her how to set up an account and so at last **lady sadies back in da house! Boooo!!!**

This I do remember – a sense of pleasure and excitement so strong that I wanted to pick up my monitor and throw it through a window, to unleash giant bubbles of laughter or sing a song as loud as I could. I wanted to shake my head around till I fell over, smoke all my week's supply of cigarettes, buy a pill or alcohol and celebrate with stomach-emptying oblivion, punch a Customer Support Officer in the tit and mock her tears. Instead, quietly and carefully, with the same tightly controlled simper of the mirrored faces above me, I composed my reply and we carried on as if Sadie were still imprisoned with me.

There were changes, of course. First, there were the black blocks of deleted text which had previously destroyed my enjoyment of my parents' attempts at communication (if anything could make them less enjoyable). But, perhaps due to the idiosyncracies of Sadie's spelling, her emails were never as riddled with them as the others I received, the recognition software hopelessly lost in the language-generating portion of her mind. And regardless of that, something about the way she wrote meant that the deletions seemed to further burnish her

24

communications with an illicit glamour. I responded in kind, deliberately abandoning my spelling bee champion's scruples and striving to insert as many errors into my texts as I could, imagining them arriving with Sadie as clean as when they were written, untouched by where they'd come from.

The most important change of all, though, was that Sadie now had news to give me. While I continued to reminisce and then, as the time grew nearer, worry about my future release, Sadie was concerned solely with the present. She was living in a 'sheltered' bedsit in a town called Coalville, which, despite its name, was in Kent rather than the North. She had her own telly, was receiving food tokens and had found a shop that would give her fags for them. She was 'seeing' the man from the library now and then and he bought her unspecified gifts of some sort. And, of course, she was nicking whatever else she wanted, her remarkable facility for relieving shops of their most precious goods apparently undiminished by her time inside. She went out to pubs and clubs, got drunk, munched pills, danced with boys, snogged, puked, all by herself, utterly singular. I could imagine Coalville crumbling around her, the blackened red brick turned to dust, the dust blown away by her approach.

I, meanwhile, was set to be released into the care of my parents – even though I had refused their visits, left their letters unopened, their emails unreplied to. These were, to my mind, the people who had put me here, who had made my destiny inevitable from the moment my brother was conceived. The people who had decided 'not to take sides' in the matter of who was right and who wrong. The people who had confided in me that it 'isn't helpful to keep going over it'. I felt more betrayed by them than I did by David. He knew I wasn't guilty, they just chose to believe I was. My emails became distorted by my anger and sense of injustice. Instead of the glitz of Coalville all I had to look forward to was compassion in Reading, the itching scab of living with understanding warders. I'm not convinced that Sadie really grasped my problem. I'm not sure that I do, looking back, in the light of everything that's happened since. But I know that my despair felt genuine, that I wrote again and again to her that I would rather stay at Yarleigh Falls than go back to them.

Did I know what I really wanted? Did I push her into it? It took weeks of my bleating before Sadie gave in and said that I could come and live with her. She explained (as I already knew) that she lived in one room with one bed, that it would be crowded and uncomfortable. That she wasn't going to babysit me. That I'd have to look after myself and put up with her moods and get out of the way sometimes. That it would be a laugh, though, **a good carck,** as she put it. How could I say no? How could she expect me to say no? I'd got what I wanted. I sat, my heart nervous fingers on a tabletop, the irregularity of the rhythms zigzagging through me.

From that moment I'd escaped Yarleigh Falls. I devoted my imagination to the topography of Coalville, the grammar of my future perfect home. PrisonWeb contained no information on the town so I rebuilt it from my friend's references. I studied and re-studied Sadie's mails, trying to piece together a landscape from the minimal information she gave me, to work out whether Tariq's shop was on the corner of the road the Crown was on or a block over, whether the Job Centre was near to Blake's NiteClub or in a different part of town. I attempted to picture the architecture – Gothic, crowding in above my head – dreamed of the yellow light shading my body between graphite sky and wet pavement, the skimpiest of dresses covering my skin, as I made my way out for the night. I fantasised about the two of us letting go in the middle of a crowded dancefloor, our skirts riding up our parted thighs, our heads thrown back, the rhythm taking us somewhere else, an appreciative crowd forming round us (the images' origin in too many hours spent watching music videos made all too apparent by the arrival of the square-jawed, sad-eyed hunk who would romance me for the rest of the night).

I was, however, sensible enough to realise that if I were to make any of these mirages concrete my behaviour in these last few weeks was all important. I threw myself into such ultra-critical auditing that Evelyn, by far the most stringent of the auditors, seemed taken aback, apologetic. She even stroked my hair once. Meanwhile, I won the Sales Award two weeks running for persuading home owners to increase their credit burden to unsustainable levels.

Most important of all, though, I had to convince my parents. At the time, persuading them to let me go to Coalville seemed to be the only obstacle to my happiness rather than merely the first to be discovered. A long, tearful conversation with my mother in which I made considerable use of the phrase 'finding myself' eventually secured the approval I needed. She had never been able to resist the pull of this quest and I despised her for having lost herself to begin with.

If I were to be asked for a word to describe my own poor character up to this point in life, I think I would choose 'diffident'. Partly because I like the sound of it, the mousy shuffle of that double 'f'. Partly because it was true. And yet, in these few weeks at the end of my sentence, I seemed to shrug off my former personality. And, as if in outward tribute to this inward change, I began a transformation in my appearance.

In preparation for my release I paid thirty carefully hoarded cigarettes to Leez Munday, for which sum she bleached my hair (Leez worked in the Domestic and Industrial Hygiene Unit and the potions she made using toilet cleaner were renowned throughout Yarleigh Falls). I considered getting my nose pierced, too, but my nerve failed me. I did have one ear done twice, Melindah Hawes assuring me that the studs she put in had been sterilised by Leez. I waited for the holes to become infected with a grim relish.

I took every opportunity to admire my bright yellow hair, the colour of additive-laden vanilla ice cream. The glint of the bronze-gold studs in my right ear consistently surprised me, the reflection not me but a better girl. There was nothing I could do about the clothes to be returned to me on my exit except grit my teeth and put up with it until the first opportunity to replace them. As for my glasses, I decided that seeing clearly was overrated and put them back into their case for good. The hollow thwock of its last closure – previously a kind of reproach – that last closing thwock rang out like a hymn. Seriously myopic, my reflected image now took on a vaseline-lensed, soft-focus aspect which made me feel sexier than I had ever done before. Not hard, admittedly.

But then, as the day crept nearer, ceased to be a kind of hypothetical and asserted its reality, then, just when I should have been most excited, fear swamped me. Although my correspondence with Sadie carried on exactly as before, although she said that everything was ready for my arrival, although she seemed as excited as I was, what if she never showed up to take me to my new home? The stories in her emails were packed with missed appointments, jokes about her tardiness, tales of standing up friends, lovers and members of her foster family. The idea that she would turn up for me at the right time on the right day seemed ridiculous, presumptuous, irresponsible. Suddenly my lack of glasses, the fogged blurriness of the world around me, made me feel exposed, insecure, as if I were physically preparing myself to be tripped up, a stooge in a silent movie. I found myself reconsidering all my certainties, questioning the decisions I had taken, longing for a way to back down, to return home to my own cell, in my own parents' prison, the photo-poster of the kittens frayed and creased but still there on the wall above the pink glow of my old, familiar bedspread. By now, though, it was too late.

I could see the blue sky, the sun illuminating the Chief Customer Support Officer's outline so that her dark form was ringed with brightness. I didn't listen to what she said to me as she signed my Certificate of Social Adequacy and my NVQ (Level 1) in Call Centre Technology & Skills. It was the usual rustle of platitudes about the importance of knowing my place, of remembering the feelings of others, the dangers of drugs, alcohol and unprotected sex, the potential within me which could be unlocked by application, diligence and humbleness. The entirety of my concentration was focused on what lay beyond the window, on whether she was out there waiting.

I was led down long, fluorescent-lit corridors, dingy after the office, left and right through set after set of unlocked and re-locked doors, and taken to a counter where my clothes and personal effects were returned to me, neatly folded into a plastic bag, the possessions of a corpse. Sweat evaporating from me in cold shudders, I undressed from the boiler suit which had become so familiar and forced myself back into civvies, my discomfort increasing with the realisation that I had grown, upward and outward, my sleeves left like tidemarks on my arms, my grey a-line skirt preposterously tight, my breasts bound uncomfortably flat by the white nylon of my school shirt. There was nothing I could do about any of it now. I stretched upwards above my old self, set my teeth and marched out, back past the desk, past the muttered good lucks of the staff on duty, out towards the surfeit of light crashing through the wide open door.

It makes no sense to think of our situation in terms of metaphors of 'imprisonment'. To be inside a prison implies the possibility of being outside it. CTRL – which crawls through our blood – offers no such possibility. We are not inmates because we are not inside anything. It is inside us.

Extract from *Ninth Communiqué of the Vanished*

2

I didn't recognise her. Not straight away. Perhaps it was just the sun flooding my retinas. Perhaps it was the shock of being outside, the steps leading down to a road, the road running in front of a park, trees caught against sky, the horizon more than twenty metres from me. More than this, though, she just didn't look like I'd expected, both my memory and my imagination letting me down. Certainly the glint of her facial jewellery should have alerted me to her presence, all holes now filled. Or her badly streaked hair. But I had never imagined Sadie in a blue-and-silver Adidas Stushsuit or white Reebok Ultra-Classics. I had never imagined her wearing make-up, her eyes two slashes of lime green, her mouth a brownish cerise smush, her already prominent cheekbones re-emphasised to the point of caricature. And I had certainly never imagined her pushing a pram.

I stumbled down the steps and past her, squinting, unbalanced, desperately scanning left and right for the person I was expecting.

'Ya lookin for, ya dippy cow?'

I turned to the stray single mum, peered up at her, my neck retreating into my body, waiting for blows or anti-social invective to rain down.

'Sorry . . . ?'

'Kin ell, Titch. They bin givin ya letric shock or sutt'n?'

' . . . Sadie?'

'Ya fink it were? Muvver Theresa?'

'I . . . The pram.'

'Thi? For you innit?'

'But. But I don't have a baby.'

She looked at me as if it was I who was insane. 'S'not for

babies. S'for carrying stuff around what ya don't wanna carry.' She glanced back up to the building behind me, its smooth blue-washed, unwindowed surface. 'I'll show ya. S'get away from these *freaks* first, though, yeah?' The 'r' rolled out like barbed wire.

I walked alongside her, the pram soundtracking our steps with its uneven grumble, the sun bouncing in dazzling flashes from her lacquered hair. Sadie was silent but I was dumb, my eyes wide despite the glare, my mind occupied with recording the moment, sure as I was that my life could get no better. Then it did. We turned a corner, Sadie slumped onto the uncomfortable plastic ledge of a bus-shelter bench and pulled back the covers. A tracksuit still on its hanger, a rich purple colour, the nylon weave unstretched, untouched.

'Wha–?'

'Present innit? Show me up lookin like dat.'

I lifted it out more carefully than a baby, the swoosh a tick, all boxes ticked.

'S'Nike. Prefer Adidas but we don't wanna look like twins is it?'

I held it up to me, feeling a prickle of static, its arms like the arms of a puppet me, moving with boneless precision.

'It's beautiful. It's perfect. Thank you.'

Nodding at the buggy: 'Z'more.'

I took the gifts out one by one. A pastel yellow Ralph Lauren polo shirt. A black Adidas sports bra ('That's the don that is. That's the don a sports bras'). A pair of white Adidas socks, the three black stripes angling down the inside ready to be turned out. A pair of very pale pink Special Edition Reebok Classic Classics with a shower of glitter somehow set into the laminate. A thin gaggle of material creating three interlinked loops, unlikely, a mistake. I held it up between index finger and thumb trying to puzzle it out.

'What's this?'

'A fong, ya norman.' She watched me watching it for a moment, enjoying my uncertainty. 'Ain't gunna wear school

34

pants the rest of ya life are ya?' My blush equal parts embarrassment and pleasure.

'Gettin changed yeah?'

'What, here?'

'Be more embarrassed to be seen dressed like that'n show a bit a skin in the street. Ya look like sutt'n from an orror film. Big doll or sutt'n.' She stood, arms rigid before her, eyes so wide the reds of her whites showed right round the pupils. 'Teacher says you bad. You bad. You must d-i-i-i-e-e-e.' Joke abandoned before I had time to laugh, she swung back to the pram. 'Wanna drink?' Ruffling further down, pulled free two silver bottles and shimmied them at me as she span, placed one of them on the ground, hooked the other on the edge of the bench and brought her right hand crashing down, some yellow liquid spilt and the serrated gash of the top's teeth forever marking the seat. I took the bottle from her, still cold, water glossing its surface and read the peeling label: *'CELEBR8!!!*™ – *a fruit flavored champagne-style cocktail with vodka'*. Sipped at its sweetness, gulped, felt it fizzying down into my stomach and up into my head. Turned back to Sadie and, clumsily, with none of her panache, clinked my bottle against her own, took one of the two lit fags she offered from her mouth.

'I can't. I can't take all this.'

'Shuddup.'

'I can't.'

'S'all nicked anyway innit? Not like I can take it back.'

I refused to change in the street, something blocking me regardless of how much I wanted to impress her, to be worthy of the uniform she'd given me. We donated the buggy to some kids we came across playing with a box of steak knives and rolled up at the station ready to leave for Coalville, Sadie laughing and doing stupid voices, I double drunk. She taught me to vault the turnstiles for the toilets and I locked myself in a cubicle to try my finery. My life's opening act of gratuitous

35

vandalism – like seeing the ocean for the first time – was throwing all my old clothes into the toilet bowl and then peeing on top of them. I emerged to a cold, appraising eye, arched brow, the corners of her mouth angling down, chin pushing forward as she nodded her approval.

'Could do wi'a bit a make-up but you'll do.'

We had another cigarette to celebrate, leaning against the sinks, and the toilet lady, one ankle elephantine, the tight blue and white check of her official overall describing in miniature every fold in her flesh, said she'd call the police unless we left. So, flicking our burning butts toward her, leave we did, up the steps, through the turnstile, past the ticket barrier in a fortuitous huddle of foreign language students waving the wrong parts of their tickets, down the platform, onto the train and straight into another toilet. Sadie explained to me that she knew someone back in Coalville who would buy my permit-to-travel from me and that it was stupid, then, to waste it on an actual journey when we could get home like this. I didn't disagree or even consider the risk of ending up back in Yarleigh Falls. All I could think of was getting to my new home. I was going home.

I needn't have worried, anyway. The guard had already lost long before he rapped his key on the door.

'Who is it?' Sadie sounding unlike herself, younger, wide-eyed, farcically naive.

'Tickets please.'

'Fraid you'll have to wait. I'm on the loo.'

'I'll wait.'

'It's *women's troubles*.'

'Oh. Well. Well. I can wait.'

'I might be a little while . . .' She paused, a master swordswoman pulling back her blade. 'It's quite bloody.'

'Oh. Oh. I'll. I'll come. Come back and. See you sitting at. Your seat . . .' His voice already fading, his being shrunk inside his smart-casual uniform. Sitting up on the sink holding my nose, desperately trying not to laugh, the plastic bubbling away from the glass of the window subtly brightening the colours around me, my tracksuit seemed to glow a vivid maroon.

Coalville was not what I had expected. One of a series of recently constructed dormitory towns feeding commuters into London, it was originally to have been called Hope, until someone high up had suggested that its name and that of its fellow newbuild conurbations should reflect Britain's Unique Industrial Heritage. Hence Coalville Newtown stood between Ironbridge Newtown and Steelship Newport on the coast. The place was built from an orangey-red brick in Victorian Barratt Home hybrid. The only employer in the town itself was the Coalville Living Mine Experience, the mine shaft having been specially dug before the houses were built around it. So, when we staggered from the station at five that day, we were met by the sound of a siren and the emergence from the gates of more than a hundred end-of-shift miners marching home with their dirty metal lunch boxes tucked beneath their donkey-jacketed elbows. There was no reason why I should have known that these were tour guides, ticket sellers and café staff and that the coal dust caking their faces was sprayed on. I found myself thinking almost fondly of my parents, who probably remembered such scenes from their childhood in the seventies.

Sadie led me through this town of identical streets, each exactly as dilapidated as the last, despite being less than five years old, the bricks already crumbling, slashes and stains of dirt and badly executed graffiti everywhere (a good amount of the half-filled, gappy bubble letters being attributed to LADY SADY). She led me past paper shops, pubs, off-licences and bookies that looked like they must have been there in spirit long before the structures which housed them were built, their windows dark and crabbed, as if something ancient were lurking just inside, their walls thick with redundant satellite dishes and home-installed security cameras. She led me over dipping hills where terraces of houses seemed to roll past, giving the impression that we were standing still and the town was moving round us. She took me to her bedsit, my eyes full of it all, my brain reeling with alcopop, nicotine and excitement.

It was a small, L-shaped room. Opposite the door was a single bed, the duvet on it crumpled round and half flung back to reveal almost-matching grey sheets. Above the bed was a picture of Leonardo Bloom stripped to the waist, thumbs through the belthooks of his low-slung jeans, golden hairs swirling up to his belly button and catching the last of the day's sun. At the bottom of the bed, a small chest of drawers with a large, dusty-looking television hanging over its edges. After that, a wardrobe in wood-look laminate, then on the next wall round, a window out onto an overgrown yard, the dusty purple cones of buddleia jostling and nodding at the glass. Along the base of the L, the thin carpet changed to thin lino, the walls were studded with a couple of half-hearted, almost empty shelves and a kitchen sink stood next to a dirty hotplate on another chipboard and plastic cupboard. Above it all, aloof, a glossy black electricity meter – by far the newest, best-maintained object in the room – ground out its rhythm. The impermanent, shoddy quality of the place made it a child's den grown suddenly full-size, magnificent. I could barely breathe. We jumped on the bed, kicked off our Reeboks and had a fag, the Fosters Extra ashtray between us, a pledge of allegiance. If I could, I think I would have happily stayed like that for an eternity. I didn't get ten minutes.

The calm evaporated even before the door opened, the rattle of an immense bunch of keys ripping through me with invented memories of a prison experience I never had. I was up and off the bed wafting smoke with the flat of my hand before the intruder had managed to get her head in, eyes lost behind the fist-sized tinted lenses of her glasses.

'Oh, sorry. Didn't real-*ise* anyone was home.'

'Never do.'

'Allason *and* . . . ?'

'Titch.' My name decided before I could speak, my mouth gaping at the sight of her.

'Titch? Un-*use*-ual. Well, I'll no doubt get to the bottom of it. Aren't you going to intro-*duce* me?'

Reluctantly: 'Titch. This is Lynda. She's the landlord.'

'That's Lynda with a "y". And I am your land-*lay*-dy.'

Perilously thin, much older than she thought she was, Lynda moved into the room like a puppeteer's spider. She flung back her parched yellow hair in a crackle of static and let me admire her – the white crease lines ironed into the front of her jeans, the sky-blue blouson jacket, the sunburst spectacles, the long, cherry red nails curling over into talons, the Mores lodged between them. The dryness about her, the creaking of evil intentions in every jerky, desiccated movement, the stick-insect tremors in her hands. I took a step back, then another, ran out of space, feeling for the wardrobe behind me, for something solid.

'Don't mind me, I'm just going to *emp*-ty the meter.' I glanced across to Sadie for reassurance, but she was too busy looking fifteen, the first time I'd seen her like that, staring at her socks, a sullen blankness slackening her features. Scared by this transformation, I watched as Lynda clopped up to the meter, chose the right key from her chain, opened it and gutted it of silver. Watched as she strolled back, her knees bending unnaturally, watched as she sat down on the bed and began counting.

'It looks like you'll be needing more tokens, Allason.'

'Y'fink?'

'Well, yes. I do.'

'Ain't got no more vouchers.'

'But your new playmate. She must have hers. You gave me to be-*lieve* . . .'

'Titch?'

I edged towards my Yarleigh Falls Releasee Orientation Pack, fiddled past the complementary condom, Multi-Faith

39

Little Book of Prayer, 'Fitting Back In' graphic novella and the debris of tester packs for new brands of shampoo and liquid soap, to the multi-coloured wad of vouchers.

'What am I looking for?'

'S'a blue one – Power an Eat. Got like a lightnin bolt frough a fire on it.'

'This one?'

'Thass it.'

'*Lov*-ely. You need to *sign* it dear . . . Then hand it over. Oh, so it's *Tilly* is it? Very nice, I'm sure. Though of course I already *knew* that. I was just *play*-ing with you, dear. These tokens' – she poured the freshly counted coins back onto the bed – 'are yours, *Tilly*.'

I picked one up, saw the same picture on its face.

'And don't try putting them in cigarette machines. The weight is all *wrong*. Not only is it a terrible waste but it blocks the ma-*chine* up, too, so that *honest* people can't use it.' Standing up in a creak of bad faith, she headed for the door. 'Anyway, I'm bored of you now. I'm going to go and do the other flats. See if anyone can entertain me any better. Rent vouchers due Monday. Don't forget and we'll all get along *fine*.'

Nothing moved in the room once she'd gone. Sadie and I stood separated in space, the excitement drained from me, a deep unease dribbling in to fill my hollowed body. The light slanting through the window greyly illuminated a quiver of airborne fluff. Sadie used her big toe to examine her discarded trainer. The noise of a plane passed over, a slow-motion sigh, its windows filled with smiling holidaymakers, every hand waving a primary-coloured bucket and spade. The plants in the garden began to wilt, the season ending before it had begun. Finally, I managed to take a breath, speak.

'How –? How often does she come?'

'Ere?'

'Yeah.'

'Well. Quite a lot. A lot.'

'Why?'

'Why? She the landlord innit?'

'So?'

'So she as to come quite a lot.'

'You mean she checks up on us.'

'Kinda. Kinda, yeah. Checks up.' A pause. 'Looks after us.'

'What?'

'Looks after us.'

'Our landlady "looks after us"?'

'Yeah.'

'That isn't her job, though. To "look after us". Why can't she leave us alone? Have you told your social worker?'

The room returned to that same writhing stillness, Sadie very interested in her footwear.

'Er.'

'Sorry?'

'S'er.'

'I don't understand.'

'She's my social worker.' Another gap, my stomach lurching down into it. 'She's your social worker, too.'

'She's not. She can't be. She doesn't even seem like a social worker.'

'Ow would you know? Ow many social workers you ad?'

'Well, I haven't had any before, but my dad's friend Jo –'

'V'ad a social worker since I were eight. An I'm tellin ya, Lynda's a social worker.'

'But I thought they were meant to be, y'know, *caring*.'

'What ya fink this is, the telly? Ya fink they're jus runnin around *carin* about ya? Ya think they ain't got nutt'n else to do except *care* about *you*?'

'I don't care. I don't like her. She gives me the creeps.'

'She's sposed ta.'

'I'll speak to. I'll speak to my probation officer and get someone else.'

'Ya can't.'

'Why?'

'She's ya probation officer as well, innit?'

'She can't be.'

'She is. *Out*-sourcin. *Down*-sizin. She bids for the contracts.'

'This is ridiculous.'

'Believe.'

'I do.'

'Don't worry.'

'But I do.'

'Ya wanna get pissed?'

I felt anger overwhelm me, rush up my throat like vomit. Leant forward, opened my mouth to let it out. Felt laughter gurgle through instead, self-pitying at first, until, encouraged by the sound of Sadie laughing, too, it grew. And then we were both at it, the whole room rattling as we let it build, the sight of each other's pinkly frozen, grotesque face lifting it still further, the tears dribbling from our red-wet eyes. Until I flopped forward onto my knees, until Sadie threw herself back onto the bed, the both of us holding in our aching guts, our faces hurting, until the world drowned in our liquid gulping.

'No no no don't look at me don't look at me –'

And we were off again.

'Stop no stop I gotta stop –'

And we were back where we started.

'Oh god oh god oh god I can't breathe –'

And with each diminishing wave this little island became ours again, footsteps washed from the beach, and we both lay panting on the pristine shore. Then we got up, pulled our shoes back on and headed for the pub.

Privacy is hardly something that anyone who has been incarcerated would ever expect as a matter of course. If it's been taken from you once you treat it as a gift rather than a given. To choose intimacy rather than have it forced upon you is a different matter again. I don't believe that either of us had really thought about how we would sleep in that tiny room with its narrow single bed. But when we staggered back in there, I with my head in a spin of sugar and alcohol, Sadie seemingly unaffected – though louder and more demonstrative than was usual even for her – there was no question. In a flurry of abandoned clothing, we both stripped to our knickers and t-shirts and squeezed beneath the covers, Sadie flicking the telly on and waving its giant remote in imperious and over-deliberate channel hops. While she settled in to watch a late-night American made-for-TV horror movie of dubious plotting, acting and dialogue, I concentrated on passing out and any awkwardness was dealt with permanently.

My bladder forced me from sleep. The television was still running, the flashes and rustles of light animating Sadie's sleeping face, her hand flaccid on the remote. Shivering, my mouth stuck to itself – the innards of a deflated balloon – I manoeuvred my way over Sadie and out of the bed. Stood, suddenly roused from bleariness by the realisation that I had no idea where the toilet was.

Trackie trousers pulled back on and door latched, I flapped my hand around the hallway until my fingers felt plastic. Plunging the round, marginally concave circle down into its base with my palm, I lit an empty hallway, my fingers the only living things in it. As quietly as I could, leaning away from other doors and dark-hours encounters with their inhabitants, I soft-footed it to the stairway. Climbed to the first landing, every creak matched in my muscle tissue. There I found Yale locks on every door, a regiment of disappointment. Climbed again, desperate now, the relief of finding a bathroom only lasting for the time it took to realise that the cord to put the light on was outside the door.

It was when I was washing my hands and looking at the way the woodchip from the wall had marked my face with pox scars that the darkness returned with an ominous click, no illumination, even, from the frosted skylight above the door.

Carefully, I turned the tap off. Felt the cold water drip from my fingers. Listened.

Perhaps it was a symptom of my fear of the sudden freedoms that I believed had been granted me by my release. Perhaps it was merely my unfamiliarity with my surroundings and, in particular, thrifty landlords' systematic use of timer switches, but that black bathroom shut me down, too.

I could picture a maniac waiting for me outside the door, one dirty hand smelling of tobacco and sperm as it fastened over my mouth, the other already pulling at the all-too-compliant waistband of my Nike sweatpants. Somehow I knew he was there. Stranded, I inched to the door, listened to the scratch of his suppressed breath. Went to the window, yanked plaintively at the painted-shut frame, the moon picking out my forearms, impossibly pale. Turned back to the door, just visible past the grey flaring of the shower curtain, sank slowly down to the floor, my knees to my chest, my arms girded round them.

I'm not sure how long I stayed there, trapping that whimper in my throat, waiting for the wood to splinter in front of his flat foot, a hot prickle of tears sticky on my cheeks. Houses make noises, mumble to themselves, so I interpreted them, each click or creak my fate coming closer, his fingers looking for purchase on the doorframe. I found myself in a slasher movie, the camera circling me again and again, slowly recording the way the light reflected from my skin and hair and tears, circling again, every twitch and snuffle amplified, slowly again, everything about myself I could ever have told anybody fixed frame by frame. Then the camera stopped circling, turned away from me, crept past the white side of the bathtub and the mould-flecked shower curtain, past inch after inch of pube-strewn lino, past the toilet bowl, brown dribble stains marking its underside, past, past until it stopped flat against the door.

Which was when the light went back on out in the hallway, a rectangle of glare filling my squinting eyes, the sounds of movement outside becoming gradually more distinct, definitely the sound of a person, of a person approaching, of a person arriving, definitely the sound of a person arriving.

The light in the bathroom now came on to reveal me cowering and then a voice spoke.

'Titch?'

'Sadie?'

'Who else it gunna be?'

'Are . . . Are you on your own?'

'Er, *yeah*. Four in the morning innit? You alright?'

'Er, yeah. Yeah. Course.'

And as we marched back down to home, my arm inveigled its way inside hers.

'Got stuck in the dark innit? She puts timers on everyfink. Wait till ya try an get a shower that's ot for more'n two minute.'

The next morning – and most other mornings after that – we went shoplifting. Sadie had picked for me a role so suited to me, to my personality and class, that I almost feared that this was what she had brought me here for. I was cast as the goody two-shoes, little Miss Direction who allowed the sleight of hand to take place.

We began by working the smaller shops, myself squeezed into a humiliating new school uniform nicked by Sadie for this purpose, marching girlishly up to the counter and, in my best received pronunciation, befuddling the shopkeeper with a succession of unanswerable queries and unfulfillable requests. I would insist that I had lost something and make them search beneath the counter. I would try to place an order for a nonexistent product (always claiming that they must have a catalogue hidden away somewhere in which they could check). Shyly, solely for the benefit of the sweating, overweight wreck behind the counter, I would bend down from the waist to examine the chocolate racks, rising with eyelashes fluttering and a helpless smile deforming my face. I would wonder, terrified, if the old lady guarding her racks of booze had seen the little sister who had run off up the road while I was talking to a friend, pulling the veteran till-jockey with me to the door to look left then right, left then right, my desperation, the obvious correctness of my upbringing, moving even to me. I would go to pay for a pack of Polos with a pound coin and flip it through my fingers so that it rolled between the shop assistant's flailing hands and cracked to the floor, skipping away under his feet, then would wait for him to rise, complain about how much he was going to charge me and ask for the money back. I would engage the owner in long conversations concerning the working conditions of the hypothetical Saturday job I claimed to be looking for. Sometimes I would just have a chat – surprisingly, I found myself genuinely interested in the lives of those around me.

And while I was occupied and occupying, Sadie would be off to my left or my right, the mouth of her bag gaping open as she filled it with drinks or magazines or beauty products or luxury food items or stationery or CDs or cheap watches or whatever else came within reach of those two steady, slow-moving, graceful hands. Because, despite the randomness of what she stole, she never seemed to rush or panic. Everything was done deliberately and carefully, reversed footage of a shelf stacker. Even her odd selection of goods in fact appeared to be deliberate, as if she were working to a plan so complex I couldn't begin to imagine it. I certainly never questioned it, choosing to see something retributive in this minor crime wave, a sense of fairness in the way Sadie stole everything from everyone, as if we were a miniature, two-girl revolt. So what if some of it ended up thrown in the bins? Who was keeping count? The shelves were always full again the next time we went in.

When I thought I had learnt every possible trick I needed to know we graduated to the big shops and the shopping centres, forested with CCTV networks, packed with security guards, both uniformed and plainclothes, and I found out I hadn't even started yet. The basis of my technique, the one-on-one, was worthless here. The difference between amateur dramatics and a Hollywood movie, it was now all about performing for the cameras.

I tried but I seemed unable to master this new discipline. I either gave too little or too much of myself. As a distraction I was insipid, ignored by seen-it-all staff, the cameras invariably sweeping over me to something more interesting, Sadie left cursing in the centre of a brightly lit aisle, skewered in the criss-cross of their sightlines. While I flapped and gasped through a faked seizure – shoppers picking their way round me, an old lady raising her foot high to step over me – a full complement of store finks and private police circled round my friend. As I mugged for the cameras in a giant overcoat, their red LEDs winked only at her. Somehow she still managed to get what she wanted, but it was due solely to her own talents, not assistance from me.

It didn't take me long to figure it out. I told her one cold morning as we hurried along the road, Sadie's feet never deviating from the kerb, my hands plunged deep into my pockets, touching sausagey, clumsy fingertips to palms, a shiver of sick fear groping through my innards. I could see the doors of Yarleigh Falls closing behind me again, imagine my last forlorn wave as they led me away from my friend. I knew I had no real talent for deception, no nerve to speak of, little in the way of courage, nothing flinty in my whole personality, just a banal need to be liked, my parents' gift to me.

'You should be the distraction and I should do the thieving.'
'Y'wha?'
'I should do the thieving.'
'Nah man.'
'It makes sense.'
'Nah.'
'It does.'

'Don't. Already got a job innit?'

'But I'm rubbish at it.'

'Nah. You shun't be nickin.'

'Why?'

'Trus me blud, I *know*.'

'Well, it's not working is it? I gotta pay my way.'

'Nah man.'

We hit a rhythm between us, a back and forth which continued for two days on and off, between further half-cock forays into the area's department stores and malls, numerous trips to the offie for more booze and fags, through baked beans on toast and an Indian and so on, through late-night TV and daytime TV, through every moment of our shared time, my repeated request slowly beginning to take hold of Sadie, an apathy snipping the muscles in her face, a heaviness caulking her, until at last –

'Alright. Whateva. What the fuck. Whateva.'

Sadie was a conscientious teacher. She took me through the basics of checking a shop's security arrangements, of spotting gaps and flaws in it. She showed me how to pick out the plain-clothes snoops, how to evade their attentions, how to be invisible to them. She taught me how to choose my moment, waiting for that seemingly fortuitous instant when camera configs, distribution of shoppers, shop assistants and security guards all fell into place and it felt, for perhaps only a second or two, as if you were the only person there. She showed me how to use the tools for removing security tags. Most importantly of all, she taught me how to take the goods from the shelves – with her own slowness and grace, without jerkiness or panic, the flow of the movement like that of an elderly Japanese gentleman exercising in a park at dawn. No sharp movement to draw the attention of a security guard to the screen.

What she couldn't teach me, of course, was guts. The first time we tried out our new roles Sadie provided masterful diversion while I stole a budget toothbrush, just one, a bottom-of-the-range piece of plastic crap. When I showed it to her the sweat from my palm had already eroded its cardboard packaging, the head pushing out through the mulch, pitiful. She slipped her arm around my shoulder, contemplated it, her mouth pulling downward, then let out a hawk of laughter.

'Thass the shit, man. Thass. Thass sick, man. Serious. S'what I need. Me uvver's fallin apart.' And then later, 'You know what I got first time I went shopliftin? Nutt'n. F all. You're up on me.' Then later still. 'Know what I got second time I went shopliftin? Nicked.'

I didn't get nicked. Instead I gradually improved. After a couple more trips, Sadie started giving me a shopping list. After a few more times I began to bring it back with everything ticked off. Something about having her nearby covering for me gave me a sense of invulnerability. I knew she wouldn't let anything happen. I knew that I was as safe doing this as I had ever been doing anything. A kind of glow caught me as I began the day's work, a warmth, every hair on my body tingling.

We returned to the bedsit one afternoon, the sun thin and shaky, the feeling still cradling me as I threw myself back on the bed, the bagful of shopping by my feet.

'That's the first time I've really enjoyed it.'

'I could tell.'

She began removing other items from her pockets – a bottle of designer perfume, a large silver watch, its strap like the tracks on a bulldozer, a fountain pen of obscene thickness and gravitas, a tiny MP3 player, a selection of lipsticks, some surprisingly understated jewellery.

'What's all that?'

'What's what?'

'That.'

'That? Jus some bits innit?'

'I thought you were causing a diversion?'

'I was. I caused it. Den I pick up some bits.'

'Well it can't have been much of a diversion then,' I huffed, a prickle of hurt shivering through me.

'Well, ya don't *need* much of a diversion. Ya can do it now.'

'*You* needed a diversion.'

'Nah man.'

'What do you mean, "*nah man*"?'

'I mean I din need no *diversion*.'

'So what was I supposed to be doing then?'

'Keepin outta trouble innit?'

'Are you serious?'

'Always serious.'

'Then fuck you.'

'Just tryna look out for ya.'

'I don't need looking out for.'

'Oh yeah. Yeah course.' She faked thought. 'Hmm. Must be why you're livin in muh yard.'

'You invited me.'

Nodding. 'Yeah. Sure. Sure I did.'

'Alright then. Alright. I'll go.'

'Where ya gunna go? Back to mummy and daddy?'

'Fuck you.'

I had walked right through town to the station, my head awash with injustice, my face stinging with perceived insult, before the gradual flap of my Reeboks lulled me, the whisper of my tracksuit soothed me, and I began to reconsider. I took from my pocket the mobile my mother had sent me and switched it on for the first time. Her messages from the last few weeks – text, voice and picture – entered the handset in a cacophony of tones. I didn't open or listen to any of them, the picture she had loaded on the phone's screen – my brother and I as kids snuggled on our parents' laps – enough to make nausea unbalance me. I turned it off, spun round and headed back to the bedsit. Back home.

From then on we nicked together without any pretence that either of us needed the help. We were constantly hungry for more, rapacious, a crime wave across the whole of the South-

East. I, for one, was drunk on it. I had never had a detention at school, never even been the target of an angry word. When I went nicking I felt bigger than myself, my heart battering my ribs, adrenalin warming my cold body all the way through. I had this desperation in me back then, whatever I was doing, wherever I was, whoever I was with. Some kind of rough-edged gash running down the centre of my underdeveloped personality, as if what there was of me might rip apart at any moment. When I was out there, lost in the floorplans of a superstore, making my way through the grid of its cameras, the feeling ceased and I was complete.

Lynda, of course, was thrilled with this combined assault on the region's retail sector. Did I mention Lynda's other job, this maven of outsourcing? She was our fence. She would park her battered TR7 on the pavement outside, enter the building, let herself into our single room, teeter to the bed's edge and perch herself there, demanding to see our latest haul, smoking and nodding with all the appreciativeness of a Rottweiler watching an untended baby. We would lay the goods out in front of her while she kept a running total on the large, cartoon-buttoned calculator she carried for the purpose. Each keytap effected with the end of her Parker Pen would be accompanied by a small, whined exclamation: 'Love-ly. Su-per. Yyyess. O-o-oh. Hmmm. What brand? Uh-huh. Did they have any other colours? Per-fect. You know I can all-ways take more of those. As many as you can mus-ter. Love-ly. Very good.' And at the end, when all the goods had been sorted and valued and the sums totted up, she would watch as we loaded the gear into the brown cardboard boxes she kept wedged into her vehicle's pokey boot and then pay us in a mixture of cash, vouchers and hash – just enough of each to keep us going until the next time and never more, however hard we worked.

With the first order of business out of the way, she would allow us to bundle into the car, each particle of oxygen heavy and black with the barbed weight of stale tobacco, and, one of us perched on the other's lap in the passenger seat, would deal with what she described as 'my social work and pro-*ba*-tionary du-ties'. These consisted of briefing us with avoidance techniques and alibi creation for use in the auditing sessions to which she delivered us twice weekly. And, although she only taught us to protect herself from any accusations of inappropriate behaviour, these lessons remain the only reason I ever had to feel grateful to that poisonous, evil old bitch.

The rest of her time was spent taunting us. Or, more usually, me. 'Your mum-my called to see how you were, Tilly, *dear*. I told her, "Mrs Parkins," I said. "This is a *very* difficult time for your daughter. A period of great change and great challenge. She has a lot of growing *up* to do. But I am *here* for her. You can re-*ly* on me. She is dea-ling with the best care there is." Do you know what she said to me, Tilly dear? Shall I *tell* you? She said, "I have absolute faith in social services. You do a *very* difficult job with very little reward and even less respect."' Turning to me, another Mores drooping from her mouth, the ash curving from the end of it like a flaccid penis. '"Thank you *so* much. Thank you *so* much for your time. I know my little girl is safe with you."'

It was two months since I'd left Yarleigh Falls.

Imagine if someone built a set of metal legs that could enable him to run inhumanly fast. Imagine if these legs moved so fast, though, that his brain could not keep up and the man lost control, so that he ended up running over a cliff or smashing into a wall, or, if he managed to avoid these cartoon obstacles, then running and running until he starved to death. Why on earth, that being the case, would others continue to strap them on?

Extract from *Fifteenth Communiqué of the Vanished*

3

There are questions I'm qualified to answer and questions I'm not. How, for instance, do you distinguish the crucial moments in your life from the quotidian? Do those critical events assert themselves as such when they happen or do you create them later, the details chosen to fit your understanding of what transpired? Is any event in actuality any more significant than any other or do we just make them so in order to improve our stories?

Cold fog up against the windows, a grey brightness smoothing all edges, our small world gripped with a comfortable lassitude. The telly talked to itself as we lolled round on the bed drinking instant coffee and passing a spliff between us. Last week's haul had been particularly good – the meter chewed its way through a surfeit of tokens and the heat in the room cuddled us drowsy, smoke dissipating beneath the ceiling. We were going nowhere and doing nothing, my new Adidas vest-top – removed from JD the previous afternoon – ideally snug, reassuringly boxfresh.

The sound of Lynda's keys being shaken free from her belt crumbled the mood, the clicks and sudden metallic tumbles as she worked her way through their complex taxonomy, the crunch of the right one entering its lock and then her face, in the room as quick as she could.

'Morning, *chil*-dren. Didn't real-*ise* anyone was home.'

And there she was again, a lazily produced stop-frame animation making herself comfortable, with just the right degree of distaste, on the edge of our unmade bed.

'I would ask for a coffee but I don't supp-ose for one instant that *ei*-ther of you has an *ink*-ling of how to make a proper cup.'

'Dun arks den.'

She sat with what she took to be a simper disfiguring her face, the cold bowls of her tinted lenses hiding the hollowness of the eyes behind.

'We weren't expecting you today, Lynda,' I ventured, her silences more painful to me than the blackboard scrape of her voice.

'No, I don't expect you were.'

'So' – Sadie glaring at me as I allowed my curiosity so easily to break our pact to keep communication with this woman to an absolute minimum – 'what brings you here?'

'Business, Tilly dear. A new *line* in fact. An exciting development for LifeStart Business Partnerships Ltd of which I, as I am sure you are aware, am none other than managing di-*rec*-tor.'

'Shit man. What ya gunna do now? Wipe our arses?'

'It's almost that distasteful, believe me.'

'Can't we have someone else? For something?'

'I don't go looking for the extra work. They came to *me*. They sought *me* out. Besides, most of the contracts have gone to debt collection companies so you should be thankful it *is* me. Better than two thugs coming round and smashing your furniture. As no one is going to offer I'll help myself shall I?'

She plunged the remains of her cigarette into the ashtray, her false nails scraping against the surface, came up with the remains of the joint and, using those extravagant plastic extensions as a kind of clip, re-lit it. Choked back a half-cough, grimaced.

'I can't believe you still smoke this . . . *rubbish*. Have you no taste at all?' Took another, deeper pull, a crackle as the seam burnt quickest towards cardboard roach. 'And, no, I don't need reminding that I sold it to you. It's a buyer's market. The choice' – her voice cartoonish, withdrawn by the effort of holding the smoke down, an over-enunciated croak – 'remains yours.' She brought her sunglasses nearer to the smouldering, spent tip. 'Does it even work?' And flicked it back where it had come from.

'I think I will have that coffee, Tilly dear. If it's not *too* much trouble?'

I found myself rising and moving to the kettle, unsure whether I'd been programmed to obey her commands or was just glad to put a few more steps between us.

'So now, where were we? Oh, of course. My new business obli-*gations*. Work to keep me at the cuttting *edge* of law enforcement and social *pol*-icy. The future, my dears, is bright. For me, anyway. I don't hold out a *huge* amount of hope for you.'

Still hot from our own cups, the kettle boiled. I poured the water over the sprinkle of granules, picturing emptying the lot on her head.

'Milk and sugar?'

'Yes please, Tilly dear. You see, Allason, how well brought up she is? Now *where* was I?'

We were drinking ours black due to the age of the semi-skimmed, but I happily glugged a lump of it into hers, stirring in the sugar with unbecoming enthusiasm in an attempt to break up and mix in the foul-smelling curd.

'Yes, I'm going to need a swab from both of you. I'll get out the kit while we talk.'

'A what?'

'A swab. A mouth swab. A sample to send, as they say, "back to the lab".' Removing plastic gloves from her bag.

'What ya sayin?'

She stopped laying out her kit for a moment, thanked me with a frowned attempt at a smile as I passed her the coffee, let out a pantomimed sigh. 'I don't suppose you two spend much time on the reading of *news*-papers do you? Do you even watch the news on *TV*? God, you're depressing. Well, anyway, it's government policy. *All* offenders and all *ex*-offenders – as if you can distinguish the two groups! – to be DNA tested and all members of their im-*me*-diate family to be DNA tested.'

'They already did that to me when I was arrested.'

'Yes, but that's just for identification. This is for science. They are intending to find the gene for criminality. Or, at least, the gene for the kind of stupid criminality which gets you caught. And then, when they have found it, I hope they will eradicate it.'

'Nah man.'

'What do you mean, "*Nah man*"?'

'I ain't givin no swabs.'

'I'm afraid you have no *choice*. Legis-*lay*-tion has been passed. I have an information leaflet for you here somewhere. And paperwork to fill out too. And, yes, *here* it is, "It is a criminal of-*fence* to re-*fuse* to give a *sample* for these purposes and will be treated *as such* by the police and courts." Surely you're not going to end up back inside over a little *spit*, are you now?'

Neither of us believed her, of course. Lynda, we knew, was a habitual liar, utterly systematic in her misrepresentations.

'Have you got the leaflet, then?' I asked.

'I wouldn't have expected any other response from you, Tilly dear. Your mother no doubt is an active *mem*-ber of the Consumers' Association. She must be *very* proud of you. On some level, anyway.'

She continued her rummaging then pulled free a handsome purple booklet, the smiling family on the cover hugging each other with the clumsy warmth of catalogue models. Above them, in embossed white lettering, PROJECT ROOT CAUSE – THE DNA OF CRIME, and underneath in smaller letters, *The UK leads the way in Crime Prevention with a Major Scientific Study.*

'I suppose you'd better have a look.'

I allowed the pamphlet to flap open into my lap as I sunk onto my haunches and, self-consciously, the silence gently punctuated by the dialogue of their crackling cigarettes, began to read.

A Message from the Prime Minister

'The United Kingdom is a World Leader in Crime Prevention and the Solving of Crime. That's something which I think we should all be very proud of. But feeling proud is not a reason to rest on our laurels, but rather a reason to strive for improvement. If you're reading this then the chances are that you or a member of your immediate family has broken the law in the past and been caught and been punished. Now it's time to put something back so that we can all benefit. So that we can make this great country of ours greater. All you need to do is give us a swab. Then let the experts do the rest. So, thanks for taking part. Together let's stop crime and make history.'

[His picture glamour-lit, greased with sincerity.]

Introduction

All crime is anti-social behaviour because crime, by its very nature, transgresses our society's norms. Over the last few years we have punished anti-social behaviour and also struck deeper and deeper at the roots of this behaviour. But however deeply we dig for causes, however hard we are on wrong-doers, the roots always lie still deeper.

Now, science offers us a new way forward. Science will enable us to reach the root of roots – to discover criminality and anti-social behaviour (which are the same thing) in our genetic make-up. With your help we can make the biggest scientific leap of the last hundred years. Welcome to Project Root Cause.

Meet the Scientist

Peter Debray, the President and Chief Scientist of Sanalex Genome Science, is no ordinary laboratory boffin. A maverick and a visionary, this intellectual colossus towers over his contemporaries in the modern sciences. An ordinary mechanic until the age of twenty-two, Debray made a promise to his

59

dying father to re-train as a Biological Scientist specialising in genetics. By the time he was thirty Debray was acknowledged to be one of the world's leading experts in DNA. His work on the Human Genome Project led to him starting Sanalex Genome Science, now considered to be the foremost player at the leading edge of genome research.

[Accompanied by pictures of men in crisp white coats, goggles obscuring eyes, pipettes as long as anteaters' tongues.]

Peter Debray says:

'We here at Sanalex Genome Science are very honoured and very excited to have been asked to conduct the historic research involved in Project Root Cause which, we hope, will change the way we look at criminality and at the genome, too. Never before has such a huge and varied sample been available to science. The possibilities are endless, the results likely to be revolutionary. I would like to thank the British people and, in particular, their government, for giving us this opportunity.'

[Debray's head shaved bald, his glasses held in place by impossibly thin wires, his smile just small enough to cause a shiver of discomfort.]

FAQs

• Do I have to give a swab sample on request?
Yes. It is a criminal offence to refuse to give a sample for these purposes and will be treated as such by the police and courts.

• Who will collect the swab?
One of our field operatives will collect the swab. All work has been tendered for by a transparent process and only the most trustworthy operatives have been employed. Your swab will not be traded or shared with any other organisation, though, at the discretion of Sanalex Genome Science, the data the swab provides and forms a part of may be.

• Will being swabbed hurt?

No! The operative will wipe the swab vigorously but carefully against your cheek to collect some cells from the surface. You may feel a very slight discomfort.

• What will happen to the swab?

The swab will be taken to Sanalex Genome Science's main laboratory in the countryside of Berkshire, where it will be analysed. The information gleaned from this analysis will be added to the Project Root Cause database. Using the most sophisticated forms of data analysis, correlations will be drawn and a picture built up of the criminal population of the United Kingdom. Slowly, painstakingly, Debray and his team will home in on discrepancies and mutations within the genome, which will lead to a deepening of our understanding of criminal pathologies as genetically predisposed.

• I have never committed a crime. Why am I included in the study?

If you're being asked for a DNA sample then someone in your immediate family has been convicted of a crime. The only way we can build up a full genetic picture is with your contribution, too.

• Do I get paid?

You don't get paid. Think of it as putting something back.

• How is Project Root Cause funded?

Sanalex Genome Science are covering all costs from swab collection onward. There will be no cost to the UK taxpayer. In return, Sanalex will own the swabs, the genetic material contained therein and any and all information and insights gained from analysis of that information etc. This information will be leased back to the government of the United Kingdom on a Favoured Nations basis.

• This all sounds great. How do I start swabbing?

Don't worry. Your Swab Field Operative will talk you through the simple process. It's impossible to get it wrong or be a bad swabber. Just relax and swab on!

Finished, baffled, I looked up from my reading matter. Lynda had lit a new cigarette and was examining her nails with the minute, all-encompassing concentration of a new mother checking her baby's breathing. Sadie had also sparked up, her head tilted toward the ceiling, her eyes focusing some way beyond it. It can only be projection of some sort which makes me remember the air in the room as thick with a foreboding I could not have understood.

'What ya sayin, Titch?' Sadie expectant, open, the decision deferred to me, a moment of control.

'Guess we'd better get on with it.'

'Seen.'

Lynda determined to ruin my passing seniority: 'See, Allason. I *told* you she was a good influence on you.' Her smirk's half-life diminishing, she busied herself with removing what she needed from her bag. 'You're my first, actually, so it may take a little longer than usual. I have an *aw*-ful lot of instructions to follow.'

'They trained ya?'

'In effect.'

'In effect?'

'Well, they sent me the kit and an *aw*-ful lot of instructions. It's quite straight-*for*-ward. You don't need to be a trained doctor. Just . . .' – flipping through the manual she had pulled free from a clinch of rubber gloves – 'just . . . *Clean. Concentrated. Courteous* and. *Careful.*'

'The four Cs,' I muttered, summoning the best sarcasm that being fifteen and scared can muster.

'Tilly, have you been reading over my shoulder?' she responded, the tone of her voice a nuclear warhead compared to my popgun.

'Should be five Cs, innit?' offered Sadie.

'Oh Allason, I hope you're not being crude. You'll make Tilly blush.'

Her face gradually subsiding into default sourness, Lynda hooked up one of the rubber gloves and raised it in front of her glasses.

'Dis-*gus*-ting things. I don't suppose you have any baby powder?'

This time I did blush, unsure why, some wheedling implication there in her voice, the other two apparently oblivious to my discomfort.

Bones bunching, her concentration absolute, Lynda tried to hitch the glove on. Wrist twisting one way and then the other, she looked for a way to accommodate the fragility of her nails within the rubber hand. Failed.

'Bloody things.'

'Can't you manage without?'

'Hardly. I mean, let's face it, imagine if some of my own cells were somehow to get into your sample and it came back saying that *I* was your mother. It wouldn't be so *bad* if it were *yours*, Tilly, but all the same. Even you are still a common criminal. No, it's of the ut-*most* im-*por*-tance that I am protected from any contamination.' With which she recommenced her hand's wriggling.

I looked across at Sadie, who, in the way that she always did in Lynda's presence, had sunk into a sort of waking coma, her motor skills still adequate for placing cigarette after cigarette into her mouth, but nobody home. My own habitual reaction to Lynda was to endeavour to get her out of our room as quickly as possible. I felt that if the sound of her nails scratching at the glove's entrance continued I was in danger of losing all control.

'We can do it.'

'I beg your pardon, Tilly dear?'

'We can do each other.'

'Oh, I'm sure you can. And do.'

'We can do the test on each other. You can supervise. Read the instructions and tell us what to do.'

I could imagine her eyes narrowing.

'I can't *pay* you.'

'That's fine. It's just. It's like. It's our duty isn't it? To society and all that.'

'Tilly Tilly *Tilly*. If you weren't carrying the criminal gene, I would be tempted to adopt you. Or sell you to a pimp.' A wistful pause before rallying. 'Anyway, what a *mar*-vellous idea. So I can just read and you two can ad-*min*-ister. *Mar*-vellous. Well, who wants to be swabbed first?'

'Best be me, yeah? Titch can show me ow it's done.'

'I don't know how it's done.'

'Yeah, but you're better wiv instructions'n what I am.'

'Hang on a second.'

Lynda plucked out a face mask, a white teddy-bear snout overlaying the bottom of her glasses, her hair helmeted above and flaring out below the line of the elastic. 'Okay, that's me set.'

'Have you got one for me?'

'One what?'

'The face mask thing.'

'Oh, that's not part of the kit. It's just there's *def*-initely an odour in here. An un-*pleas*-ant odour. And I'm going to have to sit here for a little while yet. Here's your gloves. And *you*' – signalling to Sadie – 'need to sit down.'

'Shoulda give us some chairs den.'

'Just sit on the bed and stop fussing. Tilly, will you take these gloves or do I have to . . . *stand*?' Reluctantly, I pulled them on, my fingers suddenly out of focus. 'Now you mustn't. Touch. *Any*-thing. We don't want *any*-thing to contaminate Allason's sample. We want the scientists to come to her DNA in all its degenerate, in-bred, *trashy* glory. So. Stand. *Still*. And keep your. *Hands*. In. The. *Air*.'

I did as I was told. Lynda scrabbled up her pamphlet and began to instruct, a combination of stumbled sight-reading and emphatic repetition which suggested her previous training had been rudimentary. I picked up the relevant envelope, stuck to it a label with Sadie's name on, pulled out one of the two swabs it contained, poked the outsize cottonbud into my friend's mouth and began swooshing it round, Lynda's orders rasping at my eardrums.

'"You are trying to remove cheek cells from the interior of the cheek so be *very vigorous*. *Aggressively twirl* the swab as you rub. Complete 25 *strokes* or *more*. Be sure to take more than 30 full seconds. Use a clock. Do not guess." Agg-*ress*-ively, dear. Twirl agg-*ress*-ively.'

I could tell from the bulge to Sadie's eyeballs, and the noise she managed through a mouth of plastic, that I was in danger of getting a slap if I continued with the requisite level of aggression. Carefully, I moderated my efforts, a tiny nod acknowledging the wisdom of this approach. We settled into our new rhythm and, as Lynda checked her watch, Sadie rolled her eyes toward her and offered the universal blowjob sign, her fist pushing invisible penis into her mouth in time with her cheek's swab-powered bulgings.

'Okay, I think that will probably do. I really need to get a move on. I have a *huge* amount of these to do and I have to do them pretty quickly if the whole enterprise is to be profitable. *So*: "Place the shaft of the swab in a *glass* or cup, so the *head* of the swab is ex-*posed* to air. Allow the swabs to dry natural-ly – don't use heat or blow on the swabs. Make *sure* the head of the swab will not come in contact with anything *else* that could contaminate it. Repeat with the same person using the second swab from the same slip." Do you have a clean cup or something you could balance that in while you do the next one?'

'We've only got three cups.'

'Well, then wash one up.'

'Well, *I* can't,' raising my gloved, swab-holding hands.

'An I ain't gunna.'

Lynda's physique clicked through a pipecleanered mime of exasperation before, with a withering huff, she staggered to her feet and, high-heeled leather boots clopping on the lino, carried her cup to the sink.

'Then I will do it for myself, I suppose. Although *not* with-out a sense of disappointment. Do you have a *brush*?'

'No, just a cloth.'

Her distaste growing by the moment, she placed the cup on the sink's floor, took our Lemon Fresh Happy Shopper liquid and squeezed until the cup was brimming with it.

'Lyn*dah*!'

'Oh, you can always steal some more.' With which she jetted hot water down on top, allowing it to run as the sink vanished in steam and the slow upward advance of foam, keeping it running as she turned and lit a cigarette, waiting, our meter chuntering round with the excitement, until all the bubbles had, one by millionth one, slowly burst and the sweet, citrus scent had ceased to register in our nostrils. With which she finally staunched the flow and lifted out one shining, perfectly clean mug.

'Is that how you do all your washing up?'

'Yes, Tilly darling. It's called a *dish*-washer. Have you heard of them? I expect Mummy and Daddy were too worried about the en-*vir*-onment to have one.' She was right. 'Well, stick it in there and get on with the next one.' Sitting, she returned to her instructions. '"Allow the swabs to dry for *ten minutes* or more." Oh, *really*. Oh, this is too much. I can't sit here for ten minutes waiting to do another test and then another ten waiting for those to dry. I'll be sick. This is ri-*dic*-ulous. Tilly dear, pull off those gloves and wash up your cup, there's a love. Then Allason can get on with swabbing you while hers dry. We'll just have to be very careful to keep them apart.'

Although I understand now why I did what I did, I'm at a loss to remember what I thought was my motivation then. I've looked back and can only conclude that Lynda somehow goaded me to act in a manner, which, at the time, appeared to be totally out of character. There were repercussions, though, and those repercussions seemed to change my character in such a way as to make that first act more in keeping with who I became. But whether that was a prophecy, or fate, or even a reward or punishment, who am I to say? This, though, was the start of the path which led me here, writing to you.

Sadie had finished removing cheek cells from the inside of my mouth, my swabs two ramshackle heads nodding in the cup, hers, in the other mug, lying similarly akimbo. I found myself turning, pushing my friend towards Lynda, my mouth opening, words I'd never intended coming out.

'Lynda, would you let Sadie have a proper look at your boots? I just really really like them and I was, like, hoping she could get me a pair?'

Sadie turned to me, a look of horror munching at her face, and I found myself frowning and nodding her forward and down down down on her knees to the witch's feet. There was an instant of stunned silence, Sadie looking at the boots, Lynda looking at Sadie, the absolute unlikeliness of the situation freezing the pair of them. And in that moment, I lifted two swabs in each hand, crossed my arms and dropped them back into the others' cup. Turned and smiled.

'Oh, no, it's not those ones. It's the other ones. Your other boots.'

'I don't have any other boots.'

'Oh, sorry. Sorry. I must have got you confused with someone else Lynda.'

'Are you feeling o-*kay*, Tilly?' Suspicion lapping over her words.

'Think I'm probably just stoned.'

'Y-e-e-e-s-s-s. I expect that's it. Anyway, I don't have *time* for the admiration of my footwear. I have to be off.'

Creaking and scratching, all our tiny space her pen, Lynda gathered her data, leaving us to deal with the detritus of its collection. Until finally, with ashtray a butt monument, the mutant johnnies of used gloves scattered around, curls of torn paper quivering in the draught, finally – the sky-blue blouson jacket, the carefully pressed jeans, the sunglasses, the kindling-dry hair, all a carapace obscuring the hollowness which was betrayed in every movement of her arms and legs – finally, she left. And I, giddy with release, desperate for another joint, almost unable to see through the smoke we had collectively exhaled, I sunk down on the bed and began to laugh.

'Whass funny?'

'Dunno. Nothing really. Her.'

'Whass all dat wi da boots?'

For a moment I wanted it to be my secret, for me to have Sadie's DNA, to be her, to inhabit her skin, to possess her as completely as I could. Then I remembered my upbringing and consented to share.

'It was a diversion.'

'For wha?'

'I switched the swabs over.'

She looked at me through thin eyes, hands on her hips, her face flat.

'Fuck ya do dat for?'

I thought about it carefully, a genuine attempt to understand myself. Reached a conclusion.

'Dunno.'

She looked at me a little longer, nothing moving, that stillness she could muster. Relented, flopped down onto the bed, surrendered to my uncontrollable whinnying, her own tuneless honk redoubling my volume. Gradually, the recovery graph jagged with false starts, we quietened, the day still clothed in grey, the heat oppressive, two envelopes containing our cells in a handbag in a TR7 moving gradually away from us through the fog.

'Skin up, den.'

'Alright.'

She looked at me with what I took to be respect.

'Ya nuts, you are.'

Surveillance is how CTRL produces data, the processing of which brings about our subjugation. But surveillance, this production of data, also feeds processor power. So that CTRL, surveillance and processor power form a vicious circle, or rather, a spiral. And that spiral seems as natural to us as the DNA which, we are told, contains the recipe of our existence.

Extract from *Nineteenth Communiqué of the Vanished*

4

Sometimes it's all about meeting targets. While we prided ourselves on the élan of our nicking sprees, the ludicrous nature of
some of our choices, the middle-finger audacity of our raids,
come evening we still needed fags and dope and booze. On
occasion, despite the banality of the experience, we just had to
go for the bankers. Even if it made us feel no better than crack-
heads.

So we trailed out of Boots that day with our pockets stuffed
with razor blades, Gillette Mach 55 cases clacking together
with the soothing regularity of worry beads, a trail of removed
security tags littering the aisles behind us.

Lynda was sitting on a bench opposite, hunched up against
the quiet enormity of the sky, clouds rushing up from behind
her and over us and away, the elements placed on fast forward.
She didn't like *outside*, regarding it as something to be navigated rather than dwelt in. To see her there, shrinking down into
the wood (carved and ballpoint-decorated by five years' worth
of bored teenagers), her body collapsing in on itself, the cloud
of smoke that always surrounded her blown asunder, was both
warmly satisfying and utterly unnerving.

'Wha'gwan Lynda?'

'I do wish you wouldn't insist on all this *jive* talk. It really is
in-*cred*-ibly horrible.'

'I think we were just surprised to see you. Out here,' I
explained. 'What are you doing? Out here?'

'I was waiting for you, of course. Now let's get *in*-side.'

Lynda rose, her body scraping away at the laws of physics,
and clopped urgently towards Forfars, Sadie and I sucked in
behind her, our eyes a ceaseless left right, nervous in case anyone should think that the woman ahead was our mother.

71

The door nearly defeated her, daylight sucking strength from her, us two bunching up behind, heads downcast. Then we were in, fluorescent strips feeding her vigour, her spine uncurling a little, her nostrils leading us straight past the counter to where a sign announced '*no SMOKING ARIA*' in the loopy hand of a ten-year-old girl, each 'i' topped by a heart. Lynda lowered herself into a yellow plastic bucket seat, her fingers skipping with unsettling tenderness from fag-scar to fag-scar across the table top. She motioned Sadie to sit down in the seats opposite her and ordered me back to the counter.

'Three cups of *tea*, Tilly dear. Do you think you can run to that?'

'Why she payin?'

'I'll tell you why she's paying,' Lynda replied with a snarl, 'when you're both sitting *down*.'

As I got the teas I examined the girl on the other side of the counter – a mirror of me, acne starring her forehead in an identical constellation, the draylon crackle of her uniform, the unbecoming tilt of her hairnet jolting me with a sense of good fortune.

'There isn't a Smoking Area is there?'

'Y'wha?'

'A Smoking Area?'

'There ain't one.'

'So why does that say "No Smoking Area"?'

'Dunno. Cos it is.'

'But there isn't a Smoking Area?'

'Not allowed is it?'

I slid into my seat, the icy touch of Lynda's knees against mine only partially offset by the contact between Sadie's shoulder and my own. We took our mugs from the tray, patiently waited our turn to splash torrents of sugar from the dispenser, tried to find something to do with our under-occupied hands. I looked at Sadie's as they returned to the table, the death's head on her ring, the length of her fingers, the way her nerves translated her wishes with far more grace than I could ever muster. We were sitting with our backs to the door, nothing in front of us but more empty yellow seats and tables. I found myself swivelling round, Sadie following me.

'How *dare* you?' Lynda's voice crawling out of her throat, cold outrage slapping onto the table. We turned back, shook. 'And after *all* I've done for you.'

'Sorry, I was just having a look round –'

'Oh, not *that*. Not *that*. Obviously not *that*. How *dare* you put my business at risk? How *dare* you?'

'Sorry?'

I thought I knew what was coming. In recent weeks we'd taken to siphoning off some of the goods we'd stolen and instead of passing them on to Lynda, swapped them up direct for alcopops and cigarettes at Tariq's shop. The rate of exchange was marginally better but the real purpose had been to get one over on Lynda, to show her (or rather, ourselves) that the arid bitch didn't quite have dominion over our souls, no matter how it looked. Plus Tariq was a mate, of sorts.

'Which one of you switched the swabs?'

I inhaled my tea, scalding hot liquid gushing into my nostrils and out in a fine spray over Lynda's hands. She didn't flinch. She barely seemed to notice. It was over two months since she had us scraping at each other's cheek and I'd forgotten all about it. I couldn't quite imagine what the problem might be.

'Which one of you switched the swabs?'

The room quivered. Sadie pulled herself straight, forced her chin forward, pulled hard on her cigarette.

'I don't know what you're talking about,' I said, flannelling.

'Don't *bullshit* me.'

'Really.'

'Alla-*son*?'

'Who ya fink?'

'Well it's *obvious*, isn't it? It's obvious, you sullen little *cow*. But I want to hear it from you. I want you to *tell* me.'

'It was me.' The words spilling over my lips as easily as the tea. Then silence, beats on top of beats, the two of them looking at me, Sadie frowning but unreadable, Lynda's face absolutely still.

'This true?' The question for Sadie, answered with the smallest of nods.

She leant back as far as the chair would allow, her hands rattling round her unused lighter. Slowly ratcheted herself forward over the table, planted her elbows, her face looming ever nearer, a ragged whisper dampening her lips.

'Stupid. Little. *Bitch*. Showing off to *her* were you? Trying to pretend you were a little bit "*crazy*", were you? I should have known. Your sort are always the worst.'

'Easy, Lynda.'

'I hope she at least ate you out for it.'

'EASY.'

'Did you *read* the leaflet? Did you *read* it? All *criminals* and their *families*? Did you not think that someone might find it *suspicious* when your DNA didn't match up in any *way*, *shape* or *form* with that of your parents? That they might think it a trifle *odd* when they discovered that it was actually im-*poss*-ible that your *par*-ents were actually your *par*-ents at *all*. Not so clever as you like to think you are, little Miss *Perfect*.' The 'perfect' spat out with exorcism-intensity, the depth of hatred she obviously felt for me now on show, her lips pulling back from the browned harassment of her teeth. 'And I don't for *one* moment *care* if you end up back in *pris*-on or spend the rest of your life there or get *stabbed* by some *dyke* because all you do is moon around dreaming of *All*-ason here. But this is my *business* you're screwing around with. This is my fucking *business*.' For the first time I saw her eyes, just for a fraction of an instant, as she fought for control and raised thumb and index finger to the bridge of her nose, two shiny raisins just visible in that dark intersection, her nails pointing toward them. Then the shades came down again, normal service resumed.

'Do you understand? Unsur-*prise*-ingly questions are being

asked. Questions are being asked of *me* and of my methodology. It seems it's much more likely that *I* am at fault than that *you* are a changeling. Unbel-*iev*-able though that may be. I have tried to point out that you seem the classic case of cuckoo in the nest, but all to no avail. *Oh no no.* It seems *I* have blundered in the collection of the swabs, because of course the *DNA* can't be wrong. And if at the end of the investigation which they have now be-*gun*, it proves to be my error then I will *automatically forfeit* my contract. I will be *barred* from collecting more swabs and I will not be *paid* for the collecting I have al-*ready* done.'

She paused, a shudder of anger crashing her system.

'So now we *all* need to *main*-tain this *crazy* pretence that your DNA belongs to each other. Otherwise *you* will be sent back to *pris*-on and *I* won't get *paid*. So we have a mutual *in*-terest in getting this right, don't we? We have a mutual *in*-terest in making sure that everyone believes that *ev*-erything from our end was done *ex*-actly as it ought to have been. That *some*-one or *some*-thing *else* is to blame. Are we all agreed on that?'

It didn't seem like the moment for dissent and, truth be told, I didn't want to go back to Yarleigh Falls. It wasn't clear who had who here, whether Lynda possessed the upper hand in these proceedings or we did.

'So how come they don't know we've swapped them? Can't they just work it out? If it comes out that Allason's mum and dad are mine and mine are Allason's? Surely they'll know?'

'So far they only have *your* completed results, Tilly. Your parents being the sort of people they *are*, they sent their swabs back the *same* day they got them. So now you have to go to *Berk*-shire and be interviewed and have your swab taken *again*. As a first step in determining how this *f-f-f-f-lipping* "aberration" may have happened. I, of course, have offered to *drive* you there and we have to work out a way to make sure that the swab you give them is from Allason's mouth. We none of us can afford any inconsistency. Any inconsistency spells *prison* for you and *pen*-ury for me. Of course once *your* results are in, Allason, the gaff will be truly blown. But we'll worry about that later. I expect it will take them months to get any blood relative of yours to even open the *door*. Plus of course you're *adopted* aren't you, so we can hope that will complicate matters even more.'

'Yeah, fanks, Lynda. Yeah, fanks for bringin it up.'

Another nerve-gas grin, this time to Sadie, hunching and shrugging, her eyes suddenly glossy with excess liquid, her cheeks a fetching pink, a little girl again. I decided to keep the conversation moving.

'So you think if we can make the results come out the same again we'll get away with it?'

'I don't see any *bet*-ter course open to us.'

'And we won't have to go back to Yarleigh Falls.'

'At the very least it'll buy us some *time*.'

'But Lynda. How are we going to give them Allason's swab?'

'You managed it once, didn't you Tilly? I'm sure if you put your *mind* to it you can do it again. You'll have to *try* anyway, won't you?'

Out onto the M20 the TR7 juddered, wheel bearings squeal-ing, Lynda's hands gripped tight around the diminutive cir-cumference of her sports wheel, clouds of black smoke splut-tering from the exhaust behind us, engine noise a definition of machine pain. Joining the M25, Sadie and I engaged in a com-plex attempt to swap roles, sitter becoming seat, seat sitter, my legs already dead, great crackles of discomfort cramping through them. Soon we hit our first jam, Lynda squinting, uncomprehending, at the morse of hazard and brake lights up ahead, her foot still jammed on the accelerator, leaving it later than late and a little later still before switching pedal, her body braced against the impact, lips peeling away over her face, axles apparently ready to snap as easily as one of her arms receiving a snakeburn. The jolted unprogress, windows down,

76

three red embers, Lynda unable to drive at less than twenty miles an hour and so waiting until the first horn sounded behind her before leaping forward and, almost immediately, screeching to a stop again, our faces perilously close to the windscreen, our arms, determinedly protecting our smokes from harm, jutting out like weeds in a desert. My bum now dying and Sadie's legs aching, we engineered a further switch back to our original positions. Finally the M4, budget plane after garish budget plane falling toward Heathrow, nose to tail, each one with a pun-based web address written down its length, and, at last, cars spacing out, gears being negotiated in a standard progression, speed.

I had already tried to drill myself into the seat as we passed the two previous exits but I still flinched when Lynda pulled down the indicator and careened leftward to the turn-off marked READING (W), a gulp catching in my throat, bile hiccuping at my vocal chords.

'Sup Titch?' Sadie feeling me cowering beneath her.

'Nothing.'

'Wha'gwan?'

'Really. S'nothing.'

The conversation lost in a splurge of carhorns, I found myself moving forward with the impersonal inevitability of a dream, each inch of my surroundings so pre-viewed they seemed mind-made. Just as I knew we would, we turned right at the roundabout, took the third road off on the left, followed it along through an endless modern suburb and took another right onto New Station Road, familiar faces coming out of familiar shops, every dent in the pavements known to me, everything just so. Only less imposing than I'd pictured it, a long and mournful sigh.

'This a trick?' The words squeaked out between my teeth.

'What?'

'Is this a trick?' But as I said it we reached the turn-off and this time there was no signal click and the steering wheel didn't spin in Lynda's hands and we were past my parents' road and moving away, moving away from them now again, staying moving away from them for now forever.

'What are you talking about?'

'Nothing. It wasn't anything.'

Our destination was a couple of miles further up the road, out into the countryside, dying hedgerows and bony cows giving way to a ten-foot-high metal wall, untouched by graffiti and shining despite the gloominess of the day, the razor wire along its top backlit and glinting. I remembered Brompton Manor as a guinea-pig farm for medical research, messily fortified against wave after wave of animal liberationists, notes forever being slipped beneath their door, the farmer and his family smudge-eyed and always scared-looking. The borders never so well-protected as they were today.

We were met at the entrance by two armed soldiers. A halt hand brought us to a stop and, while one of them stood back, barrel raised, desperate to punctuate our journey, the other bent down to Lynda's window and demanded our identity cards, the badge on his beret identifying his regiment as SECURECORPS PLC. Unfortunately, the electrics in the car were not what they used to be and the window wouldn't budge, a tense negotiation ensuing as to whether we could open the door *just a wee bit* to facilitate the handing over of documents. This misunderstanding dealt with, our interrogator retreated with our laminated identities and left us under the twitching gaze of his subordinate. Rather than reassuring him or distracting him, our batted eyelids and coy smiles seemed to feed his discomfort, so it was with a genuine sense of relief that we greeted the reappearance of our interrogator, returning our documents to us and waving us on through the regally paced auto-opening of the gate.

Our chauffeur, clearly discomfited to find herself bracketed with us in the face of authority, had begun muttering again about how she would make me pay for the trouble I had caused her. Sadie, whether to give or take comfort, was holding my hand, her fingers cool and smooth.

Waiting for us at the edge of the car park's gravel was a balding, middle-aged man, his brown-and-brown checked shirt tucked into his too-high brown cords, his smile so wide it closed his eyes into slits.

'Lynda? Great to see you. Always nice to meet our operatives. And which of you is Tilly? Nice to meet you, too, Tilly. Thanks for coming all this way. I'm Des Fortune, I kind of take care of sorting out any irregularities. For my sins!' Then turning to Sadie, enthusiastically chuntering on yet another cigarette, 'And you are . . . ?'

'I'm er lawyer innit?' A staccato blast of laughter. 'Only messin. Friend. Just along to keep er compny. Lynda said there might be some waitin.'

'Well, it's very nice to meet you. You're very welcome here. If I can show you inside . . . ?'

Within minutes Des 'Call-me-Des' Fortune had led me away from the waiting area where Sadie and Lynda stood hissing at each other in front of the drinks machine, down a long, empty corridor which smelt of hospitals but which looked far too clean and new to have ever been in one and so to his office. At least he said it was his office. There was nothing written on the door, not even a number like the other doors we had passed, much less his name. There was a desk with a phone and computer on it, a chair tucked up to it, another over by the wall. But beyond this the room was bare, the walls empty even of a window, no other furniture, no pens, no paper, no litter bin, no Post-It notes, no pictures of children or wife or pets, nothing, in fact, to suggest that anyone had ever stepped in here for any other purpose than to deliver the half-hearted props for whatever farce was to ensue.

He pulled the chair from over by the wall toward the desk, waved the back of his hand toward it.

'Sit down. Make yourself comfortable.' Walked round to

79

the other side of his desk, tapped the keyboard's space bar, began moving and clicking his mouse.

'Put some music on. Help us relax. It's not the sort of thing you normally listen to, I would think. Whale music. Give it a chance, though. You might like it.' He moved briskly towards the door. 'Can I get you a drink? A cola? Yeah, a nice glass of cola.' And, ignoring my attempted refusal, he was gone. With nothing else to focus on, my attention turned to the music, just beginning to drip tinnily from PC speakers.

It was very quiet at first, with long gaps of nothingness in between each emission. I would wait, listening to silence until I was almost sure the audio had stopped and then, just at that moment, just as I relaxed, the sound would come again, perhaps the sound of a creaky door being moved through three millimetres very slowly, or of a newborn kitten dying. The volume rose – so gradually that I could never distinguish any change between one sound and the next – and as it did, the sounds started to come more frequently. While I had never heard 'whale music', my mother had played me recordings of whales and this sounded like no cetacean I had ever come across.

Slowly a shape began to emerge, the beginnings of a pattern. I listened more intently. In the background I could pick out the patter of a polyrhythm, as if someone was applauding as quietly as possible. I began to notice the relation between this sound and the louder, less frequent noises that overlaid it.

It was some time before it occurred to me that these gasps and groans were coming from a human throat. A male throat, judging from its pitch, which had grown deeper as the recording had progressed. A throat of a male engaged in some kind of sex act. Whilst I personally had no concrete experience of such behaviour I had seen enough sex scenes on television to recognise the audio. But on telly, two people usually groaned together. This man had a very silent partner, I remember thinking, before the truth came to me. He was on his own. Hot static flooded up my back and engulfed my face. I was listening to a recording of a man – quite possibly of Des himself – masturbating. The man was almost wailing now, the speakers rattling. I pushed my hands deep into the pockets of my trackpants, slid my bum forward and let my spine sink down between the squeeze of my scapulas. With a shuddering, drawn out gulp-groan and the slightest of whimpers he, whoever he was, stopped. Recording hiss. A moment's silence. The door opened.

'Okay there? Here's the cola.' A plastic cup of brown placed in front of me, not a single bubble to disturb its syrupy meniscus. 'And let me just put this down here.' He gingered a cardboard box onto the desk in front of me. 'Oh, the music's stopped. Well, I guess we'll be best off concentrating now, anyway, won't we?' Pulled his chair round to the side of the desk. 'Did you like it?' I shrugged, blushing. He sat, apparently oblivious, placed his hand gently on top of the box. Smiled a little more.

'Now, Tilly. In this box I have a device called a polygraph. I don't know if you've come across one before? It's commonly called a lie detector, but I prefer to think of it as something which enables you to express the truth. What I'd like to do, with your permission, is just get it out of the box and rig it up for our interview. With your permission of course. So that we can rule out absolutely and utterly any wrongdoing on your part.'

I blanked, stalling for a response, trying to think what Sadie would do, how she would get us out of this.

'Because that's all we're here to do, Tilly. To help you. It would be so easy to blame this sort of thing on someone like you, wouldn't it? Someone with a criminal record and a history of anti-social behaviour? And I don't want that. I really don't want that. I want you to walk out of that door utterly vindicated.' He dipped his head towards me, smiled his best smile, his eyes wet with the manufacture of sentiment. 'We'll just need you to sign this form,' and abruptly, there was a pen in my hand and a sheet of densely typed paper in front of me.

'Just here . . . and here.' My hand moving forward through the air, touching down on the cold of the desk, biro tip making a single black dent in the contract, resting there.

'I can't.' Something of Sadie welling up in me. Something of me. Another tiny accident of resistance. 'I can't. I'm a minor.'

'Tilly, what you –'

'I'm a minor. I can't give consent. And I'd need a lawyer present. And . . . No, I'm sorry. This is illegal.'

'I'm disappointed Tilly. I hoped we could work this out –'

'I don't care. I'm not doing it.'

'You know how this makes you look, don't you?'

'Don't care. I've not done nothing. I got nothing to prove.'

'I appreciate that, but –'

'No.'

'All we're trying to –'

'Nope.'

'We're trying to help –'

'Don't care. No. You ain't doin it.'

'This isn't going to reflect well on you . . .'

'Listen, if you've got some questions to ask me, ask them, cos if not I'll be going.' I made to stand, my legs boned.

'Okay. Okay. No polygraph. That's fine. It was for your benefit. I do have to tell you that the interview will be recorded and filmed.' He waved up to the back of the ceiling, a camera in each corner blinking their red lights at me. 'Is that okay?'

'Whatever.'

'O-kay. Then I'll begin.'

He started with my name, my age, my date of birth, my address, my parents' names, ages (*old?* How was I to know?), address, siblings ditto. From here he took me through the swabbing process in as much detail as he could squeeze from me, the questions eerily similar to the ones Lynda had prepared me with in the car.

'Was there anyone else present other than Lynda and you?'

No.

'Did you touch the swabs?'

Of course not.

'Did Lynda follow the procedure as set out on this piece of paper? Take your time and read it through.'

Yes.

'For the sake of clarity I'm going to take you through this process step by step. At each stage I will ask you, is this exactly how Lynda did it?'

Yes. Yes. Yes. Yes. Yes. No.

'Ah, just checking you were concentrating, well done. And there was no one else there?'

No.

'And she put them back in an envelope with your name on?'

Yes.

'And as far as you're aware, there was no contamination or interference with your samples before they were sealed in their envelope?'

No.

'And you yourself didn't fiddle with or interfere with the samples?'

Why would I?

'I don't know, for fun, to get one over on Lynda?'

No, I didn't.

'Okay that's great. Now we're going to move into a more qualitative part of the interview. Do you know what that means? Yes, that's right. It means it will be more about impressions, about values, about how you see things rather than exactly what you've seen. Okay? Okay. Take your time, don't rush. It may not be immediately clear why these things are important to us, but we have our reasons. What is your earliest memory? Take your time.'

It just so happened that my earliest memory fitted perfectly. So perfectly, in fact, that I felt the first tug of excitement at the idea that perhaps this was all true, that somehow Lynda had muddled the swabs back and that I was, indeed, genetically unrelated to my family.

The memory starts now, as it did that day, with blackness, sound muffled, perhaps the distant snuffling of a child. Pain, nose pressed down. My mouth stretched wide and finding fabric instead of air, my lungs pulling and pulling at fabric, the texture of it on my tongue. My arms and legs beginning to thrash aimlessly in the complete blindness, a beetle stuck on its back. Then – without any warning, when the memory already seems to have run forever, an inevitability to its unchanging starkness – a sudden, dazzling light, sound rushing in to fill the gap, dusty bedroom air seeping down into those tiny lungs and, in succession, all three moving away from me, a red velveteen cushion gripped tightly in two chubby hands, my brother, a look of complete horror and anguish on his saliva-flecked face, two larger hands coming up through his armpits like growths, my mother, glazed with shock and fear, and yelping again and again, 'What are you doing? Get off her. What are you doing to your sister?' His answer a scream of lost control: 'She's not my sister, she's not she's not she's not she's not she's not.'

Des looked impressed.

'What single word would you use to describe your mother?'

'Pious bitch,' I snapped back, the whole interview rolling for me now, truth a minor casualty.

'I said single word.'

I weighed the options. 'Bitch.'

'What is the nicest word your father has ever used to describe you?'

'Sexy.'

'What trait would you say you and your brother most share in common?'

'Hatred.'

'Of what?'

'Of each other.'

'Does the name Valerie Charles mean anything to you?'

'No. Why should it?'

'No reason. Have you ever been to Hampstead?'

'H –? Where?'

'Hampstead. It's in North London.'

'No.'

'Who does the name "Martin" make you think of?'

'. . . My uncle?'

'Good. And the name "Mary"?'

'. . . Girl in my class?'

'Theo?'

'. . . The footballer. That footballer . . .'

'Excellent. What about Val?'

'. . .

'. . . No one?'

'Sure?'

'Don't know anyone called Val.'

'Valerie? Vally?'

'No.'

'Do your parents have any friends called Val, or Vally or Valerie?'

'Nope. Not that I know of.'

'No postcards or letters coming to the house from anyone of that name?'

'No.'

'Or from a Ms or Mrs Charles?' Suddenly sharp, insistent. 'Valerie Charles. I really want you to think.'

'Nope.'

'No strange phone calls?'

'No. Why should there have been?'

A smile. 'No reason. We're just trying to build up a picture. No particular reason. I know this is hard but you're being very helpful. Anyway, I think we've gone as far as we can with this, Tilly. And there's no point leaping to any conclusion until we've done the swabs again and verified the results.' He faked an examination of his watch with all the care of a movie star. 'In fact, it's time I was getting you over to the clinic to get that done.'

The clinic turned out to be another room much like the office, only whiter, emptier, a stainless-steel counter looking more appropriate as part of the set for a cocktail bar in a daytime soap. Standing behind it was a woman in the kind of tight-fitting white uniform-dress normally worn by dental assistants in the same sort of programme, as if we were lost in an interminable dream sequence in one of those shows. Des introduced her to me as Nurse Bridget, smiled his eye-occluding smile and left me there, as she tugged on her gloves and got ready for work.

I, meanwhile, pulled out my mobile and texted "starting" to Sadie, decreasingly confident of the likely efficacy of the "plan", as Lynda insisted on calling our on-the-hoof strategy. Three minutes later, though, as I leant against the unit and ruefully stroked my strimmered cheek, the room collapsed under an assault of sirens and bells and I could only presume that my friend had managed her part of our scheme. Nurse Bridget stood, neck askew, listening to the clamour, then, with a polite 'Excuse me for a moment', walked to the door.

As soon as it shut behind her I was moving, even more slowly and gracefully than her geisha shuffle, looking neither at the swabs nor at the camera as I circled round and positioned myself exactly between the two, barely moving as, my back framed on CCTV, I removed the swabs from the paper envelope in my pocket, grabbed mine from the drying stand on the table and put the ones scraped through Sadie's mouth in their place. By the time the nurse returned to collect me and guide me through the fire drills I was well away from the desk, a blankness on my face that went beyond mere innocence.

The corridor was empty despite the evacuation apparently in progress, the noise of the sirens making our movements silent and ghostly. We glided smoothly across this carpet of sound until we reached a junction and wheeled round to our left, my footfalls still mimicking hers. From a door just past this corner emerged a towering, overweight boy in thigh-squeezing grey trousers and dark green blazer, a walkie-talkie to his child's mouth, his hair a shaved gradation of skin tone. Little eyes flickered over us and immediately he was advancing, his arms stretched wide to shepherd us back.

'Sorry ladies, this sector's closed. You'll have to s-s-s-s-seek an alternative exit.'

We stopped, nurse obviously nonplussed, I jangling with such a desperate urge to get out of the building that I nearly ducked beneath his arm (the sleeves of his jacket barely covering his elbows) and ran for it. At the door behind him, three others appeared, bigger, older, stronger and more alert than him, veterans of one hundred private wars, the way they analysed the space around them and fanned out around their cargo an algorithm.

What they were securing was a man, male pattern cropped and browned, expensive frameless spectacles, an expensive white shirt, the top two buttons left undone to show his tanned chest, expensive blue jeans. It was impossible to be sure how old he was, his obvious health and vitality undermined by the feeling that he was preserved, somehow, a fixed quality to his well-being. The bodyguards quite clearly wanted to get him moving away from us as quickly as possible but he stopped where he was, something near to a smile on his face as he looked at me, straight at me, our eyes sucking into one another, discomfort splashing over me, a familiarity for which I could find no basis.

He tapped one of his guards on the elbow and came past him towards us, talking above me to the nurse as he approached.

'She's the one, is she?'

'Er, yes. Yes, sir.' Flustered.

His attention back on me.

'Hello, er . . . ?'

'Tilly.'

'Tilly. Thanks for coming through. My name's Peter. Peter Debray. I run Sanalex. Thanks for coming in. We're all very interested in you and your results. Hopefully we can get it all cleared up.'

'Yes, hopefully.'

'Anyway, must dash. Thanks, again.'

And he was gone, just his expensively shaved head visible over the bulk of his goons.

I found Sadie and Lynda standing with Des back out in the car park, the staff of Sanalex Genome Science morphing in and out of huddles round them like migrating starlings, the trio's posture a group exercise in social discomfort. All of them looked relieved to see me, Lynda more, even, than the others. The nurse approached Des, raised herself on tiptoe and spoke quietly into the ear he was tilting toward her, his eyes and fixed smile never leaving me. He nodded and she left.

'I hear you met our leader. What an honour! You'll come to treasure that one day.'

Lynda had taken me by the arm and was dragging me toward the car.

'Are we off, Lynda?' Des asked, ingratiatingly.

'I'm all done, Des,' I replied on her behalf. 'All swabbed an all that.'

'Well, as a whole one would wait until . . .' He signalled back toward the building and its nonexistent fire. But there was no checking Lynda's crabbed scramble. 'But, I guess, if we've got anything else we need to . . . And it is a long drive back for you. So. Well, great to meet you all and thanks. Thanks for coming. We'll be in touch.'

I waited until we were past my parents' road, past my parents' motorway junction, past my parents' town, past my parents' entire motorway and past all the other motorways, past the door of Lynda's car, past the front door and past our door, past clicking the catch on our very own Yale. Past all this and back to normality – a cup of tea, a spliff – all that passed before I piped up.

'Nice one on the alarms. What ya do?'

'Nightmare, man. Started a fire in the toilets innit?'

'You know what? It was worth it?'

'Seen?'

'I know your real mum's name.'

'Wha?'

'He told me. Kind of.'

'Old up.'

'Valerie Charles.'

The silence that followed seemed to stretch out over us and mould down onto our features, latex. Our lives trundled to a standstill, imaginary brothers forcing pillows down onto our upturned faces. Sadie just kept looking at me.

'That ain't my mum's name.'

CTRL gave us televisions so that we would measure its power in cameras. But, like the march past beneath a dictator's salute, their main purpose is ornamental. They are both a reminder of strength and a distraction.

Extract from *Twenty-second Communiqué of the Vanished*

5

She didn't mean to look like a child right then. She meant to look like she didn't care, like she was in complete control. Which is exactly what made it show.

'That ain't muh mum's name.'

'Not your adoptive mum. Your real mum.'

'Yeah, but that ain't er name.'

'What ya mean?'

'I know muh real mum's name. Found it out while I was at Yarleigh Falls. Me auditor wrote off for it for me.'

'So . . .'

'So it ain't Valerie Charles. Er name's Kaylee Fuxxx. Actually, er real name's Katalina Svorsversky. The other's, y'know, like a stage name.'

I gulped back my confusion. 'She sounds nice.'

'Yeah, right. Polish prossie.'

'You've met her?'

'Went to visit her when I got out. Some massage parlour in Kilburn. Tried to get me on the game.'

'Oh.'

'Yeah.'

'So who's Valerie Charles?'

'Dunno.'

'Don't you think we should try to find out?'

It's very easy to get hold of someone's address. Or it was. I haven't tried for years. But I can't imagine it has become harder. That would run counter to my education back then. I was to learn in those few months just how much data concerning each of us was available to other people if those people could pay. We paid.

We used to hang out at Tariq's shop now and then, not least because he would always serve us and we'd never lifted anything from there and so weren't barred. His younger brother Mushtaq was a computer expert. Not like my brother. Mushtaq worked in an IT department of a proper insurance company and wore clean shirts and designer spectacles and spent his day helping clueless staff members to fix their machines after they had opened emails obviously containing malevolent viruses, something that they continued to do however many times they had previously clicked on an identical attachment. As a result he was consistently world-weary, one hand swooping through gel-hardened hair, the other adjusting the sit of his valuable frames, his posture rounded by the daily friction not of machines but human stupidity.

Mushtaq's sole pleasure, the only trigger that would stretch his spine out, was collectible model tractors. He had eighty or so of them, all still in their boxes, all apparently identical except for the colour they'd been sprayed, but the most valuable going for well over a hundred pounds on eBay. You couldn't help but pity him.

In exchange for him using the insurance company's database to find out Valerie Charles's address, we agreed to liberate a 1967 boxfresh Massey Ferguson from its pride of place way up behind the counter of Masons Models. It says something for our priorities at the time that it never occurred to us just to go to the library and see if Valerie Charles was listed in one of the London phone books.

We knew it'd be hard to get the tractor. It was displayed on a high shelf behind and above the stooped, melted-wax figure of Mr Mason, probably the only shopkeeper to have been based in Coalville before it existed. He had managed to make his new unit instantly old – dark, cold and damp, visited only by feverish young men who came down from London to search through the slightly decaying cardboard boxes for various grails of modelling. No one local ever went in there – except Mushtaq, of course, who would stand and stare at the toy tractor which, for reasons unexplained, was never for sale.

In the end we abandoned any attempt at a plan and opted for shock and awe. One winter Friday at 5.25 p.m. we pulled on second-hand caricature masks of a prime minister we'd never heard of, burst through the door, let off a Big Smokey banger, pressed an air horn to Mr Mason's head and then, as he lay cowering on the floor, leapt up onto the counter, grabbed the tractor in its box and legged it. My ears rang for three days and, by all accounts, Mr Mason was never himself after that, either.

Mushtaq complained about a slight rip in the packaging, but still handed over the dossier he had got from a friend 'over at dunnhumby' which, as well as detailing where Valerie Charles lived and her career at the Bar, also contained considerable information regarding her shopping habits and, in particular, her penchant for ready meals from Waitrose.

'Nah. No way,' Sadie stated. 'There is no way muh mum's a lawyer.'

Even then, I perhaps hadn't realised how important this was to Sadie. It was hard for me, who spent my time trying to shrug off my family, to imagine any overwhelming appetite for finding one. And Sadie's own need to appear cold and hardened and in charge of any situation also meant that she had largely kept her feelings on the issue hidden. But the morning before our planned departure she awoke jittery and tense, one issue obsessing her.

'What my gunna wear?'

'What do you want to wear?'

'Dunno.'

'Well, how do you want to be?'

She wanted to be herself but she wanted to look classy. Wanted to endear herself without selling out. Wanted to look like the world's greatest daughter and the world's worst. Wanted to be loved, of course, but without looking like she needed to be. These contradictions resulted in a frenzy of thieving that day, alternate outfits piling up on our bed, a mountain of unsuitable couture.

By evening everything went wrong. Nothing worked, nothing fitted, nothing looked right. We moved from bony cheeriness through a dry tiredness and on into something unprecedented. Slumped amid the wreckage of our fashion attempts, Sadie had cried, make-up flowing down her face, shoulders hiccuping quietly to themselves, teeth clenched against any emission of sound.

When she cried, it transpired, she looked exactly like the lady who we were to meet in Hampstead the next morning, when the words 'We've come about your daughter' were all I had to say before I was made dumb by the resemblance.

Not that she cried straight away. First of all she screamed at us and shouted. It was only after that the tears came. Then she was crying so hard she wasn't even shouting anymore. She seemed to decide to sit down on her doorstep, but instead she fell into the doorframe and hung there, one arm above her head, the other hand next to her face. She was quiet but still crying, her mouth wide but on mute. We tried to take her inside and she let us and the three of us formed an ungainly hug and no one seemed sure who was holding up who or why. Then we were all crying. Until eventually we all stopped. Because you do, don't you? Eventually, if you do it for long enough, you just stop and, however bad the thing you were crying about, the act of crying overwrites it. So we stopped. And I made tea.

We sat now, all three of us uncomfortable, the lady drooped in her armchair, Sadie and I perching on the edge of the sofa. This young old woman owned the downstairs floor of a merchant mansion in gradual decline. The scrappily painted doors of her French windows framed an intensely green lawn and bushes, giving the light in the drawing room an emerald tint. We looked at our tea, at the delicate china cups, the matching saucers. We looked at the walls, not really taking in the pictures.

We looked at the bookshelves. Finally, the lady raised her cup to her mouth and sipped. Squinted her lips and, with effort, swallowed.

'I don't usually take sugar.'

'Sorry. It was for the shock.'

'Oh, I see.'

'I haven't drunk any of mine yet. Have mine.'

'And that's without sugar . . . ?'

'Well. No. But it's only got one in.'

'How many did this have in?'

'Three.'

'My.'

'Well, you seemed quite upset.'

Sadie just looked at her, dumb, too full of need to talk.

'So come on then. What do you want? Why did you ask . . . why did you ask about my daughter? What do you want from me?'

'Nothing. We really don't. It's a weird one. Sadie?' She shrugged, shook her head and nodded all at once, shrugged again. 'Sadie's adopted.'

'Lots of people are adopted.'

'Yeah, it's just . . . we think you might be her mum?'

'Is this supposed to be some sort of a joke?' She seemed angry. I suppose it wasn't the reaction I expected. 'Is this supposed to be funny?'

'No.'

'Why are you doing this to me?'

'We're just trying to work out what's going on.'

'Who sent you here? Who put you up to this?'

Looking at her now, even I could see that she wasn't that old. The way she dressed and did her face, the way she spoke made her seem ancient but she was much younger than my parents, much sharper and much, much richer. I wouldn't have minded her for a mother myself.

'Nobody. Honest. We're just trying to sort something out.'

'I want you to leave now.'

97

'Can I just explain?'

'If you won't leave I'll call the police.'

'Please. Just five minutes.'

She stared at Sadie long and hard. Sadie shrugged again, tried a smile that came out wrong. And we watched as the lady shrank in front of us, tried to shrink with her, all three of us deflating. We watched as her face came apart, her raised hand trying to hold it together. Watched as she struggled to speak.

'My . . . my daughter's dead.'

Valerie Charles had made a mistake. Or a series of mistakes. It was understandable when you knew the whole story, but she didn't ask for understanding, or accept it. Or for that matter, forgiveness.

Just before Valerie had started at university to study law, her parents had been killed whilst on holiday. It was a funny story, she told us. Or would have been, if it was made up. Or if they hadn't been her parents, anyway. Her father had been an exceedingly nervous traveller, the kind to avoid aeroplanes, even when the fares on them were cheaper than a day return to Brighton. So – Valerie could remember feeling at the time that it was just her luck – most of their holidays had been in the UK. These stop-at-homes had decided, however – 'just before I started college!' – to hare off to the south of France. The father wouldn't fly so they decided to drive. When they reached France, though, he had found the motorway traffic too heavy and driving on the right too taxing, had trundled back to Dieppe, parked up and bought tickets for the train. On arriving in Toulouse, they had stepped out of the station looking for a cab to take them the last twenty miles to their gîte and been run over by the shuttle bus from the airport.

She was the only child of two only children. She took care of the funeral arrangements on her own, discovered that her father's life insurance policy was worthless, was informed that the mortgage her parents had switched to in the early Nineties had grown instead of shrinking. Left with nothing and nobody, her synapses misfiring, in a swirl of dislocations, she had begun her degree. She had not known what else to do.

Unsurprisingly, she was a particularly vulnerable undergraduate, desperate to find someone to be dependent on. She had soon fallen in love with a biological sciences postgrad and, despite his supposed expertise in such areas, become pregnant by him. She tried to be sensible, considered a termination, but the father wouldn't have it, insisting instead that they could get by if they stuck together. One month before she was due to give birth he landed a job in America and skipped the country without telling her. So, desperate, she had gone to see her Moral Tutor, who had convinced her that the only right thing to do was to put the child up for adoption. Which meant that she never even touched them as they came out, yes, two of them, a boy and a girl she was told afterwards, her boy and her girl and she never even touched them.

Cut and cut through all the years of waiting and fantasising and hoping that the children would contact her. Cut and cut through the faces of other mothers on finding her looking too needily at their offspring. Cut and cut through solo ready meals after a long day at court. Cut and cut through sleepless nights. Cut and cut, cut and cut. Anything to get to the end before she did. Cut and cut right up to her receiving the letter from the Adoption Agency saying that her daughter was trying to get in touch. Because, of course, the mistake couldn't be singular. If Sadie had somehow ended up with someone else's birth mother, someone else had ended up with hers. Cut and cut to their first meeting.

'And it was just the most wonderful and painful thing to have ever happened in my life. And I felt so ashamed. And there she was in front of me. And we just sort of looked at each other. And I suppose she was sizing me up. And because there was no reason for her to trust me. And I was I was I was just bursting. And I didn't know what to say. And there was nothing I could say. And I still can't express how it felt even now. And at the same time it was awful, horrible, all those years, the betrayal, this shame still clinging to me. And yet. And yet my God, this was this was my little girl. And this discomfort between us just suddenly cracked. And we were both crying and we pulled each other in towards us. And there we were, a mother and daughter clinging on to each other. And I thought, If I die now, if I die now I'll be happy.

'But unfortunately I didn't.'

It was raining outside now, the room with that heavy daylight darkness, all three of us picking at the frayed remains of damp tissues, all three of us looking at these lumps of collapsing fibre, afraid to meet each other's eyes, the whole afternoon evaporated.

'And then they rang me. About a month later. We were meant to be meeting again that weekend, doing something together. We were meant. They rang me and told me she wouldn't be coming. I was already protesting, begging them to beg her to. But when they got a chance they explained. They told me.' I remember my own guilt as I sat there tearing these words from this lady I'd never met before. I remember how sick I felt at the moment she paused, my stomach heaving, retches spasming through my throat. 'She disappeared. Just like that. Not a trace. Took nothing with her. Never withdrew any money from the account I'd set up for her. No body. Never seen again. I hired a private investigator. The best. Nothing. Nothing. She must be dead. She has to be dead. She was so happy. She was so happy to have found me. You wait fifteen years and then. You wait and then.'

What were we to do? What did it matter, at that moment, what any DNA test might claim to show? There was a stronger proof at work in that room, water dribbling down the French windows, a rain-assisted silence emphasised by the sound of someone walking around in the flat upstairs. Here in front of us, in a black cashmere sweater and a stylishly sensible skirt, with her hair cut short and just angular enough, here sat a mother who had waited as long as we had been breathing and then found her daughter. And that vacancy was filled now, interviews closed. Forever.

'And . . . and the brother? Your son?'

She didn't look at me.

'Just have to wait . . . Just have to wait and hope and . . .'

I can't remember if it was me or Sadie who rose from the sofa first, though I find it less painful to imagine it was Sadie. There wasn't much in it. We both creaked upward slowly, as if scared of disturbing the background, our teacups clattering on their saucers as our nicotine-desperate fingers chattered, our eyes frantically crossing each other's looking for a place to deposit cold china.

Oh, I'm sorry. I'm so sorry. Don't go. Don't go just yet. You haven't explained. Sit down. None of these words were forthcoming from the chair, which is all that she'd become, collapsing into it, lost in the springs and the dust and fluff inside it. In silence we collided with one another, having chosen intersecting routes to our chosen dump zones, my cup toppling free of its base, spinning toward the floor, the last dreg of tea coming out from its receptacle, falling as a continuous blob and shattering on the thick, pale carpet.

'Sorry. Sorry. So sorry. Just dropped. Sorry. Not . . .' I flapped onto a knee, righted the cup, began agitating the stain with my tear-heavy tissue which, in turn, burst into a galaxy of brown crumbles. 'We should go. We should be going. I think we should.'

The light almost all absent now, shadow having met shadow, all contrast gone so that her face was flat, little more than a gothic embroidering on her seat back, her hands carved talons decorating its arms. Still she said nothing, Sadie echoing her again and again, perspective being sucked between these two vacuums. I raised my hand, hesitant, laid it gently under the crook of her elbow and, minutely, pulled her toward the door. Our feet began to work, the room spinning past us, the hallway looming ahead and I found myself able to imagine the world beyond these walls again. Sadie stopped, turned back to the chair.

'What she called?'

She stood, my arm stretching back behind me as my exit fantasy stalled. There was silence from the other side of the room, then a slight shuffle of sound as the mother repositioned herself.

'What?'

'What was she called? Yer daughter?'

'Suzanna. Suzanna Milding.'

Feeling panic fluttering up inside me I essayed a gentle tug at Sadie's sleeve. She swayed with it, then took a step back toward the centre of the room.

'S'a lovely name.'

Another wait.

'Yes.' Another. 'It's not the one I gave her. The one I gave her in my head. Obviously. That was a lovely name. *He* wanted to call her something else, but in my head I knew.' She sighed – a long, wistful sigh with a touch of performance about it – and then added in a sing-song voice, 'I always called her Sadie-May. Sadie-May. My little Sadie-May.'

Is it any surprise that we froze? That no air entered or left our lungs? That our hearts paused, the blood in our veins standing like wine in bottles? There was nothing that Sadie could have said that made sense of this for Valerie Charles. Whatever words came out would only make it worse. What other reaction could there be but to cease to exist or try to cease to exist? To hold on for as long as possible to being as little as possible? So we did, and a whole night seemed to pass, or perhaps a season or a geological Age. And it was only when she began to sob one last time in front of us that our biological systems booted up again and it was only then that we staggered through the door and down the dark hallway and through the door and down the dark hallway and through the door and, at last, out, out and away along the avenue, the sharp yellow of the streetlights finally reawakening me.

Outside of commuter hours, Coalville was a long way from

London. Direct trains became mythical, a fleet of ramshackle Sprinters depositing those too poor to travel in Premier time-zones at stations along the border between the south of the city and the start of the country, from where they would be collected by a squad of antique coaches whose overhead plastic nozzles belched a hot, stale tobacco-vomit smell. These, after lurching drunkenly through suburban inner cities at limit-busting speeds and then hanging round in lay-bys while the driver had a smoke, would eventually deposit you, always a little later than in your worst case scenario, in the rubbish-strewn bus station of your particular soulless conurbation.

The journey that night was as long as it could be. Sadie had sunk into dumbness, not merely failing to articulate, but completely absent, a walking catatonic. I yanked her on and off buses, past kebab shops, through clots of drunken lechery, round puddles of sick and girl-on-girl fistfights, each moment of it filmed from above and every side, camera phones swaying in and out of each other's shot. She was oblivious, gliding past sights that would usually have made her cackle with laughter or spit or punch someone and none of them registered.

I managed to nick two bottles of WKD from the off licence on the station concourse and it was only once I had dragged her onto the train, snapped the lid from one and forced it to her lips that she showed any sign of occupancy. Even then she didn't speak, taking the bottle from me without looking down and pulling on it. When she had finished she dropped it to the floor – its clonk and subsequent roll up and down the carriage drawing pursed lips on the old dear sitting opposite – and took mine from me. I didn't complain.

We were the only passengers on the bus laid on for us, so we had the back seats all to ourselves. At last the rigidity went from Sadie and her head came slowly down to rest on my shoulder. She didn't sleep. I watched the flashes of passing light reflecting in her eyes, listened as we moved across different tar-macs and concretes, my own head beginning to roll and jolt as

I endeavoured to stay absolutely still for her. We moved through a ghost England of empty streets, empty bypasses, empty shops, empty bus shelters, empty McDonalds, even those that were open drained of life. The yellow light a hollowing, moving cars devoid of drivers, only us two awake to witness it all, the silhouette of our coachman hunched over the gently swinging wheel an optical illusion.

It was gone five by the time we picked our way back through the familiar streets of Coalville and a comforting grey was beginning to rob the buildings of perspective. We linked arms and leaned into one another, me feeling happy to have been spat out here, hoping that Sadie was feeling it, too. Hoping she was feeling something, anyway. We were children, after all, and this wasn't meant to be our life.

I should have known, somehow – though why or how I should have known is as much a mystery to me now as it was then – that a day like this would find any excuse to continue. As soon as we pushed into the hall we could see that the light was on in our room, its sixty-watt gloom mothing out through the strengthened glass above our door.

We pushed in expecting to find our meter chewing through the last of our carefully hoarded tokens. Instead we discovered Lynda asleep on the bed, an empty bottle of Diamond Fruzion in one hand, in the other a spent butt burnt to filter, her arms and legs splayed out at unlikely angles, glasses riding up her forehead to reveal . . .

Animal instinct roused her and she scuffled up, right hand rising to protect her eyes, a smudge of ash left gashing her forehead. Nobody spoke for a moment, Sadie still mute, Lynda apparently as stunned as I was by the idea that she slept. Unfortunately she wasn't to be silenced for long.

'Well aren't *we* the dirty stop-outs?' She seemed to expect an answer to her rhetoric but we offered none. 'And where have we been, ladies?'

'Out.'

'Out. Yes. Of *course*. And there *I* was thinking you were hiding under the *bed*.'

'You drank our drink.'

'Well yes, Tilly dear? I have been here *wait*-ing for you since seven o'clock? I was in danger of dying of *thirst*?'

'I don't really like you coming in here whenever you like.'

'Tell that to the parole board, *dar*-ling.' She took a moment to calm herself, that tight smile insinuating its way onto her features again. 'Talking of which and back to the question in hand, where have you *been* all night?'

'I told you. We've been out.'

'Allason?'

'I'm talking and I already told you.'

'But I am asking *her*, Tilly. Allason and I are very close. Aren't we, Allason?

'*Aren't* we, Allason?

'You and I?'

She dismissed me with a flap of her hand, dropped the dead cigarette into the empty bottle, dumped that on the floor. Extended her arm toward Sadie, beckoning with all four fingers, a witch imitating a parakeet's comb. Caught the very edge of her jacket, tugged it between finger and thumb. Sadie almost fell toward her, mesmerised, spinning in the air and landing beside her, their hands linked in my friend's lap.

'Just leave her alone, Lynda. She's had a long day. Just. Just get off her.'

'What's the matter, Tilly dear? Jealous? It's very *un*-becoming. Allason and I have known each other for a long time, haven't we Allason? Long before your little . . . *fling*. So it's only to be expected that in times of great stress . . .' – she raised one set of talons and began scratching them over Sadie's hair – 'she should turn to me. Isn't that right, Allason?' Tilted her head in my direction, sneered another poisonous smile. 'After all, for all your wonderful upbringing, what are you actually going to *do*?'

I stood there, my head full of blood, its pumping noise drowning my thoughts, my tongue swelling, oozing down my throat, my arms two dry sticks by my sides.

'Allason has no doubt *told* you how we met? That I worked at the *home* when she was there? How I looked *af*-ter her? How, if she's *ho*-nest, I'm the nearest thing she's got to a moth-er? Aren't I, Allason? I'm like a *mum* to you, aren't I? Just like little Allason's *mum*-my? Now Allason. Where have you been?'

Squinting now, under this sustained assault on reality, I looked to my hero for a denial, for defiance, anything. Sadie sat with her head drooping forward, fat tears falling from her eyes and plopping onto the three hands remaining beneath. Finally, as if she was calling me on a cheap mobile, her voice tiny, metallic, she spoke.

'Went to see muh mum, Lynda.'

'The *whore*?'

More time evaporating in silence, my desperation to interrupt robbing me of speech.

'Muh real mum.'

'The *whore is* your real mum.'

'Nah she ain't. Titch found out she ain't.'

Space.

'*How?*'

'The DNA thing innit?'

'Oh, you *stu*-pid girls.' She pulled her cigarettes from her bag, offered one to Sadie. I was left standing as they lit up together. 'I thought you had understood. You *swapped* the swabs. Hence, they think that the *whore* is *your* mother, Tilly. When in fact, as only us three know, she is still very much *your* mother, Allason.'

'But she ain't. My mum's a lawyer.' The pride evident, but desperate too. I looked at her and for the very first time she seemed younger than me. The shock freed my own voice.

'You don't have to tell her anything.'

'Got nutt'n to hide is it?'

'So let me get this straight. Little Miss College Girl has somehow convinced you that you too are possessed of *bour*geois blood? And how is this supposed to have *happ*ened, Tilly dear? Was it a miracle? A *vir*-gin birth? Is Allason the daughter of God? Are we in the presence of the Mess-*i*-ah? Because these things *do* happen you know. Oh yes. You may be too young to remember it but there was the girl up the road? Worked at the shopping centre? The one that shut down? I believe she makes adult films now. Do you even know what an adult film is, Tilly *dear*?'

'I don't know –'

Interrupting me: 'No, I didn't think so –'

'I don't know how it happened. But I do know that that Des up in Berkshire kept asking me and asking me about this woman who they thought was my real mother and she wasn't a prostitute.'

'But are you sure? Could you even read the *signs*?'

'Do you want to know or not?'

'Oh, I'm sorry Tilly dear, the cut and thrust of *conversation* is too much for you.' Pulling herself into a pastiche of contrition. 'Go ahead and we will *listen*.'

'I can speak for meself,' Sadie pulling herself up, reinflating, overbite manifested. 'Fuckin arguin over who talks f'me? Speak f'meself.'

By the time Sadie had gone through it all twice and then through certain points three or four more times, Lynda's momentary show of contrition had vanished to be replaced by a crackly jauntiness, actually doling out fags to both of us, her face contorted with the effort of sincerity, her teeth – huddled like corpses in a mass grave – visible between thin, salivaglossed lips.

'So let me get this *straight*. There must have been a-*noth*-er swap as *well* as the swab swap *Tilly* here pulled off for *fun*? When you were a baby? And you *know* this or have at least in-*ferred* this from the fact that the *whore* who is sup-*posed* to be your *birth mother* isn't the same woman as the woman Sanalex matched your *DNA* with? Even though they think it's *Tilly's* DNA? But this other woman, this *Valerie Charles*, she's already been introduced to the *foundling* who she thinks is her birth daughter? And this *other girl*, the *impostor*, had gone and disappeared? Am I getting it so far? So you didn't feel you could tell *Valerie* the *truth*, what with her being in mourning and all. Although personally I'm not sure if it was the time for scruples. What with *Hampstead* and everything . . . Have I left anything out?'

'Muh bruvver.'

'Oh *yes*. Your *twin* brother. And *how*, may I ask, are you meant to have a twin you've never met?'

Sadie shrugged slightly. 'Separated at birth?'

'Prep-*os*-terous. The whole thing's preposterous. And yet in-*trigu*-ing, too.' She pulled hard at her cigarette. 'And the father? Your *father*?'

'Din't really go into that.'

'And the brother? Your twin brother? Where's he?'

'Or that either.'

'Well, the silly cow, eh? Crying over her dead daughter and you're there in front of her.' I nearly dropped my smoke, ashamed that Lynda still had the capacity to shock me.

'Anyway. Anyway. The important thing is to find the brother, right? Right. No point worrying about the mother right now. Give her some time. But the brother . . . Well, that makes more sense.' She examined our blankness for a moment, clinical.

'The brother's the key. *Typ*-ically. For one, his DNA will prove whether you're the other twin and then mummy will have to accept you into her *lovely* home. For two, imagine mummy's grati-*tude* when you deliver her only boy to her. She will *love* you for it. And you know you need help on the whole *lov*-able thing. For *three*, from his DNA you can find out who daddy is. The blessed Y-chromosone. And you may well ask why. You do not have the Y-chromosome. Just the X. But the son's is i-*dent*-ical to the father's. A positive identification is then possible. Oh, I've been doing my reading you know, since they started sniffing rou–' An abrupt halt, recalibration, continuation. 'I would imagine there's every chance that daddy is a goldmine, too. Do you follow?' Again, she looked from one of us to the other. Sloping with the disappointment of our non-reaction, she gang-showed on. 'Okay, we'll leave the whole goldmine issue to one *side* for now. The important thing is to find your dear brother. And *I* am *here* to *help*.'

'We don't know his name,' I mumbled, desperate to block her involvement.

'Ah, but we know his *sister's* name,' she countered.

'But she's dead.'

'But there are records.'

'I didn't get the impression they'd been brought up together or anything.'

'It doesn't matter. We have the birth mother's name, too.'

'I don't think it's the kind of information they give out.'

'And who is this "they"? "They" is "*I*". I am a freelance social services operative. I have contacts. It's simply a matter of putting out some feelers. Anyone would think you didn't want Allason to be from better stock than you. Although it's really not surprising. That she is. When you look at the two of you.' So I looked and it was true and I wasn't.

Shivering now, an insatiable hunger taking hold of me, I spat my last pathetic defence.

'And what's in it for you, Lynda?'

She ratcheted to her feet in painful increments, tossed her head so that the dry mat of her hair quivered, then turned on me.

'What's in it for –? Oh, Tilly *dear*. You used to be such a nice young girl. What's in it for *me*? Oh *dear*. What an up-*sett*-ing creature you have turned out to be. When the only one here who seems to have to have something *in* it for her is, of course, you Tilly dear. You and your lesbian fantasies. You and your *smoth*-ering *filth*.

109

'But oh no. But oh no *no*. *I* am the one with the hidden agenda. *I* am the one who needs something *in* it for me. What's *in* it for me! Shall I tell you? Shall I tell you exactly what is *in* it for me? I do this, all this I do, all the things that I do for un-*grate*-ful young girls like you two, all of it, I do for . . .' – her tongue lapping out as it tried to start the word, her mouth loose and obscene as it groped back and forth round the first consonant – 'I do it for l . . . for l . . . l . . . llll . . .' – a deep breath – 'I do it for' – a long exhalation and then low, a polypped tenor occupying her, gruff and sonorous – '*love*.'

'Yeah, love innit?' Sadie's voice as flat as an oil spill. 'And the gold mine.' Her eyes crossed, smoke snorting out of her nostrils.

'Really, Allason. I was hoping you had turned over a new leaf.'

'I ave. An I wanna find muh bruv. Whateva it takes, Lynda, I'll be grateful for it. Yeah? Yeah Titch? Whateva she can do.'

Circumspect, stretched between my relief at Sadie's recovery and my anxiety at Lynda's involvement, I nodded my assent.

'I will take that as an a-*pol*-ogy from both of you, then. Your feral, criminal minds have a way of perverting even the most selfless of motives. I should be used to it, I suppose. The middle classes have always been dishonest, selfish, grasping shopkeepers.'

It was fully light in the room now, a cold, moon-footage patina making Sadie and Lynda look even more insubstantial and pasty than usual. I looked down at my hand, my bitten nails, my bony knuckles, tried to imagine what it would mean to be a mulch of my parents' worthless genetic codes.

'But as a sign of good *will* on my part, I will take you both for some breakfast. Proving that I really am much nicer than you deserve.'

Lynda had never bought us anything without charging it back to us in some way. The offer confirmed to me that she was plotting. But I was too tired, confused and hungry to refuse. I walked over to the wardrobe, opened the door and looked at myself in the mirror, this changeling, acne forcing its way through powder, chipmunk cheeks, car-accident eye smudges. Shut the door and began to look for my sponge bag.

'Got to put some make-up on first.'

Surveillance is the ultimate mediation. CTRL flows through our blood, occupies our minds. We become CTRL, inhabit it so totally that, when we are reminded that there is a separation between us and it, we shudder then wave it away, because 'All these things are here to help us' and 'How could it be any other way?' At best, we fuss about an irrelevant *form* of surveillance which we believe 'invades our privacy'. As if there was anywhere still left to invade! Our physicality is hopelessly infected.

Extract from *Twenty-fourth Communiqué of the Vanished*

6

'Ya fink e look like me?'

I squinted down at the crumpled piece of paper in front of
me. Quartered by fibrous white fold lines, printed using an
inkjet purchased from a spiv down the market, taken from a
digital image of double-figure resolution, I could just about be
sure that it was a head-and-shoulders portrait of a teenage
boy. I examined it carefully, the spacing of the dots, the way
the colours had separated. Looked up at Sadie and back down
again. Up and down again. Up, down. Up.

'Yeah. He really does. I think he really does.'

'Ya fink so?'

'Yeah.'

'For real?'

'Yes.'

Lynda had been true to her word, the planet spinning the
wrong way. Two days after our conversation she had turned
up at the bedsit in the company of a fat old lady with her grey
hair in a bun and her hands plugged deep into the pockets of
her purple overcoat. She was introduced to us as Mary, greeted us with the hushed niceness of a librarian. The room almost
flickered round her edges, such an unlikely presence did she
seem there. But Mary, it transpired, had been met by changing
priorities in the workplace and was determined to rise to the
challenges presented. Having spent nearly thirty years as a
Clerical Support Worker in the County Council's Social
Services department, six months ago she had been informed
that she was no longer eligible for any pension provision.
Confronted by this setback, she had decided to loot the stationery cupboard, to start siphoning off supplies of tea and

instant coffee and, most pertinently, to sell whatever information she could find a buyer for. And she had no shortage of
information, her job being the collection and storage of client
data.

Although it was only September, we were presented with
Mary's Christmas list and told to call Lynda when we'd got
everything. Pictures pasted from catalogues and magazines,
comments, alternatives, shop addresses, opening hours – her
dossier gave a sense of how accomplished she must be at her
job. Two latterday elves, we lurched into the project with all
the enthusiasm and goodwill it demanded.

Cherry-red cashmere sweater, latest hand-held digital enter-
tainment centre, bottle of fine Cognac, microwave oven,
'Green Doll' (whose soiled nappies had to be hand washed in
the mini sink included), Hawkwind's *Live with Lemmy* DVD,
Fame Academy 10th Anniversary DVD box set, Burberry
Prorsum slippers, Mrs Milligan's Fine Conserves Christmas
Collection Basket, lavender bath salts, palmtop computer,
javelin, Home Tummy Tuck kit, train set, spillikins, glass swan
ornament, pashmina, nunchaka, maracas, vintage talking
model of B.A. Barachus, champagne flutes, case of champagne, two picture frames, two Vettriano prints (to fit the
frames), decorative candlesticks, diamond-patterned golfing
sweater, power drill, adjustable workbench, ceremonial
sword. It took us forty eight hours to tick off everything on the
list, only the spillikins inconveniencing us in any way.

Within half an hour of calling Lynda's mobile she and Mary
shuffled into the room and we all began carting the gear out to
Mary's motor. It wasn't a very big car and she had to make
two runs to take it all. Once we'd loaded her car the second
time she turned to us, unclipped her handbag, pulled out a
brown envelope and handed it to Sadie.

'It's a little crumpled I'm afraid. I have to carry documents
out of the building in my undergarments. For security reasons.' She left, the crinkling noise of her exit more than ade-
quately explained.

Lynda, however, hung round, first on the pretext of checking the meter and then quite nakedly waiting for the envelope to be opened, her movements merely serving to map its location in Sadie's lap.

'I ain't openin it till ya gone.'

'What? What *are* you talking about?'

'This. I ain't openin it till ya gone.'

'Oh that? *Oh.* I'm really not that interested.'

'Surprised you din ave a peek before we got it.'

Lynda paused, examined a chip in the paintwork on the doorframe, always eager for reasons to keep the deposit.

'She wouldn't let me. She has a very skewed sense of obligation.' A sigh. 'Well, fuck you then. Call me when you *want* something, won't you?' And, her limbs in constant reconfiguration, she was gone.

There was no sound then in our stripped grotto. We teetered in the silence, isolated in our own anxieties.

'You want a tea?'

'Seen.' Looking round the room without looking round. 'I'll skin up.'

So that at last, with smoke swooping from her mouth and nose like a tiny soul, she shook the tobacco pubes from the envelope, laid it flat, picked and pulled at the adhesive on its lip and, tenderly smoothing the flap back, pulled a battered sheaf of paper free.

'Ya fink e looks like me?'

Now there were three of us sharing the same birthday. Marcus Milding had been fostered at birth, along with his twin sister Suzanna, by Mr and Mrs Peter Milding of 32 Stork Close, Surbiton. They had applied for full adoption when the children were six months old but then, at a crucial point in the proceedings, asked for some time to reconsider. Their original motivation for adopting was their mutual barrenness, but somehow, it seemed, a rogue sperm had met the only egg ever to grace those tubes and now Mrs Milding was pregnant.

Perhaps that would have been enough to mess things up for the twins on its own, but Mrs Milding soon let Mr Milding know that the sperm was another rogue's. Mr Milding jumped into the path of an oncoming commuter train, traumatising the driver and costing the rail provider over a quarter of a million pounds in sick pay and counselling fees. Mrs Milding had the twins taken into care, where, due to a resources shortfall, they had to be separated. They were sent their own ways before their first birthday.

Marcus was then parcelled through a succession of children's homes all over the South East, each successive county council finding a reason to move him on as a result of restructuring their care packages. He was diagnosed dyslexic six months before the medical establishment decided no such condition existed. His attendance record at school was patchy from the age of nine. By eleven he no longer turned up at all, his social worker had suffered a nervous breakdown and he had received his third youth court conviction, arson joining shoplifting and housebreaking amongst his extracurricular activities. At twelve he was fostered, against the advice of anyone who had ever read his file, by a couple of Russian Orthodox Christians who weren't Russian and who treated difficult children as a kind of extreme sport.

Either they did something right or Marcus got bored of playing out the role forced on him by his personal history. He started attending school, steamed through grades, broke records, led sports teams, made friends, influenced people, the feelgood end to a movie, but there in front of you! *For real!* Teachers thanked him for being in their classes, adults lapsed into silence when he passed them on the street, girls circled round him in flutters of desire. He was handsome, intelligent, caring, tender, athletic, a fantasy. Our fantasy, only the barest of facts supporting our embroidering, both of us willing him to be remarkable, though for different reasons.

One truth we couldn't avoid was that, despite his many

achievements and accolades, our deity had vanished. A little over two months earlier his foster parents had reported Marcus as Missing. Just as we'd discovered him, everyone else had lost him. With a sense of being stuck moving in circles, our existence a giant ring road, I agreed to accompany Sadie to the satellite town on the other side of London where the couple lived.

'Are you sure you're up to this? They'll probably be really upset.'

'Belie'me, Titch, foster carers dun get upset.'

Sometimes there can be no response worth giving to a conviction honestly held. This time I packed a bag for what I was sure would follow – extra cigarettes, alcohol, tissues.

'Melanie, could you stop that please?'

He turned back to us, huge in the doorway, a round-headed man with short dark hair, black long-sleeved t-shirt, black jogging bottoms, black kungfu slippers, black-framed glasses. Smiled, adjusted the specs slightly. 'Sorry, completely missed what you said.'

'Marcus. We're here about Marcus.'

'Oh. Right. I guess you'd better come in,' he waved us through the door as he turned back and shouted at the stairs again. 'Mel! Just turn it down or I'm up there.'

The bass continued to bounce through the floorboards as we followed him along a dark hallway, no light reflecting back from the deep red carpet, the walls measured out by perspectiveless saints clad in gold leaf, none of those huge-eyed, long-nosed, tiny-mouthed martyrs apparently taking much pleasure in their proximity to God. I entered the kitchen with considerable relief – brightness, the messy retro-ruralism I remembered from my parents' house, the pinboard of photos and postcards, the wooden cupboards, even the blue-and-white bread bin, all in exactly the right places.

'Grab a stool. I've just made a pot of camomile tea. Do either of you fancy a cup?'

We both shrugged assent as we clambered onto the stools at the breakfast bar and perched uncomfortably while he busied himself by the kettle, pulling chipped mugs from a cupboard and splashing urine-coloured water into and around them from a pot with a wildly inefficient spout. When it was brought to us, Sadie asked for sugar, which I enthusiastically helped myself to as well. Then she asked for milk.

'Milk? It's not that sort of tea –'

'Always ave milk in tea.'

'I really don't think –'

'Always.'

'But it's *herbal* tea.'

'Still tea.'

'Well, if you insist. I don't think it'll be very nice, though.'

'Whateva.' Her face tensed every time she took a sip but eventually she would drink it all. Mind you, mine tensed, too.

'So, anyway, I apologise, my name's John. And you've come to see me about Marcus. Are you friends of his from school? I'm sorry, I have to admit I don't recognise you.'

'Nah, we ain't from school. We ain't from round ere at all. It's jus. I fink e's muh bruvver.'

'Your brother? I see. Well, I'm afraid there's going to be a problem. Marcus has run away, we think, although –'

'Yeah, I know. Just fought dunno you might be able ta help or sutt'n.'

'To be honest, I was hoping you might be able to help us. I was hoping you had some information or something.'

'Nah. Not really.'

'Oh. Jenny'll be so disappointed. She's been very worried about him. Sorry. I'm confusing matters. Jenny's my wife. We were very attached to Marcus. He was a lovely kid.' Correcting himself. 'He *is* a lovely kid. We're still very attached to him. He. I mean, you get used to this sort of thing. If you foster. You can't let it get on top of you. Too much.' He looked up at us, settled on Sadie. 'Yeah, I can see it now. You do look quite like him. I guess that's why I thought you were someone familiar at the door. Your face is the same shape.'

They looked at each other, my spare-part features composed as uninterestingly as ever.

'But there's nothing I can do for you.'

Their eyes twisting into each other's.

'If we knew where he was he wouldn't be missing.'

'Maybe ya know where e is an e dun wanna come back.'

'But we don't.'

'Maybe ya know why e ran off.'

'We wish we did.'

'Maybe it's sutt'n ya did.'

'Maybe it was. We don't know.'

'Usually is.'

'We did have a row, Marcus and I. But that wasn't, that's not unusual. Things were slipping. I thought he might be doing drugs again. But that's not unusual either. I really don't know whether that was the cause or part of the symptoms. I wouldn't like to guess.'

'Bet ya wouldn't.'

'Nice tea,' I interjected, surprised he hadn't chucked us out yet.

'I use the toilet?'

'Sure. It's upstairs. First door you come to. I'm really not trying to be obstructive. We just don't have any idea why he went or where he went. One day he was here and everything was fine, the next he wasn't. It's been very hard for us.'

'Sure, whateva,' Sadie offered as she left me to hold the fort.

We sat listening to the bass line's disconsonanted swoop, repositioning our cups in the stains of their former placings while I clicked through my conversational options before finally, in something like desperation, trying one.

'I like your pictures. In the hall.'

'The icons? They're lovely, aren't they? A little bit more than pictures to us. More than decoration, anyway. We're Russian Orthodox. I know, I know, we don't seem very Russian. Used to be anarchists, actually. Became very interested in Russian anarchism at the end of the nineteenth century. From there, Tolstoy, and from there the art and architecture. So we decided to go to a service and it was just remarkable, a remarkable experience. And it all followed from that.'

'Oh.'

'It's a fascinating, very deep, very spiritual religion.' He smiled at me shyly. 'Not that I expect that's of any great interest to you at your age. It wouldn't have been to me. But we all need a certain amount of spirituality in our lives. A way of making sense of the gaps. Of making sure we don't get lost in those gaps. Yeah?'

Sadie came back into the room.

'Better be goin. Sorry if I were rude.'

'That's alright. I understand.'

'You got a photo? Of Marcus? A spare one. For me?'

'Yeah, of course, I'm sure I must have. Let me have a look.' He turned to the pin board. 'Do you mind if it has other people in it?'

'Nah. Whatever ya got. Cheers.'

Extracted a drawing pin with his nails, a small flutter of bills and school letters eddying downward, ignored as he hunched over the picture, huffed a single-breathed laugh, smiled at the image. Looking up with the slightest shake of his head, his smile tightening.

'That's Jenny on the left. Marcus is on the right. But you probably would've guessed that.'

'Thanks. Dass wicked.'

'You're welcome. Sorry I couldn't be more help.'

'Worry about it. We're out of ere. See ya.'

He followed us to the door and thanked us for coming, took my mobile number in case they heard from Marcus, watched us walk down the cracked concrete of his drive and away round the curve of the pavement. Waved, called out.

'If you find him, let us know he's okay, yeah? We just want to know he's safe.'

We went right at the bottom of the road instead of left, Sadie leading us away from the station, I flickering along behind her trying to make sense of our route.

'It's the other way, Sade.'

'Not where we're going it ain't.'

'Where are we going?'

'Got a fag?'

I passed her one. 'Where's yours?'

''Ad to give it that lickle bitch.'

' . . . ?'

'*Melanie*. Only blasted twelve year old. *"What's it worth?"* Give er what it's worth.'

'I'm sorry. You've lost me.'

'Melanie. Back at the ouse. She is foster sister innit? So I arksed er a coupla question.'

'So where are we going now?'

'Down the reccy. To see Billy.'

'Who's Billy?'

'Muh bruv's mate, cordin to Melanie.'

The reccy found its expression in a length of nettle-bordered, lumpy grass, three swings – their metal chains wound back on themselves like telephone cables, the seats impossibly high – a witch's hat, removed from its pole and hanging with all the poise of a vomiting derelict, and a much-vandalised bench, its remaining slats charred at one end, the marker-penned graf fading into black. At the furthest point of this field was a small concrete bunker which had probably been a caretaker's office or toilet block left over from the time when parks had such things. Now it was just used for hiding behind, which is why Sadie was heading straight for it.

On its far side we found two boys, dressed much as we were – branded sportswear, a flash of Kevlar, double baseball caps pulled down tight over their shaved, fragile-looking crania, brims slanting away from each other. One was leaning against the concrete wall and worrying a boarded-over window frame with his Stanley knife. The other was bent forward, the lower half of his face obscured by a bright blue carrier bag, his body heaving and the bag inflating and deflating like an outboard lung, whatever filled out its bottom causing it to sway obscenely with his breaths.

'Whaddup.'

Sadie's greeting causing two turns, two flurried jumps to attention, knife and bag respectively pulled behind them. Then, seeing only two girls, perhaps a little older than them but not old enough, their bodies sloped back towards the floor, weapon and glue bag visible again. The one with the knife dropped his right shoulder further, opened his arms out until their angle matched the saints' back in the hallway, pulled them in over his crotch and hop-limped a step towards us.

'Wha'gwan shorty?'

'You Billy?'

'Who's arksin?'

'Me.'

'Who me?'

'Sadie.'

'Yeah. An?'

'Lookin for Marcus. Ya know im yeah?'

'Marcus? The Mac? E's my bredren innit?' He slapped his hand onto the board across the window. 'See?' His finger traced over the tag – MAC-US.

'All city. He was all city. Kna'mean? Gangsta. Pure gangsta.'

'Ya know where e's gone den?'

'What I just say? What'd you hear me just say? I said we was bredrens din I?'

The other kid was struggling with his focus, wistfully swinging his sack, all the muscles in his face lengthening.

'So where is e, blud?'

'Blud? S'blud now is it? Ya know what, I kinda like ya, *Sadie*. But . . .'

'But what?'

'But why should I tell ya anyfink?'

'I'm is sister.'

'The Mac din ave no sister.'

'E did. I'm it.'

'Nah man. An even if e did, I gotta arks myself, what's in it for me?'

'What you want?'

He made a show of thinking – his finger going to his lips, a little flash of tongue poking out – as he looked Sadie up and down. The other boy and I hung behind our respective leaders, equally unsure what was going on.

'Now lemme see . . . Ya like *Christmas*, Sadie? Lovely juicy turkey? A nice gobble? I do.'

'Fuck off.'

'Seriously, if you wanna know what I know, shorty . . .'

'Fuck you.'

'Well, that'd do too, but I'll be appy with a lickle gobble.'

'Perv.'

'Ya know ya wanna, anyway. Just makin it easy for ya.'

'Tell me what ya know first.'

'Yeah right.'

'Listen. You tell me what you know first an we got a deal.'

'Yeah?'

'Yeah.'

He squinted at her. 'Juss remember – I got a shank.'

'There ya go den.'

'E's in London.'

'Where?'

'London.'

'Where in London?'

'Dunno.'

'That's it? "E's in London"? What he say he were gunna do?'

'How should I know? I ain't is mum.'

'Nah, you're is *bredren*.'

'Listen, I tol ya what I knew. Now ya owe me.'

'For that? Jokin int cha?'

'Nah man. Deal's a deal. An I still got the shank.'

'Like that is it?'

He shrugged, one hand down the front of his tracky pants, the other spinning the Stanley.

'Titch – you an glue boy go wait round the corner.' Turning back to Billy. 'You – drop em.'

I was so taken aback, so appalled in my own timid way, so jealous, in point of fact, that I did as I was asked without question. Sadie had had sex a few times since I'd come to live with her and yes, I'd been forced to spend time sitting out on the stairs waiting for her and whoever she was with to finish on more than one occasion. But this was something else. She didn't even *like* him. The boy with the bag had begun inhaling again. I looked up at the sky, a low, marbled grey. Heard a noise from the other side of the hut, a tiny whine, like air escaping from a lilo. Found myself peering round the corner.

The boy was lying on the ground apparently trying to suck his whole body into his stomach. A little bit of sick shined on his cheek and puddled next to it. He seemed to be crying. Sadie was holding the knife.

I turned to find the other kid behind me, the bag over his mouth but looking, too, his eyes wide with it. Without thinking I put a hand behind his head and pushed the bolus of glue up into his face, squelching it into his mouth and nose and eyes. He twisted away from me, hands flapping at his bagged features, a high, plaintive screech coming from his sticky trap. Sadie was already moving past me, heading for the gate.

'Fuckin ell, Titch.'

I scuttled to keep up, a light, caffeinated swoosh ticking the inside of my head. 'He saw what you did.'

'So?'

Behind us the boy was still screaming, down on his knees, his fingers covering his eyes.

'So. So. So I just did it. I thought it was. I didn't think.' I glanced at her. 'At least I din't stab anyone.'

'What ya talkin about?'
'You. You and him.'
'Dint stab im. Just kneed him in the nads.'
'Oh.'
'Yeah, "oh".'
'What were you doing with the knife, then?'
'I ain't gunna leave it for im to come for us wiv, is it?'

We sat next to each other on the train, the photo on the plastic table in front of us, trying to squeeze as much information from that smiling face as we could. We discussed the way he wore the school sweatshirt, his haircut, the slight lopsidedness of his smile, the earring, whether he was leaning towards his foster mother or she was leaning toward him. When we had run through every angle we could think of we just sat there staring, burning the picture on some internal screen, my own need seemingly as powerful as Sadie's.

'Dun make any sense.'
'What?'
'Any of it. Dun make sense.'
'You mean –'
'People don't jus get mixed up. They ain't jus gi the wrong baby to the wrong muvver.'
'I suppose it can happen. Maybe they got the adoption papers in a muddle. You were all born in the same hospital on the same day. I guess it's not every day that happens.'
'Yeah, but. No. I mean. There's *systems*. Innit?'

Again, Lynda was waiting for us when we got back, anger sharpening her bones, her mouth anus-tight with irritation.
'So where have we *been* today, girls?'
'Just out.'
'Out? I know *out*. Out where?'
'Up town.'
'In-*vest*-igating?'
'Just chillin really.'

'*Chilling?* Chi – I ought. *Chilling.* And did you have fun *chilling?*'

'It were alright.'

We watched her fight herself for control, her fingers fisting up and then extending, her mouth contorting between a snarl and a smile, the room reeking of her perfume.

'I don't think you girls really understand what you're getting yourselves into.'

I preferred to let Sadie deal with Lynda but sometimes the words came unbidden. And when they did they always made things worse.

'What's that supposed to mean?'

'Oh,' she snapped back, settling on the snarl, 'it's the mouse that roared. *Again.* How tiresome. I *mean* there's a lot of interest in you, Tilly dear, and your little problem with having the wrong parents.'

'What does that mean? What do you mean "a lot of interest"?'

'I am just trying to emphasise to you that you are not operating in a vacuum. That you would be advised to tread carefully. That you would be ad-*vised* to take help when and where it's offered. That, in particular, you would be advised to turn up for your auditing and not leave me having to make ex-*cuses* for you. And that if you *are* going to leave me making excuses for you, that you make sure I know what I am excusing you *for.* I don't like feeling I'm being cut out. I can be really quite *na*-sty when I feel cut out.'

'Yeah, but what's all this about "a lot . . ."?'

'Let's just say that Allason's DNA ap-*pears* to have imbued you with a certain *value.* To certain groups of people.'

'So what, Lynda?'

'So sometimes it's best to be worthless.'

'Cool. Cool.' Sadie laid her hand on my arm. 'Thass cool. Can't *belieb* we miss auditin, eh Titch? Won't appen again.'

A smile levered back in place. 'You always were more intelligent than you let on, Allason. But – and I can't help *not*-icing this, taking *note* of this – you still haven't told me where you've been.'

'Told ya. We was chillin. Up town.'

'*Chilling* doing *what* exactly?'

'Window shoppin?'

'Allason, we both know that you and . . .' – indicating me – '*this* do not window shop. If you see something you like you take it. So *where*, I was wondering, *where* are the results of your *chilling*?'

Sadie never looked at me, didn't waver, simply tensed her jaw for a moment and then laughed.

'Bussid, innit? Went to see muh bro's foster parents. They din't know where e was. We came ome. Waste of a day. Waste a money. Shoulda arksed you what to do innit?'

Cautiously: 'Well I'm glad you can see that *now*, anyway. An older, *wi*-ser head. I understand why you perhaps felt you couldn't. But *now* perhaps you'll have learnt your lesson.'

'We ave, innit Titch?'

'Uh, yeah, yes. Yes of course we have, Lynda.'

'You're making me nervous now. Don't *o*-verdo it or I'll start to suspect you're having me on and we'll be back where we started. But *worse*.' She brushed at imaginary ash on her lap, reached into her bag for her cigarettes. 'Why don't you let me put out some *feelers* for you? See if I can track him down? While you just sit tight and serve the terms of your probation and get back to doing the things you're *good* at, like *sourcing* some new goods for me?'

Sadie nodded. 'Deal. Titch?' I nodded, too.

'Don't fuck me about.'

'We ain't.'

'O-*kay*.' Back to her bag again, her hands pulling out a purse, the purse uncatched, a riffle through the notes in there. She pulled the purple edge of a twenty up, pushed it back down again, searched a little longer and drew out a tenner. Held it out to Sadie.

'Go and get yourself a drink tonight. Re-*lax* a little. I'll take care of *ev*-erything.'

'Wha'gwan Lynda?' She had never given us anything before. Everything we'd got we'd earnt. She sighed, smiled her impersonation of a hurt smile, waved the note away.

'You're *so* . . . suspicious. It's a *gift*. Now I have to go. Sit tight. Let me handle it for you.'

''Ardly gun get us a round, that, is it?'

Lynda sighed again, re-opened her purse, pulled out the twenty.

'Very well, here you are. Ah-ah-ah,' fluttering it back from Sadie's outstretched hand. 'Give me the ten back first.'

Our travelling fund partially replenished, we headed back up to London the following morning. Personally I couldn't see the point, but Sadie had a theory. When she herself had tried running away to London she had never made it far from the station she had arrived in. And nearly all the other runaways she met had done the same. 'There or Piccadilly Circus. The resta London dun really exist.'

That she was right became clear as soon as we emerged from Kings Cross tube, the smell of agglomerated fast-food chip fat gusting round us in warm breezes, the vista before us – despite the extensive modifications and refits, the zero tolerance policing, the infinite variety of regeneration strategies – populated solely by desperate people, even the Antipodean backpackers looking lost. Sadie moved through this landscape with a confidence I couldn't hope to mimic, let alone match. As a defence against the humiliation of my tidy former life I habitually chose not to think about Sadie growing up and what she had witnessed, much less what she had participated in. But watching her composure and poise as she interacted with these people reminded me of the vast gap between us. She started with the *Big Issue* seller, presumably on the grounds that someone who had got it together to flog magazines was likely to serve as a more reliable witness. From here she moved on to the lads trying to shift the odd bag of weed, the more presentable of the prostitutes, back to the random beggars, the rough sleepers cocooned in cardboard and soiled blankets, from there a swoop through the rougher prostitutes before finally turning to the translucent ghosts dispensing narcotics to those too hopeless to get hold of them anywhere better.

She took her time with everyone she spoke to, easing into a conversation, trying for a genuine connection with each of them, even the man with a spider's web tattooed across the entirety of his face. After sharing a joke or an observation, usually concerning the dishonesty and stupidity of the feds, she pulled the creased photograph of Marcus from her pocket and asked them to have a look at it. Quietly, persuasively, asked them to really look, explained it was her brother, that she'd never met him, that she thought he might be hanging round here somewhere, asked them to look again, asked them to be absolutely sure. And all of them did it for her. With some I stood watching the thought crawling across their minds, watched as they painstakingly attempted to access databases long since deleted by their life. And I was humbled, I suppose, by the sincerity of their attempts. Or at least I should have been. Perhaps I wasn't ready to be humbled then.

Despite her efforts, though, our morning yielded nothing. No one had seen Marcus. Or, if they had, they hadn't picked him out from any of the other young strays milling through the station and its surroundings. No one knew anything. Why would they? No one, despite their geniune efforts, actually cared. Why should they? We were each of us in transit, our routes inefficiently monitored.

We lunched at McDonalds, a Happy Meal split between us, alternating sucks of Coke with pillow-soft meat and bread, crisp slivers of salted potato mulch our line breaks. We stared absently at the people moving round us, unabashed when our eyes met theirs, eyebrows automatically rising with defiance. The food was gone too quickly and already a red-shirted min-ion was lurking, determined to wipe down our tabletop and see us safely out to the street. Tired, disheartened, we rose and slouched toward the exit.

Sadie, however, stopped, her head jerking back as if her hair had been pulled. With a milky look filling her eyes, giving her a stoned aspect that bore no relation to the certainty of her turn, she moved briskly back to the counter, picking her way between nervous punters whose food couldn't come quick enough.

'Speak to the manager, plea?'

'Happy Meal?'

'The manager.'

'With fries?'

'The manager.'

'You want large drink with that?'

'The man-a-ger. Wanna speak to the man-a-ger.'

'Oh yes. Yes. I see. The *Team Leader*.'

His cap a patchwork of achievement badges, his shirt tucked into his high-waisted slacks, his glasses the chemist-bought psych-bid for quiet authority, the Team Leader came to greet us to one side of the till, paperwork sheafed out above his hands.

'Hello, a pleasure to meet you and to have served you here today. If you're interested in applying to work with us at this branch I should state here and now that we are an employer that looks for and rewards ambition. We don't consider ourselves a' – and here he crooked two fingers on each of his hands – '"fast food" outlet. We are purveyors of healthy, quality fare for people who demand great service, great value and great convenience. So this isn't a job you should be thinking about if you're just hoping to hang around and eat some of our delicious fries . . .'

Sadie raised a hand, stopped him.

'We're lookin for im. The boy not the lady. You ever seen im?'

'Oh, I see. I see. Well, it's not really my place to and, then, for another thing, isn't this sort of thing best handled by the police and, if, then, a law enforcement officer were to come in here and ask, well then, of course . . .'

Sadie kept the picture just where it was, a few centimetres from the end of his well-punctuated nose. We watched his boss-eyes focus on the surface, witnessed the pinkening of his cheeks flood out to his ears and neck, heard his nervous, dismissive snort.

'Oh yes. Yes. I know him. I know him alright.' Began shaking his head.

'Did e work ere?'

'Work?' A camped-up cackle. 'No. I don't. Think. *So.* Not in the way you mean. I had to throw him out of the toilets. On more than one occasion. On a number of occasions, in fact. Haven't seen him for a few weeks. I suppose he finally got the message. I will not tolerate these premises being used for, for, for anything other than that which the company has designated they be used for. Now if that's all . . .'

He was already moving away from us, his contempt written across his rounded back, our only lead certain we were not on his team. I felt something of my mother inside me, insidious, embarrassing.

'Excuse me.' He stopped, thrown by the stridently bourgeois note in my voice. 'It may have escaped your attention but we have just eaten lunch here and as such we are your customers.' Then, really beginning to project my words for the benefit of the queuers to our left: 'And if you aren't prepared to discuss calmly and rationally with us a complaint about the standard of food on offer on your premises, then I will have to take up the issue with your head off–' He was back with us before I could finish, ushering us away from the tills, a scared, angry, solicitous look mangling his face.

'What do you want from me?' The sneer long gone.

'We want to know where he is.'

'Well, how should I know?'

'Well think. Did you ever see him with anyone, did you ever see him anywhere else?'

'Well, I don't know. I don't know. I really don't know. Try the Gents lavs at the station if I were you. That's all I can think of. Now please just go without a scene.'

'Well thank you. So kind of you.' And we linked arms and bounced out of the place, the mesmerised-looking Poles and Ghanaians behind the counter, the Chinese and Lithuanians in their branded hairnets, all trying to control their smirks.

We set ourselves up opposite the entrance to the Gents toilets, first pretending to graze through the magazines near the entrance to Smiths, and then, when the security guard had made it amply clear that our presence wasn't welcome, moving our weight from foot to foot in front of Upper Crust. At last, a space opened up on the bench and we took it in turns to sit on the designedly uncomfortable metal lattice, our bums being chipped. A gush of people flooded backward and forward through the barriers, each of them melding with the next, my eyes itching with the effort of watching, no space to blink.

Among it all, only one person achieved any degree of individuation. A boy about our age dressed just as we were and as all the others our age were, who vaulted the barriers with such grace and lightness that even I couldn't fail to spot him. He must have stayed in the toilets for around fifteen minutes and then appeared again, floated over those barriers and vanished off out of sight. Another ten minutes later and he was back. Once again we watched him approach the barriers, a nonchalant shuffle and the spring over to the far side. Time passed, Sadie tensed forward a little, her watching a gradual rise in intensity. Then, when just long enough had passed that it had become hard to imagine what it was he might have been doing in there, out he sauntered, his vault as pristine as all the others. Sadie jerked up from the bench, hesitated, sat again, the boy already gone.

'Thass im. We need a lickle word wid im.'

'Shouldn't we get after him then?'

'Nah. E'll be back.'

Sure enough, like an elf in a fairytale, the boy reappeared soon after and glided past the barriers for the third visit of our vigil, his movements as smooth and incomprehensible to me as ever. Sadie stood, stretched, and led me over towards the toilets, showed me where and how to stand to watch for his re-emergence, positioned herself against a wall, leant there, glazed with a sleepy indifference.

As I saw him coming I gave Sadie the nod and she immediately swung round and began strolling away. The boy sailed over the barrier, turned past me and continued his predetermined route, quickly catching up with my sauntering friend. At the exact moment of his overtaking, she changed direction sharply as if remembering something forgotten and caused an abrupt – and quite brutal – intersection of their paths. I stood and watched as they brushed at themselves and began to talk, noticed the way she flicked her head, the meeting of her hand and the back of his arm, her unwavering attempt at eye contact. I observed her sudden blush, the flutter of eyelids as she finally broke her gaze and looked at the floor, the way she joined her hands and raised her shoulders to make her torso heart-shaped, her head bobbing a simper in front of it. And, quicker than you could imagine possible, they had reached an agreement. They nodded, she turned and pointed me out, waved me over.

'Titch, Dave, Dave, Titch. Me an Dave fought we should get a drink.'

'N'you're buying, yeah?' Dave's personal history distilled into a twitch which made it look as if he were trying to shake off a malignant wink. His genetics little improving matters.

'Course. Always buyin, innit Titch?'

Two bottles of L'ush Velvet Club Mix and a pint of lager with a barley-wine top (apparently nicknamed a Gordon Brown) and all our money was gone. We sat on already unstable blondwood chairs at an already rickety blondwood table beneath a gigantic skylight dappled with pigeon shit. Dave had led us to the nearest chainpub to sell cheap drinks in bright, aspirational surroundings. We, along with the rest of the clientele, were there for the cheap drinks. Cameras validated our existence. A drunk pissed himself in a nearby armchair.

Carefully sipping, we watched Dave glug and gargle at his pint, his chin wet with it, his teeth independent of one another when he threw us a smile. When he was halfway down he slapped a hand on the tabletop, rocking it toward him and almost upsetting our bottles.

'Gorra piccie then?' The scouse in his voice coming and going, a fading inheritance.

Sadie took it from her pocket slowly, glancing down at the image before extending it to him. Then, as he reached to take it, pulling it back again.

'Careful wi it. Only one I got.' The look on her face reinforcing the point, he nodded his agreement with a momentary solemnity.

'Marky Mark! Yeah, that's im. Marky Mark. Me main man Marky Mark. Lookin a wee bit straight but that's Marky Mark alright. Couldn't miss im.'

'For real? You know im?'

'Know im? We was partners. Me an Marky. Me an me main man, Marky. More'n partners. We was like brothers. Bredren.'

Marcus, it seemed, had a lot of brothers in addition to his single sister.

'Where is e?'

'Business darlin. Partners one day, next day there's like a boardroom coop. Fuckin aggressive takeover an whatnot. Times change. Things move on.'

'But *bredren*, man. Bredren's for life.'

'You wanna ask Marky about that, pet. You wanna ask Marky Mark.'

'I do wanna.'

'You do.'

'So . . . ?'

' . . . wha?'

'So' – a little irritation slipping in now, or at least beginning to show – 'where is e?'

'Search me.'

' . . . ?'

'Fucked off, asn e?'

'Whatcha mean?'

'Said e gorra meet someone an I ain't seen im since.'

'Wha? Musta said sutt'n about who it were?'

'Nada.'

'Nutt'n?'

The boy gently fingered a shining red sore on the side of his nose, eyed Sadie through narrowed slits.

'Gorra smoke?'

Sadie took one from the pack, her teeth crunching together, flicked it into his lap, from where he picked it up and unsuccessfully tried to flip it into his mouth, rescuing it from the floor between his feet. Snugged it up behind his ear, rested his elbow on the back of the chair and crossed his legs, so that he twisted away from us into feigned thought.

'I like youse. I really do.'

'Ever feel like y'eard it before, Titch?'

'An I wanna elp youse.'

'So elp den.'

He reached forward, lifted his pint and sucked at it, put it down and examined the level, quizzical. Looked over at Sadie's bottle, pointed.

'Looks nice. Can I ave a taste?'

Almost before she'd nodded he lifted it to his lips and sunk a swallow, his tic seguing into the kind of neck thrust caused by cocktails of cheap spirits and aspartame. Nodded appreciatively, eyes wet with it. Signalled his wish to add the remains to his pint by tilting it above his glass, his eyebrows bouncing. Sadie's nod small, definitive, vaguely threatening. The glass refilled, he leaned back, crossing his legs again, his smile the ugliest sight in a room dedicated to ugliness.

'Ampstud.'

His eyes flickered between us, checking to see if we believed him.

'Thass all e told me. Gorra go an see some contact up in Ampstud. Few weeks back. Ain't seed im since.'

He watched us watch each other.

'That's all I got. Ampstud.'

She continued to look at me, sighed, smiled.

'Deeja vu. Spooky, innit?'

'All technolog[ies] can plausibly be regarded as weapons.' CTRL is the technology of new technologies, that is, it is the organising principle, the *systematic treatment* of new technologies. And the organising principle of new technologies is the growth of new technologies through the input of data. We are the data. Or, if you like, the cannon fodder.

Extract from *Twenty-ninth Communiqué of the Vanished*

7

It was dark by the time we got back to Valerie Charles's house. Dave had taken pity on us and, despite our protestations that we had to get going, bought us another drink. Or, at least, scrounged it from the woman behind the bar, who could have been his sister, his lover or, most plausibly, both. And, having bought us a drink, he seemed to feel he owned us, did own us, in fact. So we sat quietly and listened to fractured anecdotes of bravado and derring-do which somehow always managed to skim round the central truth of his life, which was that he hired out his various orifices to middle-aged and elderly men who had found no better way to sate their appetites. To hear him you would have thought he was some sort of hero. But then we all want to be heroes and none of us ever come very close.

It was dark by the time we got to back to Valerie Charles's house, dark and cold. The first night of winter accompanied us, crunching beneath our feet, ghosting up round our faces in great gusts of freezing breath. We were, as is traditional for teenagers, underdressed for the conditions. Shivering, our hands budded in their sleeves, huddled in on one another, our postures unchanging, our arms linked, we trundled round into the gravel drive and approached the front door. Sadie unsheathed one finger, reached up, pressed Valerie's bell. We listened to its ring, intimately close and impossibly distant. Waited, our feet taking turns to remove their thinned soles from the icy step, even the silence sounding arctic, the big city hum a glacier moving.

Sadie stepped forward, placed her forearms to each side of the reinforced glass, rested her face on them and peered through into the illuminated hallway beyond. I stood behind her imagining how lovely she would look from the side, the light picking out her bones. She stayed there until a shiver wriggled up her spine, stepped back, rang the bell again. Still nothing. We hovered, internalising the cold, baffled by the absence. Sadie took her phone from her pocket, held it up to the light and squinted at it.

'Not back from work yet probly. Less go round da block. Come.'

So we circled, trying to pass time but always speeding up, our strolling breaking again and again into a trot, the off-licence, the curry house, the pub, all glowing invitingly, throbbing with electric bar fires, scalding hot radiators, coal-look fireplaces with genuine flames. But you can't shoplift warmth and to inhabit it you need money. We kept moving.

'Maybe she went for a drink after work. Shall we go round the block again?'

This time we slowed down only as we passed the doors, even the light from the windows taking the chill off us a little, the dogshit on the pavement unsquashable now, the patch of grass on the corner crystallised. Coming round too fast for there to be any point in crunching up the drive again, we repeated the route, back where we started with no discernible lapse in time. The bell rang in an emptiness that grew vaster with every try.

'Probly gone cinema. Or out for dinner.' With no need for the suggestion we started walking.

I have no idea how many times we made our circuit. After a while I was dizzy with it, my toes, my ears, my nose all numbed, my teeth, even. It felt like we were staggering now – just popping out, may be some time – the huddle colder than the air around us. As we approached the pub again, Sadie pulled me to the door, a frown spiking her face.

'Fuck it. Gotta be someone'll buy us a drink.'

There wasn't. The pub was airy and bright, the clientele well dressed and older, infinitely older than us. There were no groups of men, no solo drinkers at the bar, just happy, well-adjusted, mixed-sex groups of workmates and friends chatting loudly and confidently about subjects we didn't care for, or, frankly, understand. On the other hand, no one turned and eyed us when we came in, nobody stopped talking, nobody even noticed we had entered, least of all the Aussie barstaff pouring glass after glass of expensive white wine. We were invisible here, too lowly even to register.

Sadie led me to a table in the process of being quit and we hung about for a moment while they swished their long brown coats on, flung elegant scarves over well-kept necks, kissed the air around each other's faces and finally, regally, a stately procession of goodbyes and see you soons and laughs and agreements, left. Then we were down on the stools, our hands burning as we conglomerated the remains from five wine glasses into two and hunched down low over the table, the rest of the room closing over us so that we were traceless, fundamentally absent, just us and a drink that made us cough, our eyes water.

We stayed there as long as we could, scavenging, eking out an existence, until eventually one of the black-t-shirted, black-aproned staff, his fingers glittering with dirty champagne flutes, stopped, double-took, treble-took, as if we had materialised in front of him.

'How old are you?'

'Eighteen.'

'Can I see your identity cards?'

'Not on us.'

'You know that's against the law, don't you? I'm afraid I'm going to have to ask you to leave . . .'

We didn't bother to argue, just gave him the finger as we reached the door, a pointless act as by then we'd been re-swallowed by indifference.

The house looked just the same when we got back there, but I consoled myself that I knew it would. It was a house, after all, and they don't change that much.

I think we both already sensed that no one was going to answer the door, however late we called. We rang and we rang and we rang. Our bodies began to shudder and warp again under the blanket of cold, our heads jangled with the bell, became the bell, two hollow spaces with a clapper juddering between them. Sadie seemed to keep her finger there, driving the sound into us, for minutes, for blocks of minutes, for hours. When she finally pulled it back into her sleeve, the noise carried on in my head, disappointed in her.

Eventually, when she had rung enough, Sadie walked away from the house a little, limbo-ed herself back a bit and looked at the upper windows. Turned and walked to the pavement, jutted her head left then right, left then right. Stood and listened intently. Suddenly flooded back past me with a signal that I was to follow, past the door, past the dark bay window and round to the gate at the side of the building. Clicked the latch up and applied her weight, a little give there but no opening. I stood, not exactly baffled but certainly dumbfounded, while Sadie pushed my hands together, knitted my fingers for me, bent me floorward then, with her hand still on my shoulder, placed her cold, wet, muddy, leaf-mulched Reebok in the inverted, vaulted ceiling of my palms and launched herself. I staggered then remembered myself, pulling my arms upward, but Sadie was already gone. In a blink she had braced her arms, swung a leg over, pulled the other after and silently dropped from view.

I wheeled guiltily round to the road, pushing my back against the cold brick of the house, hoping to find an unoccupied shadow there, wanting this all to be over, to go. I could feel tears building in me, as if I couldn't cope when separated from Sadie even by a single wall. I didn't know whether to run or to call out for her, to tell her to be careful, to say it wasn't worth it, to beg her to climb back over to me. The bolt on the far side shot through my dilemmas, the opening gate mocked my head-whines. Sadie's hand loomed out of the darkness, grabbed my arm and pulled me through.

We swayed in the silence of the other side, the moon making us suddenly insubstantial, the yellow of the street lights left behind. Our breath mingled into one lost spirit, my contribution the heavier despite Sadie's exertions, and I clung to her sleeve as she stepped quietly down the path, her feet laid with careful certainty, my shuffling behind her the only sound. We turned into the garden and found ourselves in a fairy tale – old-fashioned, terrifying. The grass was white, preserved in ice, the only contrast the black blood spots where a cat had walked across it. The trees and bushes loomed above us, sparkling, too, but the magic in it was indifferent, impersonal. The house remained dark. Somewhere in the distance I could hear a man laughing at his own joke, his dinner party smiling with him, all this, this icy trespass, a black square beyond tasteful shutters.

Sadie went straight to the French windows, bunched her sleeve over her hand and used the stump to pull the handle down and towards her. The door opened, the moon's reflection flashing across it. With a jerk of her chin she signalled me past her, gently pushing me into the room as she shadowed me, quietly closing the door behind us.

My shivers took on a different quality as I stepped through. I had come to think of shoplifting as normality, but going in to someone's house seemed another kind of game, a dangerous provocation. Fear shuddered through me.

'How'd you know the door'd be open?' The whisper strangled.

Her hand came up to my lips, the touch of her finger as smooth and cold as a 99, the jagged set of her brow and widening of her eyes caught in my mind still, more vivid than anything I did yesterday. I didn't want her to move, so I shaped to speak again, just an intake of breath really, but enough to hold it there. I wasn't bothered by the answering shrug, the huskily whispered response.

'Juss a guess. People's always leavin em open.'

We moved across the room searching for familiar landmarks but there were none. No sofa, no coffee table, no armchair, no shelves, no books, no patterned rug. No pictures, no teacups, no tidy line of CDs. Just a dark, empty room. Only the view through the windows could convince me we were in the place we had visited before.

The rest of the flat was the same. There was no bed in either of the bedrooms, no towels in the bathroom. No fridge or cooker in the kitchen, no carpet on the floors. No ornaments on the windowsills, no photos. Emptied, the flat seemed smaller than it had on that previous visit, less sumptuous, more threadbare. We moved from room to room with caution melting into disbelief then apathy. We passed each other, our paths crossed, we milled and individually moped, our sense of direction shot. The flat offered us no clues, no hope of leads, no resolution, just a blankness of walls. The doors led nowhere. The ceilings closed in.

Gradually I realised I needed to pee. The bathroom was a windowless box off the windowless hall. Without a thought, I groped for a switch, found the hanging cord wrapping itself round my wrist and pulled. The extractor fan boomed into action, a thundering roar which seemed to shake the ceiling, rip at the night, blast our careful mission into a million tiny pieces. I yanked at the cord again, but while darkness returned, absolute now for my momentarily brightened eyes, the fan kept on rolling, as intense as any burglar alarm. I felt Sadie come up behind me.

'Shit. Sorry. Sorry.'

She reached out and pulled the light back on.

'Worry bout it. No one ere is it?'

I made a tight-legged dash for the toilet, pulled down my trackpants and knickers and lowered myself onto the seat. Sadie remained leaning on the doorframe looking abstractedly at the shower. I imagined sinking beneath hot water, the stinging above my hands.

'Weird innit?'

'Er, *yeah*. It's really weird. I mean, how long ago was it we were here? A few days? She didn't look like she was moving then, did she?'

'Nuh-uh. S'weird.'

'I mean, there wasn't anything in boxes was there? Nothing like that? There's no SOLD sign up outside.'

Sadie looked at her feet.

'So what we gunna do?'

Sadie pulled her phone from her pocket again, squinted at the display.

'Late innit? Think we should jus stay ere. Case she comes back.'

All the cold in the flat came to huddle round me. She wasn't coming back. That much was clear. We were trespassing on territory we didn't understand. The woman had evaporated. We should get out of here. We had to. My skin trying to walk off me.

But then the buts came flooding in. The woman was Sadie's mother. We were expecting to find Sadie's brother here, too. Her family. Although my own instincts were to get out, to run back through the gate to the road beyond, to keep going by bus and by train and by foot until I was at last safely cocooned in the routines of our bedsit life, I knew we'd have to stay. Sadie wasn't ready to give up on genetics yet.

We hunkered down together in a corner of the living room, facing the garden. We didn't smoke as we couldn't find so much as a saucer to use as an ashtray and weren't ready to make a mess of the place yet. While the temperature inside was undoubtedly better than outside, it still wasn't comfortably warm. We plaited our arms again and Sadie, in one of those moments of vulnerability that I cherished unhealthily, lowered her head onto my shoulder. Then we sat and tried to sleep.

A long while passed until the change came in Sadie's breathing and I remained as alert as at any point in that long, disorientating day. I couldn't move without disturbing Sadie and that was the last thing I wanted to do. I stroked her hair for a moment but wasn't comfortable with how it made me feel. I thought of my own family, of my mother and brother, my father. I tried to run through everything that had happened to us, to find the sense in it, to spot whatever it was that we'd missed. As if there was a key and only one door to unlock, my need for a simple mystery mocking me. And so eventually, with no sense of its approach, my neck creased, one shoulder held in a perpetual jut, I slept, too.

When I finally drifted from my dreams, it was with my mind already trying to recall what those dreams were about, so that they themselves seemed to be nothing more than this attempt to remember, an infinite regression. While we slept we had tumbled away from the wall and now lay twined next to it, the parquet sticking to my cheek. Cold and stiff, refusing to admit I was awake, I tried to shuffle my body closer to the glimmer of warmth Sadie was still emitting. She huffed and turned away from me. I opened my eyes.

I hadn't expected to see a pair of feet in front of me. A pair of boots. Large, gnarly, army boots, the hiss and scuff of their slight readjustments on the floor. My body spasmed up, the arm Sadie was sleeping on coming out from underneath her and sending her rolling and groping. It didn't take me long to realise this wasn't Valerie Charles. Just long enough to look up and see the black combat trousers, the black leather jacket, the black gloves.

'Okay Tilly, I want you to be calm,' she said, her voice light and relaxed, a slight smoker's roughness to it. 'I'm not here to hurt you. You, too, Allason. It's very important that you keep calm and think very carefully before you do anything. I just want you to sit next to each other on the floor there. Can you do that?' As if she were on a morning telly sofa instead of offering threats. Which were all these could be. Carefully we pulled ourselves back against the wall, just our elbows touching.

The woman crouched in front of us, all her weight on the balls of her feet. As she lowered herself she unzipped her jacket and allowed us a glimpse of the shoulder holster underneath.

'Good. That's really good. I'm sorry to sneak up on you like this while you were asleep, but I'm afraid you're just going to have to believe that I'm here for your benefit.'

It was hard to tell how old she was. She looked like a cartoon assassin – the bleached blond hair pulled back into a scraggy topknot, the nose piercing, a tattoo just visible at the base of her neck. But her skin had a stretched and papery quality to it and her smile was utterly lacking in the easy charm you'd expect from a comic book heroine.

'For now it doesn't matter who I am or where I come from. But there are people outside this building waiting for you. And I mean just outside. And if those people get hold of you it won't be very pleasant. My job for now is to get you safely out of here without those people even knowing. Nod if you understand.'

I don't know if Sadie responded, but I certainly did. It hadn't sounded like a request.

'Good. Okay. So here's what we're going to do. In a moment I'm going to ask you to stand up. Then we're all going to walk quietly to the front door of the flat. If you make sudden moves or start shouting or screaming then it's going to make the situation a lot more complicated than it already is. Once again, nod if you understand.

'Good. I'm Anna by the way. It's always a pleasure to work with girls with their heads screwed on right. So now then. Could you slowly and carefully stand up for me? Very good. Now I just want you to walk very slowly and carefully out of here and down the hall to the front door and stop there. Allason, you first, and then you, Tilly. Nice and slow and calm. That's it. That's great. That's really good. And stop there. Perfect.'

I found myself so caught up in the mechanics of this rescue, how it felt like television instead of life, that I forgot to be scared. Anna marched past us, placed her back flat against the wall, slowly eased open the door. Inched the minimum of her body round the frame until she had established a sightline, swung back. Beckoned us through with the tiniest tilt of her head.

'Follow me. Nice and easy now.'

She led us away from the front door and up the stairs, our feet thundering and clumping, hers soundless despite the size of those boots, every movement of her body precise, calibrated. And, whereas our faces were drawn behind us again and again, our eyes fluttering dust up in the light coming through the front door, she never once looked back, never hesitated as she took us up the three flights to the top of the building.

There on the highest landing, she skipped up onto the banister, poised like a ballet dancer above that drop, the wood beneath her pointed toe spiralling downward in vertigo perspective. Pushed up the hatch in the ceiling, extended the long sweep of her body a little more and pulled a ladder down. Jumped with it as it fell, her feet reaching the floor just before its own metal stumps hit, the whole operation managed without a noise. Still without talking she signalled to us to climb.

Sadie stopped, her shoulders dropping, a slap of breath ripping from her, a theatrical half-shrug.

'The fuck this all about?' Her voice booming into the vacuum of our retreat, expanding to fill it, me flinching back from the sheer scale of it. Our escort, "Anna", raised a gloved hand to her mouth, momentarily widened her eyes and gave a nod towards the door of the uppermost flat.

'So what?' Sadie bristling now, her lip curling, she took a step toward the door. 'So. Fuckin. What?'

Calmly, a flatness to her tone: 'You're going to have to trust me, Allason. Isn't she, Tilly?'

'Why? Why should I trust ya? WHO THE FUCK ARE YA?'

She kept looking straight at Sadie but her right hand seemed to glide over where she'd deliberately shown us her hidden gun.

'Well, what choice have you got?'

They faced each other, a before and after picture from an unlikely advert. My head felt like it was being pressed in on itself, my eyeballs ready to flop out onto my cheeks, my ears forced back down the stairs to where I was sure I could distinguish the sound of someone picking a lock, of someone sliding into the hallway, of someone unholstering firearms. I pushed between the two of them and started up the ladder, its metal creaks my only exclamations. When I reached the top and poked my head back through the hatch, neither of them had moved, only their dumbstruck fizzogs bobbing up at me, plastic poodles in a car's back window.

'You coming then?'

The dizzying light out on the roof, the pitch of it, my feet constantly slipping away from each other, the rapid diminution of the world laid out below me, trees' trunks dwindling, everything leaning back from me, back from this unsupported surface I found myself clinging to, back, back to give me uninterrupted access to the distant ground beneath. All of it turning slowly to emphasise its three dimensions, its solidity, the bird moving across, the woman walking her dog, the man raking leaves in his employer's garden. The frosted ground as hard as concrete and so far down.

I didn't fall. None of us fell. We skidded across that angled rink for an age, every movement apparently our last, witnessed only by chimney pots and the width of the sky. Until at last, when I was sure I couldn't go on, when I was ready to just lie as close to the slates as I could and stay there until I froze or was captured by our supposed pursuers, at last we reached an ending and over that ending found a drop of only a metre or two onto a neat roof terrace, the bushes trimmed to echo their pots, the garden furniture artfully aged. I wanted to stop and regain some degree of composure, but Anna was now ready to show us something.

'Okay, look. You see that van over there with the tinted windows? Yeah? And that guy washing the windows opposite? And those two in that car over there? And watch this one walking along the road with his newspaper. Watch him, wait for his arm to go up to his face. There. People don't usually talk to their wrist do they? There's a whole team down there waiting for you to come out. And if you're not out soon they'll go in. Okay? Satisfied?'

'Dun prove nutt'n. Jus people innit?'

'Okay. Well you go back and ask them. We're getting out of here. Aren't we, Tilly?'

'I just need to sit down for a moment,' My own lameness, my lack of suitability for this sort of situation, all too apparent to me.

'We really need to get moving now.'

'Ah whateva. Guess we ain't got no choice. Where next?'

Anna walked over to an iron ladder which rolled from sight over the side of the building. Sadie followed. 'Come, Titch.' Gritting my teeth, sick but not quite ready to give up, I followed over the edge.

The ladder led down onto a cast-iron fire escape, the fire escape, eventually, into a back garden, bigger than the one we had left behind when we started our upward journey. Anna strode through the garden, Sadie hurrying to walk alongside, I a couple of paces behind but scuttling to catch up when I saw, flapped out from beneath a bush, the four brown-and-black legs of a large dog. I tapped at Anna's sleeve, pointed.

'Don't worry. I neutralised it before I came to get you.'

I stopped again, needing a moment to compute this one.

'You killed the dog?'

She turned to me, smiling with exasperation. 'It's sleeping. I drugged it. I didn't shoot it.' Kept walking.

'Wouldn't have cared if you had.'

On the other side of the gate at the bottom of the garden, a big black SMV, its windows as dark as those of our supposed enemy, its wheelbase as wide as a truck's, the words *Princess of Persia* swirling in silver across its boot. She bleeped the doors open and the sound of those locks thunking back took me straight to Yarleigh Falls. Perhaps they did Sadie, too.

'Right, you two hop in the back and get down on the floor.'

'Nah man. I'ma sit up front wi you.'

'Sorry, it's not safe. I want you down on the floor in the back.'

'For what?'

'In case you're seen.'

'The windows a blacked out, ya norman.'

'Just get in the back.'

'What, so I carn see where you took us? Nah, I'ma sit up front or I'ma walk.'

'We don't have time to argue.'

'I do.'

Anna turned to appeal to me but was met by my head shaking. Puffed and made to punch the car.

'Alright, get in the front, then. But at least keep low in the seat. Okay?'

'You got a stereo?'

'Don't touch the stereo.'

'F'real? It special then?' Sadie clambered into the passenger seat, waited for Anna to walk round the vehicle and climb in next to her. 'Yer only friend?'

'Just sit there quietly. Okay?'

'Easy. Easy man.' Sadie turned to me, grinning as I slid into the throne of the back seat, tipped me a wink. 'Dyke innit? Dun like bein arksed about their equipment.'

'I'm warning you . . .'

'Can we just go?' My request, though limp, had the desired effect, the car lurching forward and out from the lane onto the road.

'Din mean to piss ya off, Anna,' Sadie offered as we moved. 'Got nutt'n against dykes.'

The force of the sudden movement clamping me back against the seat, other vehicles rushing up on me to the left and

153

the right, their headlights dipping down toward the tarmac, our arc through their midst slashed fabric.

'Enough.'

Sadie craned back round to me, her grin coming loose at the edges. 'Better buckle up, Titch.' With which, for the first time in my experience, she reached for her own belt, a slow long pull over, her left arm stirring a concrete-thick potion.

I followed her lead, the quickness of my movements lending my own attempt a stuttering obsequiousness. The world on the other side of our darkened windows moved impossibly fast, a film with every other frame removed. Sadie waited, her eyes unfocused, stoned-looking, until I finally clicked the belt into place. Turned back to Anna.

'You ain't gunna rape us are ya?'

'I'm warning you –'

'Put some sexy music on the stereo an rape us . . . ?' Her hand reached out to the fascia, deliberately too slow, caressing the buttons there with advert fingers, the subtext wasted on me, sunk there in the back, the world still accelerating beyond us. Snap. Anna's hand clamped on Sadie's wrist.

'That's it.'

Sadie trying to yank free, failing, of course failing, this kid fighting a trained killer or copper or kidnapper, teeth showing, anger shaping her face, the stereo flicked on in it all, some chat show on Radio 4 booming out at rude-bwoy volume and then last, last in this mix, the grace note, from my throat, unbidden and unprecedented, a high, long, sustained screech. Two faces turned to me, their mouths spilling open.

How long would it have taken them to follow my eyes back over their shoulders and through the windscreen if I hadn't pointed? Long enough that there would have been no time for the swerve, our bodies following behind, the attempted readjustment, the readjustment to the readjustment, both her hands occupied now. A chaos of images put together wrong, ordering and angles shot to pieces. The punch, all air forcibly removed from me and scattered miles from my heaving body, sound cut out, the pain instant and complete, as if I was just its wrapping. Continuing for so long, longer even than my howl, longer than my life, longer than the history of the entire planet, this one desperate attempt at a gasp dragging and dragging, a cut-out-and-keep guide to futility. Until the moment arrived when I gave up trying and resigned myself to never breathe again, settled back into moist red oblivion. The same moment, of course, that my body relented and air once again stroked my alveoli, the noise of my reinflation lost amongst the sudden conversation of sirens and car alarms and honking horns.

'Titch. Titch. Titch. Titch. Titch.'

I opened my eyes. Sadie was leaning over me, her face very pale, a fingernail of blood poking from a nostril.

'Titch. We gotta go.'

Anna seemed to be praying to her steering wheel, her forehead resting on it, words bubbling silently from her mouth. Beyond the windows, a blather of people, the new snarl of our bonnet, steam rising, something from the effects department of a post-apocalypse movie.

'Titch. We gotta go. We gotta go. Undo ya belt.'

My fingers flapped round my chest, blubbered lumps.

'Fuck's sake.'

As she leant through the gap – my hands fluttering toward her of their own volition, trying to pull her into me – one drop of red, so dark it was almost unrecognisable, fell in a perfect circle on my palm, inveigled itself into the channels it found. Then, with the sound of a flying dagger embedding in wood, the belt clicked open and I felt myself floating free and Sadie was suddenly outside the car waving at me through my window, so I waved back and I watched her pointing from wherever I was deep in this pool until gradually, so gradually, as if I was swimming up towards a surface that swam up at more or less the same pace as me, I realised she was pointing at the catch, wanted me to undo the lock. And I did. And the next moment she had dragged me from the seat and was reassuring the concerned folks who loomed toward me that I was fine and keeping me moving and moving, my legs flipping and flapping across each other's path.

The rubberneckers seemed to close up behind us, accelerating film of a wound, until our passing itself was lost and we turned a corner and were lost and we staggered down the street, drunk on impact, my sight anchored by the browning blot on my hand.

Welcome, then, to the low-intensity dystopia which, with varying degrees of awareness, we all inhabit. Which we have no choice but to inhabit, as it happens. Our souls are not merely owned by CTRL, but created by CTRL, validated by CTRL, animated by CTRL. There are no cross-roads to go to, no choices to be made.

Extract from *Thirty-seventh Communiqué of the Vanished*

8

It felt like we were going in circles. How were we to know that in actuality we had dropped another level, that we were to keep dropping, spiralling down, all our assumptions being reversed and then reversed again? How could anyone predict that? How would a child even know it could happen? To the extent I had indulged in speculation as to the geometry of my future life, I had always seen it as a line plotted steadily upward, an uncomplicated ascent equidistant to both axes.

Off the coach, through the streets, along our road, up the steps to the door, through the door, down the hall to our door, keys from pocket, keys in the lock, open the door, into the room and Lynda there to meet us, the weather different, the lighting, the time of day, all of these subtleties lost beneath the bleak shell of sameness. Her smile so tiny it was barely there, her laugh so soundless it only manifested in the patterns of her smoke.

'Look what the cat's dragged in.'

We fell into the room, hunger, fear and exhaustion pulling our legs from under us, the thin carpet, the narrow bed, the converging, jerry-built walls, all of it made wonderful by our desperation, all of it made homely, our eyes nestling in every imperfection.

'No point sitting down. You need to pack. Quickly.' Her voice dry enough to crumble the walls. 'You wouldn't listen to Aunty Lynda would you? You wouldn't listen. Oh no, you *al*-ways know best. Well, now you've made a *mess*. A right royal mess. You have upset some very important people. I've tried my best to shield you from the *re*-percussions of your actions, but no, you would not be shielded.'

We stood there panting, cornered, waterworks on overtime, our eyes reservoirs moments before a terror attack.

'Ya jokin?'

'Do I look like I'm joking? Do you *hon*-estly think I've nothing better to do than to *joke* with you? Now let's get packed and get out of here. *Please*.'

I think it was the last word that terrified me most. And presumably Sadie, too, for we did as she said, knickers and socks and t-shirts plunged into matching binliners in a frenzy of grasping, as if we were robbing our own home. Our former home? The realisation slowing us until we stood, wilting, the black sacks at our feet.

'Can we just get a cup of tea before we go?'

'No,' rising in her ratcheting way and grinding her filter down into the ashtray with unquestionable finality.

'Where we goin?'

'You'll see.'

'Are we coming back?'

She looked around before she spoke, something close to tenderness seeming to enter her voice. 'It's not a great loss, is it?'

'But are we?'

Shaking her head, more in amazement than in reply, she turned to the door and staggered her way through.

Perhaps in reading my account you're struck by how often I attribute to Sadie emotions that could only have been mine. I can't offer any real justification for this habit, except to say that this was how it worked. We were synched, our brainwaves intertwined, our thoughts, our feelings, our actions all mirroring each other's. To separate me out from Sadie seems far more dishonest than attributing my inner world to her. She *made* my inner world. How many times did I reach for a cigarette to find Sadie offering me one? How many times did we both burst from silence into laughter at the same moment? How many times did I begin to speak only to find Sadie already articulating my thought? We echoed and amplified each other, time lags minimal, a single circuit. Either that or I was just another needy, delusional teenager. I guess they're pretty much the same thing.

'Whass gwanin?' There it was again. Lynda had been circling round Coalville's ring road for half an hour, gradually getting the hang of the roundabouts, beginning to ease through the traffic less jarringly, but nevertheless generating an increasing crush of tension.

'Wai-*ting*.'

'For wha?'

'None of your *bees*-wax.'

'Well it kind of is,' I offered, 'if we have to sit in the car with you.'

Then her phone rang and we were too busy cowering helplessly away from potential accidents, trying to reverse that lurch across the lanes using only the power of our frightened faces, our four arms braced on the dashboard, Sadie's arse forcing down hard on me.

'Yes? Uhuh. Uhuh. *Yuhuh*. Should be . . . two minutes?'

We traversed the DFS car park like a drunk closing in on dropped change, a series of wobbly circles refusing to join up. And at the nominal centre, another SMV, just like the one we were in earlier that day (or was it the day before?) only with its bonnet undamaged. Leaning up against it, growing larger and somehow more real with each pass, our old friend Anna, a white square of lint sticking-plastered to her forehead, her right eye purple and lending her, in this light, an undead aspect.

'Shit.' A veteran of a thousand flights, Sadie's fingers clasped the door's handle long before mine had stopped flapping from the fright (tucked through her armpits and no doubt giving our waiting host the impression of a panicked teenage Shiva). All to no purpose, as it turned out, the plastic latch thwacking back into place, the door unmoved.

'Central locking,' Lynda explained aridly. 'One of the first cars to be built with it as standard.'

'Bitch.'

'Allason, if you weren't so ignorant I would be tempted to *slap* you.'

'Bitch.'

'Oh *dear*.' The car leapt to a stop, beyond the glass Anna's hand rising involuntarily to her forehead, a peevish smile forced half-heartedly onto her face. The engine cut, we sat in the wash of silence, the world growing out from us. I craned my neck around hoping for witnesses but there were none.

'Before I release the locks, let me explain.' She paused to light a cigarette. Continued. 'Anna and I are trying to *help* you. Luckily for you, des-*pite* your actions Anna is *still* willing to try and help you. It was me who sent her to get you in the first place. For once, listen to me. You're in very great danger. I have no reason to make this up. Anna is your *best chance*. So when I unlock the doors, please *try* not to do anything stupid.'

'The fuck ya sayin? What fuckin danger?'

'There isn't time to explain.'

'This is bullshit.'

'I don't appreciate being sworn at just because you find it difficult to understand that someone is trying to help you.'

I had played my usual mousy game but had found myself growing tired of it, tired of all the games I was ceaselessly co-opted into, tired of my failure to grasp even the basics of what was going on. So I said the first words which attached to my tongue.

'What's in it for you Lynda?'

Her sigh a tour de force, a long swoop down, sustained beyond any credible estimate of her lung capacity, as eloquent a statement of hope betrayed as you could hope to find.

'It's about your swab results. And you may remember that I have an interest in that, too. Let's just say it's in all our inter-est if you just get out of the *way* for a little while. Until things have calmed *down*. You know the drill. I'm sure you must have made yourself scarce be-*fore*.' With that we heard the clunk of the doors unlocking. 'Run if you want to. It'll only make things worse.'

We tumbled out in to the half-light watched by our newly appointed saviour and my mind found itself stuck remembering the day at school when I was eight and we'd been examining toadstools, the teacher telling us too late to wash our hands, my thumb already in my mouth. And I had run from the classroom, from the school, already feeling the poison in me, my guts cramping as I fled up the path to my own front door and knocked and waited for Mummy to come and wipe my cheeks dry and tell me what I must have known somewhere, that I wasn't about to die (not yet, anyway, though mummies are understandably vague on this point). And she did. She comforted me, calmed me, led me by my hand back to class, smoothed over my teacher's anger and alarm so that, when she left, all that was expected of me was a short apology for the natural order to be reasserted and my briefly finished, fabulously ordinary life could start again. Now, for the first time since I had left Yarleigh Falls, I wanted Mummy, not these unsatisfactory substitutes.

'In the car. In the back this time, please.'

'Lynda?' She stood by her own vehicle, neck lost in collar, a corn doll woven from filth. Shrugged a fraction of a shrug. Nodded. Then as we approached the door, each of our steps running slightly slower than the one before, our bin-bagged possessions bouncing against our legs, the sound of another engine, the sight of another car. No squeal of tyres, though, no sign of any cavalry, just the lopsided trundle of a third- or fourth-hand motor choking its way to a halt, with a very British sense of decorum, between SMV and TR7. Stillness as engine cut, the distant rattle of stacked trolleys the sole indicator of life anywhere in the surrounding miles of retail park. The doors opening, a man and a woman getting out, tan anorak, green waterproof, both sets of trousers slightly too short, shoes designed to offer comfort to people of a certain age. She hitching her handbag high up towards her neck, her fist tensing round the leather strap as they huddled together to walk between us.

'Should be ashamed . . .' – her mutter aimed at who and for what unclear, but too late now, too late now for our last best chance.

Without looking back, we climbed into the vehicle. And this time the banter was already done. We circled Lynda, static where she'd left us, and then watched her shrink as we pulled away.

Two hours later we were climbing the uncarpeted stairs of a building just like the one we had left to a room just like the one we had left (except for the en suite shower – a windowless cupboard spotted with mould, the water in the toilet bowl black, the set for a short film on the dangers of lung cancer, a step up on our previous accommodation).

'I know it's not much to look at but you'll be safe here for a little while.'

'Seen.'

Anna had trundled us through an infinite suburb of smudged houses and imaginatively named fried-chicken shops which were identified as distinctive neighbourhoods of South London only by the shout-outs delivered by the MCs of the succession of pirate radio stations our host had decided we would enjoy listening to. Any chance of us knowing definitively where we were was squashed by Anna's instruction to put our heads between our knees for the last ten minutes of the journey. I expected Sadie to argue, at least to complain, but she was as quiet as me, the pair of us folding ourselves away without comment, puppets going back in the box. And the street itself, as we walked the twenty steps from vehicle to refuge? It seemed to have taken a vow of silence, not for any high-powered reason, but just because it couldn't be bothered.

'Ain exacly Witness Protection is it? Maybe we should go to da feds, innit Titch?'

'Got your tongue back? And there was me hoping you'd

164

swallowed it. Oh well. Listen, I know it's nothing special but if you're going to lie low for a while then it's got to be pretty shitty or you'd stand out too much.'

'What ya sayin?'

'I'm stating a fact.'

'Cos if ya sayin we ain't good enough –'

'Why would I bother? You can work that one out for yourself. Fact is, this isn't the telly and this is what lying low's like and the sooner you get a grip on that the better. Now. I'm gonna go and get some food and things in. There's a TV over there. Don't answer the door to anyone. Anything you need specially?'

'What's going on?' I asked.

'What?'

'Why are we here?'

'Plenty of time for that. Dunno about you but I'm starving. Shopping first. Now, is there anything you need?'

'A shag?'

'Don't start that again.'

'Fags then. Bein as you're buyin I'ma get Marlboro. Titch? An a coupla packs for Titch, too. An sutt'n to drink. Bacardi Breezers. Four. You takin us out later?'

'I think you'll be staying in.'

'Better make it eight, then.'

As she left the room, the click of the latch was followed by the chime of keys pulled from pocket, then – so quick – the insertion crunch and the dead sound of barrel turning and bolt slamming into place. We both moved fast but it was already too late, the noise of her footsteps on the stair, the distant clap of the front door closing, the nonexistent padding away down the pavement our soundtrack as we took it in turns to waggle frantically at the handle, to rock ourselves back and forward in homage to this door's utter immovability, as we both dribbled to the floor there, leaning our scared, tired heads against triple-ply, reinforced wood.

She was gone for an hour or so. After we had checked the windows (barred), looked through the cupboards (empty) and examined the sheets on the bed (dirty), our prison held no mysteries for us and, with this knowledge, some of our fear went too. Lab rats, we followed the only course of action open to us. We turned on the TV. And there we were met by familiarity, every character a personal avatar, the sensation of watching these brightly coloured, flickering pixels ingrained in us from so early on, even before we were aware of self, that they were more comforting than a sucked thumb.

Which meant that when Anna did return we were already done with anger or despair and Sadie had found a nubbin of slate in her pocket a while back and hollowed out then refilled a fag and the sweet smell of it had warmed the room and we barely shifted our gaze from the repeat of *Fifteen To One*. And after she had locked the three of us in, she made tea and broke open a packet of custard creams and settled down to watch with us and started shouting out the answers. Was pretty good, too. And that was the first day of our second captivity.

She didn't sleep in the room with us, just waited until we were having trouble with basic motor functions and then retired to the flat next door, still wide awake, utterly straight and completely alert, ready to spend an hour or two catching flies by the wings or practising assassination yoga or inputting new information to the database she was building on us. Who knows how kidnappers pass their time? Who cared? The two of us far too wasted to even think of escaping, let alone capable of acting on any such thought, the television still chatting to itself, soothing us in the absence of any mother, as we collapsed fully dressed onto our dirty bed.

In the morning we were woken by her unlocking and relocking the door, my brain a swollen mass of poisoned blood, far too big for my cranium, grey matter pushing out of my ears, eye sockets, mouth, nostrils, the light a sharpened fingernail scratching at a membrane. And our jailer standing in the corner of the room frying bacon, the smell of it pulling us

166

upright, saliva flooding over the dusty interior of my mouth. So that from the beginning we were eating out of her hand.

We had, of course, been well socialised for imprisonment. Once the initial shock had passed we lost all interest in questioning anything. We slumped into a stupor. Perhaps we were simply glad to have someone looking after us, cooking our meals, doing the shopping, even getting the sheets washed. Most people aren't running their lives at fifteen and though they think they want to, they have no idea of the work involved. We must have been longing for a holiday from independence, even if that holiday involved being locked in a bedsit with a toilet which, we had learnt, didn't flush properly.

How many days passed like that? They were all so similar it's hard to tell. I would guess seven, partially because in the time it allegedly took God to make the world, we managed only to smoke a half ounce of hash and drink the fifty-six bottles of Bacardi Breezer Anna had provided us with. It may have been more or it may have been less because we really weren't counting, just consuming bacon sandwiches, watching telly and smoking and drinking. After the disruptions of the last few weeks, we needed to shut down. While Anna had her reasons for fattening us up, I prefer to think, though we never discussed it, that like Gretel and Gretel we chose to go with the flow only for as long as it suited us. I believe, though, that I would have happily stayed locked in that room forever, all our actions cut and pasted from that basic loop.

Then I messed it up. Not deliberately. Just stupidly. Although it was unsustainable, anyway, carried its own collapse deep within it. Or so I like to tell myself now, after all these years of struggle. I'm a great believer in the inevitability of my own actions.

Anna had left for the supermarket. Sadie and I sat, as usual, in front of the telly. Without shifting my gaze from the re-run of a vintage *Love Island* episode, I ran my fingers out across the covers searching for the cigarettes. I found the pack, but with Sadie's paw covering it. She didn't move, not her head nor her hand. We kept our faces to the screen, my fingers on her knuckles. I thought she was pulling away, but her hand flapped over and gently closed round mine. The screen bled random colours at me, all consciousness focused on the point where we met. Then she really was pulling away, except rather than leaving me the hand scuffed up my arm to my shoulder in a series of tiny jumps and then, hesitantly, touched down on the nape of my neck. Which was the trigger for my face to turn and for hers to turn, too, and we began halving the distance between our lips and halving it again and halving it again and with each halving the anticipation was more exquisite. Then there were keys rattling in the lock, the door opening, Anna's own face coming through the gap, a sudden, sharp reverse from both of us, a mutual fumbling for cigarettes, blushes.

'What's going on?'

'Nutt'n. You was quick.'

'Forgot something. What's going on?'

'Nothing. Just watching telly.'

'Anyone want a cuppa?'

'Thought you were off out.'

She took a moment to study us.

'Just thought maybe I'd have a cup of tea first. Do you want one or not?'

We both assented, careful not to look at each other. I knew I had to say something, just open my mouth and talk or I'd blow it. I don't know why it seemed so important to cover up the non-event but it did. I asked the first question that came to me.

'So, Anna. How long've you been working for Lynda then?'

I didn't mean anything by it. It's just that, in all the time we were there, we'd never bothered to ask her anything about herself (a habit learnt from dealing with screws) and when it came to it, that her and Lynda had some kind of professional relationship was the sum total of my data on our situation.

She turned away from the kettle, looked at me intently, her eyes squinting slightly, a hard smile on her face, lower teeth jutted.

'Are you taking the piss?'

'No, it's just I –'

'Me? Work for . . . *that*?'

'I didn't –'

'Think? No, I'd noticed.'

'– mean anything by it –'

'She couldn't afford an hour of my time. Let alone all this. She works for us. In fact, she couldn't even afford to work for us. Let's say she was rewarded for the information she gave to us.'

'Yeah, well yeah, I mean, that's obvious isn't it?' My embarrassment seemed a long time past now. Sadie was sitting on the bed looking down at her chewed nails, her face shut off. The television kept talking to itself. Anna still watching me, the kettle in her hands now, her fingers strong enough to crush the handle. 'What information, exactly? If you don't mind me –'

'That's obvious isn't it, Tilly?' The smile growing, not so quick you'd notice if you never blinked. So I did, repeatedly, witnessing it through these human frames, waiting for but failing to see any self-evidence right up until she said it.

'It's you.'

I think I understood but pretended not to. Something like that. Or maybe I should take myself at face value.

'What?'

'It's you?'

'What's me?'

'The information.'

' . . . but I don't know anything.'

'Not what you know, *you*. Your DNA.'

'What's up with my DNA? What are you talking about?'

'Sanalex isn't the only company working exclusively with the human genome. I represent Cheralon Genomics. We think we would've done a considerably better job of managing the

Roots of Crime project than Sanalex is ever likely to. We're very interested in some of the anomalies and mistakes which seem to be cropping up in their work. For instance, people like you who they claim to have found a whole new set of parents for. I mean, a different father, yes, that happens all the time. But a different mother, Tilly? Doesn't it all seem a little bit odd to you?'

'Well, yeah, but . . . it's like, well, but yeah it is.'

'Well, yeah, it is. So we're gathering our data – cases like yours – until the right time to release the evidence.'

I wriggled, looking for some looseness, a little bit of give which would allow me to dream of escape.

'But couldn't you just have done a swab and, like, stored it? Isn't this a bit excessive?'

'Tilly, have you any idea how much the Roots of Crime contract is worth?'

'No. Course I haven't.'

'Billions. Not just millions. Billions. They *own* all the data. And the data's what it's all about. They're not going to find a gene for criminality because there's no such thing. It doesn't even make any sense. But the *data* . . . And, of course, as DNA is just data, this pure way of transmitting data –'

'So why ya telling me now?'

'You never asked before. And anyway why not? We're going to help sort out all this mix-up. And you're here for your own safety. You don't think Sanalex want you wandering around talking to people about this, do you? That was who was waiting for you back at the house. Who knows what they would've done to you if they'd caught you. They certainly wouldn't have been buying you fags.'

'An what about me?' Sadie asked, rousing from her self-imposed stupor. 'Where do I fit in? If Titch is so important?'

'Lynda said Tilly wouldn't come without you.'

'Got that much right innit Titch?'

I didn't react. I couldn't react. I was caught in an endless moment, time suddenly twinning itself with all the decorum of a virus, my capabilities lost in this gallery of mirrors. Eventually I tried for breath, found one. Slowly forced my pupils from their paralysis and round towards Sadie, who I imagined would be standing near me, ready to catch me as I fell and fell and fell from the great height of my own socked feet. Only to see her slumped on the bed again, the defiance spent, alternating her remaining energies between chewing bottom lip and fingernails, the cigarette burning unheeded, the spot on her cheek breaking through the cloudy remnants of foundation and blusher.

I found myself oddly liberated by this lack of support, a bracing loneliness grasping me. Adolescence is, after all, the time when you are supposed to feel utterly alone and find only exhilaration in it. I turned back to Anna, my bones moving like the components of a well-designed machine.

'And that's all there is to it? I'm just another piece of data you've collected am I?' I summoned all my pride, straightened myself up like an evolutionary chart. 'Just keeping us here for the good of science are ya?'

She met my eyes with nothing other than total emptiness, the kind of expression that makes the sensitive believe in demons.

'What's the matter, Tilly? Were you hoping you were *special*? Wanted the fuss to be just about you?' And the truth was that she was right, despite knowing that the only data they were interested in belonged to Sadie and not me. I wanted the drama to keep getting bigger and scarier and more all-encompassing even while I felt I just wanted to go home. I wanted, no, I knew, that somehow it was already all turning round me, that the whole world was recalibrating to the beat of my heart, that I was trapped in this room for a reason. I was deluded, of course, but a little delusion can go a long way and the most important thing at that moment was to go a long way.

'I don't care. I don't care about any of it. I just wanna know how long we have to stay here.'

The face of the woman in front of me changed, the release

of a few muscles replacing her with a better version of herself, younger (not much older than us?), considerably more eager to please. How many selves do we consist of?

'It may be a while yet. It's not too bad, though, is it? Really? I'll go down the supermarket now. Get you something. Yeah? Some more Breezers? Yeah?'

We indulged ourselves in another silence.

'Okay. Yeah, okay. And some more fags.'

Lost in habit, we listened to her go, unmoving. Sadie broke first – a sniff, the back of her hand passed across nostrils.

'Shit man.'

'We have to get out of here. We have to find a way out.'

'Y'wha? Why?'

'I dunno why. It just doesn't make sense. What she says. It's not true.'

'So what we gun do? When we get out? If we can get out?'

'I dunno Sadie. We just gotta get out. It should be you, anyway, with all the answers. That's your job. Stead of just sitting there.'

Her face cracked into a grin, an ideal made reality.

'Enjoyin it, though, innit. Bein da boss?' She stood, faking faked enthusiasm, winging her arms and pivoting her fists. 'Right. We gotta go. Titch got a funny feelin.' She did her eye-crossing schtick again, which remained lovely, despite my attempt to pretend otherwise. 'Titch, shower room please. Get yer coat.' With which she picked up her jacket, zombie-marched, arms outstretched, into the mildewed cubicle, climbed into the high-sided half tub, ushered me through the door behind her and, straining, shut and bolted it. Stood, blankly examining the mould in front of her.

'Sadie? We're still inside? We're still in the flat?'

'Whassat?' she asked, nodding her head forward.

'A wall?'

'Yeah. A party wall. Woulda been put in when they convert-ed it. G'it a knock.'

I did as I was told, was met not with the knuckle-echo of brick but the hollow boom of plasterboard.

'Shagged a builder once,' all that was offered by way of explanation. 'Well, a plasterer, anyway. Now lessee.' She had pulled something from her pocket. With a click a triangle of silver appeared at the Stanley's tip. 'Can't belieb she never searched neither of us.'

As I leant back against the door, Sadie scored a horizontal line into the wall, paint and lumps of grey crud rippling along it. One down, another down, her left arm and cheek flush above it, her whole body straining out behind its rumble. A last line across completed the square. We both admired it in a disinterested, hollow fashion.

'Get right back against that door.'

I did. Sadie, meanwhile, slid herself against the far wall, wedging her shoulder and her head around the shower unit. Spreading her arms and her left leg to brace her, she raised her right foot and kicked, flat-soled, into the middle of the square. Both her trainer and the board beneath disappeared into the wall.

'Piece a piss.'

Once we'd removed the cracked, crumbly pieces of plaster-board, we found two rough wooden supports with just enough space between them for us to squeeze and another sheet of board nailed to the other side. Sadie repeated the process, but when she kicked this time she opened up a square of darkness, as black as a picture in a children's book.

'Ere we go, den.'

She crouched, stretched out her arms in front of her and inserted herself into the hole. I watched from the side as she wriggled – readjusting over and over – and the wall slowly ate her, her legs angling up, feet leaving the ground, these last limbs shortening with a fast slither, her Reeboks swal-lowed.

Silence, a moment for reflection, a muffled, under-played clatter. Then the stuttering, dust clogged roar of a never-serviced expelair and light coming back through the hole to meet ours. Sadie's head followed, smiling.

'Gotta see this, Titch.'

I emerged – dragged, laughing despite myself – back in our shower room. Or rather a reflection of it, everything identical but reversed, even the dirt on the shower curtain like the other half of a Rorschach blot.

A sight of the main room winded me. There was the sinkful of unwashed dishes, there was the bed, its clothing twisted to the blueprint of our restless night. There was the ashtray, a squeezed cut glass, replete with ash, generous with angled butts. There was the tangled clump of dirty knickers, t-shirts, bras. There was the telly, tuned to the channel we'd just left, its picture subject to the same flicker, its colours blessing skin with the same orange burnish, eyes like white punctures in each glowing visage.

I was ready for the door, this parallel world too near for me, but Sadie was having a bulb moment, her face backlit with cunning.

'If we ad any money where would we a hid it?'

'Let's just get out of here.'

'We need money, man.'

'The TV's on. Let's just go.'

'Where ya fink?'

'I dunno. In a drawer? Can we go?'

'Nah. In a shoe, man. A drawer ain't hidin.'

'Let's just go.' But Sadie was moving, without hesitation, towards the copy of our wardrobe, opening the door, pulling from its floor a double of one of our Reeboks, raising it to her nose for a cautious sniff, then thrusting her hand down inside it, her fingers shrimping through its interior. A sardonic, triumphant smile, lips licked as she pulled free the roll of notes, waved them for my benefit.

'S'all about the Benjamins,' she rap-sang at me badly. 'Less go, Titch.'

Out on the street we found ourselves bombarded with evidence that we had stepped into an alternate world, a place that looked the same but burst with hostility. Anyone who glanced at us was watching us, those who didn't were simply too good to get spotted. All the people behind us on the pavement were tailing us, all those in front preparing to pick us up. The glint of a mobile arcing up to head height had us flinching from concealed weapons. Helicopters were suspect, their spidering routes sinister. All the cameras followed us, as if we were magnetic. We walked the centre of the pavement, fearful of being dragged into any car that slowed on one side or any front door that opened on the other.

As we grew furtive and twitchy more attention was drawn to us, the scratches turning to free-bleeding cuts, all our assurance haemorrhaging. We stumbled on, lost but too scared to ask for help, fearful of both crowds and empty side streets. Our arms linked not for warmth or comfort but to foil snatch squads. The world around us grew and we shrank, so that first we were doll's-house people, then insects, then microbes. Our breaths became laboured, our steps intermingled, the daylight an anxiety attack. We learnt a new appreciation for escape, sucked desperately at the thought of it as we seemed to prove its impossibility. This was my political awakening (or my spiritual awakening if you prefer), though I did not know it at the time. The sleep was still in my eyes, terror draining me, so it's unsurprising that I failed to notice the difference between consciousness and unconsciousness.

Eventually we fell. Our legs crossed too far, rhythm long-since lost and, in a snaggle of confused limbs, we found the pavement reaching up to punch us. The street stopped, the carefully prepared tableau of shoppers glitching to a halt, only our continued movement capable of driving the scene. We lay, panting, eye to eye, the tears on my face echoes from childhood.

'What the fuck we gunna do? Where we gunna go?'

I looked at Sadie for as long as I dared, our faces horizontal, no plan forming in my head, no scheme to save us, nothing. So I said the only word that came to me.

'Home.'

It's unimportant whether someone is 'watching us'. It doesn't matter whether information 'falls into the wrong hands'. Our contention is that once we have been data-mined there is nothing of us left. A set of quantities is removed and turned into refined ore. This ore is stored in a bank to act as guarantor for the continued free flow of processor capital. We, the landscape the ore was taken from, have disappeared. In an absolute sense we have already vanished.

Extract from *Forty-second Communiqué of the Vanished*

9

Paranoia burst from us, an allergic reaction. How were we meant to travel the fifty or so miles to Reading when merely walking down the street gave us palpitations? Public transport was out of the question. We had tried a tube station but been sent into retreat by the careful scrutiny of a free-sheet distributor. We had boarded a bus only for the driver to examine us before consulting what we took to be some sort of blacklist in his lap, our feet threading back behind us from lowered footplate to pavement. Even with the money Sadie had found, we couldn't afford a cab, let alone trust the driver not to squawk. We sat on a bench at the centre of a low-lying open-air shopping precinct surrounded by old-timers topping up their pensions with surveillance work.

'We're fucked. We're really fucked.'

'No worries. It'll sort. Just gotta think innit?'

'We're fucking fucked.'

'Nah man. S'cool.'

'They'll be waiting for us there, anyway. Even if we do get there.'

'Maybe not. We can go an check it out innit. We ain't just gunna walk in.'

'It's a stupid idea. It's just fucking stupid.'

'Titch, you wanna see ya moms innit? Nutt'n wrong wi dat.'

I looked down at the concrete slab beneath my friendless knees, the grey comets of abandoned gum, the black coal trails leading to ground-down cigarettes, the remaining white of their paper stippled by rain.

'Yeah. I do.'

She rubbed my back, clasped her hand lightly over the curve of my neck.

'We'll go and see me bruv. Brer owes me, knamean?'

'Sadie,' the words coming before I'd had a chance to edit them. 'We don't know where your brother is. Do we?'

'Not muh real bruv. Muh foster bruvver. Well, we was both fostered innit? Kep comin frough after what e'd moved out an shit. Lives up Tottnam. Used to go there when I ran away. Cuz like I'ma used to work for im. Y'getme?'

'Kind of.' What else could I say? 'What sort of work?'

'Jus sellin a few pills an shit. Nutt'n major. Jus get a bitta stock an use some an sell some innit? Make a bitta papers? Bitta pocket money?'

She stood up, reinvigorated by her own ingenuity, bouncing in her Reeboks, an unexpected gap in the clouds behind her illuminating a few stray hairs frizzing out from her skull like tiny lightning strikes. 'We out, then? S'a long walk, Titch. Come.'

We made our way across the city slowly, seeming to move back as much as forward, but gradually, inexorably advancing. First, wide, barren stretches of houses and petrol stations, the occasional local high street a huddle of pound shops. Then, almost imperceptibly at first, the process running to hours, the roads beginning to snaggle into one another, the density of chicken and kebab and pizza shops rising, the occasional black cab trundling by between the second-hand Bimmers and dirty vans, towerblock windows framed by fluorescent light instead of tacked-up sheets and England flags. By the time we saw our first beggar our shins were already aching from repeated impact with concrete, our stomachs spaces in which only air boiled.

The sun moved too fast, so that each time it found a space in the clouds it had jumped forward improbably and light was being forced from the day almost before it had arrived. Automatons on some vast cosmological clock, we limped on, the swagger gone from even Sadie's legs, the steady patter of our trainers replaced in my head by a hollow metal knocking.

We crossed the river at dusk, two stick figures shuffling against a multi-headed determination of commuters who, drop-browed, kept sweeping us against the granite wall of the bridge, searching for breath and forced to consider jumping into the slab of sluggish grey water below.

We tried to skirt the City, each under-occupied, over-polished block alive with cameras and private security. We followed the trails of rubbish – torn crisp packets, flattened cigarette cartons, translucent chip wrappers, discarded fly-ers, broken bottles, drink cans and their deep brown content-stains – and found that the cameras vanished as the littering grew. We walked through chest-to-chest arguments between brown-faced grocers, past Middle Eastern Marxists stencilling over the proclamations of Middle Eastern jihadists, past shops selling fruit and vegetables I had never seen before, past East End theme pubs with Kray-lookalikes working the door, past take-away after take-away as the Bangladeshis gave way to the Vietnamese, the Vietnamese to the Nigerians, the Nigerians to the Turks, the Turks to the Jamaicans, the Jamaicans to the Azerbaijanis, the Azerbaijanis to the Somalis and so on, third generation white supremacists the mortar between these bricks, their claim to innate superiority posited solely on the fact that they were still here, living in areas that everyone else was trying to escape.

We walked on in darkness, the water in the sky reflecting back illumination from ten thousand flickering headlights, one hundred thousand intermittently functioning streetlamps, one million sixty-watt bulbs. Caught beneath this grey canopy – our shadows swinging past us, shrinking to be trampled on before rolling round to begin again – we trod the same streets over and over, the same cars passing the same shops, the same security staring at us from the same supermarket entrance, the same towers looming up, their disembodied heights picked out by the same lit windows. The business of commerce began to pace itself then stopped completely and we were shambling through a Coalville built twenty years before our own, the toy-town houses graffed and scrubbed so many times, the doorways pissed in so often, the reinforced glass shattered so regularly (each one an icy flower, so beautiful it made you wish the hammer was yours) that it felt as if one more intervention would crack the whole brittle structure and send it tumbling into the pit it was built on.

'Ta-da.' With a quarter-hearted fanfare, Sadie indicated a house in front of us, its windows and door blocked by metal council perma-shutters, their surfaces sponsored by a corporate loan shark.

'What?'

'We're ere.'

'Where?'

'*Where?* Muh bruv's place. "*Where*".'

'Looks kind of . . . empty. You sure he's still here?'

'Looked like that from time. Chill.'

She approached the door, pressed a bell I hadn't noticed, took a step back next to me.

'Smile.'

I followed the angle of her head up to the camera above the door – red LED pipping out a steady rhythm – and did as I was told. We waited in silence until, just as I'd decided that the building was indeed derelict, an unseen intercom crackled and released a strange room's static.

'Yes?'

'Yo, Big Phil! It's me.'

'And oo, pray tell, is me?'

'Me. Lady Sadie innit ya dick?'

'Is it?'

'Yeah. Ya gunna let us in or what?'

'I was merely askin.'

'Yeah, well *I* was just arksin if you was gunna let us in or *what*?'

The intercom clicked off and we waited again, my head involuntarily spasming round to check the street.

'Try not to look too jumpy,' Sadie offered without releasing her focus from the door. ''E's a bit para.'

Nothing continued to happen, then continued a little longer.

'You sure he's gunna let us in?'

'Sure sure.' She nodded towards the door. The metal plate shuddered a little, shook, lifted up slightly, lurched forwards, the bolts leaving ragged holes in the brick. Staggered to our left, a cartoon of itself, before keeling over towards the wall, its top hitting with a clang that echoed down the street like a medieval bell. Sadie didn't blink. A head emerged from behind the metal, prematurely bald and with a fine-haired moustache.

'Evenin Sade. Welcome, welcome.'

'Wha'blow?' She led me in and turned back to the doorway. On the floor between us was a metal cable with a large hook at one end, spooled out from a winch of some sort attached to the wall opposite. Phil crabbed back into view carrying the shutter, which he hoiked into place. Picked up the hook and posted it through the letterbox on the door, biting his bottom lip as he strained his hands in and attached it to the back of the shutter. Closed the door. Skipped to the winch and pulled it tight before jamming it in place with an iron bar. Returned to the door to treble lock and bolt it. Stood with his hands on his hips admiring the set-up, his body loose with satisfaction.

'I'm tellin you for free, no one an is dog is comin frough that.' Tenderly checked the tension in the cable. Looked up. 'What can I do yer for, Sadie?'

'You gun invite us in or what?'

'*Indoobidably.*' The Yank twang as unconvincing as the moustache. He turned to another door, unlocked it and waved us through. Smoke met me with the force of a breaking wave, the sweet smell of good weed making me salivate.

Despite the three-piece suite and coffee table, despite the huge widescreen plasma TV, the room exuded a feeling of emptiness, the camel-coloured carpet flecked with maggots of dirt, the windows bricked up from the inside. The television, generating more lumens than the bulb above it, painted the space with cold light. A thin j-builder hunched over the magazine on his lap, being eaten by the sofa. He looked up, revealing himself to be much older than his haircut suggested and acknowledged us with a thick-tongued sound, his mouth hidden behind the white strip of Rizla he was licking.

'Please be downstandin. Make yerselves comfortable. Treat it as your ome,' said Big Phil behind us. The man on the sofa shuffled himself over and, establishing eye contact, patted the cushion next to him. Sadie made for the armchair. I didn't move.

'You've failed, Sade, to do the introductions.'

'Phil, Titch, Titch, Phil.'

'Charmed. An that's Seb. Don't worry, love, e's armless. Int ya, Seb?'

'*Indoobidably*,' offered Seb, his body flickering with wheezed mirth. I made my way over and perched as far away from him as I could, relaxing a little when he passed me the joint, his gaze staying fixed on the telly, which seemed to be showing a rolling news report from a conflict in a place I didn't recognise. Big Phil made his way to the other armchair, sank into it like a rap star, his legs splayed, then slowly raised his arms, his index fingers meeting as their tips reached his lip, his hands forming a triangle beneath them.

'To what do I owe the pleasure?' Every bit the cut-rate capo.

'Can I at least get a smoke an a drink first?'

'There's Pepsi in the fridge' – offered with another mafioso tilt of his head, any attempt to seem impressive or threatening lost on Sadie, who heaved herself to her feet, came to request the joint from me then puffed her way over to the squat white cupboard humming by the arm of his chair.

'Don't get up, will ya?' Swivelling her head round to me under the arm holding the door open. 'Wanna Pepsi?' I nodded back, speech lost inside me. Seb nodded along, his eyes scrubbed.

'*Indoobidably*.' Both he and Phil creasing up again.

'That s'posed to be funny?' Lowering the lids of her eyes in contempt.

'*Indoobidably.*'

'Oh yeah, very good.'

The Pepsi was cold and sweet and sticky, my mouth expanding round it, the trails of its taste fizzing down my nerves, making me shiver. Sadie was grimacing.

'Why int ya got Coke?'

'It confuses my clientele. So as I was sayin, what can I do yer for?'

'Ow's business?'

'Business is good. Could be better, could be worse. Now what can I do yer for?'

'What ya got?'

'I got everythin innit? Whatever you want I got. An if I ain't got it I can get it. Fulfillin demand, my dear?'

'We jus need to crash for the night, Phil. An a lickle help gettin somewhere.'

'Gettin somewhere? Where yer need gettin to?'

'Readin.'

'Readin? Oh my gyosh. What the blazes ya goin Readin for?'

'Titch's yard innit?'

'Lucky Titch. So it's a day trip. Candyfloss on Readin igh street. Where'd I come in?'

'S'complicated. We can't go on the train or the bus.'

'Yer need monetary assistance?'

'We got money.'

'So what, pray, are yer doin ere? I'm a narcotics dealer not a blummin taxi service.'

'Yeah, I know. We're in a mess, Phil. I'm arksin for elp innit? I'm shook.'

'What ya done?'

'We ain't done nutt'n. It ain't what *we* done.'

The war continued on the television, the explosions punctuated by men in suits talking just beyond the camera. Seb was leaning forward smiling, his elbows on his knees, the images reflected in miniature on the water of his eyes. The joint had gone out resting in Sadie's hand. She stood now, crossed the room, handed it to Big Phil, his fingers long and thin and delicate. I took another swig from my Pepsi, heard the bubbles bursting in my head. Sadie sat down again, a long exhalation of breath, the search for her cigarettes. Lit one and began to talk, trying to find the sense in any of it.

She didn't get far before Phil cut in, laughing, his eyebrows where his hairline should have been, his moustache making him look like a big, messy, stupid kid with a glass of chocolate milk.

'No sugar!'

'What?'

He laughed again, high-pitched, disbelieving.

'No sugar!'

'What?'

'Are you tryin to tell me that young Titch ere ad a DNA test and er mum an dad turned out not to be er mum an dad?'

'Xackly.' (Sadie had stuck to our public story and it was still me who the world believed had mislaid my family).

'Ya hear dis Seb? No sucre, as they say in France.'

'What?'

'Seb, too. Seb as much the same tale to tell. Yeah, Seb?'

'*Indoobidably.*'

'Will ya pack that shit in?'

'Easy, Sade. Seb got a right to free expression, innit Seb?'

'*Indoobidably.*'

Sadie was out of the chair and standing over him, face ripped with anger.

'Ignore it,' I said, my hand reaching up to hers. 'Let's stick to what's important.' I chose to shrug off the slight slap with which she pushed me away, relieved that she slumped back into her seat.

'You were saying?' I asked Phil.

'Uh? Oh yeah. Seb's got like a *teeny-tiny-wee-wee-weeny* record for possession of controlled substances so e's called in to be swabbed an, well you know how it is when you lead a busy, active life? It takes im a *leetle* while to get round to it, to take the time out so to speak. But e goes in what? two or three weeks ago? Does what needs to be done. Makes is contribution, so to speak. Gives back. An then goes away and forgets all about it. An when e's definitely an completely forgotten all about it, then they call im back in. An it takes im a lickle while to go through again, cos is life remains very full and, I think you could even say, *rewardin*. But e opens up a window in is diary and goes back in today. And they says just what Sade says – ya mam an ya dad ain't ya mam an dad. Must a been some mix-up at the ospital. Jus like that. How old are ya, Seb? Ya forty yet? Forty years wiped out jus like that. What we was celebratin innit?'

'How do you mean?'

'Seb's dad's a judge. Lord Justice, good as. And pater and poor dear mater've spent the last forty years tryin to figure out where it all went wrong. Always been tryin to re*form* im an all that malarkey. And now' – he paused to relight – 'those days are gone.' Dropped his jaw onto his chest, drawled out his next words in what I took to be a judge's voice. 'In the opinion of the court, Seb is a *bad apple*.'

While we'd been talking, Seb had been busy building, his fingers moving with the mindless efficiency of call-centre operatives. As Big Phil reached the end of his story, his semi-mute associate had flicked out his Zippo, snapped it open and ignited, sucked lustily at his creation and then uttered his one-word embellishment of the tale in a pinched, high-pitched croak and accompanying belch of smoke.

'*In-doo-bidably*.'

We joined in with the celebration, for no other reason than we had no reason not to. We were suspended in time here, floating on top of the world, slumped in a derelict council house designed by a prince. Big Phil pulled out a bag of powder, flopping in his hand like a dead animal, and, arched over the coffee table, I took my first nose at the substance, my heart stammering with excitement, anxiety and chemical life. It seemed to scrape through me like a broom through dust and my legs quivered despite the miles they had walked, my mind pleased with itself regardless of the fear I felt, my pulls on the various joints criss-crossing me from left and right bigger and hungrier than before, so that the smoke caught at the back of my throat and I coughed and laughed all at once again and again and again.

It turned out to be a very long night, all our fingers touching over and over, cold smooth skin, the tiny friction of fingerprints on follicles, docking and separating like space ships. Sadie's and my slow surrender to the indubitable amusement of the others' joke, the four of us lost in laughter long gone beyond itself, the funniest way to suffocate. The visitors Phil went to meet out in his reinforced anteroom, his eyes suddenly focused as he came back past us and through to another locked room in which he sorted the orders. The constant music of his three mobile phones, often all of them sounding at once, strange discordant mixtures of notes and rhythms ripping into our ears and misaligning our teeth. The stories he told us, all only funny in those bulb-lit hours: of the seventy-year-old man who purchased coke to fuel his wife's and his late-discovered interest in bondage, only for his newfound hobbies to prove too much for his heart so that he died leaving his sweetheart of fifty years chained to the family bed waiting for her daughter to find her in the morning, Dad collapsed at her feet, naked but for his black leather mask; of the eldest son of a rich father who had sold a townhouse in Kensington, moved into a suite at the Ritz and stayed there until he had no more money to give to Seb (who visited daily on Phil's behalf, his courier's bag bulging with carefully packed rocks); of the local hardnut who had tried to help himself to a little of Phil's business and ended up losing a hand in a bear trap Phil had bought from a survivalist site on the internet; of the former merchant banker who had sunk so low he would hang around outside on his knees offering up blowjobs to the CCTV in exchange for another hit; of the runner for a film production company who would snort half of what she bought and then cut what remained before taking it back to whichever star had demanded it (and how Phil, respecting her bollocks, had always supplied her with his best stuff); of the well-known British actor who had been led here by the aforementioned runner for research and had ended up locked in the toilet for most of the night, finger of fear rifling through his innards; of Sadie selling pills to privately educated ten-year-olds on their way to exclusive kiddy raves; of bent feds, desperate politicians, the amount of narcotics consumed at magnificent dinner parties, art theft, clever mules, quick thinking, incompetent authority, problems with suppliers, problems with sales reps, problems with customers, until all occasional incidentals were stripped away and we found ourselves listening to yet another shopkeeper, the camera pointed down at us making it absolutely clear to me that we hadn't made it any further into the workings than the showroom.

The television the only constant beyond the free flow of drugs, showing hour after hour of shakily filmed explosions, soldiers ducking, civilians running screaming from houses, correspondents in Kevlar vests, the scrolling tickertape strip at the screen's bottom making no sense, terse bullet points from nonexistent capital cities. Seb, in particular, mesmerised by this flickering accretion of meaninglessness, grinning his mad-happy grin, his cheeks line after concentric line, his eyes dry and unblinking, his head moving to avoid incoming missiles, as if he were playing a video game which only he could comprehend.

My consciousness began to come to pieces and I laid its scraps to rest all over the room with no pattern or rationale, so that my memories of that evening become increasingly disjointed, all sense of time and ordering gone, just discrete sensations left – a gulp of Pepsi, my fingers running over the weave of the sofa's arm, Sadie unbanding her hair and working her fingers with tooth-clenched intensity through its heavily lacquered shell, the itch of my nostrils as if the hairs inside grew fairytale-fast, Sadie's hand on my cheek, the tilt of the floor, the way my feet flew up and over my head when I closed my eyes, the fading voices, preoccupied now with a quiet game of sounds, words leftovers from a more complicated time and place, words something I almost knew about without any real evidence, something we all used once, apparently, like phone boxes. And all night the dimmer switch had been brought down and down, the light lost in fractions, weakened bit by bit so that at last there was nowhere for it to go, no last place it could call its own, nothing unmediated by our grasping eyes, no point in its continued existence. Hence, it vanished.

I awoke on the couch with no idea of how much time had passed. No bird song entered the bunker, no morning light dappled my face through its brick curtains. The bulb above was still on low and through the heavy haze of cold smoke particles Seb was visible sitting in Big Phil's chair, continuing to skin up. Neither Phil himself nor Sadie were present. The television was still going, with the sound turned up slightly, though the war was over and instead a man in frameless glasses with very pale blue eyes and a shaven, tanned head was being pursued down a set of steps, the crackle of flashbulbs flattening him into a badly realised animation. Cheerfully, his English inflected with American, he uttered the doorstep mantra. *'No comment. No comment. No comment.'*

All traces of sleep had left me now, straining forward to hear the commentary, not daring to look away in case I missed anything. But I couldn't seem to make it out, the sudden heartbeat buzz of a police helicopter, the muezzin call of a nearby mosque, the squeal of a joyrider's borrowed tyres, the thud of a custom-car's booted bass bins, in a moment all these sounds came tearing in.

'Where's the remote?' Turning to Seb.

'Uh?'

'Where's the remote? The *remote*? The fucking re*mote*?'

'The remote?'

'Yeah, the remote.'

'This?' Lifting it from his lap, his eyes the fossilised remains of an ancient civilisation.

'Turn it up.'

'What?'

'*What?!* The TV. Turn the TV up.'

He smirked at me, not understanding my urgency. With no reason to understand my urgency.

'What's the magic word?'

'The m . . . For fuck's . . . Just . . .' A deep breath. '*Please.*'

'Actually it's "sativa" but I guess that'll have to do.' His arm unfurled towards the television, wrist pointing above it, hand ratcheted down, so that his sightline, his limb and the beam formed a shallow triangle.

'*. . . the maverick scientist and company CEO is, himself, famously childless, an irony –*'

'*And reach down to your toes . . .*' A familiar-looking woman in lycra top and tracky trousers followed her own instructions, the correspondent gone.

'Shit.'

'*And up. And stretch.*'

'What ya doing?'

'*And down again. And hold it there.*'

'I didn't mean to.'

'Just turn it back.'

'*Now up again and s – Ivan went up to the big house. Ivan rang the bell. Bing-bong went the bell . . .*'

'What channel were we on?'

'What?'

'*"Bing-bong," said Ivan – set of extra sharp, professional standard kitchen knives . . .*'

'What number?'

'Number? Should I know?'

'*. . . cut through – Mordrex! I should have known –*'

191

'No.'

'When Hitler gave the order for the initial –'

'Nope.'

'– to explain in terms of –'

'No.'

'– that I don't fancy you –'

'Fuck's sake, Seb.'

'*"There is nothing wrong with the science. There is nothing wrong with our methodology. The problems lie elsewhere."*'

'Voila.'

Cut back from the tanned head to the science correspondent. *'Peter Debray may be right. But without cold, hard evidence to support his claim, Sanalex will only find themselves increasingly mired in the scandal that's building around them. The leaked documents we've seen show that the few cases to come to public attention aren't an isolated phenomenon but the tip of the iceberg. It's not just science demanding answers. It's parents. And their children, too. Back to you in the studio, John.'*

'Thanks, Rory. Now, in other news, sometime "super model" and charity worker . . .'

'Great. Marvellous. You can turn it back down now.'

'What?'

'Down. You can turn it down.'

'Jesus. Up, down, up, down. I'm not your bitch, woman.'

I thinned my eyes until his features were softened by my lashes. He smiled at me, sideless.

'You're very talkative today.'

'Oh, it's the drugs. Can't talk when I'm caned. I'm very contrary like that.' He took one last puff at his spliff, waved it at me. 'Coming down now. You mind?' – indicating the TV's whereabouts with the remote.

'Whatever. Missed it now.'

He recommended a more leisurely scroll through the channels on offer. 'What's so desperate?'

'What?'

'What did you wanna see?'

My arms weighed more than the rest of me put together. I let them flop at my sides. It felt like I hadn't stayed asleep long enough. 'Nothing. Doesn't matter now. Where's the others?'

He indicated the door to the rest of the house with a lateral movement of his head, lay an index finger flat against the side of his nose, jumped his eyebrows up.

'Catching up.'

My cheeks prickled. 'What ya mean?'

He looked at me with something close to genuine sympathy. 'What ya think?'

I didn't want to think. I stood and marched to the door, yanked at the handle. It twanged through my fingers, unyielding.

'What, we're locked out?'

'And in,' nodding to the door we'd entered by. 'Though I prefer to think of it as finding ourselves blessed with a secure environment.'

'This is fucking . . .'

'Chill. We got a TV, a fridge, a toilet. They'll be down in a bit. Wanna skin up?'

I hammered on the door one two three times, shouted her name. To be locked up again, by her of all people, seemed too much, my throat swelling so that I couldn't swallow, the blood in my head pounding. And, anyway, where was she? Had she had enough of me? Was she going to leave me here? I hammered again, shouted again, my voice stretching into a screech.

'She won't hear ya. It's a steel door. You'll just end up breaking your hand.'

I opted to lock myself in the toilet, the tap running to hide the sobbing I couldn't justify. And when I got bored of my own histrionics (crying, as I've said before, being remarkably hard to sustain) I came out and skinned up. Seb, it seemed, had access to a hidden wisdom.

More than wisdom, in fact. Transport. It was as we sat there waiting, both imprisoned and excluded, allowing the telly to lull us, to round the edges, that Seb, out of nowhere, offered to get us to Reading.

'I got a bike. A *motor*bike, obviously.'

'Oh. That's great. That's. That's great.' I tried to think of a way to approach the next point without causing offence. Failed. 'Just one problem, though. Including you there's three of us.'

'And?'

'How we gunna fit on?'

'I got a sidecar. It's a classic bike. Norton. Big Phil lets me keep it in his garage.'

'Why's he called *Big* Phil? He isn't very big.'

'Should I know? It's his name . . . What about the bike?'

I knew we weren't going to get a better offer, but the thought of accompanying a constantly stoned semi-geriatric with some three-wheeled death wish didn't fill me with enthusiasm.

'What about helmets?'

'I got spares.'

'Is it safe?'

'Lovely bike.'

'I. I meant you, actually.'

'I haven't been drinking.'

'But all the . . .' I mimed smoking.

'I actually drive better stoned. Smoother.'

He nodded sagely. I examined my fingernails and promised myself that when this was all sorted I would stop biting them then nick myself expensive polish to celebrate.

'I won't be able to invite you in when we get there.'

'That's cool.'

'It's not me, it's my mum,' I lied.

'No problem, honest. You seem like a nice young girl. You should get home.'

'Oh. Thanks.'

'Delighted to be able to help. And we're in the same boat aren't we? Both lost our mums and dads?'

I didn't know what to say. I took the joint he passed me and inhaled hard. Smiled. Tried to make my left eyelid stop shivering.

Sadie joined us just as I was finishing the Mars bar Seb had thrown me from the fridge. I stared at her, both hungry and queasy for signs of betrayal. She moved across the room carefully, carrying out a sullen inspection of the floor, headed for the couch and flopped down on the far end from me, her bare feet tucked beneath her, her hands wedged between her thighs, arms straightening and relaxing, the upper reaches of their bones making acute angles with her downcast head. Raised her face to me for a moment, skin blotched with the remains of yesterday's badly removed make-up.

'Alright?' A tired smile for me.

'Fine. Wondered where you'd got to.'

'Sleepin. Not room for two of us on the couch is it?'

'Spect we could've managed.'

'Yeah, well we din ave to.'

'No.'

We both pretended to watch television. I wanted to tell her I'd seen the boss of Sanalex on the news this morning, but I was too hurt by her absence, her refusal to explain. And anyway, what did it matter? Instead I passed her the joint I was holding, happy to touch her, however briefly.

'Where's Phil?' asked Seb, dismantling the moment.

' . . . should I know?' Tensing up again. 'Avin breakfast or sutt'n.' Glancing round at me again, too quickly. 'Starvin.'

'Seb's got some Mars bars.'

He pulled a rumpled blue carrier bag into his lap from behind the fridge and began to rummage through it. 'Better'n that.' Pulled free two blue-and-silver packets, lifted one to each side of his smiling face with the wide-eyed excitement of a children's TV presenter.

'Crisps!'

Life seems a calmer, less complicated endeavour with a

mouth full of Cheese & Onion. We both fell away from the
ends of the sofa, munching contentedly, our arms touching at
some mid-point of happiness. Our faces turned to one another, each tentative, pathetic smile exactly mirrored, our teeth
speckled with potato fragments.

'Seb says he'll take us to Reading.'

'I know,' regretting it as soon as she said it. Speaking down
into her bag, by way of explanation: 'Big Phil tol me.'

The sharp demand for explanation offered to Seb met with
an exaggerated shrug. 'Big Phil knows everything.' His eyes
rolling up in his head as it, too, moved back to indicate the
camera at the top of the wall behind him. My whole body hollowing out, a retch stuck in my throat.

'You been *watching* . . .? How long've you been watching
us?'

'I ain't!' Sadie protested, but I was already in motion, my
crisp packet flicked from me, crumbs scattering across the coffee table, a graphic of my disgust. Entering the toilet I kicked
out at the bowl then crumpled down to the seat to nurse my
damaged toe. Tears came again, the remains of my eyeliner
making its final, sluggish journey across my cheeks and onto
smudged, damp, wrinkled clumps of toilet paper. This time
they were stopped by the thought that perhaps Sadie meant to
stay here, that she would leave me to go to Reading on my
own, to deal with my own fake problems in my own fake way.
A desperate fear prickled up over my skin, an immediate
weakness in my limbs. I cleaned myself up as quick as I could,
a frenzy of splashing and wiping.

By the time I emerged, the picture had changed. Big Phil sat
back on his throne, stroking his moustache and looking, to
me, more than usually pleased with himself. Seb had returned
to the sofa, engrossed again in muted twenty-four-hour news
coverage. Sadie was perched on the arm of Phil's chair, a flat
look to her face as she took the envelope from his hand, folded it and pushed it deep into her pocket.

She looked up and smiled at me and who was I to say if the smile was forced or genuine, who was I to question her methods or her motives?

'Ya set, Titch?'

I looked at her as she rose, tugging at her hair, trying to pull it back to some kind of order, a little more frantic, perhaps, than usual, her scrunchy at the ready, cigarette dangling from her mouth with movie-star ease. I watched her take a step towards me, grinning, just the slight twitch of her left cheek to show that she was nervous. I let the question sink in.

'Course, Sadie. Always.'

Outside now, the city seemed still for a moment and, as we squinted through thin sunlight, our eyes unaccustomed to such richness, I heard what I'd previously found missing in the single bubbled call of a bird, its heart below its feathers faster than the tremble of my hand.

Our physicality becomes both the originator of and the vessel for data. To remove ourselves, to Vanish, is, then, an act of war because with it we cut the supply line that feeds processor power, which in turn feeds CTRL.

Extract from *Forty-fourth Communiqué of the Vanished*

10

I date my mistrust of motorcycles to that day. Not that Seb wasn't as good as his word in every particular – better, in fact. But travelling in a sidecar is not for the faint-hearted and, despite how my story may encourage you to see me, those two words sum me up as well as any.

First, there's the noise and power of the machine next to you, just close enough you feel it could chew you up at any moment. Then there's your mode of transport – a metal box on a single wheel, the rudimentary shock absorber unequal to its job, your teeth juddering and jarring off each other so that you expect your mouth to be full of grit by the time you reach your destination. But worse, far worse than any of this is how low you sit, your proximity to the road, the way you're constantly aware of tarmac moving at flesh-scouring speed just centimetres below you, the whole exercise a continuing flirtation with deformity.

It was my own fault. Horrified at the thought of having to straddle the bike and cosy up to Seb, the insides of my thighs pressing on the outside of his, I had baggsied the sidecar, fondly imagining that I might even catch some sleep. Sadie had seen through my ploy, a single eyebrow raised in amusement, her own mounting of the machine exaggeratedly lewd, her voice baby-girl pouty as she, winking at me, observed, 'Oh Seb, your machine is so . . . *powerful*.' The shadowing of panic on his face delightful.

It turned out that Seb's parents – or ex-parents – lived in a manor house somewhere in Berkshire so he knew the roads. Furthermore, he refused to travel on motorways or through central London (too many cameras), instead patching together a route north and then around the metropolis along A-roads and B-roads, past abandoned petrol stations and unattended truck-stop caffs, beneath audiences of leaves and through a lifetime of empty fields. It could have been a pleasure, an exercise in nostalgia, like a day out back when the M25 only had three lanes. The sidecar precluded any such enjoyment. That and my fear for Sadie, who kept reaching across to tap my shoulder before her next trick, her arms and legs sticking out at right angles, her face set to comedy surprise.

Seb dropped us at the parade of shops near my former home, offering us a royal wave as he turned in a generous loop and paraded back past us. We stood for a moment, our bodies buzzing with the spent vibration of the bike, the world around us absolutely foreign, a hostile environment. An old lady with a beagle walked towards us, both so tired and peg-legged it was a miracle they moved at all. Except for the occasional passing car the only noises were the distant sigh of motorway traffic, the random sex-calls of birds and, from a hidden ladder, the quivering melody of a workman's whistled show tune. All of the endless space around us seemed to press in on me, my breathing without rhythm, Mr Brodkin who ran the newsagents (and who wouldn't let girls take paper rounds) squinting at me from the window as I pulled down the brim of my cap, caught hold of Sadie's arm, paralysed with fear or disgust or wonder, and made for Sycamore Avenue.

Sycamore Avenue looped right round Willow Close, where I had grown up, the gardens of one set of houses mirrored at their end by the gardens of the other. I led Sadie to number 43, the residence of Mr and Mrs Trowbridge back in my day, a childless couple with the stiff, uncomfortable enthusiasm of the disappointed when it came to other people's kids. Aged ten, my mother had repeatedly scolded me for taking advantage of the situation, never missing an opportunity to pop round and be plied with ice cream. It hadn't struck me until that moment that perhaps her biggest concern had been the Trowbridge's motivation and hence my, not their, welfare.

Who knows whether it was a reaction to their unfulfilled desire to reproduce or a cause of it, but both Mr and Mrs Trowbridge were keen hobbyists. Though retired, they were rarely in the house (except when entertaining me), instead collecting train numbers, improving advanced flower-arranging chops, practicing the tango, attending philately conventions, or giving recitals as integral members of Berkshire's finest hand-bell ringing group, the Campanoles, whose rendition of 'Chatanooga Choo Choo' had taken them within a whisker of a South East Regional Final two years running.

I was, then, fairly confident that the Trowbridges would be absent as I strained over the top of the high garden gate to undo the latch, the smell of creosote pulling from a corner of my memory these uninvited slivers of recollection. Both Sadie and I exuding the casualness crossed with efficiency which she had taught me makes you invisible, we passed through and set off down the garden, our pace neither too fast or too slow, the sky very close to us, everything else leaning away.

We headed straight for the far shrubbery, each leaf identically proportioned and positioned, the green so bright it shook slightly against the red-brown of the fence, Sadie looking at me looking only ahead. Into the plants we waded, I a child again, exploring the jungle of my former self. Finding the loose boards in the fence was no problem. Getting through was another matter.

Something had been bothering me since I had climbed from the sidecar, a deeper aspect to my unease. Now it was made clear to me. The fault lay not with my memory or the place I found myself in. Both were perfect. It was me. I was too big. We didn't even have to try to know we weren't getting through my former gateway.

Clumsily, doing ourselves little credit, we managed to scale the fence – which, after all, didn't present the same challenge it used to – and flopped down into the bushes at the foot of my garden, our curses uttered quietly but urgently to no one in particular. And this is where we stayed for a while, in amongst the foliage, our smoker's breaths coming faster than they should, completely hidden in the dense shade of a super-breed plant much favoured by nuisance neighbours.

Next we peeped out, two faces wreathed in green, an illustration from a more innocent age, the books I'd read and read before all this was set in motion, smudges of dirt on our faces. Children despite our bulk, the unwieldiness of our trainered feet, the unnerving changes in the proportions of our faces.

And there was Mum, moving through the kitchen, raising a nibble of unidentified food to her mouth, putting a container in the cupboard, pushing the cat down from the work surface by the sink, my mind adding the sound of claws on formica, the hopeless mew as its feet hit the floor. Through into the sitting room, back to the kitchen, Sadie and I withdrawing deeper into the leaves as she braced her arms on each side of the sink and stared through the window straight towards us. Except the focus was beyond and before me, no chance of my becoming the centre of attention. And eventually the reverie passed through her, she put the kettle on and made herself a cup of tea.

And what of me, the urchin? I was hungry, my head smoggy with the last heavy blobs of cannabinoid, my clothes dirty and crumpled, my hair crushed and misshapen beneath my cap, teeth unwashed and filmy with plaque, nose itching and irritated by whatever drugs Big Phil had allowed me to suck up, face zit-riveted, unmade and unmakeable, mind shut down to everything but fear. I wanted my mummy. I wanted my mummy. I wanted my mummy.

She was right next to the kitchen door as I staggered from the bushes, drunk on need, Sadie my twitching shadow. But instead of flinging it open and coming running, arms wide to signal me in, she jumped, backed away, knocked a vase from the table and seemed to fall upon the phone, her right index finger frenziedly pressing the keys. As I reached the door, I glanced back to see Sadie frozen in the middle of the lawn, torn between her desire to follow me and her urge to run.

There was no time. I pushed through into the kitchen and charged at my mother, a pathetic yelp of surrender escaping her mouth, her hands waving round her face as if she was fending off bees. I pulled the phone from her, made sure she hadn't had time to dial and then chucked it across the room.

'It's me, Mum. It's me.'

'Just take what you want –'

'Mum, it's me.'

'Please don't hurt me –'

'Mum, Mummy, it's me.'

'Please, please, *shit*, no.'

I raised my hands to her, lowered them under a polyrhythm of slaps. Raised them, lowered them, tears now streaking both our faces. Raised them a third time and found them batted down again. Took a step back or, at least, fell back, an action which worked as a password or the next move in the choreography because now my mother's arms opened to me, as if their outward sweep rolled away the clouds, and now I was inside those arms and now they closed around me. And for a moment we snuffled at each other's necks, locked into our wet hold, my head spinning with the smell I'd forgotten she had. Then, without warning, the muscles in my legs abandoned me and I found myself sinking to the floor, a slow process, a towerblock being dynamited, my mother subsiding with me, though at a lesser rate until, eventually, the side of my face came to rest on her breasts, emanating an unnatural warmth, and stayed there.

'It's me.'

'I know.'

Perhaps we would have remained like that forever. Perhaps we would have never said more than this. We could have crawled under the table and lived there, eating crumbs. But we parted, eventually, with the realisation that there was someone else in the room, another person breathing our breath.

It happened to be Sadie. She stood half in and half out of the doorway, her face lost in a daze of discomfort, her body unsure of its place. Her eyes skirted us in a continuing loop, trying to build a picture of us solely from peripheral vision. She chewed at her thumbnail, print parallel with ceiling, lower teeth extended beyond upper.

I felt Mum turn to bone beneath my cheek, the hardening both sudden and slow. In response I loosened my grip and she moved back from me, began to rise. Or was it in response? Perhaps it was me who broke our clinch. Perhaps she sensed I was just playing at it. The only certainty is that we both stood up and dusted at ourselves and examined the floor for distractions. And that I found the best one.

'Mum, this is my friend, actually she's my best friend and she's really been looking after me and everything and. And anyway her name's –'

In the end I didn't even have to decide.

'– Allason? You must be Allason? It's so nice to meet you. Lynda told me a lot about you. Come in. Come in. Can I get you a cup of tea or something? Or some food? You both look starving. Have either of you eaten today? I must say you're not how I pictured you. And you met Tilly at Yarleigh Falls, right? Helped her settle in? We would've liked to do more ourselves but she wouldn't let us. Wouldn't even let us visit. But then I suppose you knew that. But it was very hard for us. Do you want something proper or just beans on toast? Beans? Okay then.'

The sproing of bread ducked into toaster.

'And then when she decided she didn't want to come home. God, that hurt. That really hurt, Allason, so it was at least reassuring to know there was someone – someone a little more, how would you put it, *streetwise?* – looking out for her.'

The room waiting in complete stillness as she unlidded the tin and poured its contents into a pan.

'Mum, I *am* here.'

The clatter of pan onto hob, the controlled explosion of burning gas.

'Yes, lovely, I know you're here. I know you're here now. I know that. I was just explaining to Allason how grateful I was that you had someone to so to speak lean on, because of how terribly upsetting, how agonising, frankly, it was to not have you here with us. If you can understand that. Do you think you can understand that?'

Sadie, sat at the table, never took her eyes from her hands, as if she somehow hoped that unresponsiveness would exempt her from this conversation.

'If you'd believed me . . .'

'What Tilly means, Allason, is that if we had taken *sides*, if we had sided with her against her brother, then everything would've been different. That, if we had made that decision, we would've been allowed to support her, we would've been allowed to remain part of her life. But what she doesn't understand is that we had no choice. That as parents we had no choice. That we had to, however painful it was and whatever our gut instinct told us, we absolutely had to stay neutral between our two children. That we couldn't win. That we had to pay a price whatever we did.'

She began clattering plates and cutlery and a tub of cholesterol-reducing spread onto the table, offering Sadie's forehead a taut smile.

'We had to pay a price whatever we did.'

'Mum, there's plenty of time for all this. Can't you just be glad to see me?'

She stopped where she was, the pan of hot beans yawing dangerously floorward, and, for the first time, looked at me. Really examined me, her face older than I'd remembered it in this sudden repose.

'Of course I'm glad to see you. Of course I am.' She moved closer to the table, began spooning beans onto toast, more messily than necessary. 'Just eat up, both of you. You look starved. And then we'll have a think about what to get you for dinner. Try and feed you up a bit.' She pulled a chair back, its hind legs stuttering across the lino, sat down. 'You are staying for dinner, aren't you?'

I don't know what gave me the idea they might have cleared my room out. Wishful thinking, I suppose. I'd already wanted the decor changed before I left for Yarleigh Falls. Even for such a sheltered and cosseted teenager as I had then been the room had seemed too childish, too dated. But rather than destroying it, my mum had opted for the traditional approach and made it into a shrine. 'We haven't moved a thing,' she reassured me as Sadie and I padded our way up the stairs, my fear of humiliation the column which held me upright.

I pushed the door open, the thick pile sighing with its movement, reached forward and flicked the light on. The room was an idealisation of how I'd left it – tidied, hoovered, paint touched up, the ballerina figurines aligned just-so on their shelf, all the *Little Women* series in the right order in the book case, an army of soft toys sitting patiently on the bed, rank after rank of them looking expectantly up at me. The pink of the walls, the pink of the curtains, the pink of the bedspread visible beyond the reach of the animals, each shade complementary and only ugly, really, by association. The fairy windchime my aunty had given me for my eighth birthday. The gymnastics magazines piled in a corner. The torn posters on my wall – all mended now, each rip preserved beneath carefully applied rectangles of sellotape – of a horse, the kittens, an array of endangered species and, of course, Leonardo Bloom. For a moment I felt terribly sorry that they had lost their little girl and that she was never coming back.

'Shit, man.' I had more pressing matters to deal with for now, such as Sadie's scorn. 'Thass the go.'

'What?'

'Like sutt'n from a fairy tale innit? I never seed nutt'n like it.' Her eyes toured the room again. 'An all dis is like your stuff? An ya din't share or nutt'n?' She lowered herself onto the bed, smoothed out the covers round her, passed her hand gently from head to head of the front row of toys – puppy to teddy to teddy to kitten to giraffe to teddy. Looked up, real excitement in her movements. 'Can I ave one?'

'What?'

'One a these?'

'Yeah. If you want. Help yourself. As many as you want.'

'Only want one.'

Her hand hovered over them, they seeming to have eyes for her alone now, a mutual love-in terminating when fingers clutched the head of a squashily stuffed white rat, two goofy teeth protruding from curl of smile, eyebrows touching pink ears.

'What's is name?'

I looked at the cheaply made toy, scratching over the interior of my cranium in search of a memory to match it. Nothing there, barely a whisper of recognition and then . . .

'*Ray-mond. Ray-mond le Rat.* Said like that. I got him in France on holiday. So it has to be *Ray-mond*. Daddy named him.' All of them suddenly with names and provenance, as if I'd downloaded the data.

Sadie sat, knees together, a pursed smile for *Ray-mond* as he goggled up from her lap.

'Can't take im can I?'

'Course ya can.'

'Can't.'

'Why not?'

'S'not right is it? Ya got it in *France* innit? Ain't just sutt'n ya got in a toyshop roun the corner.'

'So?'

'So, *France*.'

'What?'

'Fergeddit.' She placed *Ray-mond* back amongst his companions.

'What? Please take it. I want you to have it. Him.'

'Nah.'

'*Please.*'

'Ya sure?'

'Sure.'

'Cheers, Titch.' She picked it up again, looked at it with an amused seriousness, shook her head a little. 'France . . .'

Mum had made us fish fingers, chips and peas for tea, just as Sadie had requested. She didn't eat but sat at the table with us, the stem of a glass of red wine twizzling between the finger and thumb of one hand then the other. She seemed a little calmer now, her smiles less forced, the set of her body less jagged. The three of us were silent as we ate, cutlery tapping cutlery tapping china. Mum had given us a glass each of sweet cider, having refused our request for Breezers. The stillness around us unsettling, the house stretching out, empty. As I huddled my knife and fork together on my empty plate I asked the question I'd already figured out an answer to.

'Dad's late. What time's he getting in at?'

She had been preparing for this moment, her words clear, carefully scripted. 'He won't be, I'm afraid. Your father and I have separated. It's been a very hard couple of years and in the end we both decided it would be best if we started afresh.'

'Oh.'

'I know this all must be very strange for you. Believe me, it's still quite strange for me, but you have to try to understand the pressure our relationship was placed under.'

'So it's my fault is it?'

'That's not what I'm saying. That's not what I'm saying at all. It happens, Tilly. It happens all the time. It's really nobody's fault.'

'You don't seem very upset.'

'I'm dealing with it.'

'Seems pretty dealt with to me. So where's Dad living. A hotel? Some horrible bedsit?'

'Your father is living with his new girlfriend.'

'Oh.'

'Yes. Oh.'

'Do I know her?'

'I wouldn't think so. She's just slightly too old to have been at school with you.'

'Oh.'

'Yes. Oh. I'll ring him tonight and let him know you're here. He's been very worried about you despite . . . Despite everything else. You can speak to him then if you want. Find out the details for yourself.'

'Don't know if I want to.'

'Up to you. I'll phone him just to let him know you're okay.'

'Mum?'

'Yes?'

'You mustn't let anyone else know we're here. Just Dad, okay?'

'Whatever you want.' Her fingers swiped across her eyes. 'It would help if I knew what you'd done.'

'We haven't done anything.'

'Allason?'

'We ain't. Honest.'

'Okay. What about David?'

'No way. If you're gunna tell him we're leaving now.'

'He comes over on Saturdays to eat and drop off his washing. I don't see how we can avoid telling him.'

'Seriously, Mum. If you tell him I'm going now.'

'Okay, so what am I meant to do on Saturday?'

'What day is it now?'

'What day is it?' Her face tightening with concern. 'Tilly . . . It's Tuesday.'

'Then ring him and tell him you're away this weekend. Where is he anyway?'

'Just in halls in town. He's at the university.'

'So you could drop his washing off on the Friday, then.'

'Tilly, seriously, is there anything you want to tell me?'

'Yeah, but not right now. First, I need you to tell me you won't tell anyone but Dad. And tell him not to tell anyone.'

'I've already told you that. Are you okay?'

'Of course I'm okay. Why shouldn't I be okay?'

'You don't know what day of the week it is.'

'What, so that's like the standard now is it? For being okay?

Knowing what day of the week it is? I just got confused. I just got a bit confused. Things've been confusing.'

We retreated to my room to smoke fags, the ash flicked into one of the many empty trinket boxes with which I had lined my shelves, Sadie offering up the opinion every time her cigarette tapped on its edge, that it was a shame, really, to make a mess of something so pretty. Mum had refused us another glass of cider. We were sober and bored, too uncomfortable here to go and watch telly.

I hadn't expected to feel out of place. I began to wonder if I was this woman's daughter at all (a suspicion she no doubt shared with me). We seemed to move from one prison to the next, nothing beyond the perimeter fence but another perimeter fence and another beyond that, not so much concentric circles as a series of modules, all our escapes defeated and defeating. The trap of our life, always awakening to find ourselves in the trap of our life. We had nothing to say so we sat and chucked soft toys at one another, each high parabola beneath the ceiling, back and forward, defining a game without rules or purpose.

I had already heard the muffle of my mother talking before I went to the toilet. It was only as I left my former room and walked across the silenced floor of the landing that I became interested in what she was saying.

'I think so . . .' She sniffed loudly and I realised she'd been crying. 'Yes, I think so . . .

'Smoking.

'No. Just cigarettes.

'Well, how am I meant to know?

'My main priority is to make sure she stays . . . not make her feel like she's being interrogated.

'That's easy for you to say, isn't it?

'Sorry. Sorry. I'm upset.

'I know you do.

'I don't know. Let me get her. Let me see.'

The tiny sounds of her moving through a house grown much too big for her, her daughter frozen at the top of the stairs. The projection of my name abandoned when she found me there, hands tucked inside the waistband of my sweatpants, posture exaggeratedly bad, bottom lip folded beneath top teeth.

'Oh, you're there. Would you like to speak to your father?'

'Gotta go toilet.' The words carefully chosen to make Mum wince.

'Okay. After that? Do you want him to wait? Do you want to call him back?'

'Nah. Maybe tomorrah.'

'He'd really like to talk to you.'

'Maybe tomorrah.'

I turned and continued to my destination, my mother's voice behind me, quieter but no less deliberately neutral than it was with me.

'Not now.

'Tomorrow.

'Maybe tomorrow.

'I'm only reporting what she said.

'I really don't want to act as go-between.'

A tightening into anger now: 'Well, perhaps if you were here? Instead of . . .' She didn't finish the sentence – couldn't, perhaps. I closed the door to the bathroom, locked it, sat down on the lidded, empty laundry basket and thought of nothing, calm stealing over me, the beginnings of a realisation. I pulled myself up and looked into the mirror, the mask in front of me without antecedent, the blackheads speckling my nose much more real than any self supposedly resident behind these eyes. Then I sat again, my knickers connecting my knees, peed, wiped, stood and re-clothed, headed back to see what Sadie was doing. My friend, my only friend.

My mother finally went to bed, a timid knock on the door and the request delivered through it that, although she would rather we didn't smoke in the house at all, if we had to then it should only be in my room. Our territory expanded, we took our chance to go and laze on the warm beige carpet of the sitting-room floor, the giant screen of the television illuminating the glasses of vodka and orange we had fixed ourselves, the bottles in the cupboard we took the spirit from fluffy with dust. After a while we decided that one cigarette between us wouldn't hurt and in all kinds of ways it didn't. When we finally staggered upstairs we left the vodka bottle empty and one of Mum's best bowls full of ash.

For obvious reasons we woke late the next day. I, in fact, would have slept longer but Sadie was busting for the loo and didn't want to bump into Mum without me there. And Sadie, as usual, was right. She was lurking, waiting for us, although only to give us a taut non-smile and say pointedly, '*Morning*.' A pause. 'Do you want some breakfast?'

When she had us captive at the table, our cups of tea shuddering as they made their way up to our mouths and back down again, she started in, nothing in her rhythm surprising me.

'Now listen to me, please. I know you're both accustomed to living on your own and doing things however you want to do them but, well, this is my house. And I don't make many rules but those I do make I expect us all to stick to. So if I ask you not to smoke anywhere in the house except your room, Tilly, then that's what I expect to happen.'

'Sorry Mrs Parkins, that were me. I'm a addict innit? Won' appen again.'

'Well, Allason, that's very nicely put but I think we all know you weren't smoking on your own, don't we? Tilly?'

I allowed myself the smallest fraction of a shrug possible before it wouldn't have existed.

'And then there's the vodka. I'm not trying to pretend you don't drink. But I gave you alcohol with your supper. I'm really not happy about you just taking a bottle of vodka without even asking.'

'Jus you'd already gone bed, innit. S'like, what's worser? Wake er up to arks or jus –' A light touch on her elbow enough to stop her, my mother and I watching only each other. Me allowing the moment to last a little longer, forcing the slightest of smiles onto my face.

'We can always go.' Giving the words time to settle. 'If you don't like it. Having us here. If the rules are too precious. You just want us to go?'

She stared at me, her face cracking apart, all its elements bursting, anger and need dismantling her. Need winning through.

'Of course not. Of course that isn't what I meant. Of course it isn't.'

It occurs to me now that I could have made things much easier for myself if I had tried harder during the short time we spent together. Having your mother appear as a witness for the prosecution saying that you were 'completely changed, nothing like the little girl I knew and loved' is unlikely to work in your favour. But my anger would allow for no tactical nuance. And how was I supposed to read the future? The tools for that are the tools of power and I had none of them.

We spent the afternoon watching my parents' old DVDs, the room's contrast obscured by smoke, Sadie nervous, her eyes on the door with every drag.

While she was in the toilet (missing one of the funniest parts of *The Big Lebowski*, a film my parents had owned for so long that sometimes brightly coloured squares of pixels would glitch into life in the middle of Jeff Bridges' forehead), Sadie's mobile rang. I hesitated, my hand moving back and forward, then answered.

'Sadie?'

'It's Titch.'

'Alright Titch. Big Phil callin. You seen Seb?'

'What ya mean?'

'E still there?'

'No. He dropped us off yesterday morning and left.'

'Din't say nuffin?'

215

'No. Why?'

'It's fucked. E's disappeared. Ain't come back. Is phone's off.'

'Sorry. Dunno.'

'It's not like im.' He sounded genuinely concerned.

'You alright Phil?'

'Yeah. It's just. It's just not like im is all. Never just goes off. E's reliable.' A space. 'E seem alright when e left yer?'

I thought about it. 'Yeah. He seemed fine.'

'Even rang is mum an dad.'

'And?'

'Ain't seen him. Can't just've disappeared.'

'I'm sure he'll show up.'

'Well, if you see im tell im to call me.'

'I don't suppose I will . . .'

'No, I don't spose so.'

'But if I do I will.'

'Do. Alright. Later.'

I demanded supper early and my mother complied, the three of us bound again in our terrible silence, as if one word would start us screaming. I don't know about Mum, but Sadie and I were waiting for dusk. As soon as it felt dark enough we scanned the road out front for unusual vehicles, curtain twitchers, nosy parkers, then, satisfied, slipped out of the door, my mother left standing in the hallway.

'Are you . . .? Will you . . .?'

'Just a walk. We'll be back later. You got some money on you? A twenty?'

Once we'd scuttled away from my street and down the alley that led to the all-night garage, we felt ourselves relax. Released into the smell of the world, inflated by cool air, children caught in gathering dark, we bobbed above the pavement, happiness sneaking through us.

Sadie limped into the shop and soon emerged onto the forecourt with Marlboros and Breezers, the clink of the bottles in the bag the opening notes of a favourite song. Our arms wrapped each other's and I led her to the park.

There the two of us rocked on the swings, the last of the day's light gone, alternating puffs and swigs so that first one face would glow behind its orange star, then the other. I kept looking forward at the dark loom of grass, growing more uniform by the instant, potholes, puddles and dogshit all vanishing, only the white of abandoned lolly sticks still showing, the gentle movement of our seats calming me, somehow, these seats I'd sat on so many times before, my mind swarming with memories of the ground around me. When Mandy Clitheroe had been mounted by an Alsatian as she tried to retrieve a ball from the nettles. The time I had fallen from this very swing and twisted my ankle so bad I had to go to casualty and my brother, who had *pushed too hard*, got his pocket money stopped for a week. Playing kiss chase and never getting kissed. Jimmy Sperry, our local nutter, chucking bangers at passing OAPs. Eating lemon bonbons from the corner shop on that bench over there, teeth sticking together. Melinda Perkins and I pretending that the roundabout was a gateway to a different world and spinning it a spell. So that, even before the four Breezers had worked their magic and my head had become thick, my speech slurred, I found myself, for the very first time, glad to be home.

My mother had gone to bed by the time we got back, though every light in the house remained on, the one in her bedroom extinguished only after she was sure we were home and safe. I was too drunk for it, but Sadie started enthusiastically on the bottle of cider Mum had left out on the side in the kitchen for us, finding some ice to make it drinkable. But, sticking to a hidden agreement, we didn't smoke, our fingers pattering, under-occupied, over the work surfaces.

I left Sadie lying fully dressed on the bed, her arms and legs flung out like discarded clothing, her open mouth ratcheting air back through her nose in a regular snort. With my left arm raised, I stroked my fingers along the wall as I walked, grateful to feel something solid. I was heading to the bathroom, determined – in a hazy, serious way – that I should at least brush my teeth before sleeping. But when I reached the door, I found myself passing it and moving straight on towards my brother's room, my legs an automaton's. I stopped, the fingers of my right hand tracing the edge of his MAKE CODE NOT WAR sticker. Then pushed in, the cold air of unradiatored space eddying out to meet me, a shiver catching me even though I knew he wasn't in there.

I turned the light on to find the room a mirror of mine – both exactly as I remembered and completely other due to unnatural tidiness, excessive hoovering, the unimaginable lack of dirty pants or empty M&Ms packets littering the floor. But everything else was there. The display of every chocolate animal he had been given as a child from the age of eight onward, each unnibbled and still in its original foil. The fantasy/sci-fi posters on the wall, visions of an airbrushed, heavily muscled, large-breasted future. His collections, both filed in the cabinet over there and displayed on his special exhibition shelf: Matchbox cars, unusually shaped conkers, stamps, stones, obsolete transistors, foreign sugar lumps, prime numbers seen on the street, rare Airfix paint colours and so on, each equivalent to a period of his late childhood and early adolescence of between six months and two years, most of them overlapping to create a complex diagram of obsession.

The only major change was the absence of a computer on the desk, no amount of cleaning ever likely to remove the silhouette of its former location. Without it the room seemed dead, empty, eerily quiet.

I pulled out the chair I'd sat in all that time before, sank into it again, feeling those rubber armrests, imagining the keyboard in front of me, my finger hovering over ENTER. Instead, all that lay on the desk was a few sheets of paper, the top crested by the University of Reading, glad to be able to offer a place in halls and, further down, giving an address. Without much thought beyond a banal spitefulness, I crushed the letter into my pocket, grabbed a gigantic bunny from the shelf and settled down on his bed to eat it.

The chocolate beneath the foil was stale and long curdled, obviously inedible even before I broke off an ear and stuffed it into my mouth. I think I must have been feeling nauseous already but just hadn't noticed. It came on me now with an abruptness that scared me, my blood vanishing from me. I lay down on the bed, weakness shuddering in my limbs, too scared to close my eyes, hoping to recover sufficiently to stagger to the bathroom, hoping to pull out of this spin.

'Tilly?
'Tilly?
'Tilly?'
Like turning up the volume on a television, oblivion slowly lost, new sensations stringing themselves together.
'Tilly?
'Tilly?'
The taste in my mouth, my head's swollen thud, the bright electric light.
'Tilly?
'Tilly?'
My father's voice. I opened my eyes to find him standing above me, hangover perspective towering him up and up. He was trying to smile.

'Ah, so you're awake? What are you in here for?' Sighing, carefully lifted a glob of colourful crushed foil and chocolate shards from the bed beside me and moved them back to their place on the shelf.

'Oh. Was that really necessary? Seems a bit petty. A bit childish.'

He brushed his hands off on each other, looked round the room without really looking, lowered himself carefully down by my feet.

'How are you, love?'

I still couldn't speak, my mind a jigsaw puzzle I'd put together only to find it was the wrong picture. In contrast to my mother, my father looked younger, although in embarrassingly transparent ways. He seemed to have gel in his hair, which he had artlessly used to spike his new, aggressively chopped cut. He was wearing a pair of Carhartt jeans very low, a huge clot of stripy M&S boxers clearly visible above his belt, and a t-shirt whose XL size and slogan ('Just Penetrate') served only to accentuate his paunch. The thought of the general public seeing him like this was exquisitely embarrassing.

'It's good to see you. I've been really worried. Your mum, too.'

Perhaps most startling of all, though, were the cracks in his new identity – the apparently constant effort to keep his eyebrows from their habitual frown, the deep lining of his face, the grey, flaky quality of his skin, so that it seemed as if someone had tried to trendy up a toddler with a dreadful ageing disease.

'You okay?'

Croakily, gradually dislodging the night-time gunk that had accumulated in my throat, speech came back to me.

'I bet.'

'I'm sorry?'

'I bet you were *really* worried. What with shagging your new girlfriend an all.'

He looked down, disappointed, up again to offer me a meek smile.

'I guess I expected that.'

'Was it *really necessary*?'

'Try not to be angry with me. Not for that, anyway.'

'What *should* I be angry with you for, then?'

He looked over to where the computer had been, the chair still rolled back from the desk, the room quiet enough for me to hear the bed's amplification of his body's readjustments.

'I just want you to know how much we love you, both of us.'

I said nothing, my face warming itself.

'We really do. We love you.'

'Don't.'

'It's important that you know.'

'Please. It's embarrassing.'

'Despite the test. Despite the DNA result. You're still our daughter. To me and your mother you will always be our daughter. Whatever they say.'

'They told you, then?' I asked, surprised now that Mum hadn't mentioned it.

'Of course they told us. Not straight away. Not when we first enquired. But the DNA isn't what's important. Not to us. I can't speak for the other parents going through this. But not for us. We took you home from hospital. We watched you grow up. You're our little girl. Nothing can change that.'

I so wanted to be that little girl right then, to explain the mistake, to explain it all, to let the grown-ups sort it out and change these clothes for something sensible and complete my diploma and go to college and get a good job and a flat and a boyfriend and forget that any of this had ever happened.

'And I'm not even going to abdicate my own responsibility and say that somehow your genes are connected with your behaviour over the last couple of years. Even though I guess there's science to support that idea . . .'

His thought, or at least his articulation of it, stopped. My moment passed.

'That it?'

Jerked back into action, breezy, assured. 'Probably not even true, though, is it? There's hundreds of cases now. Most likely explanation is it's just a mix-up at the lab. All just a terrible mix-up. And all this fuss will have been for nothing. But I just wanted you to know that either way we love you. Whatever happens. Now I need you to come downstairs with me.'

'Dad?' I said, as we left my brother's room behind us.

'Yes?'

'I *am* childish. Because I am a child.'

I never had a chance to find out whether he took this seriously because I never heard any response. I stepped down the stairs to see those boots, those pressed jeans, that blouson jacket, those dark glasses and that hair. Lynda looked as uncomfortable and out of place sitting on the sofa with her cup of tea as Sadie did next to her. Her body jerked as she watched me descending, a malign Pinocchio. Sadie didn't look up.

'Ah, Tilly, *dear*. I've been *so* worried about you,' every bit the digital-channel reality-TV contestant. 'Come and sit with me here?' She patted at the cushion with a transparent heartiness, her smile a parody.

I stayed where I was at the foot of the stairs, my father moving past me. 'I'm sorry, love. It's for the best.'

'*Keen* to get going?' Lynda enquired. 'I can understand that. No point dragging these things out. The fare-*wells* and so on. Time to be off, Allason.' And she began to lever herself upright.

'Are you sure about this, Will?' my mother asked my father. 'Are you sure we're doing the right thing?'

'I thought we'd discussed this?'

'Well . . .'

'It's just now's not really the moment for second thoughts.'

'We didn't really "discuss" it, at all, though, did we?'

'If she doesn't go back she's in breach of the terms of her parole and she'll end up back in prison. Is that what you want?'

'Of course not. But –'

'Lynda is trying to help us here. She's willing to bend the rules a little bit to keep our daughter out of jail.'

'I know but –'

'But what?'

'I know.'

'So that,' Lynda interrupted, her spiked cheeks lifting her

glasses up and pressing them in to her forehead, 'is decided. And very wise, *too*, if you don't mind me saying so. Don't *worry*. I'll look after them.' She clicked through an ill-formed arc. 'Come along girls. We have a long journey.' However you looked at it she was no Julie Andrews. That much should have been obvious even to people as dazzled by authority as my parents.

I kept staring at my father, moving neither my body nor my gaze until he looked round at me.

'You're not my dad. She's not my mum. The whole thing was a mistake.'

We have been gripped by Schism, by purge and counter-purge. The Vanished have been cleaved in two. Some of us have long been suspicious of those who wait 'to be taken'. There is no point in waiting. Frankly, it's unbecoming. There will be no more 'Take me too'.

Extract from *Fifty-first Communiqué of the Vanished*

After my mother's house, the interior of Lynda's decrepit, tar-stained TR7 made me gag, a nausea which wanted me inside out. I tried to seek comfort with Sadie but she wouldn't look at me, struck dumb by my father's betrayal. She climbed into the passenger seat and turned her head from me as I lowered myself in on top of her, Lynda chucking her mobile onto the dashboard and leering beyond us for the benefit of my parents, her face creaking as she exclaimed, 'Just like old times!'

Then the car started and we began lurching backwards down the paving slabs of this suburban drive and, with each jolt, my parents, standing in front of the house, half a metre between them, became a fraction smaller, a tiny bit more distant. And as I watched their shrinkage I saw my mother begin to cry, my father raise his hand to her shoulder to comfort her, my mother push it away with a vehemence I didn't recognise in her. Then we were gone, moving forward and away and, except for at court, I would never see them again.

'We're like a family, really, when you think about it,' Lynda finally offered. 'We may argue and disagree and so on, but at heart, when it comes down to it, we all pull in the same direction.'

The rumble of the car gulped down the words, the protestations of its overworked engine making them seem more abstract, less offensive than they were. Neither Sadie or I bothered to respond.

'When the chips are down. Or when we all stand to gain.'

We'd been driving for twenty minutes or so. Lynda had avoided the motorway and instead become ensnared in a succession of ring roads, sub-ring roads and bypasses originally designed to siphon traffic away from the town centre but now a destination in themselves, the verges crowded with the primary-coloured blocks of retail park warehouses, the slip roads cluttered with invitations to dine at monumental TGI Fridays, Pizza Huts, Taco Bells and so on, a vista so undistinguished that we could have been on the outskirts of almost any town anywhere in the world. There was no chance that Lynda knew where she was or could find her way out. The only road signs here were corporate and franchise outlets were the only place.

'I know that in some way you two feel I've be-*trayed* you. In fact, nothing could be *further* from the truth. I *have* profited from the predicament you find yourselves in, it's true. But only by giving people what they wanted and no more. No unnecessary information has been forthcoming. Nothing about the little *swap* you two . . .' – her face contorted for a moment – '. . . *scamps* perpetrated.' A sigh of unclear purpose. 'There are cigarettes in the glove compartment.'

We lit up, both of us trying to ignore the thrust of Lynda's insinuations, the appeal to complicity. Instead, I watched the hard shoulder, carrier bags rising and falling like yogic flyers, a thousand spent cigarettes flung from a thousand car windows, a used nappy, the black tyre-diagrams of traffic accidents, broken glass shaped into modem chatter, a knackered chair, weeds and grasses using macadam as soil. There was to be no escape. Not until the end was there to be an escape.

'Well, I'm glad at least to see you'll still take my cigarettes. That's *some*-thing I suppose. Despite this *sulk* you both seem to have fallen into.'

I felt Sadie's legs shift under me and tried to lift myself so she could get comfortable. Heard the air move through her teeth.

'Come den Lynda. Whass gwanin?'

We jarred and jolted our way toward a roundabout, pulled out, right indicator ticking, and began to circle, Sadie and I pushed over to the door, Lynda intent.

'Sorry, just trying to get my *bear*-ings. You're from round here, Tilly dear. Which way should I go?'

'Dunno. Tell us what's going on and I'll have a think about it.'

'More of this un-*warr*-anted *an*-ger. Dear me.' She swung a little harder at the wheel. My cheek squelched against the cool glass of the window. 'Didn't Anna explain it all to you?'

'What she told us, Lynda, was that we were important because we proved that Sanalex messed up its results and the people she worked for wanted to prove that cos they wanted the Roots of Crime contract instead. But there's hundreds of people with messed-up results now and it's been on telly and everything. So that doesn't make sense anymore, does it?'

'No, I don't suppose it does.' She exited the roundabout heading back the same way we'd come, us two falling toward her. Picked up her phone and glanced at the screen before putting it down again.

'Waitin for a call? Ain't gunna try an pull dat one again?'

'I suppose I can understand your feelings of distrust, *hurt*-ful though I find them. I'm merely trying to find the best path to our destination.'

'And where's tha? Ya fink if ya talk all reh reh we ain't see frough ya?'

The car accelerated a little, my head moving back, a weight attached to the top of a spring. The children in the car in front waved at us, stuck out their tongues, disappeared sniggering from our line of sight.

'The answer is I don't *know* exactly what's going on. And I talk "all *rare rare*" because that's the correct way to talk, isn't it, Tilly? But I have used my *head* and tried to work out what could be going on.'

'And?'

'Well, there have been a lot of people from a lot of different companies *sniff*-ing around for you, Tilly, offering con-*sid*-erable *sums* of money for information. Particularly regarding your *where*-abouts. And as you *say*, there are a lot of other people who seem to have mislaid their children. So it can't be anything general. It must be something specific to *you* and your case. Or rather, to *Allason* and her's. And it strikes *me* that as I said all along, it must have something to do with the father.'

'Why?'

'Well, you met the mother and it wasn't *her* was it?'

'I don't know.'

'Believe me, it's *never* the mother. It's going to be the father.'

'How do you know?'

'Well, the mother's *gone*, anyway. So we need to find out who the father is.'

The kids ahead reappeared and gave us the finger with the kind of abashed care which suggested they had no idea what it meant.

'Nah man, thass out of order. Kiddies innit? Need to show some respec.'

They were lapping their tongues in and out now, their chins wet with slobber, four chubby middle digits dancing like puppets.

'Nah man. Tellin ya, thass a diss. Come, Lynda.'

'What?'

'Put ya foot down. Bring us up nex to em.'

'What?'

'Drive up nex to em. Their dad fink we don't know e knows? Knamean?'

'Not really. But if it'll make you happy.' None too smoothly she accelerated, the children's mania suddenly evaporating from them as they witnessed our approach, their glistening chins falling, the whites of their eyes growing until, without communicating, they both turned and dropped into their seats, only the dishevelled tops of their heads showing.

'See how *keen* I am to help?'

Lynda crunched the car out into the next lane and edged it closer to them, the boys' eyes flickering across towards us while trying to stay straight ahead. Then, with no warning we were past them and Lynda – having looked up to the red lights in front of us – brought her foot down hard on the brake and,

I with my forearms squashed against the windscreen, the two cars came to rest next to each other.

'Moon em, Titch.'

'What?'

'Moon em, man.'

'Haven't we got –?'

'Quick!'

I think I mainly did it because Sadie had asked me to, because she hadn't spoken to me or even looked at me since it became clear what my parents had done, also because it seemed funny and straightforward and subject to only one interpretation. Uncomfortably, I angled myself round, raising my arse and lowering my head and quickly, before I lost my balance, pulled my trousers and knickers down over my cheeks.

'Oh, *really* . . .'

'Put it on the glass!'

Pushed myself back onto cold window, the sensation surprisingly pleasant. Sadie reached round both sides of me, middle fingers offered with considerable conviction. I stretched and, somehow, through the melee of limbs and displaced clothing, caught sight of three faces, a gaping father and his gaping sons, amazed, disgusted and quite probably titillated all at once.

'Thank *God*.'

The lights having apparently changed, our driver set off fast, a screech of lost traction, Sadie and I a laughing tangle.

'Now, per-*haps* we can *fo*-cus?'

I expect this seems like a meaningless incident, a distraction, at best an example of our frivolousness and stupidity, the vulgarity of our limited world view. We never saw the people in the car again, we never knew who they were, they never had any direct impact on us, or on the story I'm telling you. And yet, looking back on it all, it seems like a crucial moment, the two of us heaped like that, the hot breath of our laughter stroking each other's hair, me trying to hitch my thong back into place. The atmosphere in the car changed, the despair suddenly lifting from me, recklessness taking its place. Without it, I would never have done what I did next.

'Go on then, *Lynda*' – the word spat with contemptuous relish – '*fo*-cus for us.'

'I'm not sure I see the need for your tone, but since you ask, I *will*. We're back to where we were at the start. The only way we can find out who the *fa*-ther is is by finding the brother.'

Outside, we were passing Carphone Warehouse for the third time. I wondered if Lynda had any idea of where she was going. Or even where she wanted to go.

'We tried. E's vanished.'

'*Van*-ished? I don't think so. No, I *beg* to differ.'

I began to wonder if her whole pitch was just a desperate attempt to stay in the game, somehow, a futile last bluff.

'You know where he is?'

She careered the vehicle back and forth across lane markings, her attention never leaving the road despite the lack of difference it made. Behind us, a parade of vehicles hooted, swerved, flashed their lights, our escort other people's anger.

'Not exactly.' Trying to tease us, a fork scraping round a plate. 'But I know someone who does . . .'

'Another of your "colleagues" in social services?'

'Sort of.' She spangled her head around in a sinister approximation of an excited prom queen, then sung out, 'It's *An-na*!'

'Ah shit.'

'Lemme out the car, ya crazy bitch.'

She patted us down with a lazy wave of her hand, searched for a soothing tone of voice. 'Now now.' Failing. 'I'm not about to sell you to her. *Again*.' A roll of the eyes and imitation laugh. 'No, I think I can do better out of all this if we cooperate.'

'Ya kiddin int ya?'

'She's *armed*, Lynda.'

'And so are we. Armed with *info*-mation. We know things Anna hasn't even *dreamed* of. For instance, that Allason is the one she's after rather than you, Tilly.'

She had given me an idea. Another tiny move closer.

'So? That stops bullets does it?'

'No, but if Allason and I were to meet her to negotiate . . .'

'What, and then she snatches me while you're meant to be "meeting" and you've still got Sadie? I don't think so.'

Beneath her sunglasses she squinted a little. Tilted her head then straightened it up.

'Not a bad i-dea, actually, Tilly. I always suspected that beneath your rather bland exterior you might possess a talent for this sort of thing. But no. That's not what I'm planning.'

Gradually, as carefully as I could manage, I lifted my right hand, flickered my fingertips until I found the lip of Sadie's jacket pocket.

'Then what are you planning?'

Slid my hand in, Sadie's belly stiffening slightly as she felt me.

'I plan to do a deal with Anna. For all of us. And then, if the opportunity arises for us to double-cross her, well I don't imagine you'll object to that.'

'What sort of a deal?'

'Well, it's hard to be sure until we know exactly what she's after. A mutual exchange of information.'

'Yeah, but Sadie is the information.'

'Nah man. Why should she care?'

'I'm sorry, Allason?'

'Why should she care? Don't make no sense. If ya sayin it's about muh dad an she's got muh bruv, an e's the one with the chromawhatsit why she need me? She can find out who muh dad is better from im.'

'What do you mean?'

'The chromathingy. I ain't got it, is it? You was the one dat tol me. The son's the one wid it.'

My fingers on the handle now, the texture of its grips, the cross-hatching of the metal.

'That's a good point, Sadie.' She seemed to push herself deeper into the seat. 'I don't expect we'll really know the answer until we know who your father is. Perhaps you're insurance. Or maybe they just want the complete set.'

My hand closed – its weight and diameter.

'Either way, our best chance of finding out is through Anna.'

Thumb made its way along the top edge, felt the serrated grumble of its catch. Pushed down and forward, imagining the triangle of steel growing at its tip.

'Alternatively, I could just drive you straight back to Yarleigh Falls. Because that's your only other option.'

My voice came out gruff and phlegmy: 'You don't even know where you are.' Smoothly and with a calmness which surprised me even as it possessed me, I pulled the Stanley knife from Sadie's pocket, raised it and placed the isosceles of blade firmly but carefully against the liver-spotted dewlap of Lynda's neck.

'Shit, Titch.'

'If you try anything I'm gunna cut you.'

I imagined her eyes flustering down and back to the road. 'What is it?'

'It's a knife an if you don't shut up and do as you're told I'm gunna cut ya.'

Pictured her eyes coming down again, for a little longer this time, until the car dodged left of its own accord and she was forced to look up.

'Listen, Titch man. I ain't sure –'

'I know what I'm doing.' I angled the blade round so that its unsharpened side could be pressed more energetically against her skin, enjoyed watching the resulting flinch.

'Not so chatty now, are we Lynda?'

She didn't respond. Her face seemed to be rattling slightly, as if internal g-force was shaking her. Her mouth was working, making shapes which could have been words. Her hands seemed to be trying to break the steering wheel.

'*Titch*.'

'We can't trust her, Sadie. We never could trust her. We just have to trust each other now.' I was almost laughing, my head bursting outward, the sun coming through the windscreen in threads. 'Ya see?'

I turned my attention back to Lynda, her jaw moving with the ruminant intensity of a speed freak, the neck beneath it staying very still.

'Now. I want you to tell us what's going on and I don't want any shit.'

'It's just what I told you. I don't know anything else.' Some kind of West Country burr cracking through her well-constructed accent. I pressed a little harder still, the loose skin bulging round the blade like dough.

'Come on, Lynda. You can do better than that.'

'I can't because that's the *truth*. That's the *truth*, Tilly. What you want me to *do*?'

Just for a moment I thought of actually cutting her. Not to cause her pain or get something from her, but with a kind of distant, abstracted interest in what it might feel like beneath my hand, what it might look like as the pouch split.

'I want you to try. I want you to try to remember. Cos there's no way you weren't going to fuck us up.'

She gulped, the blade riding the undulation of her throat. 'Tilly, I think you should put the knife down. I really think you should. This isn't going to help anyone. Is it, Allason? *Allason*, help your friend here?'

'I ain't sayin nutt'n.'

'Come on, *Lyndy*, spill.'

She seemed to be trying very hard to control her temper, an epic struggle between anger and fear. She fought to start her next sentence three or four times, but all that would come was a series of disconnected plosives, as if she was soundchecking a microphone. Then fear won, definitively.

'*Pleeeease*.' She moaned it quietly, an exotic mantra. '*Pleeeeease*.' A tiny whine as she drew breath. '*Pleeeease. Pleeeease*. I don't *know* anything. I really don't know *any*-thing. I *don't*. I don't know anything. I only know all I know is what I told you. That's all I know.'

'No it isn't.'

'It *is*. I'm just trying to make a living, I don't mean any harm, just trying to make ends meet, keep the wolf from the door. You're my girls. My *fave*-ourites. My *children*. I'm not saying I haven't made mis-*takes*. I really wasn't going to *do* anything to you. *Really*. I really wasn't.'

It only took a moment for my enjoyment of Lynda's grovelling to turn to disgust. Even her fear offended me.

'Well, how you gunna prove it? What can you do for us to convince us?'

'*Pleeeeease*. What do you want me to do?'

I'd never expected to enjoy all this so much. My initial plan had merely been to escape from her, or at least I thought it had. But now that didn't seem enough. Now I wanted more.

'Take off your glasses.'

'What?'

'Take off your glasses.'

'Tilly, you *can't* . . . I *can't*. I *can't* take them off. They're *med*-ical. It's not –'

'Take them off.'

'I won't be able to see. I won't be able to see to *drive* properly.'

'You can't drive properly anyway. Take em off.'

'I have an allergy. To daylight. It's a medical con-*dition*. My eyes will swell up. Allason knows. Allason?'

'Titch, she does got a problem with er eyes . . .'

'My arm's getting tired, Lynda. Take them off.'

'I could be *blind*-ed. I'll crash the *car*. *Pleeeease*. I've got money.'

'I just wanna see your eyes. Now hold still.' Pressing as hard as I dared with my right hand, I brought my left up, hesitating for a moment before grasping the frames and yanking them free of her face.

She squealed, the high-pitched sound of a small creature being disembowelled, and her hand came up to cover her face, the car slipping its leash and ducking sideways, Sadie yelping with fright. The self-preservation instinct was strong in Lynda, though, and, just as our impact with the metal crash barrier at the edge of the road seemed inevitable, she pulled the wheel over and trammelled us into the slow lane. Rescued from our own fear, Sadie and I looked across at Lynda's face.

Without glasses the terrain had changed completely, rutted pits revealed beneath those shining convexities, her nose longer and more prominent, her other features bunching in on themselves. She had always looked old, but now seemed impossibly ancient, as if she'd been hustling for a thousand years. But it was her eyes that made me gag – shiny black circles, like the buttons on a teddy bear's face, her eyelids folding round them like a tongue round an obscenity. They shuddered in their sockets, animal.

'Ah shit. Fuck's sake. Pull over. Pull over at the next slip road.'

The car had begun to accelerate.

'Ya hear me? Pull over. The next exit?'

Engine puffing itself up, faster still. Lynda's face suddenly set, her non-human eyes glistening, her jaw clenched.

'You're not going to cut me. I'm driving too fast. You touch me and I'll kill us all. I'll drive us off the road.'

'Just fuckin pull over.'

'No.' The crash barriers flickering, all other vehicles in reverse, the regular flash of tripped speed cameras.

'Just pull over.'

'Not so clever now –'

'*Titch* –'

'What you gunna do, Lynda? Drive like this forever? You're gunna have to stop sooner or later. Just take the next exit an let us out.'

'No.'

She was lost in a private film projected straight through the lenses of those eyes, collision impossible, no gap too small, speed an effect. By comparison my threat seemed prosaic, medieval. I flinched back from the bonnet, a looseness round my chest where no seatbelt held me.

'Alright, alright, point taken. Point taken. Stop the car. Stop the car an I'll give you the knife.'

Satisfied with this concession, or believing that my tone of voice indicated that she had regained control, Lynda swerved for the exit, her smile returning, body bracing back into the seat, the whole panto ready to reset and start all over again, all ready to start again.

There's no way to ascertain the causes of what happened next. Perhaps Lynda misjudged the speed she was travelling at. Perhaps she was deliberately trying to unbalance me and drive home her temporary advantage. Perhaps it was simply another example of her habitual clumsiness behind the wheel. Whatever the reason, as the car left the dual carriageway, Lynda removed her right foot from the accelerator and punched it down onto the brake.

We stopped with an immediacy completely at odds with our speed, but the sudden arrest of momentum seemed to last an age, that tiny episode cut from the narrative of life and pasted over and over again, already a repetition of an earlier event and now a repetition of itself, the anticipation of impact stretching like the screech of the tyres on the road beneath. Then – everything compressing, snapping together, the power of it taking not just my breath from my lungs, but the thoughts from my head, the bones from beneath my skin, my whole being outside itself – we were still.

I found my body bent forward, my hands held up to my bleeding nose, the engine stalled and, slowly, a whole world of sounds beginning to leak in at the windows again. I knew that I was missing something but wasn't sure what it was. I felt at my nose to see if it were broken, watched the blood spot onto the white sleeve of my tracksuit top and blot there, heavy rain drops on a summer day.

'*Fuck.*'

Angled myself round to check Sadie was okay, the bones of my neck crunching across one another, metal-mouthed, a swollen, dribbly smile. But Sadie wasn't looking back at me. Sadie was looking past me, to her right. Sadie was looking at Lynda. And Sadie was looking scared. Which was when I remembered the knife I'd been holding, my own competitive advantage, which must be now in Lynda's hand.

Very slowly, very carefully, my empty fingers hovering above my lap, I twisted my neck past the passenger window, past the wing mirror, past the sun flap with vanity mirror, past the hole where the stereo had once been and round until I faced her.

It turned out she wasn't holding the knife, not exactly. Her hands scuttled forward – more lifelike independently than as part of her – grabbed her glasses from the dashboard and scrabbled them across her eyes, one arm protruding like an aerial, the bridge lying wonky on her nose. The hands then moved to her neck, wafting through the air toward the Stanley's handle, which hung there limply, its weight pushing at the skin above its entrance so that the shape of the blade could be seen beneath the surface. The act of locating this irritant by touch was enough to dislodge it and, with a slight slurp, it fell.

That was when she screamed, the blade lodging firmly in her thigh so that she completely ignored the blood now beginning to gloop from her neck in her desperation to pull the knife from her leg. It came out easier than she was expecting, the grey metal handle being propelled upward by her two clenched fists with enough force to shatter the left lens of her newly reinstalled glasses.

Lynda looked up at us, surprised – an electrical beetle who'd seen better days – and the blood pumped from her neck. To the extent that I had ever thought about it, it had always been my assumption that if a major artery was cut, the victim's life fluid would spurt from them like foam from a can of silly string. Instead it glugged out, double cream forced through a tear in a balloon, the lips of the wound opening and closing as if it was a mouth trying to talk to me or seduce me. Huge quantities of liquid escaping like this, so that by the time Lynda noticed the exact focus of our eyes and raised her fingers to find them dabbling in this flow, a large proportion of her sky-blue jacket, her favourite and/or only jacket, her pride and joy, was dyed purple.

She raised her red fingers and looked at them for a moment, rested their tips on her chin and lower lip and stiffly inhaled a gulp of air, almost as though she believed that this one small action could, on its own, stop the tiny, disparate movements of her malfunctioning body. And, having somehow achieved at least a part of this basic desire, she opened her mouth to speak to us, to lambast us, or ask for help, more likely. But instead of any words, all that came from her mouth was a small, bubbly, baby gurgle. The incongruity of hearing it come from the drowning throat of this bloody old woman was so total that I bashed at my forehead with the flat of my hand, as if everything wrong was internal to me.

That was when we lurched out of the calm which seemed to have held us. Sadie began rattling at the door handle, her curses mixing with mine, my hands pounding on the windscreen as if I could somehow explode through it and escape by flying straight up high, high into the cold, thin air of the sky. Lynda, meanwhile, seemed intent on auditioning for a part in a horror movie, massaging at her wound suggestively, her movements strobed, her head working free from her shoulders.

'You gotta . . . reach across er . . . Titch . . . to do the locks.'
'Oh fuck *no*.'
'Quick. We're trapped.'
'Oh fuck.'
'Just do it.'
I looked at Lynda's face, her fractional gyrations, the browning smears of blood over her increasingly white skin. Managed to breathe. Lunged across her before I thought too hard about it. As my fingers closed on the plastic toggle of the lock I felt her arms tighten around me, one set of bony fingers

kneading into my tits, the other digging into my stomach. I pulled the catch and, with a desperate wriggle, tried to lever myself back across the car. I couldn't move, Lynda proving remarkably strong for a presumed sexagenarian in the process of bleeding to death. Her arms corseted me, wet breaths coming closer, the sound of her filling lungs. Unable to stop myself I turned my face toward that noise. And that was when she began to kiss me.

I think that's what she was doing. Maybe she was trying to bite me. All I can say for certain is that her wet lips oozed back and forth across my cheek as if I were a napkin and she a stroke victim eating soup. The panic this caused in me was so great that I stopped struggling, a drowsiness embracing me, all the events that had led to this moment fading from me, the shock paralysing me, my nerves burning away, central command left trapped in my head.

'Get the keys. Titch, get the *keys.*'

Her lips sliming into me, the gap between my face and her mouth shrinking, blood and spit and flesh all melding

'The keys. Titch. The *keys.*'

until I knew that we had one head, Lynda and I, were in fact the same person

'The fuckin *keys.*'

had always been the same person, this sharing of genetic material mere confirmation

'Titch. Get the fuckin *keys.*'

except for this voice, this voice, this Sadie's voice somewhere behind and away from me and us

'Get the keys, man.'

until I opened my eyes and there they were, hanging in front of me, the slightest lateral swing, so small it was almost a shudder. My hand reached out, a spindly weed to sun, held them, pulled.

'Ya got em?'

I could barely hear her, my left ear in Lynda's mouth, part of Lynda's mouth.

'Titch, ya got em?'

'Yes.'

There was a thud above me, the long slurp of lost suction, Lynda's arms loosened and I felt a tugging at my ankles. Pulled feet first back into my own body, unique, separate, the conjunction over, I scrabbled from the car, my hands wiping and striking at my head and face. *My* head and face. My head and face. Sadie slammed the door behind me.

'The keys.'

I gave them to her, watched her turn and lock, the always-satisfying clunk as the catches riveted downward spoilt by Lynda as she loomed up at the window, her hands rising to the very top of the glass, as though she hoped to prise it open, then descending slowly, palms a flat yellow-white, red left behind, a child's fingerpainting. And as the last of her long, thin nails finally clicked from the pane, her head came to rest in the bloody daub she had created, a circle of contact on her eyebrow and her cheek, her nose bent round and flattened by the pressure, the chestnut filter of the blood adding an unreality to the tableau so that it seemed like a reconstruction in the display case of a museum. And then, with Lynda staying so very still, we turned and ran.

Despair is our weapon. Which is another way of saying that it is the only weapon available and, hence, our only hope.

Extract from *Sixtieth Communiqué of the Vanished*

12

Lynda's keys floated in the air for a moment, the sun flashing from the flatness of their spinning surfaces with all the quick intensity of encryption. Then they descended, hit the water with an unexpected neatness and sank. The problem with ornamental fountains as a medium for evidence disposal is a lack of depth. Through the unnaturally emerald tint of the liquid they remained visible, shimmering with weed, waiting for a new ignition. We didn't care, didn't give ourselves time to care. We ran.

We ran through car parks as though they were fields, the crop an endless permutation of four-by-fours, jeeps, Sports-Military Vehicles, Armoured Personnel Carriers converted for family use, bachelor tanks, runabouts the size of trains. We were dwarfed in amongst them, two Alices without a growing-cake between us, so that none of the men or women we saw hefting sacks of shopping into their boots or unstrapping impeccably dressed children from their restraining devices even noted our presence, let alone the sweat dribbling off our foreheads, the fearful workout of our eyes.

We ran through the gaps between the car parks, the networks of private roads which twined their way over the shattered lumps of abandoned factories to superstores and incinerators. Without pavements, we stumbled and staggered over feral plants, concrete, rusted coke cans and flintless lighters, the regulation drone of passing cars keeping us wading.

We ran behind billboards, through brambles, thorns eager to keep us, grey paper sticking to our feet. We jumped back from disturbed rats, sent magpies twisting up into the air. We emerged, wheezing, from each wasteland to find ourselves on the edge of yet another.

We ran across piazzas raised to the glory of shopping, tables and chairs chained out like starbursts from their individual coffee retailers, the customers hunched against wind and petrol-burnt free radicals and flying carrier bags as they sucked at their foaming milk. Our feet left unscuffed the quotes from Shakespeare, Yeats, Blake and Whitman with which they had engraved their paving, the air funnelled between the surrounding buildings and then released into these open forums marking us more deeply than we had ever marked our surroundings.

And although we ran and kept running, although my heart felt itself being peeled, though my throat tightened so that my breathing yelped, though I felt giddy and nauseous, we got nowhere. We never got anywhere. There was nowhere to get.

Until eventually, when our progress consisted of a minced half-stepping which only the sharp-elbowed positioning of our arms made running, we stopped. We found a wall of concrete sandstone in front of us and to the left of us and to the right of us and it ran so far and was so tall and we were so tired that the possibility of getting round it never occurred to us. And this was where we rested our arses, our legs braced then buckling, our upper bodies piked forward, our vomit slapping round our feet, the sky trundling over us so fast that I could feel it forcing my forehead to the ground.

When we had finished rolling on the floor we propped ourselves back against the wall, grateful to it now, and shuffled ourselves away from the twinned maps of our puke. Stayed there, able to breathe hard by this point, the grain of the stone gradually working its way through our hair to our scalps, our dis-synchronised panting the loudest sound in our world. Giant aeroplanes left tiny trails between clouds, pointers to escape fantasies far beyond our imaginative means. We stuck with our wall and our wall stuck with us.

Eventually we felt unwell enough again to smoke, the cigarettes dangling loosely in our mouths, the tips wobbling with each drag. The nicotine revived us, the tar soothed our muscles, our hands touched, then our fingers locked tight round each other's and soon we found we could look at one another again.

'Shit, Titch. What ya do that for?'

'I didn't. It was an accident. Honest.'

She drew breath to speak, checked it and then exhaled.

'Ah whateva. Gotta get ya cleaned up innit?'

I took off my baseball cap and tracksuit top, both soaked in blood. After a careful study of the jacket's surface, Sadie found a clean corner, sucked it and licked at it, then began dabbing and wiping at my face, the tip of her tongue showing against her top lip, her eyes crossing slightly with concentration. When I began to shiver with cold and shock she took off her own coat and wrapped it round me. The damp rag kept coming down from my face pink, Sadie looking for another clean patch. She, on the other hand, was untouched, not a single drop blotting her. Her face had an overheated flare from running which reminded me of the daydreams I had increasingly begun to play out in my head. She was so calm, her attention to me so all-consuming that I nearly forgot its purpose. Finally she wiped her hands, chucked the mess of my former clothing away from us toward the puddles of sick, took me by the tops of my arms and looked at me – intent, careful. I was about to extend my neck and kiss her when she spoke.

'Thass as good as it's gunna get.'

She removed her own cap, handed it to me.

'Pull da peak down lower'n usual. Gotta find a toilet innit? Wash proper.'

It didn't take us long to locate the nearest Starbucks, housed in a huge building which, I now recognise, pastiched the Kremlin, its cheap red towers against this sky making it look more like a new-build mosque. We entered beneath the giant drapes used to lower the ceiling, the warmth and coffee-smell mingling with the mood music to make us feel instantly cosy yet sophisticated, free and yet safe. People searched for porn on wireless laptops, ignored their baby buggies whilst trying to chat glamorously, or pretended to read. While Sadie made for the counter, I peeled off and headed for the Restrooms, trying not to take my gaze from my feet, wondering whether the other customers would look up from their complimentary books and newspapers, from their complimentary shining lives and note the blood-spattered ASBO in their midst. Without an accompanying adult we remained invisible.

Relieved to find individual disabled toilets with their own sinks and metal mirrors, I locked myself in and stared at my face, water already trickling beneath. I barely recognised what I saw. Sadie hadn't so much removed the blood from me as worked it in, so that it looked as if a heavy-handed beauty technician had tried to renovate my face with thin brown paint. But beyond this, there was no connection to the face of the little girl the police had come for all that time before, nor to the mask I had created for myself from Sadie's make-up. Instead, I looked exactly like what I was, from the blue thumbprints beneath my crazy eyes, to the uneven teeth in my too-mobile mouth. I looked like a criminal. I covered my hands in strawberry-scented liquid soap, scrunched up those eyes so tight I hoped they'd never see me again and began to wash.

When I emerged, I found Sadie waving to me from an armchair, sunk back into it so that it appeared to be eating her, the grin on her face slightly wolfish, as if she was taking the piss but didn't quite know it. I followed her beckoning between the tables, still too scared to look at anyone, and perched myself on the edge of the chair next to hers.

'Got ya drink.'

'What is it?'

'Latt grand wi carmarel sauce.' She raised an identical cup to her mouth, sucked noisily at it, wiped the foam from her top lip. 'Bit a sugar, too.' Another gulp. 'Well nice. I'ma come ere again.'

And there we sat, one of us hunched and scared, the other smiling at the occupants of nearby tables, tapping a hand to the latest batch of authorised acoustic ELO bootlegs, seeming to enjoy the coffee-house experience so thoroughly that she would never want it to end. When I could wait no longer I spoke, as nonchalantly as I could manage, my mouth still sticky with warm, sweet milk.

'What are we gunna *do*?'

She stretched back even further, the leather-look pvc of the cushion squeezing up round her face like cartoon character hair, levered her fist into her pocket and pulled out a mobile, pushing it forward between her fingers and waggling it at me as if she was advertising it.

'Ta-da.'

I looked from the phone to her, to the phone and back to her again.

'I don't understand.'

'Lynda's celly innit? Took it fore I got out.'

'And . . . ?'

'And . . .' – she turned the phone to her, began thumbing at its keys – 'while you was in the toilet I ad a look at the address book . . . and guess . . . whose name . . . I found?'

Flipped the screen back round towards me.

ANNA

A retch of milk and bile jumped into my mouth and only a concentrated effort put it down again.

'You joking?'

'Lynda's right. S'the only way we gunna find out anyfink.'

'Yeah, well, yeah, but maybe. Maybe we *shouldn't* find out anything.'

'Runnin away ain't worked is it?'

'Sadie, this is crazy. Surely there's. . .' But I already knew she was right, had known it even before Lynda had said it, even when I was trying to play happy homes back at Mum's.

'Don't sweat, Titch. I got a plan.' And with that she pressed DIAL and raised the phone to her ear.

'Hello Anna? *Lyn*-da here.' Her imitation so accurate I almost screamed.

'Yes, *yes*, of *course*. Of *course* I've got them.'

The shape of her face contorting to accommodate Lynda's vowel sounds.

'Slight change of *plan* on that. Nothing to *wor*-ry about. But I need to *talk* to you.

'No, *face* to *face*.'

She raised her eyebrows to me, her forehead wrinkling and then relaxing, crossed her eyes, all the while listening.

'Well, that's the *deal*. You come and meet me *here* or it's all off.

'Okay, yes, you have a *think* about it. And while you are I'll call . . . *Des* is it? over at *San*-alex?

'Oh, you *are* free now? How *won*-derful. We're at the very large Starbucks in Forest Meadow Retail Park.

'Twenty minutes? *Mar*-vellous. And can I get you a coffee?

'*Ser*-iously. Let me get you a *coff*-ee. Anything you want . . .

'Of *course* . . .'

She clicked off the phone, clattered it down on the table and smiled a satisfied smile at me.

'How did you know where we were?'

'Cos while you was playin around wiv Stanley, I was readin the signs.' My incomprehension clearly showed. 'The road signs, ya div. Now we gotta get ready.'

When Anna walked in the first relevant data she harvested would have been my position, waving from the comfy chair. Her eyes continuing to scan the room with all the single-pixel thoroughness of a computer, she would then have seen Sadie, spinning slowly round from the counter, her tray carrying one very tall glass, the brown liquid in it swirled through with white. Last, she would have checked and re-checked again for our leader – the dearly departed Lynda – bending down, perhaps, to tie her shoelace or retrieve a twenty-pence piece from the floor, or to vomit from nicotine-withdrawal in this scrubbed-up, smoke-free environment.

'Where is she?' Wasting no time with niceties, her face

clogged with suspicion.

Indicating Sadie, trying to project a sunny foolishness: 'She's just getting your –'

'Not her. Lynda.'

Winced, circled my palm on my tummy. 'In the toilet, Anna. Musta been something she ate.'

'And she just left you here?'

'Didn't have a lot of choice, is it? I think she's took something. She'll be alright in a bit.'

'Wassup, Anna.'

'Hello, Allason.'

'Your drink, as ordered.' She slid the tray onto the table, admired it, the motion of the liquid sluggish. 'One grand mocachyno wiv extra whipped cream.' She pushed it towards Anna, who, with smooth, unhurried sweeps of her head, continued to assess the space around her as she lowered herself into her seat, placing car keys and phone on the table between her two hands.

'And Anna, if ya don't mind me sayin, it ain't the drink I expected of ya –'

'Don't start.'

'Nah man, I ain't being funny –'

'Leave it.'

'It's just it's proper *lady*-like, innit? Fought you'd be more a black-coffee type.'

'I don't have to justify myself to you,' she said, raised the glass to her mouth and took a defiant gulp.

Sadie watched her happily. 'Nah, ya don't. Ya certainly don't.'

We all took a moment to have another look around, examine the fixtures and fittings, hum quietly and tunelessly to the music, our three sightlines wandering like the beams in a random laser display, occasionally crossing but never meeting.

'She be much longer?'

It was Sadie's turn to grimace and rub at her guts. 'Allergic to shellfish innit? I told er but she weren't listening. She's all

"Speak to the and" so what m'I gunna do?'

Silence returned to us like a recessive defect. We sat, soaking in discomfort.

Sadie's eye flickered up to mine for an instant, such a fraction of a look that I knew it had to be a cue. I lowered my chin slightly, opened my eyes as far as they'd go.

'Lynda says you've found my brother.'

I saw her try to be angry, but – maybe tired of her peripatetic lifestyle, the necessity of hardnut posturing – she coughed out a dry laugh. Took another swig at her drink.

'Yeah, we found him. Turns out we had him all along.' Tilted the cup slightly. 'It's not very hot.'

Even that couldn't phase Sadie.

'Fer real? Want me to take it back an get ya nuvver?'

'No. I'll just have to drink it quick,' and she took another pull, us two trying to stop ourselves staring. I waited, trying to time it all as well as Sadie would.

'What ya mean?'

'What?'

'What ya mean you had him all along?'

'Oh that.' She shrugged out another mirthless laugh. 'Long story.'

The music tickling at the inside of my skull, each note a separate hook, the urge to smile at the people around me barely resistible. Forward and backward, forward and backward my body rocked, all my energy not to keep watching her cup.

'Well. We're not in any rush are we? What with . . .' I wafted my hand in the direction of the Restrooms. She rolled her eyes and drank at the same time.

'No, I guess not.' Tipped the mug right back, her throat contracting. 'I guess not.'

'So?'

'So I should tell you?'

'Why not?'

Her shoulders dropped just a millimetre underneath the

leather. 'Turns out he already works for us. For a subsidiary, anyway.'

'As a . . . ?' I couldn't say the words.

'Rent boy? No. He's given all that up. Moved on to a higher calling.'

'What you mean?'

She gulped at her drink again.

'He's a Primary Supplier of Reproductive Genetic Material.'

'Sorry?'

'A sperm donor.'

'Seen. Makin power moves,' Sadie interjected sarcastically.

'Actually, it's on its way to becoming a pretty good career option if you haven't got any qualifications,' Anna offered, amused by our naivety. 'IVF's cutting into demand, but all the scare stories about kids turning up on donor's doorsteps's knackered the supply, especially for top-end stuff. Nuclear physicists and all that. So now they emphasise the quality of the DNA and it turns out, Tilly, you and your brother rate pretty highly considering you're total fuck-ups. Seems someone at the Hampstead offices of Ballemtonor – that's the company, the subsidiary I was talking about – had this idea of swabbing rent boys and what have you on the basis that they'd do the actual donating relatively cheap and your brother's DNA – and I don't want you getting a swell head about all of this – was so good they made him a permanent.'

'What's a permanent?'

'Y'know. A live-in supplier. On tap.'

'No shit?'

'No shit.'

'You can do that?'

'You can.'

She leant forward, scrunched her face up then widened it as far as it would go, rubbed at her eyes, shook her head a little, turned and looked behind her, each movement separate, staccato.

'You alright?' Sadie examining Anna with forensic care.

'Absolutely. Absolutely. Abso-bloody-lutely. Where was I? Ah yeah. And the best part is he's here in Reading. They thought it'd limit any chance of relapses. Lifestyle-wise. Best to get him out of the city. Thought you might like to meet him . . .'

The smile left her face as quick as it had come. Something on the tabletop seemed to draw her attention from us, something tiny and important.

'Ya eaten anyfink today?'

'What?'

'Food. Ya eaten anyfink?'

'As it happens, no. Why?'

'No reason.'

I don't know why I said it. Maybe it was just to fill the gap. Maybe I thought I could get us out of it as easily as that.

'Why d'ya need me then?'

The question seemed to jolt her, her head up again and rallying between Sadie and me.

'What? What?'

'Why do you need me if you've got him? Lynda says you can only prove who our dad is through him.'

'Why would we want to prove who your dad is? We already know that. That's why we want you. Where's Lynda? She's taking too long.'

With which she stood, her head birding left and right and people on the nearest tables beginning to glance.

'But you were just –'

'Nah, she's right, man. Should go an check, Anna. Make sure she's alright.'

Anna grabbed me by the collar of my shirt and stared at it so long I was sure there must be blood on it. Then she yanked me up. People definitely looking now.

'You're coming with me.'

She put her hand on my spine and pushed me in front of her, a human shield, my heart pumping though I knew no ambush awaited us. I glanced across at the counter, saw the gradually distorting smile on the manager's face as he watched our progress, the trainee baristas exchanging observations behind the immunity of their hands. All the light in the great dome above us seemed to wheel round, conversations at the tables we passed stalled, my ears filling with the bath-water sound of self-awareness.

Despite the twitches and sudden lapses of concentration Anna managed the search with considerable professionalism. At no point did she unholster her firearm, not even when the door of the third Restroom gaped as she approached and unleashed a red-haired non-combatant. And if her posture became a little martial-arts-defensive at this point, it was nothing that couldn't be smoothed over by her forcing of a smile and the reasonably weighty play-punch she deposited on my upper arm. It was only after she entered the fourth room and had become lost in examining the taps for much longer than any aspect of them merited, her finger tracing the route of its own reflection with eerie repetitiveness, that even the reflexes of her training began to fray. Eventually she dragged herself away.

'She's not here.' Her voice musty with unnatural confusion.

'Maybe we missed her.'

'What do you mean?'

'Maybe she's back with Sadie?'

'How's that work? Only one exit.'

'Maybe she was at the counter when we came in? Getting herself a coffee?'

'I'd've seen her. I always see everything.'

'Are you alright?'

She shook her head out, bugged her eyes again, the pupils so large now that her corneas formed a thin circumference.

'Fine. What you saying?'

'I just think we should go back to Sadie and check.'

'If she's sold me out . . .'

'Why would she leave us here?'

'True. Alright.'

She took me by the elbow now, her fingers grinding into my

bones, her face spraying defiance at the masks upturned toward us, each thudding back down over its coffee under the force of her gaze. Sadie didn't watch us or wave this time, her eyes doing the old one-two, this way and that, following a flickering pendulum of suspicion.

'She's not there. Where's she gone, Allason?'

'Anna, jus siddown nice an quiet, eh? Not too much fuss.' Her gaze running circular routes. Anna doing as suggested, her body tensing as her hands came into contact with the tabletop. Me joining them, the three of us pushing our heads in towards the centre of the table, only the lack of physical contact between us preventing it from becoming a huddle.

'What?'

'Don't wanna *alarm* ya or nutt'n but I fink some a these people ain't really *customers* at all, yagetme?'

'Which?' Her hand jumping off the table over and over.

'Well . . .' She looked straight and hard at Anna, trying to gauge what she could get away with. 'Most of em, innit?' Leant in a little closer. 'I fink we been set up.'

Anna's eyes began to roll and for a moment I feared that our story was reaching its conclusion too quickly for the cargo in her veins. But then her hand came up to her forehead, shielding her eyes from those around her.

'Of course. Of *course*. Why didn't I see it? I knew something was wrong.'

'Yeah, I could tell you was feelin sutt'n. Got like a six sense for this, ain't ya?'

'Just got to think for a moment. Just got to think. I've got out of worse.'

'For real?'

She picked her phone up from the table, stared through it. Put it down again. Spun her head round, a wave of averted eyes, coughs, rustled newspapers rolling out across the room from her.

'Just have to think.'

'Tell ya what –' Sadie's smile offering up a sudden revelation. 'They aint after me, are they? So I'ma stan up an move over there an *cause a diversion*. An when it starts you two go for the door. Yagetme?'

And before anyone could get her or not get her, before Anna had a chance to question this 'plan', before I could allow the fear in me to rise up and swallow me, Sadie pushed her chair slowly and smoothly back and floated away from the table, her head dropping forward slightly to look at her feet, her movements preordained, calming, well-rehearsed. Until she stopped and the whole room stopped with her. The sly look leaving her, her brain abandoning any attempt to make the muscles in her face work. 'F –' A gulp, her mouth gaping, another gulp. Then, very quietly, 'Anna. Try an stay calm, innit, but there's sutt'n on ya leg. I'll jus . . .

'FUCK!'

Expletive yapped, Sadie lurched back, her hands coming up to cover her face as Anna – all reason emptied from her – let out a roar of protest and fear and, tipping her chair backward, put her fingers under the table and launched it upward, curling and rolling as she fell, so that by the time she reached the floor the gun was in her hand and was pointing at her feet.

'SHHHIIIIIIIIIIIIIIIITTT.'

As if I were stuck on a DVD which a malevolent viewer kept moving back and forward, frame by single frame, I watched Anna's keys rise from the pond of the table, make their own sparkling progress through the air and eventually land in my palm, their impact stinging as I closed my hand around them and fell from my own seat, the least dramatic of the three of us, a subsidence floorward.

If you had expected screaming at this point, mass panic, the toppling of one hundred chairs, you would not have been dis-appointed. Through this sudden outbreak of chaos – women begging for mercy, men soiling their pants, hillocks of human-ity lying on the ground playing dead, one poor soul even strug-gling to fit a lid to his cup as he transferred its precious load for take-out – crawled Sadie and I, left and then right, left and then right, zigzagging through the wreckage. Quicker than I had dared hope, the doors rose in front of us, the chapel of the sky visible beyond. We shouldered through the plate glass and rolled down the steps, the slow-close mechanisms gradually fading from us the noise of panic, the prayers, the beseeching, Anna's animal wailing, so that when we stood it was in complete silence and the only sound to follow us to the car park, ducking and scuffling between walking and running, was of our own feet.

Sadie led us straight to Anna's SMV, its windows showing negatives of the clouds above, its lock release bleeping out as she pulled the key from me and pressed its button. That was when the shots started behind us, distant booms, the sound of girders being smashed into concrete.

'You think you gave her too much?'

'Yeah, fink so. Problem wi Phil's blotters is you never know if e's burned ya. Sometimes they as strong as fuck an sometimes they ain't.'

'And this was a strong one.'

She whistled, nodded.

'You didn't put it *all* in?'

'Saved us a couple.'

Which is when the windows started coming through, huge panes turning white then black as a million stars of glass fell from the sky onto the huddled masses below, sound leaking out now, thin ribbons of screaming and sobbing insinuating themselves into our ears.

'Fuck. Keep yer ed down.'

As soon as I got into the car I relaxed. I couldn't help but feel safe, the weight of the doors alone a reassurance, the solidity beneath me better than the tarmac beyond, all that noise shut out again. I sat, breathing heavily, mesmerised by comfort.

Sadie started the engine, its roar piped in from speakers all around us. It was only then that the absurdity of this escape plan struck me. 'What you doing?'

258

'What ya fink?'

'You can't drive.'

'Says oo? Eard of a lickle fing called joyridin?'

'Yeah, but you never –'

'I never did wi you, nah. Cos I was going straight then innit? Don't mean I never.'

And before I could speak again, the car was pirouetting backward from its bay, the sound of rubber left on road the ideal accompaniment to the view through these screens. And if we clipped the vehicle to the left of us and if, at the end of that first turn we cracked into the vehicle behind, and if the sound of their car alarms reached even us, well, still we were away, moving away from that coffee-splashed floor, a convoy of private security vehicles, blue lights spinning on their roofs, heading past us, back toward whatever was left behind.

'Above all, I must take care not to give too much information to just anybody.' Unfortunately, there are stooges, police informers, agents provocateurs, spooks, 'scientists' and data-miners everywhere. Most of the readers of these communiqués are, consciously or unconsciously, intent on betraying us. Hence, what we say is not always what we mean, anymore than what CTRL says is always what it means. You will forgive us this equivalence. We aim for erasure over consistency.

Extract from *Sixty-second Communiqué of the Vanished*

13

Who was driving? It was Sadie and yet it wasn't. Although she sat there, pushing at the pedals, pulling at the wheel, to me it felt as if we were on a conveyor belt round a restaurant, had in fact been on it all along, and where we came from and where we were going were all already decided, markers on a pre-drawn diagram of vectors.

It took us only a couple of minutes to ring a 118 service and get an address for the Ballemtonor clinic in Reading and, although I couldn't remember having seen it, I knew the street name, felt the car take each necessary turn before I called it. Sadie encouraged me to check the glovebox and there I found – left for us, its only purpose as a clue – a black exercise book in which Anna had scribbled names and addresses and notes relating to her life, including, towards the last few filled-out pages, DR MANTRICLE and a phone number, enough of which matched with the one we'd been given by directory enquiries to suggest it was a direct line from the same switchboard. And so we plunged forward, pleasing everyone but ourselves, it seemed, in our urge to follow this course through to an inevitable end. Because nothing goes on forever and ever, there has to be an end, and perhaps that's what we were there to learn, a glimmering of future consciousness, obvious to everyone but children.

The positioning of the street was familiar, but the bare casing of the Seventies-built office blocks had been re-skinned with tinted, light-sensitive glass, plasma screens and titanium struts, a sci-fi fascia that, when it fell from fashion grace, would be easy and cheap to remove and replace with another. The biggest screen of all showed a foetus growing and developing from an egg into a baby at alarming speed, a smile clearly visible before the film re-set and the starting amoeba bloomed again.

Sadie deposited the SMV at an angle across the pavement on the far side of the street and we sat there for what seemed like hours, watching people coming and going, silent as if for the last time, nothing to discuss as we already knew what we were going to do. When I could no longer find any justification for our continuing stasis, I opened the door, climbed down into the bright noise of the street and stood, waiting for Sadie to come from her side of the car and clamp my elbow in Anna's same harsh grip.

The lobby was bright, high-ceilinged, fresh flowers on every surface, a waiting room filled with well-dressed middle-aged couples flicking through copies of *Vanity Fair* and the *London Review of Books*, the men's heads kept unnaturally low, a refusal to meet even their partner's eyes. The women, on the other hand, were animated solely by a need to connect with each other, solicitous, apologetic smiles flickering back and forth, career-woman empathy addicts with shrivelled eggs nudging shamed husbands possessed of substandard sperm motility. Suffice to say we didn't fit the client base and the receptionist, a failed beauty queen, was tracking us from beneath her highlights as soon as the doors pushed back to reveal us.

Maybe we didn't make for the counter quick enough for her liking, but before we'd reached it, she boomed out as loudly as she could, 'Can I *help* you?' – her smile a textbook demonstration of gatekeep ice.

Sadie didn't blink, certainly didn't smile, just manoeuvred me to one side and said, dismissively, 'We're here to see Dr Mantricle. It's Anna. From Cheralon Genomics. He's expecting us.'

I had just enough presence of mind not to turn and gape at her. For the second time she proved herself a mimic. All trace of her usual accent, the exaggerated patois, had gone. She was

264

as neutral as the room. And the mention of Cheralon or the doctor seemed enough to puncture the showroom moo's sense of self-importance, shrivelling into shit-eating mode before us.

'Of course. Would you like to take a seat?'

'No. We'll stand.'

'And can I get you anything?'

'You just wanna make the call?'

'Of course.' Her face flushing even beneath the brown of her foundation.

Doctor Mantricle didn't look as I'd expected when he appeared from the lift. He was young and tan, filled his skin well, his smile matching the gleam of his white coat, the black and silver stethoscope slung round his neck with the casual precision of a prop. As he reached us, he stopped and vogued, a high-end stripogram. Behind us, the room vibrated with excitement.

'*Anna.* Good to see you. Would you and . . . ?'

'Tilly.'

' . . . like to come through?' He opened his palm and swung it toward the chrome of the elevator's door, holding himself freeze-frame still until we drew level, then pivoting with our passing and strolling alongside Sadie.

'You're younger than I expected.' He spoke without looking round.

'So are you,' Sadie replied.

'So we have something in common, then.'

'Maybe we should discuss it over drinks.' A hardness in her voice hinting at sarcasm.

'I might hold you to that.'

'Do.'

'I will.'

As he pressed the button to summon the lift, he spun non-chalantly, rested his back against the wall, placed a hand in the pocket of his chinos, his thumb clipped over the edge to point at his crotch. And as his sleepy gaze drifted beyond us, I couldn't help turning, expecting security guards to loom at our backs, his flirtations a cover. He was genuine, though, it seemed, a handsome man soaking the last drops of adulation from the room beyond us, offering a sensuous wave to the barren as they waited upon more personalised attention. We walked into the lift.

'Seriously, how about that drink?'

Sadie ignored the question. 'Are you taking us straight to him?'

'I think we should go to my office and deal with business first, don't you?'

'If you wish. How is business?'

'Business is good. The Sanalex scandal is hurting us a little, but there's always desperate people.'

'How do you mean?'

'I mean the urge to reproduce seems to transcend reason.'

'Not that. The scandal?'

'Oh, it's just it's undermining people's faith in the science a little. Made people more nervous about trusting what we have to say about' – he adopted a continuity announcer's voice – '*the Primacy of DNA in determining Favourable Offspring Outcomes*. Your eyes look lovely in this light. How old are you?'

'None of your business. Twenty-two.'

'Twenty-two? My favourite age. Here we are.'

He ushered us out into a space as bright as the one we had left, nurses in too-small uniforms wiggling past, desks cascading with tropical succulents, womb music pulsing from concealed speakers, the air twinkling with moisture-borne pheromones.

'Come through to my consulting room.'

He led us across the floor, an advanced choreography causing every object and person in our path to fall back and facilitate our access, the music beginning to slink. As he raised his arms, double doors opened in front of us and then closed behind us.

266

'Now, Anna, can I suggest that you sit with me on this couch? And you, you'll probably be best off in my examination chair. It's really very comfortable if you get your feet in the stirrups.'

The walls of the room were covered in canvases of naked couples embracing, particular attention having been lavished on their nipples and tongues, the effect desexualised but nevertheless acutely embarrassing to a fifteen-year-old. A cabinet to one side appeared to be stuffed with ancient fertility objects, jutting stone phalluses and wooden holes.

'Shall I dim the lights or did you want to talk money first?'

Sadie hesitated, calculated, spoke, a new harshness in her manner. 'I think there's been some mistake.'

'I do hope not . . .'

'We're here for Marcus Milding. We're not . . .' She scanned her head for the right term.

'What?'

' . . . *sex workers*.' Even with such provocation her accent unruffled.

He allowed himself a gurgle of incredulity. 'I'll have you know I've never paid for it in my life.' Self-satisfaction dripping. 'I meant our little deal? What we talked about on the phone?'

Sadie didn't allow her face to move.

'My sourcing fee?'

She hesitated for a moment, but only for a moment. Then, without any signal that she was making this up as she went along, she extracted the remains of the money we had stolen from Anna back at the bedsit, walked to the desk and let it flap down.

'Is it right?' he asked as he opened a drawer and began sweeping it in.

'It is now.'

'Doesn't seem very professional. Did you run out of envelopes?'

Sadie's tightened face just so, as if she'd spent a lifetime

267

watching TV dramas and soaps and films all for this exchange.

'You wouldn't like me when I'm professional.'

'Well, anyway, no need to let it spoil a beautiful friendship. Why don't we all sit down and make ourselves comfortable?'

'We need to see the boy now.'

'I was hoping we could get to know each other.'

'Another time. I'm working.'

'I'll hold you to that.'

'You do that.'

'I will.'

'Do.'

He sighed ruefully. 'Very well.' Picked up the phone receiver, pointed out a few keys, raised it to his ear. 'Nurse McMelk? It's Dr Mantricle. I'm sending a couple of people up to see . . .' He glanced round at his computer, flicked and tapped and moved his mouse, 'PS212A. Just take them to the room and leave them to it.'

'He'll be leaving with us.'

He flattened his hand over the receiver. 'I'm sorry but I'm really not sure I can allow that.'

'Do you have any choice?'

'He's our best supplier . . .'

'You'll be compensated. Someone from Cheralon will be in touch. Don't want to upset head office do you?'

He exhaled again, spoke into the phone again. 'And he may be leaving with them . . .

'Yes. Yes, I know.

'Well you'll have to get the paperwork ready, then.

'I know. Just be a darling.

'I'll send them up now, then.'

He put the phone down, snapped his fingers and smiled as the room grew brighter.

'I'm afraid I'm going to have to love you and leave you. An emergency appointment. I'll see you to the lift and Nurse McMelk will meet you up on the tenth.'

In the event, Dr Mantricle walked right into the lift with us.

'Last chance, girls,' he schmoozed, addressing only Sadie. 'We could stop this between floors and do what comes naturally? No? Okay . . .' He inserted a key into a slot beneath the lift's control panel, turned it and held it there as he pressed 10. 'Restricted access,' he offered by way of explanation, removing his key and skipping back through the already closing doors. 'Don't be a . . .' – and he was gone.

The tenth floor was a different building. The doors came back to a strobed view of dilapidation, the fluorescent's malfunction revealing stutters of taupe walls, darkened burgundy carpet tiles, an uncanny sheen to everything, as if covered in a layer of saliva. And in the centre of our view, her hand preventing the lift from leaving, some sort of six-foot troll, her hair tied up in two greasy, permed knots, her teeth sharp and poisonous-looking, the folds of her corpulence filling the entire volume of her matching dirty grey sweatpants and sweat-top.

'You must be here to see Marcus?'

The sudden dichotomy too much even for Sadie. 'A . . . a . . . y . . . you?'

'I'm Nurse McMelk, silly. Who'd you think I was?'

Sadie recovered fast. 'Sorry, it's just you're not wearing a uniform.'

'Oh yes, I know, it does confuse people. But uniforms tend to overexcite the residents.'

We stepped out of the lift, instinctively drawing our necks into our bodies, the ceiling bearing down on us, a musty, unfamiliar smell working its way into our heads.

'Lovely lad, Marcus,' offered the nurse, as she turned and led us deeper into the darkness of the corridor, her fat redistributing itself with every deliberate step, her body a cotton-lined water bed over which a giant was walking. 'Very quiet. Easily pleased, you might say.'

'How many people have you got up here?'

'Residential suppliers? We can manage up to sixteen. Got nine at the moment. But it's about quality more than quantity.

269

High-end clinic like this. We get celebrities, y'know.' She tapped at the sprouting mole on the side of her nose. 'Can't say who.'

The corridor appeared to be tapering, the walls and floor and ceiling all closing in on us, so that we stooped more the further we walked, an organic feel to our surroundings, more like the inside of someone's body than a converted office block, the light a pulsing magenta. I watched the numbers ascend on the doors we passed and when we reached 16 I knew that we could go no further, the green glow of a fire exit all that lay ahead.

'Here you are then. Best suite we have. Best for the best. Don't be surprised if he's a bit drowsy.'

'Why should he be drowsy?'

'No reason. They just get like that after a while.'

She knocked on the door, a delicate rap between knuckle-duster rings.

'Marcus?' her voice high and flutey now, designed for rousing children, 'Your visitors are here? Sweetheart?'

No sound came from beyond the door.

'Go on then. You going in?'

Nurse McMelk stood and watched us, her fists on hips so wide that her elbows touched the walls. Slowly, her hand shaking slightly through nicotine withdrawal and, maybe, fear, Sadie reached forward and turned the handle.

The door swung in with the slow ominousness of the entrance to a haunted house. The room beyond was very dark, even from this gloomy vantage point. The nurse, if that's what she really was, chivvied us forward before our eyes could adjust.

'As I say, he may be a little drowsy. I'll leave you to it.' And she closed the door.

The space slowly took shape around us. There was light in the room, though, there being no window, it was generated by the blackness of the empty picture on the huge television. Scattered in front of this centrepiece, picked out in a silvery monochrome, was a chaos of magazines, flapped open and over each other, piles and landslides, airbrushed female flesh and silicone jobs just visible on every surface, a contortion of overlapping poses and fuck-me eyes. Beyond this flotsam was the dark bulk of a large bed, the satin sheets glinting hazily beneath the TV's grey beams. And on the bed, under the central scrunch of the sheets and further print media, was a body, also seemingly two-dimensional, a black cut-out, the negative of a crime scene.

'Marcus?' Sadie's voice shivery, thin. 'Marcus?' A step towards the bed then a step back again. 'Marcus? You awake?'

A rustle of crushed mags, the figure suddenly solid in movement.

'Marcus? Ya there?'

Another crunch of movement, the sound of phlegm being cleared from a throat, then a voice rumbling out, deeper than I expected.

'Y'ere to do me?'

'What?'

'Y'ere to do me again?'

'What ya mean?'

'To do me . . . Ya know . . . Same as always . . . Comes round quick innit?'

'We ain't. We ain't. We jus visitin.'

'For what?'

'What for what?'

'Visitin for what?'

'See you.'

The room was silent again. 'Don't get many visitors.' Another pause. 'Cept I'm gettin done.'

'No one's gunna do ya.'

The gap between words unfurled itself even further. A floorboard creaked as I shifted my weight to my other foot. Sounds from outside filtered in to us, so slight and disjointed as to seem machine-generated, a computer beyond the door creating a serviceable reality for us.

271

'Shame. May's well go back sleep then.'

'There a light in ere?'

'Why?'

'Need to see ya.'

'Why?'

'Jus do.'

'You *are* gunna do me, in't ya?'

'Jus put the light on.'

There was another break in the exchange while the boy pulled himself up into a sitting position, the sheets writhing round him.

'Ain't got one.'

'What?'

'A light. Ain't got one.'

'Gotta be a light. Ow d'ya see?'

'Put the telly on, innit?'

'Go'n then.'

'Now?'

'Yes fuckin now.'

'Ya sure?'

'Yeah.'

'Ya don't mind?'

'Mind what?'

'What we watch?'

'Jus puddit on.'

'O-*kay* . . .'

He clapped his hands above his head once, twice, three times – a caliph – and the screen bloomed coloured light.

The first girl had something big and long and bright green in her fist and was inserting it into the second girl's bumhole. You couldn't see much of the second girl beyond that, but you could hear her panting and moaning and saying, 'Oh yes, yes, deeper, push it *deeper*.'

'Fuck's sake.'

'Warned ya.'

'Ya turn over or sutt'n?'

'Can't. Jus gets piped in innit? Don't get no choice.'

'For real?'

'So there's two of ya. Y'*are* gunna do me innit?'

'Lemme look at ya.'

She moved closer to the bed, her shadow huge across the wall behind her, arcing over the ceiling, advancing in slasher flick swoops. I found myself unable to keep from looking back round at the telly, fascinated and horrified in equal measure. 'Yes, *yes*, yes, get it *in*.' Sadie knelt at the bed, squinted forward at his face. The first girl was squeezing and kneading at her unlikely left breast. Sadie was reaching out to him.

'S'me Marcus. Ya sister. I'm ya sister.'

'Ya gunna take ya top off?'

'Y'ear what I said?'

'Sutt'n kinky?'

'I'm ya sister. For *real*. Nutt'n fuckin kinky.'

'Nut –? Gettin done by ya sister definitely *is* kinky.'

'You int gettin done. Marcus, will ya jus listen? I'm ya twin sister. I been lookin for ya. Me an Titch. We been lookin for ya.'

'She gunna take *er* top off?'

'I'm gunna take your fuckin ead off in a minute. You ain't safe ere, Marcus. Yagetme? It ain't safe.'

'Dun even know ya.'

'I'm ya sister. Ya twin sister.'

The girls had swapped places now. The second girl's hairline was too high, her eyebrows painted on wonky, her lips replete with collagen. Sadie reached out and, hesitantly, placed her hand on top of his.

'Look at me. I'm ya sister. Look at me.'

Like mine, his eyes stayed stuck in slow passes between her upturned face and the television, caught between the fascination of her tears – slow and plump as film peasants – and onscreen rimming.

'It's me, Marcus.'

Her hands never leaving his to rise to her cheeks, so that

273

the track of those tears remained untouched, each wobbly line distinct, the slight repositionings of her head as it slowly fell forward fanning them one by one from her ear to her nostril.

'*Family*, Marcus. Can't tell me ya don't want family?'

The head angled sharply to one side so that the pierced tongue, curling slightly with the sheer effort of its extension, could be seen circling round over the sheening genitalia, the girl's eyes rolling toward the camera and looking both straight at me and through me, no hint of consciousness present.

'Marcus? Please . . . ?'

His hand scuttling back from hers – slowly, an absent-minded withdrawal – leaving Sadie holding only satin, her head just above her empty hands, her frame folding in on itself.

'John says to say ello. Sends is love. Says to say Jenny's missin ya.'

With which the TV suddenly lost its power and never mind what they were doing now, Marcus was looking only at Sadie.

'What ya mean?'

And I was freed, too, the sick feeling dissipating, my compulsive gulping done, the images abstract.

'John. Ya foster carer. When we saw im. When we was lookin for ya. Give us a picture.'

She ruffled in a pocket, pulled out the crumpled print and, trying to smooth it, held it out for him.

'Ow I know it's you.'

Marcus took the photograph, his second hand finally appearing from beneath the sheet and coming gently to rest on the woman at the centre of the image.

'What did Jenny say? She been worried?'

'Yeah, I fink so. We din see er. She were out. But John says she were missin ya. Innit Titch?'

Placed his thumb and forefinger on either side of the drawing-pin hole while I nodded.

'It off the board? In the kitchen?'

274

'Yeah.'

He squinted at the picture again, smiled, half-shrugged as the smile stopped being one.

'I keep it?'

'Depends.'

'On what?'

'If ya comin wiv us.'

Putting the photo down on the opposite side of the bed from Sadie, he now turned and looked at her with care.

'I don't got a sister ya know.'

'We're twins.'

'An I certainly don't got a twin.'

'Ya do. It's me.'

'Ya don't look much like me.'

'Well we ain't *i*dentical twins, is it?'

'Yeah but –'

'We do look alike,' she said turning her face to me, a hunger there I pitied. 'Dun we, Titch? Dun we?'

I took a step towards them, my body made from wooden parts and joined together by string. Creaking, I knelt in front of them, the floor just distinguishable beneath the slide and crunch of glossy paper. Stretched out my hands, palms upward, a spoof of the icons we had seen back in this boy's former home. Took their fingers between mine, one hand each, and pulled them gently towards me. Looked from face to face and face to face and face to face, trying to satisfy all my own needs in this one examination.

'Yeah. You do. You definitely do.' There was no doubt. Not when you saw them together. Not if you knew like me. 'You definitely are.'

I thought he was going to start crying. That they would hug. That, as they clung to each other kissing and snuffling, I could somehow inveigle my way into the huddle and lose myself in that wet warmth, too. Instead, he laughed.

'So what? Even if we are, so what? Big deal innit.'

'What ya mean?'

275

'It's not like anyone cares is it? Even if it is true?'

'I care.'

'It's not like it makes any difference.'

'Does to me.'

'Where are *Mummy* an *Daddy* now, eh? Not like they wanna find us is it?'

'Mum did. She did wanna. I fought she found ya. I fought that's where ya'd gone.'

'Not me. No one's ever found me. No one's ever come to the rescue is it? Cept this lot.'

'W'about Jenny? An John. Eh? You was killin it dere man. *They* wanted ya.'

He looked at her coldly. 'They jus like a project innit? Ole fing fake.'

'I'm ere. I've come. We can find Dad.'

He seemed to consider it for a moment, his head tilting.

'Where's Mum?'

Sadie hesitated. 'I dunno.'

'I fought ya said –'

'I did but –'

'She done a runner . . . ?' The ghost of a laugh. 'Really proved ya point innit?'

'It's not like that,' I added. 'She didn't do a runner. There's something funny going on. That's why we're here. You're really not safe here.'

'Whateva.'

'Really.'

He looked me up and down, his lip curling.

'Ya fink I were safe when I were in London? Ya fink I were safer then than I am now? D'ya fink anyone was running arter me den? Do ya? Lickle *gel*.'

That was when Sadie hit him. Not that hard. An open palm, the ball of her hand shoved into his bicep. But hard enough.

'Talk to er like that.'

'What, she ya sister, too, is it? Nuvver twin?'

'Fuck you, man. Fuckin ras claat.'

276

'Ya what?'

'You eard.'

'Wha?'

'Y'eard me man.'

And then he laughed again, high-pitched with surprise and delight. A child's laugh. And we became kids and the room receded from us and we all began laughing into our hands, sharing this momentary vacation.

'Maybe it is,' he said, dragging the moment out.

'Come wiv us.'

'Nah man. Can't.'

'Why not?'

'On too good a fing ere innit? Somewhere to live, all me food, a telly. Sorry . . . Dun even know ya name.'

'Sadie.'

'Sorry Sadie. Sorry sis.'

'Ya believe me then?'

'Dun matter if I do or not is it?'

'Ya gotta come.'

'I ain't.'

'Not jus the . . . what we said.'

'What then?'

'I need you to find out about Dad.'

'Why?'

'Cos ya chrosowhatsit's –'

'Nah. Why ya wanna find im? Why would e want ya ta find im?'

'Not about what e wants.'

'No?'

'No.' They stared for a moment, their faces parodies of each other's, close enough together that the TV's flicker hit them uniformly.

'Shoulda said. Thass all ya need I can do that easy.'

'So ya comin?'

'Nah man. You, *Tits*, whatisname. There's a drawer in the bed down near ya.'

I scrabbled to find it, located its edges and the upholstered handle, but didn't pull, just nodded a noddy-dog nod.

'Open it, den.'

It trundled out, the material lining rucking again and again on the base, so that it moved in random stops and starts.

'Swabs.' The drawer neatly divided between paper envelopes and rank upon rank of miniature white soldiers, their heads fluffy and clean.

'What you got all these for?'

'Tell ya, man, they always swabbin me. Always. Fink they fink they got it wrong. Chuck us one over.'

My hand shuddered over the drawer as if it mattered which I picked. Finally, careful-clumsy, I rolled one between thumb and finger and raised it to him. He took it with a smile and, eyebrows up, began to attack the inside of his mouth, his cheek bulging and vibrating. It went on and on, this jiggling, and I found my attention drifting back to the telly, where a man had appeared now, layered in tattooed muscle, his head oddly tiny on the thickness of his neck. His back faced the camera, the first girl dragging his thong over his buttocks with her teeth.

'Tits? If ya can stop watchin that for a minute maybe I can get a envelope?'

I jolted back to the drawer, flustered one up at him.

'It's Titch. *Titch*.'

He took a moment to stare at my chest and then plucked the proffered envelope from me.

'Yeah. Whatever. An another swab. Control, innit?'

I felt compelled to return to the television set, my mind consumed, my body heavy. The camera tracked round him, panning back as it did so, the first and second girl drawing back in admiration.

'An another envelope, square eyes.'

I scrabbled round by touch, waved it in their direction, blind to anything but the sight of his erect dick.

'There ya go, sis.'

I had seen penises before, of course. My brother's when we

still shared baths. My father's, though I had no recollection of it. The cutaway diagrams used in school sex-education classes. But never a real, grown man's erection.

Sadie tried again. '*Please*. Please don't do this.'

It was horrible. It hung out from his body, throb-veined and misshapen, an irregular lumpiness to its entire length, its top an obscene, shiny purplish-pink bursting from folded skin.

'Please come wiv me.'

Its base bristled with hairs, its bobbing and nodding uncontrolled, dumb. My stomach jumped.

'Can't. Even if I wanted.'

The first and second girl seemed to see something different to me. They cooed and groaned and stroked themselves before their fingers, of some private volition, closed round it, kneading and squeezing as if assessing its exact density.

'Ya mean ya *can't*?'

Then the second girl brought her head into shot, opened her mouth and slowly, so slowly, so that every individual motor function involved was made clear and distinct, closed it around that hideous thing.

'Look.'

She was trying to smile and suck at the same time, like the sweetest lollipop she had ever tasted, all honey and heather and fresh air and cream, was enwrapt by her tongue, instead of this.

'*Fuck*. Fuck is it?' Sadie's voice confused, uncomprehending, something in it enough to pull me from my self-suffocation.

Marcus had pulled back the sheet and lay naked on the bed, his pale skin glowing in plasma light, his ribs seeming to run in reverse order, even his arms thinner now I could see the rest of him. He was smiling again, a small smile, saintly and lost and unconnected. And where his own hard dick should have been there lay instead a metal tube, slightly narrower than a tin can, a light, brushed chrome, its top rounded and leading to a thin plastic hose, the hose spiralling over the hairless part of his

279

thigh, across the shiny sheet and down over the edge of the bed and out of sight.

'Ya like it?'

'Fuck is it?'

He adjusted it slightly, a delicacy to his actions, unclear whether the solicitousness was for the cargo or its casing.

'Fink of it like a milkin parlor innit? An I'm the cow.'

'What ya mean?'

'State a the art. Controls the temperature of muh bollocks, carries out hourly assessments on em, decides when it's best to arvest the crop. An also stops me from fiddlin wi meself the resta the time. Cos ya gotta wait till the right time. Then, when I'm ready somebody comes and does me.'

'Can't ya jus take it off?'

'If I could do that I'd jus take it off when I wanted a wank, wouldn'I?'

'Or unplug it?'

He shook his head. 'It don unplug cos they don't wanna lose anyfink.'

'Like what?'

'Like if I jus go off. Wet dream or sutt'n. I dunno. Anyways, it never comes off.'

'Why dun't they jus stop all this shit?' She indicated the TV. 'If they wanna stop ya "just goin off"?'

'Experimental, innit? They reckon it increases the yield.'

'Ya need to get out of ere. For real.'

'I love it ere, sis. I ain't goin nowhere.' He lay his head back onto the pillows. 'You, though, you need to get goin.'

'What ya mean?'

'Well, I'm gunna guess you lied to get in ere. An they the kinda people what like to check shit. So if I'm right, ya better get out before me nurse comes back, cos you don't wanna fuck wiv er, yagetme?'

'Marcus, *please*.'

'Can't sis. Ya got the swabs. Jus go. Ya can come back an visit innit?'

Sadie stood up. Looked at him sitting there, her face warping with anger and disappointment.

'Fuck ya then.'

'Don't be like tha . . .'

'Nah, fuck ya. Fuckin retard. Come, Titch.'

'Sis . . .'

'Don't even go dere. Fuckin loser. Titch.'

She was at the door now, the light planing off her cheekbones, looking dangerously thin and desperate and noble to me. I stood and scuffled after her, my feet sliding, glanced down at him, his interest already drifting back to the television, his arms sprawled palms-up by his sides, his brow smooth, his eyes, reflecting that sucked penis, full of wonder and surprise.

'See ya then.'

'Fucking *talk* to im. *Ee*jat.'

The corridor seemed to have shrunk still further, a definite veining to the walls now, a thousand red tributaries across its surfaces. Sadie looked left and right, her knees bent, a thumping throbbing pushing on my eardrums. Turned to the fire exit, slammed down the safety bar and pushed through.

Light. Light so sharp that we stood swaying at the very top of the metal steps, our hands sweeping outward trying to grasp any solidity. Sound. The birds and cars and planes of normality. Air. Wind patting ineffectually at our faces, the smell of space.

We began our descent as OAPs – hunched over, grasping the banister, scared of slipping. As we went down our eyesight returned to us, our confidence grew, the exhilaration of escape (however temporary) gripped us and suddenly we were falling, two or three steps at a time, the clatter a chorus of support. I wished as we went that we could keep going down forever, that no pavement, no British tarmac, no planet earth would ever come to meet us. But it did.

How long did it take? How long to run those ten floors

down? How long for Sadie to stop at the bottom, to gulp out that this wasn't right, that she had to go back and make him come with us? How long for my helpless assent? How long to trudge back up each of those metal steps, our legs aching, lungs rasping, our footsteps' echoes a pursuit now? How long to pull the fire escape door open, step back into that tunnel, make our way as quietly as we could to the door of number 16, how long to push it open?

You want the simple answer? Too long.

Marcus wasn't in the room we came back to. Nor was the bed, nor the television, nor the magazines. Not even the carpet remained. We stood in any empty concrete box, the walls and floor rough and dusty. Confused, we looked at the number on the door, sniffed at the air, searched the corners for pipes or aerial sockets. We wandered round in narrow circles hoping that this would somehow generate sense. I went back and again checked the number on the door. Sadie stumbled out onto the fire escape to make sure we'd come to the correct floor. She peered into the room opposite and the next one down, each an identically hollow space.

Bafflement filled me, a deep unease twitching inside. Sadie must have felt it, too, our actions mirroring one another's, our movement increasingly frantic, as if all we were concerned to do was fill this sudden void with motion. We were no longer looking, we didn't speak. An impossibility had taken us by our throats, this absolute impossibility we were moving through. Occasionally one or the other of us would stop, pull ourselves up straight and then, realising that the explanation had failed before it had begun, start forward again. Everything seemed to have stalled, our minds unable to make the leap across the gap which had opened up in front of us.

Eventually, long after it had become clear to us that we would find no clues or meaning here, and that if there was a point then this was it, we saw Nurse McMelk thundering towards us through the corridor's miasma, her tiny face angry and twisted, a roar of fury rumbling up from every fat-coated alveolus of her fat-encrusted lungs. So that all we could do was turn and run.

And Marcus? It made no sense, couldn't be true, as if the whole room – the carpet tiles, the furniture, the wallpaper and the plaster beneath the wallpaper – had been folded in on itself, screwed up and thrown away. Marcus was already gone.

'Yes, death is no matter if the time has come.' We have been libelled by the PR department of CTRL as a death cult. We are no cult. We freely publish our arguments and deny the sovereignty of any Higher Power. And as for death? Our forefathers came close but missed the point when they wrote, 'A single choice: suicide or revolution.' Why not 'suicide and revolution'? Or even 'revolution through suicide'? It is the act of Vanishing we admire, this violent secession, not how that Vanishing is achieved.

Extract from *Sixty-eighth Communiqué of the Vanished*

14

When he opened the door I butted him. Hard.

I hadn't expected to. Had never done it before. But the sight of his face, the vacant smile of superiority there before he'd even realised it was me, triggered something inside me, an adopted tribal memory of how this sort of thing was done.

It hurt. I made contact just above my hairline, much higher than I should, and from that point emanated line upon line of pain, as if I'd cracked my egg-head into a thousand pieces. I staggered forward trying to hold cranium together, tears bursting from my eyes, teeth grinding.

'Ah fuck . . .'

He was lying on his back, embedded in twists of dirty clothing, mould-lidded cups and the thick blocks of advanced programming textbooks. His hands were dabbling with the red mulch of his broken, bleeding nose and he was whimpering slightly. I waved the bread knife I had picked up in the communal kitchen down the hall, near enough to him to make him flinch.

'Alright David? Gunna invite us in?' Sadie shut the door, clocking round the latch until it was locked.

'Sadie,' I announced theatrically, the knife whistling backwards and forwards through the air in front of me, 'meet my brother.'

None of what was to happen had been planned. As we were acted upon so we continued to react and as we reacted so we brought more actions upon us. That was our helix, the path of a swingball on the beach, escape always becoming return, gravity always pulling us down.

We had emerged from the alley at the side of the

Ballemtonor clinic to find the car gone, an emptiness of pavement in its place, my fantasies of driving to Scotland and hiding out motoring off with it. After what had happened upstairs it seemed less than remarkable, the heaving of our lungs the only reason to stand and examine the space where it should have been. We knew, though, not to stand too long, that whoever or whatever wanted us was closing in.

Where to go, though? We had no car, no money, no one we could trust. Our first instinct was to head for the shopping centre and lose ourselves amongst our fellow sportswearers, to blend in and feel fifteen again, perhaps engage in petty larceny or just check the boys, chew gum, smoke fags and arse around. But as we scuttled down side streets and through pedestrian walkways, I sunk my hands deep into my trouser pockets and there I found a folded piece of paper and as I grasped on to it I remembered what it was and as we walked I made a decision. Eased it out and checked the address, thought it through, began to modify our path, so that we skirted back away from the centre, tacking, block by block, with increasing certainty towards my brother's halls of residence.

I expected getting in there to be difficult. We had no swipe card, no reason to enter we could admit to and, most damning of all, looked nothing like students, who favoured a bland, unbranded branding which they mistook for sophistication. Security, however, consisted of nothing more than a buzz-in door and we didn't have to wait long for Sadie to get her foot in as someone left, his curdled frown suggesting that he knew we shouldn't be there but didn't dare question us for fear of appearing *uncool*. Either that or he was checking Sadie's bum.

We found David's room number from the pigeonholes, went to the right floor, washed up the knife amidst the wreckage of a student kitchen then sauntered, scanning the other doors and the hall behind us, from patch to patch of neon light, and finally to his door.

I stepped over him, still whining and fiddling with his nose (as if it had been so marvellous beforehand), trawled my feet through his junk with a deliberate disregard, bent down over his desk and yanked out the plug for his computer, watching with satisfaction as all the information on the screen shrank to a central white dot and blipped out of existence. Behind me, my brother yelped and flailed upright.

'What you do that for?'

'Well, I know what you're like with your machines, David. Don't want you getting up to any mischief do we?'

'You could've just shut it down. You didn't have to –'

'You can never be too careful, though. Can you, David?'

It was only then, I think, that he really looked at me, his blinking stilled, his lower lip spasming.

'Shit. I didn't recognise you.' He was probably faking it. 'I've been half expecting you, but . . .' Laying it on for effect. '*Shit*.'

I stamped forward onto my right foot pulling fisted knife up to head height, his duck away from me gratifyingly genuine, hands rising like kites.

'Sit on the bed.'

'What are you going to do to me?'

'Ain't decided yet. Just siddown and shuddup.'

He did as he was told and as he did I felt inertia settle over me. I crumpled into his chair, weakness pulling at the knife, the urge to continue my fall to the floor almost irresistible, to curl up in the litter and sleep.

'I'm bleeding.'

'It's a *nosebleed*, David, don't be such a baby.' I couldn't stop saying his name. Kicked up a dirty pair of pants from the floor. 'Use that to stop the blood.' He did as he was told. I remembered my manners.

'This is Sadie. Sadie, this is David.'

Sadie sat down at the other end of the bed, David twitching away from her and shuffling himself along nearer to me. He opened his mouth to speak.

'Shuddup.'

289

Closed it again.

The three of us sat, Sadie watching the floor, David watching the blade, his nose hidden under bloodstained pants, me watching the blade, too, wondering how long it would take him to realise you can't stab someone with a breadknife. Though, on the other hand, you can saw their head off.

'Smoke in ere?' asked Sadie.

He looked to me. I nodded.

'You're not meant to.'

'But people do?'

'Presumably.'

'Presumably?'

'Yes. I mean, yes. They do.'

'And it doesn't set off the smoke alarms?'

'Apparently not.'

I nodded to Sadie – 'Chuck us one over' – and we both lit up, I channelling my first lungful of smoke in to his eyes, enjoying the discomforted lid-flutter.

'Lenses playin up?' I enquired without enquiring.

'The smoke . . . ?'

'*Diddums.*' Another whoosh.

We sat for a little longer, smoking and being smoked at, evening drifting in with slow certainty, the room and its occupants being flattened to a series of silhouettes, each of us intimate and alien to the other all at once. Beyond the window momentum held sway, a vast mechanism of moving parts, each constituent element going about its business, continuing to fulfil its function, the sights and sounds of these endeavours reaching us with the soft, distant coolness of stars.

'Why were you half expecting me?'

'What?'

'You said you were half expecting me. Why?'

'You ate Marjoram.'

'What?'

'Mum rang this morning to say she was really sorry but she'd accidentally broken Marjoram while she was cleaning in my room. So I said to keep the pieces and I'd fix her. And she went all weird and said she'd chucked them. And somehow I *knew* it was you. Cos Mum'd never do that. Not chuck her away.'

'*Marjoram?*'

'Don't pretend you don't know what I'm talking about. The big gold one with blue eyes?'

'I'd forgot you gave em names.' Sadie coughed. I shrugged theatrically. 'Chocolate rabbits. He collects things.' Even with the pants covering most of his face I could see him blush.

'So anyway, what do you want?'

'We just need somewhere to stay for a night or two, innit Sadie? And I reckoned you owed me.'

'Do I have a choice?'

'"*Do I have a choice?*"' I mewed back. 'No you don't have a fucking choice. I'm ungry. Got any food?'

'Usually ring out for pizza.'

'Better do that then. What you want Sadie?'

'Pepperoni?' A kid asking Santa for a present.

'Yeah. Why not? Two pepperoni pizza. I hope for your sake you got enough money.'

He sighed a prolonged, perfectly weighted sigh, the kind I had heard over and over at our breakfast bar, our dining table, in the back seat of the car, in front of the telly, in the back garden, on the swings, the sound of his imagined superiority.

'I expect I can manage.'

'Believe me, you better.'

It was unsettling to find myself staring at that wrong reflection – younger, chubbier, make-up free, but still indubitably me. Sadie's was less embarrassing, fresher of face, yes, but essentially unchanged. Though actually, that first time we saw them, we were less interested in our appearance than what was being said about us. It was on the repeats that we really studied them.

We had ordered pizza on David's confiscated phone, paid

for them with David's confiscated money, then, having tied his wrists with the power lead from his own precious machine, sat in front of him dangling slices of pepperoni under his nose before popping them into our own mouths, our expressions of delight merrily exaggerated. That was when he launched into his first plea for mitigation.

'Why are you doing this to me?'

'You know why.'

'I don't.'

'Erm, the small matter of, ha, *prison*?'

'I didn't put you in prison.'

'You made the virus!'

'Making a virus isn't a criminal offence. It's an exercise in programming. Releasing it is.'

'You set me up.'

'And you have a much fuller grasp of PCs than you make out. I always made a point of telling you to leave my machine alone. I don't see how I can have set you up if you do something I've expressly told you not to do.'

'Because you knew I'd do it anyway.'

'We went through all this in court and it didn't do you any good.'

'Which doesn't mean it isn't true.'

'No, it doesn't, but it isn't. I told you to stay off my machine.'

'Just shut up. Shut the fuck up.'

I shoved a slice of pizza into his mouth, which he chewed at with an unexpected appreciation. Sadie was looking at me funny. I felt guilty for having such a hateful brother here in the room with me when she had just lost hers.

'Sup?' I queried, more accusingly than neccssary.

'Nutt'n.'

'Serious. Wassup?'

'I said nutt'n.'

I swept round and turned the telly on to cover for myself. Except there I was staring straight back, that young me.

' . . . of *Securilux Policing, the company responsible for the section of road in question, says that officers are very concerned for the safety of the girls and would like the opportunity to speak to them as soon as possible.*' Sadie's mugshot replaced mine, her cockiness soothing me a little. '*Securilux went on to stress that the girls may be dangerous and that members of the public should not approach them. If you do see them, or have any information as to their whereabouts, please call this number confidentially –*'

I flattened my hand over the button, watched the picture return to black, my ears filled with the imprint of that tinny voice, the other two staying very still, perhaps watching how I tapped the blade of the bread knife impatiently against the outside of my thigh dot dot dot dash dash dash, the only morse I knew.

'Oh dear.' My brother's voice absolutely neutral, expressing neither sarcasm or concern. 'You seem to have got yourselves in quite a mess.'

We offered no response.

'And do you honestly imagine that hiding here is some kind of answer?'

Sadie returned to an examination of her feet. I began to drop the blade rhythmically along the edge of the bookshelf, each dent another year in an incarcerated future.

'That being here threatening me is going to help in any way at all?'

Five, six, seven, eight, nine . . . How many years would I get for murder? Could they give a fifteen-year-old life? I began to saw down each time the knife landed, the notches becoming progressively deeper and more deliberate.

'That if you stay here for a day or two all your problems will be solved?'

Swivelled my head round to look at him, his glassy eyes, that hollow, arrogant way he had of staring.

'What makes ya think we're only here for a day or two?'

His face had grown so that his nose almost fitted it. While

personal hygiene issues meant that his forehead was still sown with the black scabs and livid pink of acne and his indifference to razors accounted for the gossamer stranding which obscured his all-new jawline, I could see, for the first time, that with a little more effort he could turn out to be quite a handsome man.

'Well, it's hardly sustainable to stay indefinitely, is it?'

'Why?'

'There's the cleaner.'

I looked around me, shaping my brow for amused contempt. 'I don't think the cleaner comes in here too often, does he David?'

'My friends.'

'Be serious.'

'My lectures. My work placement. The police. Don't you think the police might come and check up on me if you're wanted for . . . for something?'

I looked at him long and hard, trying to assess this stranger's sincerity, and it suddenly seemed preposterous to suggest I had run naked round a beach with him, been given my first marbles from his own collection, had played in a sheeted den for a whole day when we were at home with chickenpox, both our torsos crackling with dried calomine.

'Murder,' I finally said. 'I'm wanted for murder. So I guess you better hope they don't come. Unless you wanna be a hostage.'

He laughed a short, nasal snort and I had no idea if he was mocking me or admiring my insouciance. I decided not to ask.

'Maybe you'd better ring Mum and tell her you're going away for the weekend.'

He looked concerned again.

'Where are we going?'

'We're not going anywhere, ya dick. S'just so's the feds don't show up here.'

He reddened and with it became more familiar – his awkwardness, the perpetual misalignments of his body, his sensitivity to any potential embarrassment.

'It won't work. I never go anywhere.'

'It will. Tell her you met a *girl*. Tell her she's into computers, too. Tell her you're going to an advanced HTML workshop together. She'll be pleased. She'll be too relieved to question it.'

The blush reaching his neck now, capillaries rupturing with the pressure, love bites from his imaginary squeeze.

'I can't.'

I moved behind him, scrolling through the stored numbers on his phone. Found **HOME**, brought it to his ear and pressed **CALL** just as I stroked the serrated edge of the blade across his throat, riding it over his jumping Adam's apple with the calm assurance of a surfer waiting for her dream wave.

'Oh, I think you can.'

As it turned out he did it well, only balking at inventing a girl-friend. Without my shanky prompting my mother may have gone to her grave thinking her son incapable of forming an intimate relationship. Despite our differences I'm glad to have given her that false succour. I almost cried with suppressed laughter as she encouraged him to describe his mythical lover.

'Er . . . Tamsin. Tamsin . . . Yeah . . . She's . . . nice . . . Yeah . . . Nice. What's wrong with nice . . .? Yeah. Yeah. Course. Course she's pretty . . . Brown . . . I dunno, just brown . . .'

Then I looked over at Sadie, leaning next to the window, her hand inching a gap in the curtain so she could look down on the lamplit street beyond. And it didn't seem so funny. I pressed the blade so hard into his neck he squeaked.

'No. No I'm fine . . . Er, yeah. Yeah she is . . . Yeah, I should . . . See you next week, then . . . Yeah, I will . . . Yeah, I'll ask her . . . Bye, Mum.'

He began to say 'I love you' but I switched the phone off before he could offer up such a blatant clue, cuffed him gently, almost tenderly. I had spent the last three years thinking of him as a brilliant, monomaniacal manipulator, the villain in my

295

own film, so it was stickily comforting to be reminded of what a loser he was.

The night stretched itself out with the slow, indefatigable certainty of gas. My brother's skill with communications technology made me fearful of leaving him unobserved for a moment. Even tied to a chair, he wouldn't take long to get a message out of the room if we gave him any leeway. I wasn't sure that Sadie appreciated this, so I gave her the early shift, telling her to wake me at three.

But I couldn't sleep. Sadie put the TV back on and kept flicking to the local news bulletin and each time it began I found myself turning my head to watch the shot of Lynda's car, where we had left it but decorated now with police tape and surrounded by yellow-bibbed officers, trying to look like they were discussing the intricacies of the case and not just the cross-dressing headmaster they had caught dogging up in the woods the night before (the programme's lead story). And with each repetition the words of the report became more fixed in my head, so that this interpretation saved over what I thought had been my experience and I felt myself erased from my own story. It scared me then, that I found a lightness, an exhilaration in this disappearance. I was drunk with it. Every minute became an hour of escape. I stretched and writhed in my brother's bed. Even the room felt impermanent, his face lit like Marcus had been, the flatness spreading, the shadows painted on.

As soon as he was sure Sadie was asleep, David started up again.
    'So what are you going to do now?'
    'Whadda you care?'
    'I'm trying to help you. I want to help.'
    'Bullshit.'
    'I do . . . I really do. I don't expect you to believe me but I do.'

'I don't believe you.'

'Don't blame you.'

We stared some more. His eyes looked just like Grandma's. People had said it when we were kids but it was only now that I could see it. She was in a nursing home these days, unable to speak since the stroke, dribble leaking from the corner of her mouth, the nurses brutally mock-cheerful. At least I thought she was. It seemed like years since I'd heard any mention of her. Perhaps she'd died? I decided that if I could stay running long enough I would go and visit her. The cool silkiness of her hands' loose skin.

Our eyes fell from each other's, dropped to the floor and rolled round there looking for something easier to focus on.

'I owe you.' So quiet I was sure I'd misheard.

'What?'

'I owe you. I never thought they'd lock you up. It was a joke and it got out of hand and I'm sorry.'

'Sorry?'

'Yeah. I am. I never expected it to be so . . . effective. So then I was scared. But I honestly thought you'd just get a caution or something.'

'Sorry? Fat lot of fuckin good that's gunna do me.'

'That's why I'm saying I want to help. So's I can make it up to you.'

'*You?* Help me?'

'You need to trust me. I know that's hard.'

'*Trust* ya?'

'If you can give me just one chance I can prove it to you. I can prove that I mean it. You only have to give me one chance.'

'There's only one thing I'm gunna give you an it ain't gunna be a chance. What ya fink this is? We're not on telly. We're not just gunna kiss and hug and make up.'

'Try to look at it rationally –'

'Don't tell me what to do –'

'You need help.'

297

'An you need to shuddup. Fuckin Judas. Think I'm gunna fall for that shit?'

The light inside and beyond the room had become permanent, unaltering. A line of it traced the shape of David's face. Another drew round my fingers. The TV, sound down, cut from shot to shot without us – a man standing on a small bridge in a town which could be Amsterdam, a close-up of his face, a passenger jet rearing up, its wheels out, coming in to land, a woman in a long camel-hair coat hailing a cab outside an airport. Beyond us, sleep, a billion sighs and snuffles weaving through each other to make the sound of air.

I tried as hard as I could not to think about what he had said, the muscles of my neck tightening, an internal noose. Because the truth was I wanted help, wanted to hug and kiss and make up, wanted my happy ending. The warm rasp of Sadie's breath the only thing stopping me, a companion for my fear.

'I was relieved, y'know, when Mum told me.' His voice sounding simpler now, a flatness to it.

'What?'

'About the mix-up. Your not being . . . your not being *blood*. Not being my sister after all, in some sense. The DNA.'

I stared at him, felt a dry and mirthless laugh snake through me.

'Everything kind of fell into place. Why you're so different. That, dunno, *uneasiness* between us. How I feel about you.'

I rattled my head, so surprised it was all I could do to keep breathing. With unseemly haste he formed a misinterpretation.

'Don't get me wrong. I meant what I said. About owing you. It's just . . . The way you responded reminded me.'

His words trickled out, each one calcifying on contact with me, these layers of rock holding me there, my mouth wide open, my cheeks pulled into a smile, my vision prismed with liquid.

'Don't you think? That it's interesting? You must have felt so different to the rest of us. I mean, let's be honest – and this is a good thing when you think about it – you don't even look like any of us. And we're all very analytical whereas you, well you don't need me to tell you you're no good at maths.'

I managed to cough up another laugh, short and weak, the runt of a deformed litter.

'Sorry. I'm not trying to be hurtful' – and he really wasn't, which made it worse – 'I just presumed you'd see it the same way. I thought it was self-evident.'

I was determined to set him straight, crush his assumptions, taunt him with it. Except that somehow he seemed to be straight already, as if once again I'd stepped into another universe and everything I might have thought or believed was wrong. Wasn't this what I'd wanted, after all? Not just since he condemned me to prison, but forever, from the moment I knew who I was? To be free of him and them, to escape not just the life I'd lived, but every trace of it, even in my blood, even in the data my cells carried. To be scrubbed clean of them, liberated.

I couldn't stay on pause any longer so I spoke.

'You're right. It is. Self-evident.'

He smiled at me.

'There. That wasn't so bad was it? It's better this way round. I kind of had a funny kind of a thing for you. So it was a relief for me. Thought I was some kind of per –'

'That's enough. I don't wanna talk about it anymore.'

'I was just –'

'Enough.'

'Okay. Okay Tilly.'

'It's Titch. No one calls me Tilly.'

We waited in silence, Sadie snoring gently on the bed, and I hoped that he would sleep. Instead he stared at me and I stared back and if someone had seen us perhaps they would have assumed we were in love rather than trying to explode each other's mind.

'I need to go to the toilet.'

'You'll have to go in the sink.'

299

'I can't.'

'What, ya bashful?'

'I need a shit.'

'You'll have to hold it.'

'What, indefinitely? I can't.'

I knew he was right. And anyway, I needed to go, too.

'Alright. You fuck with me, you're dead.'

'Yeah, I think we're clear on that one, Scarface.'

I nosed myself out into the corridor. The moon slashed huge shadows down from the skylights, the ground between them shining and pallid. Silence, as still as a print. Grabbed him by the elbow and pulled him out, his eyes black ravines in his cheeks. Pushed him ahead of me, my left arm braced on his spine, my right straight at my side, the knife extending my reach to my knee, our steps a sarcastic applause in this brittle hush.

He seemed to push back on my hand, his shoulders rolling round it. I shoved a little harder. He pushed back with more force. We repeated and repeated until I raised the knife and prodded at his side. He let out a high, undignified exclamation but stopped the power game. I was just congratulating myself when the door to our side opened, yellow light bleeding out all over us.

I turned the bill of my cap toward the silhouette, his beer bottle clinking against the keychain flopping from his pocket, glass mirroring steel.

'Zzup?' An over-laden drawl. I raised my head enough to see him looking at David's bound wrists, incomprehension bouncing into a smirky, complicit grin.

'Respect mon.' His smiling face stilled by the cost of his schooling. 'Whatever turns you on, yeah?' And the light closed out again, door filling itself, my brother's desperation caught in darkening profile as he gaped at his lost chance.

I wouldn't let him shit on his own. I was scared of what he might do and, after the incident in the hall, I was angry with him, too. So I untied his hands then stood trying to humiliate him as he strained, his face inflating slightly with each attempted motion. But all it did was remind me that when we were kids we used to lock ourselves in the bathroom together and that he would sit there just like now and recount to me in intricate detail the plot of whatever book he had just finished. Which reminded me in turn of how remarkable he had seemed to me then – how big and clever and assured and wise and wonderful. Wonderful, my throat clogging.

'You've been seen now,' he said.

'What?'

'Him, out in the corridor.'

'Don't think he'll remember in the morning.'

'There's CCTV out there, too.'

'There's CCTV everywhere. No one watches it.'

'You've had it.'

'So've you then, Einstein.'

'There's no point in any of this.'

'Too fuckin right.'

He was shaking his head, a quick violence inside him, so sudden and so strong you could feel it rolling off him. I chewed at my gnarly thumbnail, the polish chipped back from the edge in an ugly zigzag, raked my vision round the ceiling.

'You know you said you wanted to help?'

'Yeah?'

'Did you mean it?'

'Yeah. I said so.'

'You swear?'

'How old are we? What d'you want? "*Cross my heart and hope to die*"?'

'Yeah, why not?'

'I swear, then. *Cross my heart*. What is it?'

'You know there's those kids whose dads are sperm donors? And they like find out who their dads are just with a swab of their own and the internet?'

'Yeah . . . ?'

'Could you help me find out who my real dad is? And before

301

you say it, we know all about the Y-chromosome an all that and we've got a swab from my *real* brother.'

He smiled then and I wasn't sure I liked that smile. There was something sly about it, a lazy relish which made me shiver, anxiety squeezing at my insides.

'Your *real* brother?'

'Yeah. What?'

'What do you mean?'

'What you smiling at?'

He glanced away from me, a dreaminess coming over him.

'I don't think you'll need the swab. Let alone the internet.'

I didn't reply straight away, studied him, hoping to discern his angle.

'What ya mean?'

'Where do you think my work placement is?'

What was I missing? What was there in all this that was so hard to understand? I rubbed at my face, the skin only lightly connected to someone else's bones.

'I don't know. How should I know?'

'Sanalex. It's the company that did your DNA test.'

'I know who they are. I've even been there.'

'Oh yeah, I know. Des told me he'd had you in. It was him who gave me my placement. They're very interested in you. That's why I got the placement, I think. That and I guess the settlement with Mum and Dad.'

'What settlement?'

'They were very angry about the whole thing. Having to give the samples, you being treated as a criminal rather than someone with a *"problem"*, you know what mum's like. And then that woman who was looking after you tipped them off that there was some sort of issue with the test results –'

'What, Lynda? Lynda told Mum and Dad?'

'She told *my* mum and dad.'

'Why would she do that?'

'I dunno. Perhaps she thought they deserved the truth? So anyway, they began to push to get the results and finally

Sanalex had to give them to them. Just like all the other families. And Des met me through that and I think he liked me, my mindset and all that, but also it probably just made sense to have someone from the family onside.'

He sat, knees firmly together, his forearms running along the tops of his thighs, t-shirt hitched up to reveal a shadowed belly. Somewhere in the building someone else was flushing, water sucking up and down through pipes.

'So how can you help?'

'They have all the data stored there from the whole project. All we have to do is go and get it.'

I looked at him, his comfort as he crouched there in front of me, the pleasure he seemed to be taking from all this.

'What's the catch?'

'No catch. No catch exactly. At least I don't think you should think of it as a catch.'

'What are you talking about?'

He leaned back a bit, pulled himself straight, his legs separating slightly.

'I just wondered if you could maybe help me with something?'

'What?'

'A favour for a favour so to speak . . .'

'What is it?'

'I don't want you freaking out again.'

'I'm not going to freak out. I need to find out who . . . who my dad is.'

'And it's not like we're related anymore, is it? So there's nothing that weird about it.'

'What?'

He had pulled himself back even further, his shoulders almost occluded behind the sudden convexity of his chest, my eyes following the thin white line of his arm to where his hand rested between his now-spread legs.

'What do you think?'

'What do you *mean*?'

'You know what I mean. You know what I mean, Titch.'

And, of course, I did and, of course, it made perfect sense. He smiled again, blushing, bashfulness sweeping over him.

'Don't want to be a virgin forever, do I?'

Those of you who have been ideologically or spiritually committed enough to acquire the texts of the Vanished have been persecuted with every weapon available to CTRL. CTRL has beaten, arrested and imprisoned you. CTRL has forced tubes into your stomach and fed you against your will. CTRL has mocked you and made you the subject of documentaries and sitcoms which don't bother to hide their scorn. CTRL has downgraded your credit rating, CTRL has invalidated your passwords. Everything they do to you proves the truth of our position. You can't wait for it to happen.

Extract from *Seventy-third Communiqué of the Vanished*

15

I remain unsure whether these were the same soldiers who had met Lynda, Sadie and I at the gates to Brompton Manor all that time before, fear having telescoped our daily existence from a couple of months into years. They certainly looked the same. They had the same drabs, the same corporate cap badges, the same guns. I found it hard to concentrate on anything but the guns. Guns are a great leveller.

The officer squeezed his eyes and scrutinised us, took our identity cards off to his hut and either analysed them using sophisticated computers or simply put his feet up and had a cigarette while we sweated. I remember this – his hand shook as he passed them back through the window and waved the SMV onward.

Another SMV. Not that remarkable in itself, the country's roads fat with them. But this particular one was identical to Anna's, the sight of its tinted windows enough to send Sadie and I flinching back into the lift as we had emerged into the underground car park where David kept it. It was Sadie who grabbed him by the throat of his coat and clattered him against the mirror while I had hammered at the buttons, glancing round to see them book-ended in the glass, their profiles almost touching.

'What's wiv da car, Dave? The fuck's wiv da car?'

The swelling round his nose and the purpling of his lids giving him a comical aspect, his eyes shiny and fearful and overactive peeping between this damaged flesh.

'It's mine. It's theirs. They gave it me to use. To get there.'

'Who?'

'Sanalex. Des. There aren't any buses.'

I found myself laughing, without complete control, as I held my finger down on the button to keep the door open.

'How many days a week you do?'

'What?'

'At Sanalex.'

'Oh. Two, usually.'

I sniggered again, ugly.

'You do two days a week on a work placement an they give you a company car? Bit weird innit?'

He puffed up. 'I thought they just really wanted me.'

Sadie squashed him back against the wall again, her face leaping into a snarl.

'Well, I fink ya lyin. An I fink you wanna fuck us up. An I'm tellin ya, you try an fuck me or Titch an I'll fuckin kill ya, yagetme?'

David tried to sink into his reflection, more fearful now than he had ever seemed with me.

'Yagetme?'

'Y-y-y-yes,' his voice quavery and nondescript, exactly the same as mine. We exited the lift and got in the car, liquid still sloshing inside me.

Sadie had been in a mood since I'd woken her. Dawn sludged the room in nondescript light and the birds, after a night of serenading street lamps, had gone to sleep. I shook her, less gently than I would've done if we were on our own, embarrassed both by the tenderness of my feelings and the clumsiness of my actions, terrified of her discovering what she'd missed. In retrospect, of course, I should have made sure that the first thing she saw was not David sitting at his restored computer, unbound and tapping away as if the night just passed had never started. Combined with my eager, apologetic smile – the abnormal flush of my cheeks – it was bound to be unsettling.

'The *fuck*?' She was moving, the duvet smothering over me before I could speak. Not even bothering to pull on her kicks,

308

she slithered under the desk.

'No!' My bark stopped her, her hand on the plug. 'It's cool, Sadie. He's doing it for us.'

Her hand didn't move. 'Doin what?'

'He's gunna help us find out what's going on. Who . . . who my dad is.'

'*Your* dad? Ya jokin yeah? Ya jokin me?'

'Honest.' I opened my eyes as wide as I could.

'I am.' The sound of his voice yanked her up.

'You. Shuddit.'

He recoiled from the finger Sadie poked from her fist. She snapped her face to mine, the tilt of it heavy with anger.

'You says we gotta keep im off dat shit.'

'Yeah, but that was before –'

'You says we can't trust im.'

'Yeah, but –'

'That pussy ho got you put away. You did *time* for this mu'-fucker.' She seemed to tower over him, her anger feeding her and diminishing him. 'You don't let im do *nutt'n*. E don't deserve *nutt'n*.'

She stood there, pushing forward on her feet, angry for me, all the outrage a gift for me, everything from her posture to the smudged remains of her make-up, everything so perfect that I didn't want to think about what she was saying, but concentrate solely on how she looked and felt right then, to remember it, to hold it always close to me. And when I was sure it was fixed in me (and it was and it is, fixed in me until this day) I turned my gaze to David, in the same way you might rest your eyes with darkness after studying every brush stroke of a masterpiece. And my face split apart with the silliest grin when I went back to Sadie, and my eyeballs were drowning when I spoke.

'But then I'd've never met you. Then I'd've never met you.'

She had to relent, had no choice. Fought it and failed. The snap went out of her limbs, she emptied her lungs. Searched for her cigarettes, took two, lit them, passed one to me.

Returned her attention to David.

'What ya sayin then?'

'I . . . I it –'

'Ya hear me?'

'He's just adding our names to the Approved Visitors List.'

'?'

'So's we can get in.'

'What we gettin *in* to anyfink for? E's got is blasted machine right dere.'

'I can't log on to the database from here. The data's too sensitive to attach it to any external network. It can only be accessed from the building.'

'What buildin?'

'The Sanalex building. Where we went before.'

'Ah shit man. Jokin ain't ya?'

'It's the only way we –'

'Bullshit. S'a set up, Titch.'

What did I believe right then? It's hard to be sure, knowing what I know now. I think I thought that Sadie felt threatened by this new alliance and perhaps she did. It never really occurred to me to check if her analysis was correct. I was too enamoured of this short cut to a solution, the ease of it, the possibility it held of finally knowing something, to want to question it. Far from its neatness troubling me, it was exactly what attracted me. I wanted to believe that what I'd done was worth it.

'Remember what you said to me? In Starbucks? Running away isn't working.'

She wiped at her face, her eyes still plump and crumpled with sleep, shook her head to dislodge the idea, pulled her Marlboro right down to the filter. Took a step toward the curtained window, David shrinking from her, then a step toward the bed, finally an empty step toward the door.

'Need a shower.'

'Ah . . .' Pleased with himself but scared of showing it.

'What?' Me, quick to enter, keen to avoid further strife.

'It's just I already booked our arrival time in. On the AVL.

310

Wouldn't want to risk changing it again . . .'

'So when we gotta go?'

There was little attempt to make his ingratiating shrug-and-smile routine convincing. 'Now.'

'Tellin ya, Titch. Mistake, innit?'

Despite the company and its employees acknowledging no God but genetics, Sunday morning was quiet at Sanalex. Perhaps the first replicating molecule of sugar and phosphate had chosen the same day to rest. No bio-suited technicians spidered over the grid of pods, no luxury cars rested their clean tyres on the uniformly raked gravel of the swooping forecourt at the front of the house. When the engine was turned off and we climbed from the car, the only noise was from the crows, the rips from their throats drowsy in the morning sunshine. The stones grumbled beneath our feet, unhappy to be disturbed. The sky lit the sandstone, a biscuit wrapped in bright blue foil, so that it looked like the set from another, more genteel telling of our story. The trees behind us and the sun between their leaves were all that showed in the repeating extravagance of window panes.

'Come on then. Just be cool, OK?'

'You tellin *me* to be cool? Should check yaself.' Sadie's contempt sweating off her.

'I didn't mean it like that. I meant exactly that. Just to be calm and keep quiet.'

'You tellin me to shuddup?'

'Chill, both of ya' – me, definitively, sure that the cameras mounted between the gargoyles were moving.

The lobby, too, was empty. Not merely lacking visitors. Empty. The reception desk, where on our last visit a trio of greeters had sat, vacant. The striplight's flat illumination unable to locate even a cleaner to shine on. There was no distant sound of laughter from an office, no clash of trays in a kitchen, no rousing music from a boardroom presentation, no squelch of mop on grimy floor tiles. Only the hum of air conditioning, the building's iron lung.

I turned in time to see David's rapid blinks of consternation, his fingers riding up his nose to re-anchor the specs he no longer wore.

'Alright?'

A jump, minor, then a smoothing of his hair, his hand rolling over his crown as if looking for purchase.

'Yeah. Yeah, sure. It's a little unusual for no one to be on reception. But then. Then, I'm not usually in on a Sunday. I guess it's always like this.'

'Yeah man,' Sadie offered her sarcasm with a resigned quality. 'What wiv all dis top-secret data an shit.'

'Anyway, we'd better sign in.'

'What for?' My unease manifested as exasperation.

'So the records all match up.'

'What's it matter? I don't think they'll be worrying about the records.'

He looked at me then the way he had throughout my childhood, that blank certainty that resisted all argument.

'Humour me.' Walked to the desk and hitched himself over it, a little at first and then a little more, until gradually his feet were inched up above the floor. Hung much longer than should have been necessary before returning with hands bereft, his head swinging, a full-scale fluster on him now.

'It's not there.'

'No shit.'

'It doesn't matter.'

'It's always there.'

'Maybe they lock it away when no one's working?'

'Should lock im away . . .'

'But then how would they know who's been in and out of the building?'

'*Uh*?' I waved my hand up at the nearest cameras.

'The instructions were quite clear. Sign in. Definitely to sign in.'

312

Our voices echoed up above of us, cold, forlorn.

'What instructions?'

He gave me that look again. Held it.

'When I started. Here. When I started here.'

'What we do now, Rain Man?' Sadie's time with my mother's DVDs hadn't, it seemed, been entirely wasted. The insult was lost on David, but it seemed to jolt him from his tizzy.

'Keys. This way.'

He led us through a swing door to the right of the desk and immediately we found ourselves in a different building, recessed bulbs of limited wattage glooming unenthusiastically over walls runged with pipes, the pipes in turn grumbling and bubbling to themselves. Round one corner and then another until we were lurching down brick stairs with only their murmurs to reassure us, the ceiling descending quicker than we could manage, so that by the time we were back on the flat again, both Sadie and David had to stoop beneath it, their ears no higher than their shoulders.

To the end of a long, low-lit corridor and into a small room, its pull-string light revealing it to be decorated exclusively with yellowed newspaper cuttings of young girls with no tops on, their breasts like none I had ever seen, each one pumped full of misshapen hopes and dreams, their eyes glassy with need. Beneath the lowest rank's pierced navels, a work surface strewn with screwdrivers, pliers, widowed lengths of wire, a tannin-stained mug reading BEST DAD IN THE WORLD, a tin troved with different-sized washers, a hammer head and a soldering iron.

'This ya lickle den is it? Where ya come to beat ya meat?'

Trying to contain his outrage, David pranged his head on the metal lightshade as he reversed his crouch, fluttered his hands after its rotating swing, caught and stilled it.

'It's Jim's office,' he announced, as if welcoming us into a government war room.

'What's e? The company paedo?'

313

'He's head of maintenance services.'

'Ya mean the *caretaker*?'

He ignored her, brought an old-fashioned biscuit tin up under the fixed gaze of Mandy Blap ('She's GAME for anything, so get your BALLS out and check out her SUCKER skills'). Trundled his hand through bolts and pulled out an ancient tobacco tin. Took off the lid, stirred the contents with one finger before beaking in and bringing out a key.

'And Jim is the only person to have a copy of this key.' The expectant look of the coup-meister before his audience.

'Whossit for? Ya chastity belt?'

Silence between the three of us, a momentary freeze, Sadie turning to me expecting sniggers and finding only blushes.

We reversed our route to the lobby, that dead space amplifying the sound of our feet, breaths running slightly too fast, blood bumping in over-waxed ears. He headed for the lifts, arched himself round a number pad and, presumably, entered a security code, his face flashing back at us to check we'd stayed the requisite distance from him.

'Does it matter?'

'What?'

'If we see it?'

'It does to me.'

'Tell ya, Titch. S'a set up.'

There was a sign in the lift detailing the departments on the building's three floors. As we ascended I tried to guess where he was taking us. Accounts? Human Resources? Marketing? Public Relations? And then, with no discernible change in our surroundings, no thinning of the air, no sounds of distress from beyond the doors, we continued up beyond Three to a fourth that wasn't supposed to exist, the final number flashing as we ascended past it, our canned trio. Up and up, fear leaping through me, my imagination flying out of the top of the building, knowing already that reality would be worse than anything I could make up.

'What the fuck?'

'Don't worry. I know what I'm doing.'

'You better.'

'That's why it's best if I just know the codes.'

'Y'what?'

'Cos I know what I'm doing. *Chill*. "Innit"?'

We emerged onto thick carpet, even our footfalls abandoning us, the window at the far end a distant promise of escape. The walls were smooth and unadorned, just one door visible up ahead on our right, options fleeing from us with every step.

'You've heard of Peter Debray, right?' David's voice swaggering now, aching with his own importance.

'Yeah. He owns the company.'

'Uh, yeah, *and* . . . ? *And* used his own DNA for mapping the human genome? *And* was instrumental in creating the first DNA database for scientific research? *And* has boats trawling the world's oceans for undiscovered bacteria so's he can map their genome? *And*'s worth over a billion dollars? The man's a genius.'

He stopped in front of the door.

'And this is his office.'

Wagged the small piece of metal in front of us.

'And this is the key.'

The two windows behind the desk ran from floor to ceiling, offering us a view of infinite sky. Clean light from the windows first blessed the desk in front of them, imposingly bulky, much-polished, its traditionalism offset by a sleek flatscreen and ergonomic keyboard. Clean light stroked the shelved walls running from each side of the desk to each side of us, the books' spines just disordered enough to make them seem real, *The Origin of Species*, *What Is Life?*, *The Double Helix* and so on laid face out across the others. Clean light picked out the edges of the spiralling molecular model hanging from the ceiling, all tubes and spheres, its beauty in what it implied rather than what we saw. Clean light warmed the dodo skeleton, the quizzical tilt of its head animating the bones as it perched on a low table, sofa and armchair angled round it, an audience at a performance.

The doorway seemed to block us.

'Dunno about this. This is asking for trouble. What we gotta come up here for?'

'It's the only terminal with full access to the database. *If* you know the password.'

'And how would you know that?'

'Even geniuses can be careless. I had to bring him something and I saw him enter it. I'm very good at that. I only have to see it once and I remember.'

'What were you doing up here?'

'Bringing him something.'

'What?'

'Just something.'

'What?'

A twitch, then his eyelids lowered.

'A cup of tea.'

Sadie and I dropped into the same snort of laughter, tension flapping off of us.

'Ya bring im a biscuit, too?'

We entered the room and dissipated, Sadie and I bouncing slowly from wall to wall, our feet lost deep in the natural fibres supporting us, the books soaking any sound from us, the dodo's empty eyes following us. David made straight for the computer, sat, braced his hands and began. He was full of adulatory noises for himself, the praise welling out of him in gasps and puffs as he did his routine at the keyboard, us two the muses attending to him with all the rigour and customer service skills of our time. I felt sorry for him, sickened by him and oddly affectionate for him all at once. It moved me in ways I can't fully explain all this time later.

'There. Done. There you go. It's all yours. All you need to do is hit Return and all the family data will come up.' He pushed himself back from the desk with the faked smugness of the social inadequate.

Sadie's head shook on her neck, a spasm which seemed to travel down inside her and lodge there. The book she had taken from the shelf slipped from her hand and quietly met the floor. She took a step not toward the desk but away from it, to the door. Another, another. Span round, her arms peeling from her sides and re-joining, peeling and re-joining. A step back the other way. A sudden march forward past the desk to the windows, where she flattened herself, yanking and tugging, trying and failing to pull the sash up, a scene from a comedy with no jokes.

It went on longer than it should have done, this lost battle, David and I unable to move, our heads telling our limbs they were stuck in a dream. I'm not sure how and have no idea of the time it took, but eventually I did reach her, did raise my aching arm, did lay my hand gently between her shoulder-blades.

Her own hands slapped down from the window with power-cut immediacy, swinging gently with unspent momentum.

'Just me or is it ot in ere?'

We stood there, she looking down at the grass below, I – my palm and fingers still drawing warmth from her – leaning in closer to her neck, smelling her, the sweet fruit-drop smell of her. And maybe that's why we allowed time to pass – because there were worse places to be, worse ways to be, than this. This. And this. This here. This now. And this.

Eventually she moved, the small of her back imprinted on my hand, that hand drifting in air now, cooling, as empty as it had ever been. She turned and focused on the screen.

'I'd. I'd like Sadie to look for me.'

'What?'

'I want Sadie to look.'

'What?'

317

'What part don't you understand? I want Sadie to look for me.'

'Well, it's your life but it doesn't –'

'Shuddup. Just leave it.' I quietened my voice to a caress. 'Sadie?'

She nodded her head.

'We'll leave you to it, shall we? We'll go and wait outside?'

'Nah. S'cool. Stay.'

'No, I think we should.' I believed I was being adult, that it was the right thing to do.

'Stay.'

'I need to keep an eye on him.' I thought I was letting her have her own needs.

A shrug, a momentary smile and then, as we neared the door, a cough.

'Give her the key, David.'

'Why? What's going on here?'

'Just give her the key.'

As she shut the door she smiled at me again in the shrinking space left to her, her browned, overlapping teeth showing, her eyes glittering with unspent tears, her face occupied almost exclusively by hope. Then she was gone and all that was left to me was the sound of a lock turning and David's eager face, close up and hungry for gratitude, for acknowledgement of the intimacy he thought we'd shared.

We stood uncomfortably for a moment, unsure of our roles both in relation to Sadie and to each other. Then, bored of thinking, we leant ourselves on each side of the door and devoted our energy to a scrupulous examination of the blank wall opposite.

The digital ticks from David's watch grew louder, spread out, until the gaps between them seemed unbridgeable. I turned my head to the distant window, hoping that the light would change, clouds would roll across like scenery, the silhouette of a bird would drag my eye through the space. Nothing, the greenish-blue block of light so uniform it could only be paused. Looked at my bitten nails, the pieces of skin I had chewed away from their corners. Squinted at my kicks, noting the scuffs and scratches and stains which now mapped them. Found a loose thread on my cuff and yanked at it. Removed the cap Sadie had given me, examined it, baffed some dirt from the brim. Replaced it, pulled it straight, worked it back and then forward until the end of its reach formed a black line across the top of my sight. Allowed my eyes to boss against the blankness of the wall, making double images of nothing. Checked my pockets for loose change and counted it. Dug out an ancient receipt, soft and feathery, unfolded and read it, balled it up and dropped it to the floor. Whistled quietly and tunelessly between my teeth. Scratched at the side of my nostril, grimly resisting the urge to pick.

It didn't register as a noise at first, just as a greater increase in my unease, as if the vibrations, the growing rumble, the approaching roar of air being sliced and dismantled and rebuilt as towers, as if all that were inside me. I glanced at David, his chin pointing to where wall met ceiling, his eyes looking straight up. The noise definitely a noise now. Already painfully loud. Above us.

'Fuck's that?'

David shrugged but didn't look down. 'Helicopter?'

'What's it doing?'

Shrugged again. 'Landing?'

I ran to the window, my legs flaring out from my knees, the crushing noise still lowering down on me, the corridor lengthening to match my pace. I continued to draw no nearer and draw no nearer, the carpet beneath an exercise machine, my heart being squeezed between my ribs, until my face flattened on the glass. And then I recoiled as if the pane was burning hot.

The ground below had morphed, hundreds of human figures rising up from the lawns, their uniforms shadows moving across grass as they formed into lines and the lines into columns, stretching between and then round the dazzling whiteness of the pods, the sun, with its customary lust for violence, focusing on the bayonets attached to their rifles. Each face beneath each drab green cap seemed to look at me, mouth gaping, and now there was pointing, too, their hands coming up towards me, iron filings to a magnet, and I could imagine shouting, orders being issued, the deployment of snipers, boots smashing through glass as abseilers from the hovering machine above moved in to finish us off. So I fell away from the window, turned and stagger-ran back the way I'd come. And it felt like time had reversed itself because as I moved the rumble went from the sound above me, so that only a thin, ear-twisting shriek was left and the pitch of the shriek descended as if falling and the volume dropped away so that just as I reached David – still propped on the wall, still admiring the ceiling – it stopped, my eardrums thundering with the silence.

'The fuck's goin on?' I managed to force out with the rhythm of my exhalations.

'It's nothing to worry about.' Still hanging from the ceiling, refusing to engage.

'Nothing . . . ? There's half the fucking army outside.'

'There's no need to panic. She'll be done soon and we can get out of here.'

'How?'

'How what?'

'How are we going to get out of here? The army's outside.'

'It's probably unrelated. And anyway, it's not the *army*. They'll be Sanalex security.'

'They still got guns.'

'And I, of course, have an exit strategy.'

I looked at him though he still wouldn't look at me. Hammered on the door.

'Sadie, we gotta go.'

Waited, listening hard for her approach, for her voice, for assent. A snort from David.

'I knew you shouldn't have given her the key.'

Knocked again, trying to keep it within ordinary parameters. My voice quickly undoing the pretence of normality.

'Sadie? *Sadie?* Fuck's sake. *Sadie?*'

Stopping to listen again, a final time, one last chance to find I'd made a silly mistake. The silence getting louder, too much to fit in my ears, welling out now and soaking my body, pushing down my throat and blocking it, blurring my vision, sucking the marrow from my bones, pulling me to the floor. Until I was thrashing around in it, the club of one hand thumping the door, the other twisting the handle, my face there against the wood, pleading with it to open, for it to show me her standing there, for me to be angry with her and her locked-room joke. For us to be sitting on some swings after dark, the moon making me attractive, the smoke from our cigarettes silver thread by its light. For the late film to be about to start, us lolling proximate on the bed, a fresh Breezer sweating water onto each of our hands. For security cameras to be sweeping above us as we moved through endless aisles, taking our shopping like vows. For it to be over. Sadie Sadie for fuck's sake Sadie just open the fucking door open the door open the fucking door Sadie Sadie Sadie Sadie please I am begging you open the fucking door now now now please please please oh shit oh shit oh please just please just please open the fucking door now.

I only stopped when they started speaking. I hadn't noticed the lift opening, the discharge of its passengers, nor their advance. I had abandoned listening, it seemed. I jumped back from the door as though the handle had electrocuted me.

Four men in military gear – their chins jutted, their eyes focused upon death on some distant battlefield – flanked two others. The first was Des Fortune, not so full of bonhomie as when we last saw him, dark sweat stains crimping out from the armpits of his too-tight pale blue shirt. The other I recognised as Peter Debray, a half-smile occupying his mouth, his arms encircling a large and glittery pink teddy bear.

'Where is she?'

'Here,' David replied, pointing to me. 'The other one's locked in the office, I'm afraid.'

'Aah,' said Peter Debray, joining in, his body snittering with unreleased tension, 'but I have the key.' And he waved it through the air just as David had done. Handed it to one of his fake soldiers. David – a young man standing beside me – looked confused, completely unfamiliar to me now.

'But she's here,' he said.

I stepped back across the door. 'Yeah, it's me you want, not her.'

'I'm afraid it isn't, Tilly,' said Des.

'It's my swab.'

'We know you swapped them. We knew that as soon as Allason's results came back with your parents' names.'

'I actually knew before that,' interjected Debray. 'I knew it couldn't be you as soon as I saw you. Please don't take this the wrong way but the way you look, your colouring, the shape of your face. It's a terrible thing to say but you just looked too common to be my daughter. I knew there was something wrong.'

I moved, resistance sucked from me by the revelation of my worthlessness, the mercenary with the key pushing past me. Des had his hand on David's shoulder, whose stranger's face was very white. His eyes looked at me as if they were unconnected to the rest of him, bulging, obscene, the shape of his face glitching.

'Good work. Well done,' Des said.

David didn't smile, didn't seem to even acknowledge the praise.

'You swapped . . . ?' He gaped, computing. 'Why . . . Why didn't anyone tell me?'

Instead of waiting for an answer he pushed past us as he began to gag and ran towards the lift, his shoulders jumping, his hand raised to cover the zero of his mouth.

I had more important things to worry about.

'Your *daughter* . . . ?' My surprise a corset in my skull.

'What are you going to do to her?' The lunk at the door was down on one knee fiddling. The window seemed further away than ever, no bigger than a widowed cufflink.

'Do? I'm not going to do anything to her . . . Is there some problem?'

The securi-soldier raised his big, dumb, nodding face. 'She's left the key in the lock.'

'So knock it out with mine.'

'It's at an angle . . . it won't shift.'

'I did advise you to fit one of our standard security doors,' Des offered.

'Oh, what, just in case my long-lost daughter decided to lock herself in? Hindsight is a wonderful thing, isn't it, Desmond?' He returned his attention to the soldier. 'So knock it down then. The door. Straight away.'

'What are you going to do to her?' The panic sloshing up inside me shivering through my words.

'Not with your shoulder. Use your rifle butts.'

'What are you going to do?'

'Make sure the safety catch or whatever's on first.'

'I think we should step back a bit.' Des's hands sweeping us gently away from the door.

'What will you do?'

The first hammer thump as metal met wood, the noise splintering my skull.

'Tilly, my dear girl, I won't do anything–'

'It's Titch –'

'She's my daughter –'

'Not Tilly –'

'A long time ago I made a terrible mistake. I was only a very young man –'

'– no one calls me Tilly –'

'– and I thought my career was more important than anything –'

'– not anymore –'

'– so I abandoned a woman I said I loved and left her to

323

have my children – *twins,* two of them, not even just one – on her own –'

'– just Titch –'

'– and long before I'd even begun to regret this, when I still thought all this was all that mattered, those children had been adopted and there was no way back –'

'– cos of my height –'

'– no way to repair the situation –'

'– though I'm not so small now –'

'– just this endless wait, hoping that one of them would contact me –'

'– but it's still Titch –'

'So the answer is, Tilly, that I don't want to do anything to her. I just want to meet my daughter. Spend some time with her. Find my son. Spend some time the three of us. See if there's any way in which we can be a family again.'

The dribble of words finally stuck in my throat and I pulled myself up and examined him. The bear looked like he'd won it at a fair but, though I didn't believe Peter Debray, his expression seemed sincere, or at least a higher class simulation than I was used to. I found it hard to control my contempt.

'Is that what all this has been about?'

'I'm sorry?'

'The swabs? The criminal gene thing?'

His whole body empty of comprehension. Click. 'Oh, the project? No, that's for the database. And the money, too, obviously. There is no 'criminal gene'. Genetics doesn't work like that. The data, though, is priceless. It massively expands the government's security database and as for the research possibilities . . .'

I don't know why it occurred to me to ask and why I asked then.

'But who owns the DNA?'

'We do, of course. The DNA *is* the data. That's all DNA is.'

'But it's all wrong. There's all these people. Proper mix-ups. Real mix-ups.'

'No there aren't. We have the affadavits to prove it now. Hundreds of them. It seems swapping babies around on maternity wards has been quite the rage amongst staff. Sometimes by accident, often on purpose. The safeguards are flawed. Mix-ups, yes, but not ours. Not that it matters to us. We just want the DNA. That's what it was all about. Finding Olivia was a fortuitous by-product.'

It was my turn with the bafflement. 'Olivia?'

'Sorry. That's what I'd decided to call her, before my disappearing act.'

The sound of wood snapping from behind us, the rhythm and uniformity of the blows lost in a moment, each of them doing damage.

'That's how I've always thought of her. Olivia. Little Olivia. Lost Olivia. Olivia Oblivion. My dear, sweet daughter Olivia. He was to be Francis. The brother. My son. Obvious, really.'

'And Anna? Cheralon? The people chasing us?'

'It's a big contract. I think they thought they could get to me through you. Luckily they were always chasing the wrong one of you.'

'Lucky for you.'

'Yes, lucky for me. And for Olivia, too.'

A last thundering crump, silence, then the choreographed stomping of boots, four by four by four by four. Another much longer silence. Those four sets of feet wandering and stumbling with no purpose, the faint sound of wonky circles being drawn. The footsteps too sharp, somehow, something wrong about them being there at all. Something even more wrong than before.

The voice behind us. 'Sir?' His face blank beyond subordination. 'She's not there.'

How surprised should he have looked and sounded? More? Less?

'She's probably hiding.'

His man not even hesitating, scared by how easy the answer was. 'She's not. Sir.'

'You're sure?'

'Oh yeah. Yes. Yes sir.'

'And the windows? You checked the windows?'

'The seals are still in place, sir. I think. I think you'd better come and look, sir.'

And so I watched Peter Debray and Des Fortune enter the room – stepping one after the other between the soldiers – and in the moment before their faces disappeared from my sight I saw them switch from annoyance and unease to the same mixture of confusion, fear and awe. I stood for a moment in that corridor, alone now, momentarily freed of all the others' thoughts and needs and understandings, breathing slowly and deeply, focusing solely on the movement of my lungs. And then, when I had finally become used to the impossible sound of footsteps in that expensively carpeted study, I pushed my knees upward and stepped into the room.

I listened to the scratching of my feet on the grey lino. I ran my fingers over the rough plaster on the unshelved walls. I walked through the space where the desk had been. I smelt the dust in the air.

The sky had clouded over, the empty room around me flattened by grey light. The soldiers were out in the hall receiving orders for pointless searches from Des. In the middle of the room, sunk on the floor, his shop-dummy legs spraying out beneath the bear, his chin pressing down on its head, sat Peter Debray, only shock holding his face before grief stuck, as if his expression would now never change.

I found myself next to him, standing above him, not looking down but round, finding here the best place to survey this unlikely emptiness, my gaze spinning slowly over and over, a woozy swoop. And it was as I stood there, engrossed in this absence, that I felt him take my hand, his own warm and damp. And after a period of my neither disentangling myself nor squeezing back, I felt him pull it to his face, hold its outside to his cheek, as if he hoped it would absorb the water placed there. Held it there gently, but with no chance of release.

And that was when I began to laugh.

We know, intimately, the romance of imagining the Vanished gathered together in some jungle redoubt, each new member trekking across land and sea to reach us, following clues left by those who have gone before until, one day, she pushes back thick foliage to reveal a secret valley stretched out before her, her sisters and brothers running up the slope to meet her and catch her as her legs finally give way. We understand this urge for a physical escape, for sanctuary, because we have felt it, too many times and too many times again.

It remains, though, a fantasy. There is no Tora Bora, no Alamut, no Chiapas, no Eden, no Valhalla. There is no Heaven on Earth, let alone in Heaven. There is nowhere on this planet to vanish to. And it's the Vanishing that matters.

Then again, it also stands to reason that if we wished to remain hidden this is exactly what we'd say.

Extract from *Seventy-fourth Communiqué of the Vanished*

16

Now my story ends, the patter of my fingers on the keyboard almost ceased. I look back for the last time before I save this file, close it and upload it. You'll forgive my sudden brevity but I'm going to have to hurry.

I turned sixteen two days after my arrest, so when I was charged and placed on remand, I was sent, for the first time, to an adult jail. I was too tired to be scared and perhaps something about me indicated that I no longer cared about the specifics of my life, because I was left alone, an exclusion zone growing between me and the other inmates.

I sank back into the routines – so similar to Yarleigh Falls – with a shamed sense of relief. I wanted my life to be taken from me, sucked the fug of incarceration into my bloodstream, hungry for it, shuffled to and fro as I was told, loose-limbed and vacant. My main aim, if I could be said to have an aim at all, was to forget, to obliterate, to make my mind stop. There is comfort in CTRL. False comfort, but comfort nonetheless.

The process of summary justice took a little less time than the cycle of my pregnancy, such that I had barely been sentenced before I was dragged off to a private hospital and chained to a bed as my baby was cut from inside me and handed to her new parent, the screen erected to shield my eyes from the gash in my stomach hiding her, too, so that all I ever knew of her was the sad, tiny whine of her lungs inflating.

What else was I to do? She would have been taken from me whatever I wanted, placed in care for the decade until my release – brutalised and rejected again and again instead of only once. I couldn't win. I had to pay a price whatever I did. There was no choice. And the truth is, despite my lack of options, I wanted this baby gone. Although I thought what I'd done with David had been for Sadie's sake, her disappearance had led me to view my actions as treachery. The baby, the fruit of my disloyalty, had to go. I would have aborted it if I hadn't denied its existence for too long.

It was here, as the wound healed, that everything changed.

Peter Debray had sent me the television. He had proved to be as good as his word, given me on the day he found out I was pregnant. Having lost his daughter he took mine as a replacement, agreed never to reveal to my parents that they were my blood (only David knew and, for obvious reasons, I was certain he would never tell), hired me a lawyer and began paying me a monthly stipend. In return, all Des expected of me was my complete silence concerning any involvement – real or imagined – of Sanalex in the events leading up to and following on from the death of Lynda DiPalmer by my hand. That was his job, after all. And although I was never permitted to see Peter again, to discuss the terms of our agreement or attempt to make any contact with my daughter, at least he always tried to send me what I needed, or even what he thought I needed.

I wasn't aware that I wanted a television. I thought it crass when it was delivered to my hospital room. But without it, how would I have navigated my adult life? The day the Vanished animated my screen, boxed together by riot shields on a London street, that was the day I became full grown.

I watched Sadie's face bounce past on one of those boards, saw Val's and Seb's and Marcus's too, my pupils dilating. I listened as the demonstrators began their chant, what guts I had left beginning to manoeuvre inside me. The pumping of my blood accelerated as I saw the joy of conviction inhabiting their features. I began to pant, suddenly grateful for consciousness, as the tear gas canisters exploded on the screen, as smoke and screams and panic flooded my senses. I sat, rapt, as it cleared again, that slow reconfiguration. I watched the space appear where previously there had been people, I saw the flat faces of those they had gone to meet on those boards on the ground. I witnessed the fear on the face of the first police officer to remove his mask, the way in which that Vanishing already haunted him. I luxuriated in the silence, even the reporter quiet for a moment. And I understood. I finally understood.

I surely don't need to tell you how much I missed Sadie, what a space her absence tore in me. But I suppose what I wanted, if I couldn't have her back, was meaning – for that stripped room above the fields of Berkshire to signify something. Meaning or hope. And the Vanishing gave me both.

The following morning, for the first time since my imprisonment, I asked for the papers, determined to read the reports of what I had seen, to find out how others had made sense of it. And there, printed in full, was the First Communiqué of the Vanished, emailed to every news desk in the country at exactly one o'clock the previous day, as the starter pistol fired.

Of course the First Communiqué was widely dismissed as a prank, the whole episode as art-school performance, and if none of the one hundred and seventy-nine signatories to that document could be located, all that showed was that it was well-executed, not that there was any truth in it. No one took it at face value, at least no one that mattered. That was left to people like me.

Desperate for more – not just more information, but to feel again how I had felt for those brief minutes – I engaged a little with my fellow inmates, asked if anyone knew or had heard anything about the events of the previous week. I soon found that many of them were asking the same questions as me and offering answers, too. My first discovery was that I had been mistaken to read 'CTRL' as an acronym, the name of some covert, repressive state organisation. A keen puzzle-solver was kind enough to point out that it was an abbreviation taken from the computer keyboard.

A few of us began to talk informally about what the

Vanishing might mean, what the Communiqué told us and what it hid from us. Frustrated by the lack of information, we began to read, every word an attempt to explain the absence without reducing it. Debord, Mathers, Cravan, Deleuze, Seneca, Bin Laden, Benjamin, Poe, Mishima, Llewelyn-Davies, Plath, Szasz, Woolf, Czerniakow, we tore through them all and many more, taking what we wanted and burying the rest.

Before I had completed a year of my sentence I had stopped thinking that I was imprisoned, instead choosing to believe I was enrolled at university, a university where you invented your own course, worked out your own reading lists and set your own essays. I refused to take part in auditing, stated my case in my new theoretical terms and was told that non-attendence would bar me from any consideration of parole. I laughed at them, mocking their certainty that I would continue to play their games by their rules, or even care if I was on the board.

It was here, in my cell, that I composed the Second Communiqué. It was far from perfect, lacking the self-effacing brevity of the First, its flat refusal to engage and – as that was the very nature of the First's engagement – was flawed on its own terms. But it had energy and a certain rigour that, judging by its reception, spoke to an audience. And once I had developed a reasonably efficient way to get my propaganda out of the jail, my productivity increased.

All of the Communiqués of the Vanished except for that very first one were written by me. Through them, I suppose, I formalised my rejection of my daughter. But I believed what I wrote, too, clung on to those ideas like a girl overboard clings to driftwood. Eighteen years of work and thought. Eighteen years of a fellowship predicated on disappearance, a solidarity of desertion. Hours spent searching for the perfect words for the expression of our ideas, days spent developing those ideas. Still more time taken deciding what to tell and what to withold. No one instructed me in what to write. No order was given.

No authority sanctioned the Communiqués' release. It was in the nature of our movement that anyone who could be considered more senior was already gone.

From early on there was a tension within our growing, shrinking band. On one side were those who felt that we should wait for the inexplicable, the supernatural, that a Vanishing was only valuable to the extent that it was beyond comprehension. On the other were the more practical, less spiritually inclined, who saw vanishing as a revolutionary act which had to be chosen by its protagonist. The latter tended to win the argument in that they went quicker, but in doing so they lost, too.

Personally, I waited to be taken. I willed it to happen. I wrote about it. I dreamt of it. In fact, I demanded it, every message I sent to the outside world a plea to whatever power had removed and was still removing people from this earth to *choose me*. And, let's be honest – because disinformation serves no purpose now – I waited to be taken to or by Sadie, convinced myself that somehow I would see her again. I imagined over and over pushing back thick foliage to reveal a secret valley stretched out before me and seeing her run up the slope to meet me and catch me as my legs finally gave way, my cheek cradled on her chest. I left clues to my identity, hints to bring her to me, but she never contacted me, never showed me the way out. *Take me too, take me too, take me too.* Eighteen years of being left behind.

I stayed in prison for ten of them. When they could keep me no longer they let me go. I found myself in my second bedsit, on my own this time, where I stayed for another eight, writing, always writing. Finally I gave up on rescue and began to advocate the act of leaving, deciding that the arguments of those already gone were beyond improvement. I came to the realisation – painful, destructive of my self-esteem, but obvious when I thought it through – that I was not one of the Vanished at all and that I certainly had no right to represent or project their opinions. Not while I stayed.

But even then I stalled. I was the reject. I had invested everything I had to give in the Vanished and all they did was walk out on me. Sadie never came. She had abandoned me so absolutely that to think of it left me unable to breathe, a paper bag clamped over my face. I continued to write. I carried on the pretence of speaking from a Beyond I didn't even understand. Slowly, with reluctance, I started to make the necessary preparations, piecing together a personal exit strategy, a much harder, bleaker process than I had ever imagined when my head was full solely of books and the fantasies of escape. Then, like all the other Vanished before and since, finally, after all the waiting, finally I was gone.

Except, of course, I am not gone, not quite, because if I was gone I couldn't write. No, I'm still here, if only for a little longer. It's hard to be sure who's been unfaithful to who. I've played at being Vanished, faked it, spent my whole life on this deception, this fundamental failure to live and die according to my principles and there was nothing noble in it, nothing heroic. I was waiting, always still waiting, not for any Vanishing, not for any revolution, not for my ideology to triumph, not for CTRL to crack asunder, but for you.

I had no choice.

I tried to see you, Olivia. I tried to see you so many times. I don't care what I signed. I don't care if he stops paying me. I know I'm no mother to you, nothing beyond a half of the narrow pool of genes from which you were scooped, but still I tried to see you. I wrote to you, sent you birthday cards, parcels, postcards and then watched them all come back, my mat thick with my only mail. I spent days lurking outside expensive private schools and country retreats and company headquarters and the entrances to first-class airport lounges, but I never got a glimpse. I know I'm no mother to you and yet my cells tell me different, the pain inside my body, not my head. I tried to turn my back on you but it wasn't allowed.

So here it is. My confession, my final justification. This was the story of why I left you, why I vanished and was vanished from you. The explanation of why your father is your uncle and your aunt your mother. I can't make it any clearer and I don't know if it makes sense. This is it.

I lean back in my chair at my tiny desk and let my eyes pip along the queue of white tablets laid out in front of my keyboard, this final line of full stops. I raise my Breezer to my mouth and gulp its remains greedily, replace it and uncap the next. Take the cigarette from the full ashtray, pull it down to the filter and let it fall back. Each foot helping the other, I lever on my Reeboks, old and scuffed and dirty now, the soles thin, the sparkles scraped off, my ankles marrowing from them. Gently, carefully, but with complete commitment, I raise the pill between thumb and forefinger, drop it beneath my tongue. It lies there, my mouth hanging open, while I lift the bottle, cold as when I shared it. In the liquid swills – sweet bubbles burning at the tablet's edges – before I jerk my head back and feel it travel down my throat.

One more time I try to picture Sadie but find my impressions fading, so that I don't know if I will recognise her now even if I should find her waiting, her face replaced in my memory by yours.

Yours.

Success and failure twined round each other, finally I got my sighting. Two weeks ago, the day of your eighteenth birthday. When, for the first time, you disobeyed Daddy's commands and after lessons, instead of stepping behind the tinted windows of the waiting limo, you and your friends staggered and huddled through the school gates, your arms interlinking, your hands rising to each other's ears as you whispered your perfect secrets and laughed. And yes, even though I had never seen you, I knew you amongst them. And even if it made no sense that you looked more like Sadie than me, even if you overwrote her there and then, it was a nonsense I was dumbly grateful for.

I followed you onto the tube and then off again, the rocking of the carriage mimicking the rocking of your intimacies. I ascended the escalator into the station concourse behind you, the light from above making haloes round each of your heads. I trailed you to the ticket machines and bought the same return, my fingers touching the buttons your fingers touched. I entered your carriage by the door at its other end, sat forcing my eyes shut, allowing the rain of your voices to cleanse me. I alighted behind you, close enough in the queue to smell the perfume from your neck. I followed you down the long hill to the sea, rising like a wall in front of us. Careful, suddenly afraid, I shadowed you out onto the pier and watched the drop grow in the gaps beneath my feet. I sat on the far side of the bar from you, sipping at lime and soda while you sank rum and cokes. I scuffed along behind you, hands in pockets, as you picked your way between the fairground rides and threw hoops to win another teddy bear. I watched you all stand, looking up at the gigantic, shining, steel and perspex tower of the double helter-skelter, the tubes coiled round each other, heard you laughing at its name, your friends nudging you what with Daddy's line of work. I saw them encourage you, looked on as you broke away from them, paid and went through the turnstile.

This was our chance, our only chance to be alone together, to meet, to talk, the sole intersection of our lives. I ran after you, up and up that spiral staircase, my breath wheezing through my blackened lungs, not enough left in them to call to you, my ankles buckling beneath my weight, my thighs rubbing. Until, finally, the brain in my head falling over backwards, my eyes smudgy with hope, I emerged into the anteroom at the very top of the tower to find, instead of you, emptiness – a brushed-steel dome with only the two black circles of its exits to mark the walls and a pile of brown mats flung on the floor at its centre. So that without having time to think or catch my breath, I had to decide which hole you'd chosen, grab a mat and dive down it in pursuit.

And I emerged into bright sealight already knowing I had chosen wrong because as I flew down, down, I could hear your scream of terror-pleasure as you span down, down, always on the other side of the tower from me, down, down, our separation staying the same beneath the gulls in that cloudless sky, down, down, always coming nearer to that voice as it moved further away, down, down, our distance a perfect co-ordination, down, down, the whole world turning round us as we rode those perspex tubes, down, down until we reached the floor.

I lay there for a while, the sun reeling above me, already aware of what was to come. Then I got to my feet and walked slowly round to the other exit on the far side of the tower. You and your friends gone, the space I'd expected there waiting for me.

Perhaps you'd felt queasy after your descent with a stomach full of rum. Perhaps your friends had seen me acting suspiciously. Perhaps the security Daddy detailed to you had finally caught up.

Perhaps you were never there.

I trotted down the pier after you, sifted through the crowds on the promenade. Came back to search the bars and cafés, the haunted house rides and toilets. Carried on my mechanical hunt until the sun fell into the water. Caught the train back to London without you, a new ambivalence growing inside me. Why would I wish for you to find me? Why would I wish for this?

This last confession, Olivia – my final betrayal is that I want you to betray me. For love, betray me. For my love, betray me. Betray me with happiness, kindness, goodness. With light and hope.

I want you to go to college and excel solely on the terms laid out for you. I want you to ask questions only until it's better to stop. I want you to surround yourself with friends who reinforce whatever you believe. I want you to enjoy art as a diversion. I want you to find my manifestos laughable. I want you to meet someone you feel safe with and never let them leave. I want you to have children who cling to your legs when they play at being scared. I want you to work and believe you increase the sum of human happiness. I want money to be such a constant it's vulgar to mention it.

I want the lump in your breast to be benign. I want him always to be faithful to you. I want your children never to stop kissing you. I want them to rest easy in the world. I want them always to ring. I want you not to need it. I don't want you to worry. I want you to have time to appreciate it. I want you to be warm.

I want you to age with grace and grow more beautiful. I want your bones to buckle gradually, painlessly. I want your skin to become silky smooth. I want your hair to be snowy white. I want you to live in a bungalow with parquet floors. I want them to visit every Sunday. I want them to bring their babies. I want you to rest the soft claws of your useless hands in the softness of those babies' hair. I want you to live. With gladness and appreciation, I want you to live.

And if your offspring should ever ask where Grandma is?

Don't say that I'm gone. Let me be perfect, just this once. Say I never existed. Tell them that you are a miracle and that they are, too, and that, finally, irrevocably, you prove science wrong. Tell them this is no betrayal but only love. Tell them that there is only love and love and love again. That there is only love and there is only love, over and over, and that it is love and love alone which flows, unceasingly, unsparingly from my never-ending silence.

Acknowledgements

The Vanished quote from the following sources in their *Communiqués*: Marshall McLuhan, Guy Debord, Osama Bin Laden and Raoul Vaneigem. Louis Scutenaire's words are taken from a translation by Shaun Whiteside.

Help, encouragement, logistics, sympathy etc have been forthcoming from the following sources: Nick Midgley, Jamie Collinson, Simon Skevington, Matthew Shapland, Patrick Walsh, Lee Brackstone, Walter Donohue, Helen Francis, Neal Price, Alex Kirby, Lesley Felce and everyone else at Faber.

As ever, thanks to Leila, Miriam & Saul.

B